Barbara Galler-Smith
and Josh Langston

EDGE SCIENCE FICTION AND FANTASY PUBLISHING
AN IMPRINT OF HADES PUBLICATIONS, INC.
CALGARY

Druids
Copyright © 2009 by Barbara Galler-Smith and Josh Langston

Released: October, 2009

EDGE

Edge Science Fiction and Fantasy Publishing
An Imprint of Hades Publications Inc.
P.O. Box 1714, Calgary, Alberta, T2P 2L7, Canada

In house editing by Dave Gross
Interior design by Brian Hades
Cover Illustration by Rachel Haupt
ISBN: 978-1-894063-29-6

EDGE Science Fiction and Fantasy Publishing and Hades Publications, Inc.
acknowledges the ongoing support of the Alberta Foundation for the Arts and
the Canada Council for the Arts for our publishing programme.

Library and Archives Canada Cataloguing in Publication

Galler-Smith, Barbara, 1948-
Druids / Barbara Galler-Smith and Josh Langston.

ISBN: 978-1-894063-29-6

I. Langston, Josh, 1950- II. Title.

PS8613.A4596D78 2009   C813'.6   C2009-905409-4

FIRST EDITION
(w-20090903)
Printed in Canada
www.edgewebsite.com

DEDICATION

For Annie and John — our best friends, helpmates, confidants, shoulder-providers, cheerleaders, closest companions, and our partners for life. Without you, this book and those which follow could never have happened.

Annie, there is no way to thank you adequately, no hug great enough, no kiss long enough, no smile sincere enough. Let this be a start. — Josh

John, I can't express how deeply grateful I am for the sacrifices you made so I could travel the writer's path. You are truly the best man I have ever known. — Barb

We both wish we could personally acknowledge the scores of people who helped make this novel what it is and who helped and encouraged us in so many ways over the years. Thanks to the CompuServe IMPs who nurtured us, and where we wrote tens of thousands of words together before even meeting face to face. Deep gratitude to those readers who gave us the benefit of their expertise and insightful critiques.

Barb gives special thanks to a decade of students in the Sturgeon School Division who consistently cheered her, Mike Resnick for mentoring, and to the friends in the Cult of Pain Writer's Group who made a difference and sustained her: Ann Marston, Barb Geiger, Marg De Marco, Nicole Luiken, and so many dear others. And for my Dad, who taught me to persevere.

Josh gives special thanks to his most senior readers: Ted and Lydia Langston who filled in most admirably for Wayne and Jean, who never had the chance to read the manuscripts. Also Karen, Lloyd, and John — my siblings and the world's greatest advocates for good fiction, especially when it's written by their little brother.

PROLOGUE

Quintus Sertorius was of a noble family, born in the city of Nursia, in the country of the Sabines; his father died when he was young, and he was carefully and decently educated by his mother... whom he appears to have extremely loved and honored. He paid some attention to the study of oratory and pleading in his youth, and acquired some reputation and influence in Rome by his eloquence; but the splendor of his actions in arms, and his successful achievements in the wars, drew off his ambition in that direction... He maintained his ground, with the military skill of Metellus, the boldness of Pompey, the success of Sulla, and the power of the Roman people, all to be encountered by one who was a banished man and a stranger at the head of a body of barbarians.

— Excerpt from *Sertorius*, by Plutarch (75 A.C.E.), Translated by John Dryden

✠ ✠ ✠

They who call us barbarians call themselves men, these Romans, for whom women are chattel, gods are a convenience, and freedom is but a commodity.

— The Book of Mallec

1

A god walked among us today. He came disguised as a length of wood from the cavern in the mount. Because it came from such a sacred place, we brought it into the open and left it near the sentinel stones of the Ancients where we might examine it when Lugh's great chariot hauled the sun into the sky. At first light the wood changed. As we watched, it took the shape of a man. We knew it must be Lugh himself, transformed by the power of the fiery orb.

We fell down before him in supplication, offering prayers and praise, but he answered us not and looked upon us with fear as if we were the gods and he the mortal, nor could he speak to us in any tongue we knew.

— *Stave One of Jaslon, 18th Master of Mount Eban Enclave*

Castulo, Iberia 96 B.C.

The Roman soldiers working on the road had stripped to their waists as they toiled under the Iberian sun. Rhonwen imagined she could smell them, although she was barely close enough to hear their voices. The white-washed village of Castulo, and the people waiting for the medicines she bore, stood on the far side of the new road and the Romans building it.

She could avoid the *togas* as her mother admonished, or find a thinly manned section and scurry across. She glanced at the workers, their ranks stretching to the horizon. A detour meant a long hike in the late afternoon heat and would delay her return home until dark.

"Crow scat!" the girl muttered. "There must be some place to cross."

Shading her eyes, she peered across the valley. She saw only Romans and a handful of children playing at war, dodging makeshift missiles while climbing over, under, and around a battery of standing stones left by the Ancients.

Drawing herself upright, Rhonwen re-tied the cord holding her thick curly hair behind her head. Thus prepared, she walked toward the children.

She touched the pouch that held the silver druid's token Orlan had given her. Rhonwen murmured a prayer as she strolled toward Castulo and passed the workmen.

Their catcalls brought a flush to her cheeks. When one of the men leaned on his shovel and leered at her, the centurion in command broke into heavily accented Latin. "Trajan, you ugly pig-poker, get back to work."

Rhonwen regretted not taking a different path. A chorus of whoops and laughter made her glance over her shoulder. The one called Trajan still watched her. She retrieved the silver token and squeezed the edge into her palm for composure before slipping it back into the pouch. The man's gaze slid over her like a serpent in a cradle.

She hurried away and did not relax until she drew closer to the children. A new battle began without warning. Dirt clods, laughter, and war whoops flew from both sides. One of the smaller boys stood when he should have stooped. A fist-sized chunk of dried mud struck his forehead, and he fell to the ground weeping. The others played on. As any five-year-old knew, battles didn't stop because someone got hurt. The child on the ground whimpered louder when he saw her.

"You don't need me, Arvan," she said. "Get up and defend yourself. Where's your spirit?"

Arvan rolled to a sitting position and probed his forehead. "I need a healer, Rhonwen." He held out his bloody hand. "See?"

She set her basket down and knelt beside him for a look at his injury. The other children crowded around her.

Rhonwen sat the boy on one of the ancient tumbled stones and examined his wound. She clucked at the smear of dirt and blood and wiped the spot clean with a handful of damp moss from her basket. "You'll have a bruise you can be proud of."

His face lit up. "Will it scar?"

Rhonwen tried to frown the way her uncle Orlan did, but his heavy eyebrows and long mustaches gave him an aspect of authority she could not hope to match. "It might," she said, "but you'll have to keep it clean."

He looked at her with undisguised suspicion. "Will it scar worse if I don't?"

She wrinkled her nose at him. "If you don't keep it clean, I'll have my mother, Driad Baia, tend you next time."

At the mention of the healer, Arvan drew back in apprehension and grew somber. "I'll keep it clean. I promise."

Rhonwen laughed. "You're better off doing as I say." She stood. "Now, I've got to be going."

"But I'm hurt, too, Rhonwen," one of the other children cried. He grabbed his head and swooned.

"Me, too," said another, staggering into the first. Soon, Rhonwen and a few stones of the Ancients were the only things standing.

She tickled the nearest boy. "Your only hope is magic."

The children stared at her for a double heartbeat and then clamored for her to show them.

Rhonwen retrieved the druid disk from the pouch at her neck. With her palm down, she rolled the silver token over the backs of her fingers. The disk skipped across her hand and sparkled in the sunlight. She snapped her fingers to draw their attention and let the disk fall into a hidden pocket in her tunic. She extended both hands, empty.

Arvan's mouth dropped open. "Where'd it go?"

"The gods have it," she said. "They'll give it back whenever I need it." She looked over the heads of the children as a pair of mercenaries trudged toward them pulling a cart. She recognized the larger man as Trajan, a brooding foreigner with a coarse beard. The men paused to rest while the other members of their detail, and the centurion who commanded them, plodded toward the encampment. A red-cloaked Roman tribune stood near the closed gate watching their approach.

Rhonwen's pulse quickened, and she scowled at the children. "*Togas*," she whispered. "Run along now."

The mercenaries glanced at her and bent their heads together in low conversation.

"Make the druid's disk come back!" Arvan stood in front of her with his arms crossed. "Show us."

Rhonwen stole a glance at the men, who continued to watch. She turned her back to them and held the silver token where only the children could see it. One side of the disk bore a design of Orlan's: an oak tree with low-hanging branches entwined with its roots in an endless knot.

Eager to be on her way, Rhonwen hurried through a simple trick, making the disk vanish from her hand and reappear in her mouth. Delighted, the children demanded another. Then they stopped laughing and stared past her. Rhonwen's heart thumped. She didn't have to turn to know the mercenaries stood only a few feet away.

"What've you got there?" demanded Trajan.

"Nothing," Rhonwen said, switching easily to the Roman tongue, which every druid student learned. Pretending to swap the token from one hand to the other, she drew their gaze away and dropped it in her concealed pocket. Orlan's disk meant more to her than anything else she owned. She had no intention of surrendering it.

The man swept a hand at Arvan, grabbing him by the arm. The other children scattered and ran toward Castulo. Rhonwen followed them for a few steps but stopped at Arvan's terrified cry. The soldier gripped the squirming boy in one scarred and dirty fist as he gestured for Rhonwen to come closer.

"Come here," Trajan said.

Rhonwen's mouth went dry. "Let the boy go." If the mercenaries hurt Arvan, the Castulans were honor bound to seek revenge. If these men died, the Romans who commanded them would demand reprisals. More than one Iberian had been crucified for failing to submit to their demands.

The smaller man sidled around behind her, and she turned to keep them both in view.

Trajan shook Arvan hard enough to make him cry out in pain. "Come here, girl!"

Hot with righteous anger, Rhonwen reached for the boy. Trajan thrust Arvan aside and seized Rhonwen's wrist. The boy scurried a few feet away and then stopped.

"Run!" Rhonwen shouted. Arvan bolted down the road, and she turned her attention to her attacker.

"Let go of me," she said through clenched teeth. Blood pounded in her ears. She tried to pull away, but he squeezed harder, twisting at the same time. "Where's the coin?"

Gasping in pain, Rhonwen opened her empty hand. The smaller man grabbed her other wrist, but she spread her fingers wide before he could hurt her. "I have no coin."

"She lies. She's hiding it," lisped the second mercenary through missing teeth.

Trajan shoved her into the thinner man's arms. "Hold her while I look."

The second man grasped one of Rhonwen's arms and forced it up behind her back. Trajan ran his hands up and down Rhonwen's body, searching. He found the pouch and jerked it free. Trajan dug his fingers into the thin pouch and ripped it open. Angered to find it empty, he grasped the neck of Rhonwen's tunic and yanked. The linen tore easily, and he pulled it aside exposing her breasts. He pushed his face close to hers. "Where's the coin?"

Rhonwen struggled in the second soldier's grasp. These animals had no right to touch her, a free woman and someday a driad. Although she had been unclothed countless times in the company of others—in ceremonies, at work, or merely bathing—until now, she had never felt so naked.

Trajan's breath washed over her like a hot fog, and she smelled garlic and wine in his sweat. She drew herself up in defiance, her voice steady. "I have no coins."

He grunted and tore her tunic away entirely. He ran the thin material through his hands until he felt the token, and then he ripped the tunic again to remove it. He squinted at the silver disk and glowered, his face close to hers. "This is no coin."

Rhonwen rammed her forehead into his nose. It gave a satisfying crunch. "I told you that already!"

Trajan's hands flew to his face. His eyes watered, and blood dripped over his mouth. "Bitch!" He backhanded her.

Pain lanced across her cheek and released a flood of tears. She squeezed her eyes shut to keep the traitorous drops from revealing the depth of her pain.

The mercenary put the token into a leather pouch of his own. He wiped Rhonwen's blood from the crude ring on his middle finger.

"What is it?" asked his companion.

"A pretty piece of silver, Paulus, but I doubt it's worth much."

"We should make her give us something of value," Paulus said.

Rhonwen fought against the man's grip. Her grimace brought a renewed stab of pain in her cheek. "You've already taken the one thing I value."

"I doubt that," Trajan said, staring at her breasts. He grabbed a handful of her hair and forced her head back. He licked his lips and grinned at Paulus. "I think she wants me."

"What if someone sees us?" Paulus asked. "We're dead if—"

"The Iberians are cowards," Trajan said, "and there aren't any officers around."

Paulus poked at the three-armed spiral of the student's tattoo on Rhonwen's shoulder. "I think she's a priestess."

"So? It's not her prayers I'm interested in." Trajan palmed her breasts.

His hands, hot and rough on her skin, made her shiver with loathing. Spitting and kicking, she struggled to break away, but Paulus pushed her arm higher behind her back. Trajan pawed at her, leaving smears of dirt and sweat.

"Besides," he said, "as comely as this one is, I'll bet she's toppled a dozen boys. It's time she had a man, don't you think?"

Paulus jerked his head toward the slabs of stone piled all around. "Let's take her behind those rocks."

Rhonwen could not stop the shaking that grew from someplace cold deep inside. She forced her voice past parched lips in a desperate bluff. "Let me go, or you won't live through the day."

Trajan snickered and turned toward the rocks. As he did, Rhonwen stamped on Paulus' toe. He bellowed in pain and relaxed his grip. She twisted to run, but Trajan blocked the way.

He balled a fist and landed a blow to her wounded cheek. She hit the ground hard and struggled to open her eyes. Her vision blurred. Desperate to regain her wits, she forced herself to stare at her attackers until she could see them clearly.

"Get her things," Trajan said as he dragged her behind the standing stones and shoved her over a slab. The rough surface scraped her stomach. She put her hands on the cold rock to push herself upright, but Trajan knocked her down again and knelt on her calves.

Pinned, Rhonwen swung her fists wildly at the man behind her. He deflected the blows with ease.

"Grab her hands," he growled.

From the far side of the slab, Paulus yanked her wrists until the dark stone scored the tops of her thighs. Rhonwen let out a scream of fear and rage that Paulus cut short with a jab to her ribs.

The explosion of pain left her whimpering.

"Keep her quiet," Trajan ordered.

Paulus shoved part of her ruined tunic in her mouth and resumed his hold of her wrists, pulling her up against the rock.

Her face and ribs throbbed. With the cloth packed tightly in her mouth she could barely breathe. She closed her eyes and cursed them. *Ancient Goddess, may your crows eat their dead eyes before the day is done.*

Trajan jabbed a calloused hand between her legs, his fingers cruel and insistent. Rhonwen snarled in impotent fury. The mercenary hiked up his short tunic.

"Get on with it," Paulus said. "I want my turn."

Rhonwen's muscles strained as she willed herself to iron and prayed. She expected the pain of Trajan's first thrust at any moment when his weight on her legs suddenly lifted.

"Sertorius!" Paulus said, his voice a terrified whisper.

Paulus released her wrists and stood. Her legs too weak to trust, Rhonwen pushed herself up, rolled back against the slab, and pulled the cloth from her mouth.

A tall, lean Roman tribune held Trajan by his hair with one hand and pressed the edge of a long knife to his neck with the other. Eyes wide, Trajan reached ineffectively toward his attacker. Rhonwen heard Paulus run, but she could not take her eyes from the men in front of her. Half a dozen legionnaires flanked the tribune. None of them moved to chase Paulus.

"I can explain, Sertorius," Trajan said.

"There's no need," said the officer. His cloak swirled about him like the wings of a great red hawk.

"But, Tribune, I—"

Sertorius pressed the blade tighter.

Angry shouts preceded the arrival of a dozen villagers. Arvan and the other children ran alongside them. Two village women knelt protectively on either side of Rhonwen.

"Hold!" shouted Cormac, an iron smith. He waved the tip of a spear in Sertorius' face. The Roman soldiers behind him stepped forward as one, but the tribune motioned them back.

Four villagers stood guard over Paulus, who bled from several minor wounds. He struggled as fiercely as Rhonwen had.

Arvan dodged past the men to retrieve the rest of Rhonwen's shredded tunic and gave it to her.

She accepted it with a trembling hand and strove to quiet her hammering heart. She covered herself as best she could with the ruined garment.

"This is Roman peace?" Cormac's voice was flinty.

Sertorius turned a calm face toward the angry men. "You'll see I keep my word."

Rhonwen stared at the tribune. The villagers murmured in surprise that Sertorius spoke the local tongue, although tinged with a Roman accent.

"These are my men," he said, "and they know my will. They've disobeyed my orders."

"By being caught?" Cormac narrowed his eyes and kept the spear point poised.

Sertorius drew his knife sharply across Trajan's throat. Cormac stepped aside to avoid the shower of blood. The dying mercenary moved his mouth soundlessly. Sertorius released him, and he staggered forward with both hands clamped to his neck. Blood pumped between his fingers and bathed him in red as bright as the tribune's cloak.

The reek of wine and garlic wafted over Rhonwen, and she clamped her jaws in disgust. Trajan dropped to his knees in front of her and released his bowels in a final vile summation of his life. The stench shocked her into movement, and she stumbled to her feet. The village women steadied her, as a barrel maker removed his tunic and handed it to her. She slipped it on.

Wide-eyed children peeked out from behind the Castulans and stared from the dead to the living.

Sertorius turned to Paulus, still in the grip of four enraged Iberians and frowned. "I said the people were not to be harmed."

"It was all Trajan's idea!" Paulus cried.

"You disobeyed my orders."

Paulus stared at his dead comrade, then back at the tribune. "But, they're barbarians! I'm nearly a citizen. I'm entitled to—"

"Justice," Sertorius said, "no more or less than they are." He looked first at Cormac and then caught the eye of everyone present. "Let it be known that my justice is fair and swift."

He stabbed Paulus directly under the ribcage, slanting the long blade up toward the heart. He gave the hilt an additional shove, burying the entire blade inside the mercenary's chest.

Paulus gasped and let out a bubbling wail as his blood poured onto the ground to mix with Trajan's. The Castulans released him, and he folded his arms around his ruined chest as he collapsed.

No one said a word. Rhonwen, still shaking from her ordeal, stared at the bodies with grim satisfaction. The goddess had answered her prayer with Sertorius. As far as she knew, no Roman officer had ever before punished his men for crimes against the people they governed. The men under Governor Fufidius were known for their drunken brawls and assaults on village women. Everyone assumed all Romans allowed and perhaps even encouraged such things to humiliate the people and keep them dispirited.

She stepped forward and pointed at Trajan's pouch. "He stole something from me."

Sertorius retrieved the pouch from the dead man and found the druid token.

"That's mine," Rhonwen said.

Sertorius handed it to her. "It's magnificent."

He nudged a corpse with the toe of his sandal and called to the men behind him. "Drag these vermin back to the camp. Leave them where they can be seen. I'll decide later whether they're to be buried."

Sertorius stepped between Rhonwen and the retreating soldiers. He studied the skin of her face, arms, and legs, scraped raw by the rocks and stained with sweat and dirt from the mercenary's hands. The barrel maker's tunic hung below her knees. Tatters of her own clothing lay in the fresh red mud at her feet. He scowled. "Those men had no wealth, yet I cannot let their debt to you go unpaid."

"Do what you will," Rhonwen said.

Sertorius removed his light cloak and wrapped the bright red cloth around her, then pressed her hands together until she held it closed beneath her neck.

"How badly are you hurt?" he asked, touching her cheek. To her surprise, he used her own northern language.

She put a hand on the spot where Trajan hit her, startled to find a deep cut. Unlike Arvan's wound, this one was sure to leave a scar. She dabbed at it with the sleeve of her spoiled tunic.

Sertorius took the garment from her, poured water on it from a leather bottle, and wiped the blood away.

"Where did you learn my language?" she asked.

"I served in Cisalpine Gaul before I came here. In the mountains north of Rome, I learned it's wise to understand one's enemy. Later, perhaps he'll be a better friend."

Rhonwen frowned. "Both northern Celts and southern have been Rome's enemies since the war with Carthage. Now you kill your own men for harming me. Why?"

"Because they disobeyed me." Sertorius took her elbow and directed her away from the carnage. The villagers and the children dispersed, leaving Cormac to follow at a short distance.

"I saw you fight, despite great odds, a girl against men." Sertorius said. "You must be a noble."

Rhonwen flushed. Although of the druid class, she and her family were far from what a Roman might think noble. "Oh, yes, I'm the Queen of Iberia."

The tribune bowed deeply, and the smile lightened his somber features." I am Quintus Sertorius, simple soldier, and you're the first queen I've met."

Rhonwen suddenly remembered she still had work to do and cast about for her basket. All she wanted was to go home.

"What are you looking for?" he asked. "Is there anything I can do to help?"

"I'll see she gets whatever help she needs," Cormac said, pulling the red cloak from Rhonwen's shoulders and handing it to the Roman. He put a protective arm around her. "I'm takin' ye home, lass. I've already sent yer basket on to the village."

With a brief bow, the Roman marched away, his long legs bearing him straight toward the encampment. Rhonwen smiled at Cormac but wished Sertorius were the one to take her home.

✠ ✠ ✠

The wind shifted and blew a gritty dust cloud past Druid Orlan's head as he turned his donkey cart toward the shade of a great elm standing beside Healer's House. Shifting winds could represent either an omen, usually ill, or the act of a capricious god. In light of the urgent message he'd received from Castulo, he assumed the worst. Orlan had abandoned his search for herbs and hurried to his sister's home to halt any efforts she might make to mount a counterattack. He pitied anyone who earned her wrath. Baia could be as fierce in her retribution as she was dedicated to her healing.

Orlan flexed his fingers to loosen the joints. He wished there was a salve to soothe his swollen knuckles, but he hadn't found one yet. He doubted ever finding a cure for his gnarled knuckles and the threads of white hair sprouting from his brows and temples.

Baia's voice reached him before he entered Healer's House, and her tone confirmed their conversation would be unpleasant. Taking a deep breath, he forced a smile and stepped through the door.

Orlan blamed Baia's implacable temper for the pale gray streaks in her once black-brown hair. Though younger than he by half a dozen years, she could have been his twin. Their flight from Roman armies in the northern mountains had been hard on her, and the hordes of Roman settlers and merchants in the south had only increased her animosity. With her mouth set grimly and her hazel eyes blazing, she looked more like a warrior than a healer.

"Where's Rhonwen?" he asked. "Is she all right?"

"Of course not," Baia snapped from across the room. "She's been raped and beaten."

Rhonwen sat on the stout low table the healers used for meals and the treatment of patients. She appeared calm if bruised and scraped from the assault. He felt his own anger flare as he saw the cut on her bruised cheek. Unlike his sister, however, he refused to let emotions rule his head. He brushed Rhonwen's dark curls from her face, took her head in his hands, and gazed into her nut-brown eyes. "Tell me how you feel, child."

"I'll mend," she said.

"After being defiled by Roman scum?" Baia said.

"The rape failed, Mother." An errant curl fell unrestrained across her cheek. "Besides, the men who attacked me were mercenaries, not Romans."

"There's a difference?" Baia made a warding sign in the direction of Castulo.

Orlan put his arms around Rhonwen and wished the mother had more of her daughter's practicality. He gave her a light squeeze. "I thank the gods they didn't kill you."

"I thank the gods for sending the tribune who saved me."

"Who saved you?" Baia put her hands on her head. "Who do you think brought the mercenaries? If your father were still alive, he'd be riding at the head of a war party this very moment. Any *toga* who showed himself would be butchered like winter meat."

"Winter meat in the summer?" said a voice from the doorway.

Orlan smiled at the sound of his nephew's voice.

"Telo!" Rhonwen said, slipping off of the table. She hurried across the room to hug her brother. Though two years her junior, he stood taller by a head. Lean, like the rest of the family, Telo had only just begun to take on the bulk of manhood.

He pushed gently away from Rhonwen, his eyes intent on her wounds. "What happened?"

"Romans happened," said Baia.

"Bastards! I'll kill them," Telo yelled.

"Calm down," Rhonwen said. "There's nothing to be done. The men who attacked me are dead. The gods will deal with the Romans in their own time."

"I'm tired of waiting for the gods. We must settle this on our own."

"We could, you know," Baia said. "There are men ready now. And Telo's in training with Tarax, the Gyrisoenian warrior." She touched the scabbard at his side.

The hilt of the sword on the boy's hip brought back old memories. The last time Orlan saw it, Baia's husband held it. "That's one of Senin's blades, isn't it?" he asked. "I thought they'd all been buried with him."

Baia pulled the weapon free of its scabbard and tested the edge with her thumb. "I saved his favorite sword for his favorite child."

Telo winked at Rhonwen. "His favorite son, maybe."

Rhonwen smiled back, but Orlan saw the hurt before she masked it.

"Who's Tarax?" she asked.

"An arms master," Telo said. "I've worked with him for only a fortnight, but Tarax says I'll be ready."

"Ready for what?" Orlan asked. Foolhardiness came easily to the young, and the Gyrisoenians made matters worse. A hot-headed clan, they continually stirred up trouble, and their efforts only resulted in more Roman soldiers being sent to the region. It would be different if the Gyrisoenians were strong enough to defeat them, but not even the armed might of Carthage could manage that.

Telo looked at Rhonwen. "Tarax says the Romans grow more insolent by the day. What we don't give them, they steal. They eat our food and drink until they can't even stand. We should kill them all."

"Not all of them," Rhonwen said.

Rhonwen's persistence in defending the one Roman intrigued Orlan. "Tell me about him."

Baia scowled. "He intervened, so she thinks he's a hero."

Rhonwen turned to her mother and took a deep breath before speaking. "He executed the men who attacked me."

"They're all evil, Rhonwen. How can you feel differently after what they did to you?" Telo's eyes burned with a righteous fire.

He pointed to her cheek. Dried blood marked the ends of Baia's thin poultice, which held the ragged edges of the wound together. "You're lucky to be alive. Others have paid a higher price. They've pushed us too far, and now we're going to do something about it."

Telo's bravado worried Orlan. With so few Iberians armed and trained, the Romans had little to fear. They did not tolerate rebellion.

Rhonwen stared up into Telo's face. "What is Tarax planning?"

"What must be done." Telo crossed his arms. "The Gyrisoenians have promised to help us drive the Romans from Castulo. I'm fighting with them."

"No," she cried, gripping his wrists. "You can't!"

"I have no other honorable choice."

"That's not true. There are always choices, just not always easy ones."

He wrenched away, his hand on the hilt of the sword. "I've got to go, or I'll be late." He touched her cheek. "I'll make them pay."

His face grew solemn, and Orlan saw the warrior father in the boy.

"Telo—"

"Hush, Rhonwen," Baia said. "Can't you see how determined he is? Just like his father."

"The Romans killed him for it as I recall," Orlan said.

"Don't try to stop me, Uncle," Telo said, his face reddening. "There'll be a reckoning no matter what you and Rhonwen think." He stalked to the door, his back stiff.

Stubborn, thought Orlan, just like his parents.

"Don't be a fool, Telo!" Rhonwen called, but he left without looking back.

Baia stared hard at her daughter. "You'd try to dissuade him? You're the fool."

Tears welled in the girl's eyes, but she held herself as if Baia's words had no bite.

Orlan took Rhonwen's hand and led her to the door. "Walk with me. It's too fine a day to be inside. The warm sun will comfort those bruises of yours."

"By all means, go with him," Baia muttered.

He guided Rhonwen through the doorway. "Wait for me outside. I'll be along in a moment."

✠ ✠ ✠

Rhonwen paced outside, impatient to have someone to talk to who didn't starve truth to feed hatred, someone whose love for one child didn't blind her to another. Several minutes passed before Orlan emerged from the house. At the sight of the man so like her mother in looks yet so different in heart, she rushed to his side. "She makes me so—"

Orlan's eyes twinkled and he put a finger to his lips. "Hold a moment. If I know your mother, she's straining at the door behind me to hear every word we say."

His words rang true. Though Baia remained hidden from view, Rhonwen bit back her remarks.

Orlan walked south, and when Rhonwen hurried to keep up, he shortened his stride. "You started to say something back there."

Rhonwen ached all over but refused to voice any complaint that might add fuel to her mother's fire. "It doesn't matter."

"No?" Orlan frowned. "I've spent years looking for plants that can help people, and I've found quite a few: plants for pain, plants for fever, plants to calm an angry bowel. But I've never found one that'll cure word poison."

"There's no such thing."

"Poison or cure?"

"Either."

Orlan slipped his arm around her shoulders, but when she winced he released her. "Then what are you suffering from?"

"Being attacked by mercenaries!"

He shook his head. "That hurts, of course. But I think Baia's words hurt you in places no salve can ever reach. Such wounds last longer than any bruise the Romans leave."

Rhonwen blinked to stop the tears that threatened to flow from her eyes. She gripped his hand. "Why does Mother hate me?"

Orlan looked at her with surprise. "You? No, child, it's the Romans she hates."

Rhonwen held back no longer. "How can I think otherwise? She applauds every silly thing Telo does, including this newest insanity. She suggested it's my fault those men attacked me." And it was, she thought miserably. Baia had warned her to take the longer path to avoid trouble.

"That's nonsense!" Orlan scooped up a handful of pebbles from the road. He tossed them at nothing in particular as they walked. "What can I tell you about Baia that you don't already know? She loved your father dearly, and when the Romans killed him, she nearly went out of her mind with grief. She might have attacked them herself if it weren't for the baby."

She didn't have to ask. "Telo."

"She was still nursing him, and you weren't much bigger than an excuse." He tossed a stone and watched it hit a tree thirty paces away. "She loved you both then just as much as she does now."

"She has an odd way of showing it." Baia's pride in her son overshadowed everything Rhonwen tried to do. "No matter what, in her mind I'll never be as good as Telo. She may have loved me once, but she's changed."

Orlan threw the last pebble and dusted his hands. "Could it be you're the one who's changing?"

She squinted at him. His remark put her on her guard. Somehow he always managed to smooth her ruffled feelings, and right now she wasn't sure she wanted them smoothed.

"You've turned into a woman, Rhonwen. Though you're still young, you're smart and beautiful."

She felt herself blush.

"Just as Baia was." He stopped and made her look at him.

"You think she's jealous of me?" Rhonwen laughed. "She's the best healer in the province, maybe in all of Iberia. People come to her every day. They don't care if she's pretty. They only care about her ability."

"True enough, but I suspect when she sees you, she's reminded that there's more of her life behind her than ahead. And you must admit you've also grown hard-headed. You don't listen to her advice as closely as you used to."

"How does that explain what she's doing to Telo? He's got no business playing warrior."

"He has every right," Orlan said. "Just as you've become a woman, he's becoming a man."

"He's a boy!"

They reached the well in the center of Castulo and stopped. Orlan took the cup from the hook on the post, dipped it into the water bucket, and drank. "If that is what you think, then you don't know him as well as you suppose."

She hated it when Orlan pointed out her blind spots. He handed her the cup, and she drank. "It appears I don't know much of anything anymore."

"Quit feeling sorry for yourself and recognize that there's passion in our blood. Sometimes it makes life interesting. Sometimes it makes life hard."

Sometimes too hard, she mused.

They walked in silence as they approached the gigantic oak Orlan had used as a model for the design on his druid token. He captured the essence of the oak's thick, intertwining branches. On the disk they formed a thread that encircled the trunk. Now, in the deep red of autumn, the tree breathed with the same fire the setting sun imbued in the silver disk.

Rhonwen slipped the token from its pouch and rolled it across her fingers. While Orlan watched, she made it appear and disappear as deftly as any druid. Of all Orlan's students, she was the only one adept enough at all her studies to receive it.

She recalled the Roman tribune who had returned it to her, Quintus Sertorius. The man had treated her as a woman, an equal, something no one had ever done before.

"What are you thinking?" Orlan asked.

"Nothing."

Orlan arched an eyebrow. "That flush to your cheek suggests otherwise."

"I was just thinking of the Roman tribune."

"Ah." He pursed his lips. "He sounds like a decent sort, but one to watch carefully. Not every hound is fit to guard a flock. Be wary of any man in a hurry to dispense justice."

Rhonwen nodded, but her thoughts remained on the Roman.

Orlan turned her around and peered at her, putting her reverie to an end. "You may think I'm old, and I don't have all the answers, but I've heard most of the important questions. You're still young, and most of your questions seem new. You trust people, and that's usually not bad, but when it comes to Romans, you can't listen to your heart."

Rhonwen forced a smile. "Don't you think I know that?"

Orlan's face remained grave. "No, I don't."

✠ ✠ ✠

Sound carried well at night in the damp autumn air. Rhonwen heard the rider's approach long before he clattered to a halt outside Healer's House. She and her mother had just settled in front of the hearth for an evening meal of duck eggs, dark bread, and watered wine. It was the last of the bread, and mold gave it a dusty flavor.

Baia sighed. "If the Romans trusted their own healers, we might get an evening of peace once in a while."

Rhonwen flicked a pinch of mold into the fire. "They call us demons when we tend our own. How is it we suddenly become worthy when it's their wounds that need stitching?"

Baia gave Rhonwen the ghost of a smile. "The Great Mother has made it clear I need to eat and so allows me to take their food or coin."

The Roman rider hailed the house. Without waiting for an answer, he pushed through the leather drape covering the only opening. "Governor Fufidius bids you come with me. Your skills are needed."

Rhonwen recognized Marcus Vedius, the messenger the *togas* always sent.

"I'm well, Vedius. Thank you for inquiring," Baia said without moving from her place by the fire.

"We've not finished our supper." Rhonwen found a green-spotted heel of bread and offered it to their visitor. "Care to join us?"

Vedius ignored her. "I've brought an extra mount. You two can ride double."

"And will we be allowed to ride back here when we're done, or will we have to walk as we did the last time?"

"That's not up to me," Vedius said.

"I see." Baia swirled the liquid in her wooden cup. "I'm getting too old to work all night and follow it with a long walk home."

Vedius pointed at Rhonwen. "Does she have your skill?"

"You aren't taking my daughter," Baia said, her eyes cold.

"It grows late. We must go."

"We're not walking home."

"I'll—"

"Explain it to Fufidius, I'm sure."

"—bring you back when you're done."

"Fine," Baia said. "We'll leave as soon as we finish eating."

Vedius stepped closer. "If we don't go now, Fufidius will have me standing guard 'til I'm an old man."

Rhonwen popped a piece of bread in her mouth. "You'd ask us to give up a meal like this? We can't work hungry."

"I'll bring you something to eat later if you'll just come now!"

"Meat?" Baia asked.

"If I can find some." Vedius fidgeted with the hilt of his sword.

"Never mind. We'll eat here."

"Yes, meat!" he shouted.

"And wine?"

"Yes, yes, just come now." He hurried to the door and lifted the drape.

Baia nodded and Rhonwen emptied her cup on the fire.

"How many of your men are wounded?" Baia asked.

"None."

She glared at him. "Is it the dark sickness?"

"It's nothing like that. The governor's mare has broken a leg."

Baia sat down again. "Then you'd best kill the beast. There's nothing we can do for it."

"Fufidius knows that, but the mare is ready to foal. She was bred with a stallion belonging to the great Sulla. Governor Fufidius commands you to save the foal."

Baia bustled through the building gathering supplies. "Why did you waste so much time? You should have told us our patient was a horse."

Rhonwen turned so the Roman wouldn't see her smile.

✠ ✠ ✠

The stable, warm and bright with the glow of a dozen lamps, smelled of fresh straw and burning olive oil.

As Rhonwen and Baia passed through the door, three stable boys barred their way. Baia, her arm a lance, struck one boy in the chest and sent him sprawling.

Angered, the two others grabbed the women. Rhonwen twisted away from one and elbowed the other in the ribs. He released Baia as if she were aflame.

"Hold, you fools!" Vedius called from the doorway. "These are the healers Fufidius summoned."

Baia smoothed her robe. "Where's the mare?" she asked a man holding a lamp.

He pointed toward a middle stall on the left. A cluster of men loitered there, whispering.

The mare lay on her side, breathing heavily. Every few minutes she tried to raise herself. Unable to put weight on her injured foreleg, the animal fell back. A Roman stableman stroked the horse's nose.

"How did this happen?" Baia asked.

"Kicked by another mare."

Rhonwen understood all too well. They'd ministered many a healing potion to a cut caused by a hoof, or a deep bite on the neck of some filly who dared defy the herd's dam.

"Do you think it's the splint bone, mother?" Rhonwen asked without much hope. A broken splint could heal.

"Nay. She'd be able to stand with that bone broken. This is much worse." She rummaged in her herb sack and pulled out a handful of setwell plaits and turned to the nearest lamp bearer. "Some fire, please."

The stableman looked up at Vedius. The Roman nodded, and although apprehension etched deeper lines in his stoic face, the stableman held the lamp steady for Baia. The plant smoldered, then flamed. She let it burn brightly for a minute then blew out the flame, fanning it to generate smoke.

Baia slipped into the stall and waved the smoke toward the mare's head. At first the horse stared at her wild-eyed, but as the mare inhaled more of the smoke, she began to relax. Baia extinguished the glowing brand and sought something else in her sack. She took a few minutes to mix a mash of other herbs and potions.

This time she offered it to the horse to eat. Much to Rhonwen's surprise, the animal took what Baia offered, licking at her fingers as if relishing a sweet apple.

Baia sat back on her haunches and studied the horse. Rhonwen watched too, unsure what she was looking for. Finally Baia beckoned her closer.

"Come over here," she said, "and kneel beside her head."

Rhonwen obeyed, although the stableman beside her did not move away.

"Speak kindly to her, stroke her here, and here," Baia said, patting the horse's heavy cheek and neck. "While you do that, I'll examine her."

Once Rhonwen settled beside the horse and patted her as instructed, Baia moved toward the horse's leg. She looked up at the men assembled. "Who is her handler?"

"I am," said the man nearest the horse. "What can I do?"

"Help keep her head down while I examine her leg and belly." The man knelt at Rhonwen's side and added his own soothing voice and touch to hers.

Baia probed the leg, and the horse flinched only once. Sitting back on her heels Baia looked at the handler. "You know, don't you?"

The man nodded. He hid his hands as if to keep Baia from noticing how badly they shook.

"Mother?" Rhonwen said. "What will you do?"

"I'll hasten her death and make it painless."

The handler balked. "You must save the foal at all costs," he said, his voice tinged with anger. "Fufidius demands it." He combed his fingers through the mare's long mane. "Kill her, and you kill the foal. It's not ready."

"I won't let this animal lie here with a broken long bone until her foal is born. It's an outrage."

The man shook his head, and something hard flashed in his eyes. "If you don't keep her alive until she foals, more than just two horses will die here."

Vedius pushed forward. "Spanus is right. With Sulla's own stallion the sire, Fufidius insists on whatever it takes to keep that foal alive."

"Fufidius is a fool!" Spanus said.

Vedius cuffed him. "He's our governor. We do as he bids, or our lives are forfeit."

Spanus met Vedius' eyes and did not touch the place on his cheek where Vedius had struck him. Rhonwen's hand went to the pink scar on her own newly healed cheek.

"There are better men than he to lead us," Spanus said.

Vedius stamped away, and Baia furrowed her brows at Spanus. He shrugged. "It's wrong to let her suffer."

Baia nodded, and for a moment Rhonwen thought here, at least, was one Roman her mother respected. Baia touched his hand. "We'll be swift. I promise."

"I raised her from a newborn, taught her to accept a rider, and cared for her every day of her life. I'll be the one to take that life from her, not you. Then, when Fufidius discovers his loss, only I will answer for it."

Baia waited while Spanus retrieved a lance and set it against a timber. When he returned, she took him aside.

"Spanus," she whispered, "I have an idea that might save you from the governor's wrath."

"Impossible."

Baia shook her head. "I propose to deliver the foal tonight."

"It isn't due for almost two weeks."

"I'll cut open the mare's belly and pull the foal free."

Spanus stepped back. "How could a healer even think of such a thing?"

"Have you never heard the tale of Brosia?"

Rhonwen understood. This old story she knew well. Pulled from his mother's womb after she'd died, Brosia lived to become a great hero. If it had been done before, then she had confidence her mother could do it now.

Spanus looked uncertain. "Brosia? The one you call the Otter?"

"Brosia the Trickster, Brosia the Bold, he's known by many names. His birth came after his mother's death. I propose to do the same thing. I can make the mare sleep. We'll take the foal, and before she wakes you may send her to the Otherworld."

"This will work?" he asked.

She shrugged. "If we take the foal this way, it has a chance to live. If we don't try, it'll have no chance at all."

Either way, Rhonwen knew neither Spanus nor her mother would let the mare suffer past this night.

He consented with the barest of nods.

"No," Vedius said, "it's too risky. Keep the mare alive. If the foal dies, you die."

"I'll take that risk," Baia said.

Vedius looked at Rhonwen. "And you'll risk her life, too?"

Baia frowned. "Leave us, Rhonwen."

Rhonwen crossed her arms. "I'm staying. How else will I learn?"

"It's a bad idea," Vedius said.

A withering look from Baia smothered further objection. "Do something useful, Vedius. Get these men working on finding us clean straw and hot water, and find another mare with a new suckling."

At her words, the men scurried away. When a bucket of water arrived, Baia stepped back and gestured to the onlookers.

"Those of you without lamps will leave us."

Spanus didn't move. "I stay."

Baia spared him a tight smile. "Of course."

Half the men left, grumbling, as her mother laid out two sharp blades. Baia's largest and best butchering knife, sharpened to a fine edge, glittered in the lamp light.

"Timing is important," Baia said. "We must work quickly. If the foal isn't breathing on its own in a minute, two at the most, it will likely die."

In the subdued light, Baia stripped out of her white tunic and laid it over the wooden barricade of the stall. In the firelight, her druid tattoos in intricate swirls reminded Rhonwen her mother was not merely a village healer but a driad as well. The men in the barn, all locals, quieted. Druids were held in great respect, and it had been years since most of them had seen a woman of Baia's stature. She gestured for Rhonwen to disrobe.

Rhonwen glanced at the men.

Baia gave her a defiant nod. "We're going into battle."

Rhonwen followed her mother's lead, wishing she had more than the one triskele tattoo she'd received at age ten when she started formal training. Without hesitation she pulled off her new tunic, the one she bought with the young tribune's money, and delicately placed it over her mother's. Something inside her tingled when she thought of Sertorius, and she quickly shoved the feelings aside.

In a gesture of respect for Baia and Rhonwen, Spanus also stripped out of his tunic to face the ordeal.

Baia knelt beside the mare's belly and probed with both hands around the edges of the foal's body. It hadn't yet turned head down. Rhonwen guessed Baia sought one of the foal's legs pressing on its mother's womb as an indicator of its position.

Rhonwen trembled. Spanus sat beside her, ready to snatch the newborn from between the folds of flesh.

"Rhonwen, take that last length of setwell and let it smoke completely in the mare's face. She must be full asleep."

Rhonwen covered the mare's nose with a piece of leather to keep all of the smoke close to the horse. Then she inserted the smoldering plait beneath the leather near the mare's nostrils. With each heavy breath, the mare's muscles grew slack. When she was fully unconscious, Baia nodded.

"Let's begin," she said.

2

The god Lugh has lived among us for weeks, and still he refuses to speak. He accepts our offerings of food and drink but ignores us when we entreat him to perform a feat of magic. Some in the enclave have asked the Great Mother to explain his presence. To this end we have sacrificed three goats and a calf, yet nothing has been revealed.

— Stave Two of Jaslon, 18th Master of Mount Eban Enclave

Atuatuca, Belgica 96 B.C.

The last fight of the day would begin with the selection of a final opponent and a nod from the sword master. Mallec held his breath and looked away from Galan, the brawny youth waiting in the middle of the practice field. Aching from one too many skirmishes with older boys, Mallec prayed for the gods to spare him from this final encounter. Galan had already beaten him twice that afternoon, once at close knives and once at long swords. Thrice beaten meant dishonor.

If allowed to fight with a staff, he had a chance of landing more than a blow or two. Against anyone but Galan he had a good chance to win. The sword master scorned the staff for his students, preferring the spear and knife. Only druids bore a staff to battle, and then only to exhort the host. None dared attack a druid, for doing so meant banishment at least. When Mallec earned his druid's robe and staff, custom would protect him. Until then, he was subject to the same rigors of training as any other clan youth.

A swallow swooped through the late afternoon sky, an ambivalent sign at best. The appearance of a wren or a raven would have meant the gods took an interest. Mallec was on his own again.

A firm look at the sword master usually signaled a desire to fight. Mallec locked his gaze on the grizzled warrior and, with an effort of pure will, denied himself any retreat from pain or fear.

Something unreadable crossed the man's face. The sword master's look penetrated Mallec and moved on. "Hegedor will face Galan," he said.

The other boys cheered the hapless Hegedor, hoping to raise his spirits before he faced the favored Galan. Mallec knew such cheers would not be raised for him. Those were reserved for warriors. Galan made quick work of Hegedor, disarming him and battering him to the ground. With a nod, the sword master dismissed them.

Wanting distance from the practice field, Mallec followed one of the streams that fed the clanhold until he found a wide spot. He groaned as he peeled off his sweaty woolen tunic and inspected his ribs. The latest bruises from Galan's wooden practice sword had already turned dark, crisscrossing the lighter brown ones he'd received a few days earlier.

If he just had time to heal before facing Galan again... He let the thought die. At sixteen, he knew the difference between bravado and ability. Even if he had an entire season to prepare for the older, stronger Galan, he knew he would still limp away defeated. Worse, he would leave the field struggling to hide his emotions while Galan laughed.

Among the Eburones, every boy trained for battle. The clan's survival against marauding bands of Germanii depended on it. He only wished he liked it half as much as the others did. He wanted the studious life of a druid, not a life spent fighting, no matter how glorious that life might be.

Mallec's frown dissolved as he thought of Driad Seva applying the cooling salve to his bruises. The fragrant balm did nothing for his pain. It was Seva's motherly touch that made him feel better, made him feel as though someone cared. He shook his head at his own foolishness. She didn't care, of course, she was a healer and would have done the same for anyone, but it was delicious to think she did, even for a moment.

Every day he wished he'd been fostered to Seva instead of Galan's father, Talorec. Mallec would never be a true warrior, yet Talorec, a war leader, insisted he train with the other unblooded members of the Eburone clan. Every Eburone was a warrior first. Every Eburone but Mallec.

Tall and too lean, Mallec had none of Galan's heavy muscles, and although he might have matched the older boy's speed, he lacked the stamina and proficiency extra training provided.

While Galan and the others grew stronger working in the fields or tending livestock, Mallec spent his time studying with Seva.

He stripped off the rest of his clothes and stepped into the water, then lay on his back and floated. The early evening songs of larks and the buzzing of insects became indistinct as he relaxed, closed his eyes, and let his mind drift with the slow eddies.

The image of a girl soon dominated his thoughts, and although he couldn't see her face, he knew she wasn't an Eburone. Nor was it simply her slender frame or the mass of coal-dark hair that distinguished her from the giggling, pale-skinned girls who fawned over the young warriors he'd left on the practice field. Who was she? He tried to concentrate, but her image became hazy. Even so, something about her felt comfortable. As quickly as the vision came, it left.

A frog added a guttural comment that made him smile. "What do you know about it?" Mallec asked.

With the sun low on the horizon, Mallec ventured from the stream. Though his muscles had stiffened from the cold, the bracing water restored his spirits. Wet, he slipped into his breeches, draped his tunic over his shoulder, and began the walk back toward the clanhold. He gripped his staff and tapped the ground in time to match his steps.

He passed unchallenged through the gates and turned down the side path that led to Seva's house. She and her young son, Ambioris, shared a compact log dwelling near the main hall. Few people roamed the streets so close to dark, for the setting sun released a multitude of spirits. Evening also brought men and women from the fields indoors for supper. Mallec's stomach grumbled.

Seva, a proud, squarish woman who wore the red spiral healer's tattoo, stood grim-faced in the doorway. She watched Mallec but made no sign of greeting as he trudged toward her. When he nodded, she blocked the entry.

"What's wrong?" he asked.

Seva stared at him a moment longer before responding. "You know very well what's wrong."

Mallec did a quick mental tally of his chores and found them all complete. He tried to think of anything he might have left undone.

"I'm talking about Ambioris," she said, her hands fisted on her hips.

Mallec had done nothing to Ambioris. He liked the boy. There was definitely something special about the lad.

"I've told you before I'll not have you filling his head with nonsense."

Mallec frowned. "What are you talking about?"

"Do you deny telling Ambioris he'd be a great war chief one day?"

"Oh that! I merely told him about a dream I had."

Seva slapped his face. "You have neither the right nor the training to mention your visions to anyone, let alone my son. You don't understand how easily children his age are misled. When you told Ambioris you've seen his future, he believed you."

"He should," Mallec said, rubbing his cheek. "He'll be a great leader."

"You're no druid yet, Mallec, to prophesy to me or mine in my own house."

Mallec flinched at the insult. He wanted to be a druid with all his heart, and Seva's reminder how easily that dream could be turned aside bruised him more deeply than Galan's sword. Still, an honorable man defended himself.

"It takes no great skill to know the difference between the kinds of dreams everyone has and those brought by the gods."

Seva's eyes narrowed. "Who taught you anything about divination?"

Mallec raised his eyes to meet hers. "You're the only teacher I've ever had, Driad Seva."

"And what, precisely, have I taught you about visions?"

He bit at his lip. "Very little."

"Less than that."

"I know you're a healer first, but have the gods never spoken to you?" Mallec asked, his cheeks hot with his conviction. "I see Rhiannon nearly as often as—"

"Silence!" Seva whispered. "I refuse to discuss your visions of the Great Goddess in public."

Mallec stepped forward to enter Seva's house, but she stopped him with a hand on his chest.

"Come back tomorrow. If I'm no longer angry at you, my door will be open. Otherwise, stay away."

"But—"

"Good evening, Mallec," Seva said. "I wish you a night free from dreams."

As Mallec stood facing Seva's house, the leather skins covering the door seemed as impenetrable as stone. He turned toward Talorec's house, although he didn't relish Galan's recounting of the drubbings he'd given Mallec on the practice field. The more he thought about it, the more he realized a meal wasn't worth the humiliation. Mallec ignored the lane leading to Talorec's home and walked toward the solitude of the ceremonial grove at the far end of the commons.

Most people feared to enter Druid's Grove. Its giant oaks stood guard against all intruders, their limbs carved with the faces of protective spirits. Just as he felt separate from the daily life of those around him, so Mallec felt a part of the great mysteries of the gods. He found the power of the place comforting, especially at night.

Lacking another human with whom to discuss his dreams, Mallec intended to leave his mind open to Rhiannon. Perhaps she would provide an answer. It certainly wouldn't be the first time. The goddess often came to him in his sleep and he knew her gentle face as well as he knew Seva's. Perhaps she'd send him another vision of the dark-haired girl.

Darkness closed around him before he reached the stone altar ringed by father oaks. He bumped into the altar, ran his hands over stone still warm from the sun, then eased himself to the ground and leaned against it. Mallec gazed up into the overcast night sky and willed himself to relax.

He clasped his fingers in his lap and closed his eyes. Sleep came quickly, as did his dreams.

Lugh beckoned, and he followed. Time peeled away as the god pointed to a gathering of Eburones, unmistakable in their coats and cloaks of green and pale yellow, shades that blended well with the fall foliage. Piles of fresh vegetables, newly picked fruit, and casks of cider bespoke the harvest season. Amidst the crowd, Galan and a dozen other unblooded warriors vied for the privilege of riding an immense horse standing near the stone well at the clanhold's center.

The animal was magnificent, both in size and decoration. Its shoulder rose above Galan's head. Someone had woven a garland of ivy into the animal's black mane and strapped sheaves of grain to its massive flanks. Short scythes pointed outward from the beast's neck and legs. The place of honor at the feast went to the first warrior to ride the horse to the clanhold gate to signal the start of Lughnasa, the harvest festival.

At a sign from Talorec, the crowd fell back to give the youngbloods space. As the contestants struggled with each other, the horse, and the sharp blades, the crowd cheered. After much pushing and cursing, Galan climbed the stone wall surrounding the well and leaped atop the beast's broad back. Instantly, the horse went from docile to demon. Warriors scattered as the animal reared, and Galan rolled backward over its rump. The horse kicked and drove him into the stone well. Galan's skull split like a gourd under a hoof. His limp body slid to the ground and lay still.

Horrified, Mallec turned toward Lugh, but the god no longer accompanied him. Instead, the Great Mother stood nearby. She pointed at Mallec and then at his dead tormentor.

Mallec awoke from the dream with the image of Galan's exposed brains as vivid as if they dripped off the altar behind him. He shivered. Unless he intervened, Galan was doomed.

Instinct told him to seek out Seva, but he stopped before he had gained his feet. That door remained closed, at least for the night. He slumped back against the altar stone. "Why show this to me?"

He waited, but he already knew why they'd sent him the vision. The gods loved to test mortals.

Mallec wanted to be a druid, but not because he desired to sit in judgment or administer the law. Nor did he long for the life of a bard or a healer like Driad Seva. His dream was to speak with the gods, to learn from them and from the world. It took years to become a druid, and training conducted away from home cost dearly. A clan sometimes paid for it but only for the most promising students.

The gods had granted Mallec an opportunity to prove himself worthy of the clan's investment. By giving him a glimpse of the future, they also gave him the chance to alter it, provided he had the will to force a change and face the consequences.

He shifted against the rock and winced. His ribs were still sore. If he ignored the knowledge gained from the dream, Galan would die, and the beatings would stop. Yet, if he succeeded, Galan would never believe his life had been spared. Mallec also knew that if the young warrior survived, the beatings would continue.

Somewhere at the edge of his mind lurked another possibility. What if the dream meant nothing more than the unfilled wishes of a foolish youth with more bruises than sense? Mallec stared up at the darkened sky. The churning clouds were a command. The gods demanded action!

He rolled to his feet, his mind set. What were a few beatings in exchange for the company of gods? Banishing doubt gave him the heady feeling of enormous power, as if lightning were about to sprout from his fingertips. The gods had given him both the signs and the intellect to understand them. Mallec would live his dream, and no power on Earth could stop him.

✠ ✠ ✠

"Do away with the harvest ride?" Talorec stared in disbelief at Mallec. "My father showed me the scars he earned the year he rode the harvest horse. I did it before I was blooded, and Galan's spoken of little else since he learned of it. Now you want us to cancel it?"

Mallec's heart still pounded from his run from the sacred grove. He regretted he'd blurted out his idea before warming Talorec up to the discussion.

"The gods sent me a vision," Mallec said. "In it, I saw Galan killed when he leaped upon the horse's back."

Galan sprawled near the fire with a horn of cider and the remains of a pair of roasted rabbits spread on a low table. "I wonder if that's really the vision you saw," he said, tossing a bone to the hound at his feet. "More likely you saw a boy pretending to be a druid so he wouldn't have to show the entire clan how worthless he is."

Mallec glared at him.

"Where and when did you have this vision?" Talorec asked.

"Earlier tonight, by the altar stone. Lugh showed me how Galan would die."

"And how will that be?" Galan asked. "Will I be trampled by a herd of cowards?" He put the back of his hand to his forehead. "Wait, I'm having a vision! I see Mallec in a druid's robe hiding behind a woman."

Talorec laughed, but his merriment soon subsided, and he frowned at Mallec. "Have you discussed this with Seva?"

"Not yet," Mallec said. "I came here first."

Galan rose from the floor, a rabbit leg bone in his hand. He tapped the bone against Mallec's chest. "Take your visions elsewhere. Do not stand between me and the horse. I'll climb right over you to get what I want."

"I understand." Mallec pushed the rabbit bone aside. "Where would you like to be buried?"

Galan dropped the bone and reached for his knife, but Talorec put his arm between them. "I think you've both said enough for one night. Mallec, go discuss your vision with Seva. If she thinks something should be done, she'll call a council."

"Go! Run to Seva's house," Galan said, "it's a good place to hide."

3

The Dark Lady spoke to Jaslon, now master of the enclave at Eban Mount, and revealed that he whom we thought to be Lugh, son of Dagda, was no god. When the members of the enclave learned of the deception, they sought to strike down the false god with blade and stone. Jaslon dissuaded them saying it was enough merely to drive him away.

Jaslon followed the impostor to the mountain where he gathered a quantity of a useless plant known as baneweed and then traversed the passageways into the heart of the sacred place. In the great cavern he marked himself with woad and prayed in his strange tongue. He burned the baneweed and let the smoke drift into his face, and lo, as he once changed from a stick to a man, likewise did he change from a man to a stick.

— Stave Three of Jaslon, 28th Master of Mount Eban Enclave

Iberia

The rest of Fufidius' stables remained dark while the healers prepared for the foal's birth. Rhonwen settled beside Spanus, hoping to take her cues from him.

As Baia dragged the point of her knife down the length of the mare's belly, a dark red line welled up beneath it. The skin parted and Baia cut again, through the tight muscles beneath and into the womb. With rapid and firm strokes, she cut through the womb's tough muscle.

The head of the foal slowly eased into view. Baia worked feverishly, but the rest of the foal remained hidden.

"Can you feel the shoulder?" Baia asked.

Spanus reached inside the mare, his fingers probing for a fore-leg. He found one and pulled. Baia cut once more, and the entire front of the foal popped up.

"Pull!" Baia cried.

Rhonwen didn't know what to grab. Spanus pulled. The foal slid out and across the mare's belly onto the clean straw.

Baia handed Rhonwen a small knife. "Cut away the birth sac. Quickly! It must breathe."

Rhonwen grasped at the slick tissue and ripped the sac. She pulled and cut, and at last the wet muzzle of the foal found dry air. As she had with kittens and puppies, Rhonwen wiped the wet away from the foal's nose.

"Breathe," she said.

She rubbed it with a handful of straw, and when she heard the sweet sound of its first breath, Rhonwen let her tears flow unchecked. Not only would the foal live, so would those who brought it into the world.

At the clear first whinny of the newborn, the men watching cheered. Baia raised a hand to silence them and nodded to Spanus.

He staggered to his feet and retrieved the long boar lance.

Rhonwen looked from the sharp blade to the hard set of Spanus' jaw. Spanus said nothing, but the corners of his eyes watered as he gripped the lance.

The second of Baia's two knives lay unused. Rhonwen offered it to Spanus. The Roman blinked and shook his head.

Baia patted her arm. "'Tis better done quickly."

With one swift jab, Spanus drove the point of the lance deep into the mare's heart. Her death was swift as he had promised.

Baia's lips moved in prayer to the White Lady to see the noble animal into the next life.

Rhonwen gathered the wet foal in her arms as she rocked back and forth. A filly, not the treasured colt Fufidius sought, but the fine offspring of a prize mare and the stallion of Rome's greatest general. This horse suited someone better than Fufidius.

Only when the newborn lay sleeping in a clean stall with a brood mare did Baia rest. Spanus claimed the foal as his to raise.

Once Baia and Rhonwen washed and dressed, the healer called to Vedius. "I don't know about you, but we could use a meal."

"With meat," Rhonwen added.

"With meat," Vedius repeated without joy.

"Cheer up," Baia said. "Fufidius will make you a captain for this night's work."

Rhonwen smiled as she smoothed the fabric of her new tunic. Meat was always a bounty, but her smile widened at the prospect of going into the town where Sertorius lived.

Stars sprinkled the moonless sky as Rhonwen, Baia, and Vedius passed beyond the gate and into the heart of Roman Castulo. A few lamps lit the narrow passages between dwellings, but between them lurked deep shadows. Vedius pulled his horse to a stop beside one flickering light and turned in his saddle to face the two women riding double on the horse behind him.

"It's late," he said. "Don't blame me if we cannot find anyone willing to serve us."

Baia pulled back on the reins. "I'm too tired for such games, Vedius. Just give us a few sistercii for our labors, and we'll be on our way."

The Roman gave them a sour look but reached for a pouch at his waist. He dug out a few coins and held them in his open palm. "I'll expect you to bring the horse ba—"

The choking sounds Vedius made startled Rhonwen. A curtain of blood descended the front of the Roman's tunic as he struggled to remove the spear transfixing his throat.

As he toppled from his saddle, an Iberian warrior caught the end of the spear and yanked it free. Vedius hit the ground like a sack of wet grain. The warrior turned toward them and waved the gory spearhead.

"Why do you ride with this pig? Are you slaves?"

Baia fixed him with an angry glare and pulled her cloak open to reveal her robe. "Don't you know a driad when you see one?" She looked down at Vedius and shook her head. "What've you done?"

"I killed a bit of vermin."

"And how do you think the Romans will react? You've endangered us all!"

The warrior nudged Vedius with his spear. "When they're all dead, we'll have nothing to fear."

Telo's pretentious words came rushing back to Rhonwen. Apprehension replaced the sympathy she had for Vedius. "It's happening," she whispered to Baia. "Telo spoke of a plan to attack the Roman garrisons."

"Go quietly if you want to avoid trouble. Our night's work has just begun." With a wave of his spear, he disappeared into the shadows.

Rhonwen stared down at the young Roman sprawled on the cobbled street. When he moved his hand toward his neck, she slipped down off the horse and knelt beside him. Taking his cloak in both hands, she ripped off a length and pressed it against his wound.

"We've no time to tend dying *togas*," Baia snapped. "Get back on the horse!"

"I can't leave him like this," Rhonwen said as she looked into the young man's fear-bright eyes. He moved his mouth to speak, but no sound emerged.

"I'll wait for you at the city gate," Baia said. "You can take his horse." Baia kicked her horse and guided it away.

Shouting men drew closer, and Rhonwen heard the clash of blades.

"I wish I could do more for you," she whispered, but Vedius' eyes had already locked on the Otherworld. She closed the lids and left him.

His mount shied as she struggled into the saddle. As sounds of fighting erupted around her, she kicked her heels into the horse, but in the darkened lanes the frightened animal refused to run.

Curses mingled with cries of pain and rage as the carnage grew. She passed one of the many Roman barracks inside the town and watched as legionnaires by the dozen stumbled into the street where screaming Iberians cut them down. Hate-crazed warriors set fire to the buildings, clogging the lanes with dead Romans and burning debris.

Rhonwen yanked the horse around more than once to avoid similar killing grounds. As she backtracked to avoid another, a panicked Roman pulled her from the saddle. He threw himself onto the horse's back and rode away.

She walked until the main gate came into view. A crowd of warriors stood in front of it. She saw Baia near the edge of the crowd and worked her way through the mob until she reached her side. Baia acknowledged her with a nod. Rhonwen heard no more Roman voices, and boastful cries replaced fearful ones. The battle had turned into a hunt, the hunt a slaughter. Every Roman found inside or outside the walls had become a target. The few still alive now wore chains.

A warrior wearing a cloak woven with Gyrisoenian colors lurched in front of them. He held a wine skin in one hand and waved a bloody sword in the other.

"Whoever could have imagined a time when Roman blood and Roman wine would flow in equal amounts?" he said, slurring his words.

The warriors at his side laughed and passed their own wine skins around.

Baia looked down at them with disdain, but she did not speak until the laughter subsided. "Who leads you?" she asked. "What chief has brought you on this foolish errand?"

"We need no chief to tell us who to kill," growled a huge man carrying a mesh sack bulging with Roman heads. "Nor do we need anyone to tell us how to do it!" He dropped the sack to lift his drinking skin with both hands. His companions cheered as wine splashed into his mouth and leaked down his chin, a pale imitation of the blood that ran down Vedius' chest.

Rhonwen stared at the bag of grisly trophies and wondered if it also held the head of Marcus Vedius. Suddenly she realized none of the warriors near the gate were Castulans. Fearing Telo had joined the fighting, Rhonwen scanned the growing throng. "Where are the Castulans?"

"They had little stomach for tonight's sport," the first warrior said. "Luckily, we Gyrisoenii do. We'll gladly see the *togas* off to live with their gods!"

Congratulations were thick on their tongues as more of their comrades joined them at the gate. A contingent of Castulans finally appeared. Rhonwen searched their faces.

"Have any of you seen Telo?" she asked when they drew near.

An aging craftsman with a gash in his side answered. "Aye. He fought beside me, and fought well."

"Then where is he?" Baia demanded.

"Mother! Rhonwen!"

The two women turned at the sound of Telo's voice. Rhonwen ran to embrace him, but he shrugged her away.

"Are you hurt?" she asked.

With a smile wider than the crescent moon, he danced in the light from a dozen torches. "I didn't get a scratch. We should've attacked the Romans long ago. We had nothing to fear."

Satisfied that Telo was safe, Rhonwen's thoughts shifted to Sertorius. Surely of all the Romans, he deserved to live. She pitched her voice low. "Are all the Romans dead?"

Telo nodded proudly. "All we could find. Some of the barracks outside the walls were empty, the men probably out on patrol." He slashed his sword in the air. "But we'll be ready when they return."

Rhonwen pointed to the drunken warriors all around them. "Can you be sure of that?"

"You begrudge us a little happiness now that we've thrown off Roman chains?"

She cleared her throat. "I see you're still carrying Father's blade."

Telo brandished the weapon with a proud smile.

"I'd hoped you'd wait until you were big enough to wield it with one hand," she added.

"I can!" Telo cried, swinging the weapon wildly.

The mob near the gate cheered as more Gyrisoenian warriors arrived with a short row of Roman prisoners. Several men kept the line moving forward by poking the soldiers with spears. Each prisoner bled from a dozen spots, and the mob's laughter increased with each new cut.

"Where's the honor in tormenting unarmed men?" Rhonwen cried.

"Shut up, girl," said the man with the sack of heads.

The leader of those who brought the prisoners stepped in front of them and with arms upraised addressed the crowd.

Baia dismounted and led the horse to Rhonwen and Telo. "That's Alfonsus," she whispered. "He once claimed your father as a friend, although since Senin died, I doubt he's raised a single ale to his memory."

"This is a glorious night," Alfonsus cried, "a night the bards will sing about. The Romans have learned about the ferocity of the Gyrisoenii and the wisdom of the Castulans who invited us here." He turned and waved at Telo and the small band of warriors from Castulo.

"Tell me," continued Alfonsus, his face twisted in a parody of a smile, "how many of you spilled Roman blood tonight?"

He stepped toward them and began an inspection. Anyone whose clothing or body bore no trace of battle was shunted toward the prisoners. When they shoved Telo along with the others, Rhonwen's breath caught. Soon, nine unmarked Iberians stood facing ten bound Romans.

"I see we have an extra," Alfonsus said. He drew his dagger and plunged it into the stomach of the nearest Roman. The man groaned and doubled over but did not fall. Alfonsus gripped the hilt of his knife with both hands and jerked it upward. Blood spurted freely across both men. The Roman's cry ended with a gurgle as his knees buckled and he dropped to the ground.

Alfonsus pulled his blade free and wiped it on the dead man's back. He straightened and waved at the Castulans facing the remaining prisoners.

"Kill them," he said.

No one moved. Several of the Romans attempted to back away, but the Gyrisoenii behind them used their spears to check any retreat.

"Do it!" Alfonsus screamed.

"There's no honor in it," said Telo.

Alfonsus approached him. "What brave warrior is this?" He rubbed his chin as he circled Telo. "Why, it's the son of Senin, come to teach us about honor!" He slapped the boy on the back hard enough to propel him into the line of Romans.

Alfonsus stood with his hands on his hips and rocked back on his heels. "I'm waiting," he said.

Telo straightened, and although his face and ears flushed full red, he kept his boyish voice steady. "There's no honor in killing unarmed men."

The big warrior scowled. "What honor did the Romans call upon when they stole our crops and raped our women?"

Telo rested the blade of Senin's sword on his forearm, as if at ease. "Honor isn't something a man can trade, nor is it something he can buy."

Rhonwen had heard those words a hundred times from her father before his death at the hands of Roman mercenaries. He would have been proud of the man his son had become.

The men watching the exchange passed hurried whispers back and forth.

"I may not have earned much honor yet," Telo said, "but if I do as you say, I'll never earn enough to replace what I lose tonight."

Alfonsus gripped Telo by the shoulder and yanked him out of the way. As the Roman in front of him shrank back, Alfonsus raised his sword over the Roman's head in both hands. Men all around began shouting, some for, some against.

"Silence!" bellowed Alfonsus. "I want the gods to hear this man die, and all the rest after him."

"No," Telo said.

Alfonsus whirled on him with his sword still raised.

Baia's voice carried over the heads of the assemblage as well as any bard's as she moved toward Alfonsus. "Move another muscle," she shouted, "and I'll see to it the Dark Lady visits you every night for the rest of your life." She poked him in the chest with her forefinger. "And each time she comes, she'll take a piece of you away with her."

"You lie," Alfonsus said.

Baia reached for his long mustache and with a firm jerk pulled his face close to hers. "Just remember whose son you murdered the next time you need a healer to patch the raw oozing wounds left by the Dark Lady." She released him and nodded toward Telo before making her way back to Rhonwen. She stared hard at the others and waved both hands in warding gestures. The dozen men nearest her stepped back.

Alfonsus lowered his sword. "My war is against Romans. I'll take no sport from the boy." He sheathed the weapon. "Drag this scum back behind Gyrisoenian walls and guard them while we celebrate." He looked directly into Telo's eyes. "Don't fool yourself into thinking you've won any honor at my expense. You're still no warrior."

He directed his men to give their spears to the Castulans. Like water pouring through a breached dam, the crowd of warriors flowed behind Telo, the prisoners, and the guards, pushing them out of the gates to begin the journey to the Gyrisoenian's clanhold.

When all the warriors had disappeared, Rhonwen turned to her mother. "What can we do?"

Baia took Rhonwen's hand. "We'll follow, of course."

After helping her mother into the saddle, Rhonwen pulled herself up. She would ride double all night to the Otherworld if it meant getting her brother home safely.

Baia swore most of the way out of the town.

"On this foul night, I'd rather the company of Vedius and his ilk than that of my own kind. May they all be destroyed if my son is harmed." She spat on her palm and clapped her hands together to seal the curse.

✠ ✠ ✠

The Gyrisoenians, jubilant with victory and pillaged Roman wine, advanced toward their town. Even if they maintained the drunken pace set by the warriors, Rhonwen despaired of reaching any place in which she and Baia could pull Telo away from the others. Her stomach twisted in hunger and kept her awake as she leaned against her mother's back. The horse plodded forward, rocking her into brief naps, but with each stumble of hoof over stone, she jolted awake. Eventually, sleep eluded her altogether.

"Why didn't you speak up sooner?" she said. "It's plain that Alfonsus fears you."

"Keep your voice down," Baia whispered.

Rhonwen made a face. "These men don't care what I think."

"True," Baia said, patting Rhonwen's knee, "but I've no desire to draw attention. I wait only for the chance to find your brother and head home before he gets into more trouble."

"Then you should have spoken sooner. Telo could've been killed."

"Or worse."

Rhonwen smothered a short bark of laughter. "What's worse than death?"

"Dishonor. Do you think your brother would have been better off hidden behind my skirt?"

"He's just a boy!"

"You saw what he did. I'm proud of him. He carried a man's sword tonight, and he made a man's choice. He'll always be my son, but he's no longer my boy."

"But you gave him Father's sword!" Rhonwen said.

Baia turned her head sharply. "He's of the age where he must learn to fight, and he did well this evening. That doesn't mean I think he's ready for a battle."

Rhonwen eased forward, encircled her mother's waist, and rested her cheek on Baia's back. She couldn't relax knowing her little brother marched ahead of her in the dark.

As the night sky gave way to the first pale tatters of morning, the walls of the Gyrisoenian clanhold emerged from the shadows. Mist hung over the valley, bathing everything in gray light. The main gates stood wide open, awaiting the return of the victors.

The revelers pushed their prisoners through the unguarded gate. Each man, Roman and Iberian alike, shuffled with weariness. Telo remained in the center of the line of men guarding the prisoners, although the exhausted Romans offered no threat of escape.

The ragged crowd of Gyrisoenians directed their charges through the gate and out of sight. Roughly half their number had passed through into the city when shouts of alarm roused Rhonwen. Men ran back out through the gate, weapons dragging or thrown aside as they collided with their comrades in their haste to escape the clanhold.

"What is it?" Baia asked. "Can you see what's going on?"

Rhonwen squinted into the murky half-light. "They're being attacked from inside the city!"

Baia spurred their horse away from the battle and sought refuge in the safety of a nearby copse of trees. Rhonwen leaped from the horse and ran to the edge where she dropped to the ground and inched forward for a better view.

The bodies of fallen warriors littered the area near the gate.

"The Gyrisoenians have turned on each other," Rhonwen cried. She turned to her mother who'd crawled beside her. "Why would they do that?"

"Those aren't Gyrisoenians chasing them," Baia said.

Rhonwen turned in alarm. "How can you tell?"

"Look," Baia said pointing toward the gate. "They're fresh, and sober. And look at the way they fight. They're Romans wearing Iberian clothes." She paused and laid a trembling hand on Rhonwen's. "Did you see Telo come out?"

"No," Rhonwen whispered.

Baia groaned as if struck.

"He may be safe inside," Rhonwen said with a conviction she didn't feel. "We'll find him."

Baia nodded, but she wept as she watched the blood bath outside the Gyrisoenian walls. Exhausted and drunken Iberians proved no match for the disciplined Roman soldiers. When the battle finally ended, the Romans walked among the fallen and summarily dispatched both the grievously wounded and any who offered resistance. They chained all the others and left them huddled in the open. As the sun crept higher into the sky, Rhonwen could not see Telo among the prisoners outside.

The women left their horse tied to a tree and walked toward the gate. Most of the dead were Gyrisoenian, of whom they recognized only a few. Alfonsus sat among the chained prisoners. The big man beside him no longer carried the mesh sack full of Roman heads. Both stared into the dirt as the women passed them.

As Rhonwen and Baia approached the wall, the Romans ushered the rest of the Gyrisoenians out into the morning sun. The Romans drove hundreds of people, mostly the old, women, and children, before them like swine before pig boys. Any who stepped out of line they thrashed into submission. Rhonwen cringed when a young boy, no older than eight, stumbled in the line of prisoners and suffered a beating for his clumsiness.

A Roman approached Rhonwen and Baia with his sword drawn shouting, "Get into line!"

"But we're not—"

Baia grabbed Rhonwen's arm and towed her toward the herd of prisoners. They joined a knot of elderly men and women. A child wailed, its plaintive cry disturbing the unnatural silence of the throng.

"We've got to find Telo," Baia whispered.

Rhonwen looked around at the soldiers already securing the prisoners with slave chains. "We need to be more concerned about ourselves right now." A lean Roman officer caught her attention.

Baia turned to follow Rhonwen's gaze. "What is it?"

"Sertorius!" Rhonwen waved at him.

At the sound of his name he looked up, and a smile lit his face for the briefest moment. He spoke to one of his men and pointed at Rhonwen. The soldier strode into the mass of Gyrisoenians and walked straight to her.

"Come with me," the soldier said. He tried to push Baia away, but Rhonwen grabbed her hand and held on tight. "I'm not leaving without my mother."

The Roman shook his head. "Sertorius only wants you. Come along."

A vision of Telo's defiance flitted through Rhonwen's memory like a butterfly. She could be no less brave in the face of death. "No." She clutched her mother's hand.

"Fine," he said. "Bring her along. Sertorius can settle it." The man pushed people out of his way to clear a path. He positioned the women in front of the young officer and stood aside.

Sertorius bowed slightly to Rhonwen. "What are you doing here, my little queen? Do you too make war on Rome?"

"Of course not," she said. "We came to find my little brother."

Sertorius looked at Baia for the first time. "Who's this?"

"My mother," Rhonwen said. "Driad Baia, a healer."

The tall Roman nodded and crossed his arms over his chest. He looked out at the people being put in chains. An already hot morning sun beat down on them relentlessly, and many of the children whimpered.

"Why shouldn't I make you a part of that sorry lot," he asked. "You aid my enemy."

"We did no such thing. Neither did we attack you or your men."

He gestured toward a rank of prisoners, each of them too old, too young, or too sick to fight. "Neither did they."

"Mother and I delivered a foal for one of Governor Fufidius' horses when the battle in Castulo began. We knew nothing about it. We've only come to find my brother, brought here by the Gyrisoenians against his will."

"I suppose he wasn't involved in the fighting either," Sertorius said.

"I—" she began, unsure of how much to tell him.

Sertorius touched her lips with his fingertip to keep her silent. "Say no more. Later you may still claim you've never lied to me."

He beckoned the nearby soldier. "Stay with these women while they search through the living and the dead. When they find whomever they seek, escort them all to safety."

He turned back to Rhonwen. "Make your search quick. When the buildings no longer cast shadows, you must leave or risk being burned with this village."

"Thank you," Rhonwen said.

Sertorius walked away in silence. Baia pulled Rhonwen along, and the soldier had to hurry to catch up with them.

✠ ✠ ✠

Rhonwen and Baia worked their way through the bodies strewn about the entrance to the clanhold. The autumn sun burned with the fervor of summer, and flies, emboldened by the ample supply of dead, plagued the living as well. The coppery smell of blood filled Rhonwen's nostrils.

Near the inner gate they found a mass of dead Castulans. Rhonwen saw with dismay all those men unbloodied at the first battle in Castulo now lay bloodied in death. Telo's body sprawled among them.

Baia wailed, her shrill cry smothering Rhonwen's sobs. They hauled him out of the pile of bodies, impeded by the arrows that pierced his body. Rhonwen, overcome with grief, sat numb and silent, unable to do more than watch as Baia broke the wooden shafts and forced the pieces from her son's limp body one by one. Four arrows, but only one had killed him. Baia touched her finger to the end of the shaft protruding from his heart. Her tears mixed with the dried blood on his tunic.

"There's not much time left," said the soldier with them. "You can't take him with you."

Her face set as hard as marble, Baia shook her head. "I won't leave him here."

"You can't carry him all the way to Castulo."

"If I have to drag him on my cloak, I'll not leave my son behind."

"I'll fetch the horse," Rhonwen said.

"What horse?" the Roman asked. "Where is it?"

She gestured toward the east. "We left it out there in the trees. I'll get it."

"Impossible. I can't guard both of you at the same time," he said. "If something happens to you, Sertorius would crucify me."

A group of Romans trudged by, and Rhonwen recognized them from the previous night in Castulo. One of the men spit on the corpses of the Iberians.

Rhonwen screamed at him. "Is this how you repay the bravery of those who saved your lives last night? Have you no shred of honor?"

One of the men gazed down at Telo. At length he looked at the two women and their Roman guard, and then he turned to the others. "She's right." He pointed at Telo. "When that mad Gyrisoenian would have butchered us, this boy stood up to him."

He cleared his throat and looked away. "When my turn came to face death, I ran. When they broke into the barracks, I looked for a place to hide. This boy was more man than I."

"Then help me get him home," Baia said. "Go with my daughter to retrieve our horse."

Without waiting for her guard to agree, Rhonwen grasped the soldier's arm and dragged him back through the gates. It seemed that she ran in a dream, unable to draw closer to her horse or farther from the city walls, yet at last she found the animal where she'd left it and climbed on its back. With the Roman behind her, they rode back into the city.

By the time Rhonwen returned with the horse, the buildings ceased to cast more than a hand's width of shadow. With the help of the two Romans, they loaded Telo across the back of the horse and made their way out of the clanhold. Both soldiers stayed with them until they were a safe distance away. The guard returned to Sertorius, but the other paused long enough to hand Rhonwen a coin.

"For his passage to the gods," he said. He turned and walked away.

✠ ✠ ✠

Telo's body lay across the saddle, his coltish arms and legs dangling as Baia and Rhonwen led the horse homeward.

As the horse plodded into the village, and they drew closer to Healer's House, the sides of the road filled with silent watchers. Worried mothers and wives asked after their men, but Baia only shrugged in answer.

"Dead or enslaved," Rhonwen said again and again as they turned to her.

She wondered how long it would be before the world knew of Sertorius' ploy. The Roman soldier who went with her to find their horse told her how Sertorius had roused his men from their barracks before the attack. When he discovered the identity of the attackers, he disguised his men as Iberians, marched on the undefended Gyrisoenian clanhold, and captured it.

Baia and Rhonwen had passed the gate of Roman Castulo earlier that day. The Romans, too, made preparations for burials. Scores of legionnaires had been killed in their beds, an equal number slaughtered in the streets. She and Baia had witnessed the killings of many unarmed men, including a score of merchants and their families. Many of them likely deserved to die, but she remembered Vedius and how he fell. She hoped he'd had enough time in his last few moments to prepare his spirit for death. She made the crossed motions for the sign of Rhiannon. Even a Roman deserved to see his death coming.

Rhonwen stopped the horse at Healer's House where two women she recognized as former students of Orlan ignored their weak protests and lowered Telo gently to the ground.

"I must prepare my son for burial," Baia said.

Orlan stepped out of the house looking as exhausted as Rhonwen felt. "No," he said, his voice gentle. "We'll care for him until you're rested."

Rhonwen wanted to tend to her brother during his last moments among the living, but two nights without sleep robbed her of the strength.

Baia, with dark circles under her eyes, looked at Rhonwen and agreed. "Only a little rest."

At Orlan's command the women ushered Rhonwen and her mother into the house and put them to bed. Rhonwen fell asleep before the others left the hut and knew nothing more until Baia roused her.

Particles of dust danced in a shaft of afternoon light. Rhonwen had slept long but had no memory of dreaming. Her body ached as she yawned and stretched.

Baia stood near, her face marked by new lines of grief. Get up," she said abruptly. "We must finish preparing Telo."

Memories flooded back as Rhonwen dressed. New tears welled up and she sought comfort in her mother's embrace, but Baia pushed her away. "Come, our work's not done."

Rhonwen splashed water on her face from the pottery bowl warming by the fire and followed her mother to the building that housed Telo's body.

Thanks to Orlan and the two women there remained little to do. Telo's body was already washed, clothed in clean linen, and laid out in preparation for burial, his weapon at his side. Rhonwen sniffed. He'd been killed so suddenly that his sword never left its sheath.

Baia placed a wreath of woven ivy on Telo's head and kissed him farewell.

Orlan appeared in the doorway. "The cart is here." It would take Telo to the burial place.

Baia raised her head. "This is too soon."

He wrapped her in his arms. "The cart is needed for the others, too."

Baia's eyes darkened. "The Romans must pay."

Rhonwen knew that Gyrisoenii and Castulan stupidity were the reasons her brother lay dead.

"How?" Orlan asked. "Would you have more boys sneak into Roman barracks?"

"I only know my son died because of Roman arrows."

"His death was stupid," Rhonwen said. "He shouldn't have been there in the first place."

Baia fixed her with a stare. "How convenient that your Roman comrade allowed us to fetch him home."

"What do you mean?" Orlan asked.

Baia's lips barely moved as she spoke. "I've been thinking about it all night. Rhonwen is friendly with the man who killed my son."

"That's absurd!" Rhonwen cried. "Sertorius attacked those who attacked him. We would do the same."

"How is it that he alone escaped with all his men unless he had warning of the attack?"

Rhonwen shrugged. "How should I know?"

"You said his barracks were empty by the time our warriors arrived. He circled around and cut many of them down from behind. Dressed in garments taken from our dead, he marched on the Gyrisoenii clanhold and waited for them to come to him."

"That's what I was told," Rhonwen said.

"Someone warned Sertorius."

"What are you saying?"

"I think you did it."

Rhonwen's jaw dropped in astonishment.

"That's why you stayed behind, pretending to look after Vedius, but he was already dead. You went straight to Sertorius. Everyone knows he gave you money, and in Gyrisoenia you were the only one he spared from enslavement."

Rhonwen recoiled in horror at Baia's accusation. "I had nothing to do with Telo's death!" Anger washed over her. "You gave him Father's sword and encouraged him to train with Tarax. What did you think would happen? You gave Telo raw meat and sent him to play with lions."

"Sertorius could have stopped the fighting. It wasn't Fufidius who ordered the massacre." She crossed her arms. "Sertorius did."

Rhonwen's chest hurt and she pressed hard on her heart. In this, at least, Baia seemed right. In the way of her people, Sertorius was responsible for her brother's death.

"Yes," Rhonwen said slowly, "I suppose so."

Baia's expression changed from grief to anger. "What do you intend to do about it?"

"I don't understand."

"Neither do I," Orlan said. "What are you asking?"

"When someone kills a kinsman, the family deserves its vengeance. Rhonwen must avenge Telo's death."

Rhonwen hesitated. "I can't."

"Shame," Baia hissed. "My own daughter sides with *togas*!"

"That's not true!"

"If you loved your brother, you'd vow to kill Sertorius and feed his body to the crows."

Rhonwen turned away. How could she make such a vow?

Baia grabbed Rhonwen's hand and pressed her palm against Telo's cold flesh. "Swear it," Baia cried. "On your brother's dead body, swear it!"

Rhonwen stared down at Telo's still form. The dark places where the Roman arrows pierced him mocked her reluctance. If his spirit needed something to help him through the Cauldron to another life, then she must be the vehicle.

Orlan took Baia aside. "I can't permit this."

"It's not up to you."

"Let her accept a geas when she's older. She's barely out of her childhood."

"Am I supposed to stay here and wait?" Baia's face contorted with grief. "How can I remain where the man who killed my son still lives?"

Orlan's face softened. "Go away from here. Take Rhonwen and finish her training in the hill villages to the north. Come back when she's ready for her Healer's tattoo and can accept her vow."

Baia pushed him away. "I'll leave this place, but not before Rhonwen swears to avenge her brother. He was all I had to keep me in my old age."

Bile rose in Rhonwen's throat. Even dead, her brother still came first to Baia. Rhonwen whirled on her. "All right, I swear it. I swear I'll avenge Telo's death!"

Baia slumped forward as if she'd just fought a great battle. "Blood for blood."

Rhonwen swayed with anguish. The oath lay thick on her tongue, and nothing felt right about it.

Baia reached a shaking hand toward Orlan, ignoring her daughter. When he took it, Baia hugged him close. "Yes," she whispered. "We'll go far from this place of death. May the gods watch over us until Rhonwen returns and buries a blade of vengeance in Sertorius' heart."

4

Once the false god had again hidden in a piece of wood, Jaslon applied woad to it so that the stick would not likely be misplaced. He vowed to repeat the impostor's magic. To test his skill Jaslon selected a serving woman's child, born mute and left in the care of the enclave.

Jaslon led the child into the mountain and there marked him with woad in the manner of the impostor. He bound the child with heavy cord and waved the baneweed fumes toward his face. In moments the transformation was complete. Jaslon placed the small stick of the child and that of the false god beside the Sentinel Stones where he waited for dawn.

— Stave Four of Jaslon, 18th Master of Mount Eban Enclave

Belgica

"**G**alan." Mallec spat the name like venom. "I've never wanted to fight anyone so much in my life. I'm neither coward nor liar!"

"I know," Driad Seva said as she poured him a mug of sweet cider. "Now calm down. A druid must never show emotion over something like this."

"But Galan—"

Seva put a finger to his lips, and Mallec clamped his mouth shut.

"For druids, there is only one place to show emotion: on the battlefield. There your task is to direct the power of the gods to flow through the warriors. That is the time to raise your voice and shake your fist, to batter the spirits from the air with your staff and frighten the enemy into hiding with your battle horn." She settled beside him on a large wolf skin near the fire, opened her jar of salve, and motioned for him to remove his tunic.

"If I had called him a coward—"

"He would have thrashed you," Seva said.

"But I'm not allowed to touch him?"

"It seems to me you get the chance to do that every week."
She probed lightly at his ribs and when he winced, smiled. "Some
things haven't changed."

"I've changed," Mallec said.

Raising an eyebrow, she leaned away from him. "Tell me how."

"The gods have set a test for me, and I won't turn away from
it."

With deliberate motions she rubbed more salve on his weary
muscles. It felt good to be in her care again. He tried not to flinch
as she touched the new bruises. "How can you be angry at me
for one vision and not another?"

"Because your latest vision isn't about my son. I don't want
you putting ideas in Ambioris' head. Let the gods show him his
path when he's a man. As for Galan, he can choose his own."

After storing the unguent pot, she settled beside him, leaning
against a willow backrest. "Tell me your dream again."

"You've heard it three times already."

"And I may have you tell it a dozen times more," she said.
"Most people can't remember their dreams past breakfast. Why
should I think this one of yours is any different?"

"Because the gods sent this dream."

"The gods send everyone dreams."

"Not like this one."

She pursed her lips. "Tell it to me again."

Mallec repeated his vision, striving to include everything.
He told her of Lugh and the Great Mother, of the stone well and
the great horse, and finally of Galan's fatal fall.

"Did you recognize the horse?" Seva asked.

"No, but I'd know it if I saw it. I've never seen one so big."

She smiled. "Perhaps you would have if you spent more time
plowing."

Mallec exhaled in exasperation. He remembered how angry
she'd been at him earlier. This was the driad speaking, not the
mother of a little boy. "You don't believe me either, do you?"

"Of course I do."

He looked up in surprise. "Then you'll help me?"

"No. You said it yourself: it's your test, not mine."

"Talorec said you'd call a council if you thought my vision
had merit."

"I could do that," she said, "but then what chance would you
have to demonstrate the strength of your convictions?"

Mallec pondered the question. "What if I fail?"

"If your vision is true, then the Eburones will be deprived
of a young warrior."

She walked to the door and pulled her red healer's cloak from a peg. "The weather's begun to turn. If you expect to wear the ovate's robe, you'd do well to solve this problem before the harvest season."

✠ ✠ ✠

The days leading to Lughnasa sped by, marked by regular beatings from Galan on the practice field. The larger boy delivered each blow with a steady dose of invective. Ridicule made the cuts seem deeper, the bruises more tender.

Mallec's repeated efforts to prove his case to Talorec failed. When he dared approach Galan's friends for assistance, they laughed harder than Galan had.

He considered various solutions, but most, like finding the horse and hiding it until after the celebration, offered no reward for the risk. The replacement could just as easily throw the rider. He considered digging up the area in front of the well or scattering sharp stones across it to keep the horse from coming too close, but the well was central to all activities of the clan. Anyone who saw him laboring there would stop him.

He considered putting something in Galan's food to make him ill, but the headstrong youth would likely compete anyway. Desperate to stop Galan, Mallec approached Cativolcus, chief of the entire clan. Cativolcus told him to mind his own affairs. "What the gods will, will be," he'd said.

The day of the harvest ride came, and Mallec still had no idea how he could prove his vision true without getting Galan killed. He busied himself stacking willow and hazelwood branches for winter cook fires. Finished, he spent a peaceful noontime with Ambioris in the nearby field as the boy practiced slinging stones at sheaves of wheat.

As the afternoon event drew closer, people began to gather on the best spots for observing the contest. Mallec sent Ambioris home to Seva. He waited until Ambioris was out of sight before settling in a spot on the stone wall surrounding the well. Then he waited.

A commotion near the clanhold gates caught his attention. Shouts of "Eburones!" and "Lugh!" preceded a group of mounted warriors. Talorec led the procession and blew repeatedly on his battle horn to begin the ceremony. The warriors entered first, and then came the contestants, with Galan in their vanguard. Each had dressed as if for battle, swaggering in the clan's yellow and green striped breeches. Each wore his limewashed hair stiff enough to stand up like a cropped horse's mane. Wisps of mustaches fringed their mouths, and some had painted their naked torsos with blue woad or red ochre. Gold and bronze neck torcs gleamed in the sunlight, and everyone wore bracelets of bronze and silver. They carried the weapons of the clan: long sword, knife, sling and spear.

As the men entered the commons, women and girls called to them from the sides of the road, urging them to fight well. Many offered a night of passion to the victor. The feast of Lughnasa was a man's festival, and every male old enough to carry a blade proudly walked or rode as an escort for the horse. Mallec was the only exception.

Talorec and the veterans tethered their mounts on the grassy commons and ranged about the high ground for the best view while the contestants drifted toward the well. As the crowd grew in response to Talorec's horn, Mallec decided on one last attempt to avert the coming disaster. He stood and walked straight toward Talorec.

"I'm surprised to see you here," the man said. "Galan thought you'd prefer to hide."

Mallec ignored the bait. "I'm here to do what I must. Nothing has changed. Either I act, or Galan dies."

Talorec sobered. "What do you want of me?"

"I would borrow your horn," Mallec said.

"What for?"

One of the warriors sneered. "Have you ever blown a war horn? What makes you think you could make any sound?"

The others laughed, and Mallec felt a flush of blood to his face. He clung to Seva's advice. Showing emotion would only harm his cause. "I'll blow it because I have to. Before the ride begins, I must gain the clan's attention. I'm going to tell them what I saw in my dream."

"They'll laugh you out of the village," Talorec said.

Mallec shook his head. "That doesn't matter. They laugh at me anyway. If I'm right, that will change."

"And if you're wrong?"

Mallec reached for the horn.

Talorec pulled the instrument away. "What if you're wrong?"

"That's not possible."

Talorec held the war horn behind him and returned Mallec's gaze with an expression of approval he normally reserved for Galan. "I'll sound the horn," he said. "Once to quiet the people so you can have your say, and once to begin the contest."

Mallec nodded and walked back toward the well. On the way he stopped at a cart heaped with fruits and vegetables and selected a soft melon. Talorec joined him. Soon, Talorec put the war horn to his lips and blew a prolonged blast. The crowd settled down.

"This is Mallec," Talorec yelled. "He lives with me while he studies to be a druid. He has something to say."

Mallec stepped forward and Galan shouted, "Spare us your prattle!"

Talorec fixed him with a glare as sharp as any blade. "Close your mouth, boy, or I'll close it for you."

As Galan retreated, Mallec cleared his throat. "Several weeks ago I had a vision of this day." As he spoke, he hefted the ripe melon, tossing it a hands-width into the air. "In that vision, I saw the young warriors competing for the honor of the harvest ride, and I saw the first one to climb atop this huge animal."

"Who was it?" cried someone in the crowd. "I still have time to change my wager!"

Mallec waited for the crowd's laughter to subside. "I didn't say I knew who won."

"What happened to the first rider?" someone else asked. The crowd quieted in anticipation.

Mallec hesitated. He'd never experienced so many people looking at him, many obviously eager to hear what he had to say.

"The horse threw him." Mallec stepped back and hurled the melon at the stone wall. It splattered, leaving a sticky mass of dripping pulp. "Afterward, his head looked like that."

Whispers rippled through the crowd, and he raised a hand to silence them. "This ceremony is an ancient tradition. I can't stop it. But the person I'm talking about knows who he is. This is his last chance to save himself."

"You can't frighten me," Galan said stepping forward. "Children have bad dreams. No one believes they're real."

"My dream—"

"Is crow scat!" Galan shouted. "Father, blow the horn. It's time to begin."

Talorec looked at Mallec. "Are you done?"

Mallec nodded. "But I'm not leaving. If I stay near the well, I may be able to break Galan's fall."

Talorec smiled. "You've more courage than I thought. I will stand beside you."

Mallec slipped down from the wall.

"Warriors, stand ready!" Talorec shouted. Galan and the others immediately began to jostle for position. Talorec raised the metal horn and blew. Instantly, the contestants dashed toward the horse, all thought of Mallec's warning forgotten.

⌖ ⌖ ⌖

In his dream, the battle for the horse ended quickly, but the actual event took much longer. The observers crowding the makeshift arena surged back and forth as the combatants swarmed around the animal, kicking and fighting each other for a chance to grab the saddle. Blood flowed from dozens of cuts as the scythes attached to the horse's legs sliced the unwary.

Mallec shifted to keep himself between the horse and the well. Though Talorec laughed at the folly of the timid and yelled encouragement to Galan and anyone else who appeared to make progress, he stayed close beside Mallec.

Several times the swirling mass ventured near the well, and twice someone broke from the pack to stand atop the wall in hopes the horse would come near. Galan eventually adopted the tactic, and Mallec's stomach tightened. He touched Talorec's sleeve to reassure himself of the man's presence.

From his position on the wall, Galan's feet shifted on a level even with Mallec's belt. The young warrior put his foot on Mallec's shoulder and shoved him to the side. "Stay out of my way!"

Mallec obliged him, intending to regain his position once Galan left the wall. By the time injuries and exhaustion had reduced the number of competitors to a half dozen, the action moved closer to the well. Galan crouched in anticipation.

He leaped from the wall to the back of the huge horse. The animal panicked. As Galan struggled to hang on, the beast whirled completely around, scattering the remaining competitors, then reared straight up on its hind legs.

Just as Mallec had seen it in the dream, Galan rolled backward off the animal's back. Mallec bent his knees and tensed for the impact. The horse rocked forward and kicked out with both hind legs. The thudding sound of hooves striking human flesh sickened him. Galan's limp body crashed into the young druid and Talorec, throwing them against the rough wall.

So great was the ache in his stomach Mallec felt as though the horse had kicked him instead of Galan. Mallec gazed down at Galan, whose bloody head rested on his thigh. Everything stopped, including the horse. In the absence of noise and disorder, the animal stood quivering.

Though Mallec had not seen her among the crowd, Seva suddenly appeared and knelt in front of him. She gave the downed warrior a hurried examination.

"How is he?" Talorec asked, his voice husky.

Seva waved him to silence as she put her ear to Galan's chest. "His heart's still beating," she said a moment later. "But I don't understand how."

"Why not?" Talorec whispered.

Seva looked up at him, grief and awe contorting her face. "Because the horse crushed his skull just as Mallec prophesied."

5

At dawn, Jaslon implored Lugh to smile on both the child and the impostor. He waited until the sun had traversed the sky, yet the two souls remained bound. In anger, Jaslon threw the woad-marked stick into his campfire and was surprised to hear it shriek as if tormented. He therefore retrieved it and returned them both to the enclave.

Some days later, the child's mother claimed she could no longer bear his absence. Jaslon gave her the stick and advised it was Lugh's will the child's soul remain imprisoned. After much lamentation, the woman traveled to Eban and there built a shelter near the Sentinel Stones where she could daily beseech the god of light for her child's resurrection.

—*Stave Five of Jaslon, 18th Master of Mount Eban Enclave*

Iberia 91 B.C.

"Uncle?"

At the sound of Rhonwen's voice from the doorway, Orlan looked up from his drum-making. He beckoned his niece to enter the small hut he called home. He thanked the gods daily since Baia and Rhonwen's safe return to Castulo after five long years spent healing and studying among the clans in the mountains. He delighted in having both of them home again.

Now Rhonwen was a woman well-schooled in the healer's art. She'd learned much, including, he suspected, a few things he'd not heard of. The Order of the Wise incorporated many skills, and no one druid mastered them all, but Baia made sure Rhonwen had a taste of each. That didn't surprise him. Since she grew old enough to talk, she'd been his best and most uncompromising pupil. Her accomplishments made him proud.

He indicated the bearskin beside him. "Come, sit. I'm making your initiation drum and need another pair of hands to tie the sinew."

Rhonwen eased herself down beside him and knotted the cords.

"My fingers get more useless by the day," Orlan said. "I wish I could find something to loosen these stiff joints."

Rhonwen kissed his cheek and playfully pulled the sparse hairs growing on his chin.

He winked at her. "Is it wise to tug the wisdom hairs of an elder?"

She laughed. "Mother says wisdom hairs only grow on the faces of women, for if wisdom were as common as the beards on men, there'd be no trouble in the world." She smoothed a few hairs on his balding pate. "Rather than finding a potion to relieve stiff joints, find one to grow hair on a man's head. I'll wager some would pay handsomely for that secret."

"I have no doubt," he said, running a gnarled hand over the bald spot on the top of his head. He lifted the drum, nearly three hand spans across, toward Rhonwen and indicated a loose strand. "Hold this."

He tucked the other end through the remaining holes poked in the hide as she pulled the sinew tighter at each hole. When finished and struck with a leather-tipped birch twig, the drum would emit a deep resonating thrum.

The silver bracelets on her wrists tinkled like cymbals with each pull. It made the work of securing the hide to the wooden frame pleasing and quick. Orlan pulled the last sinew, tied it off, and set the drum aside.

"Now, what brings you here?" he asked.

"I've come to tell you the time set for the ceremony is good. My moon blood has arrived."

"Ah, excellent," he said with a satisfied nod. "If only all my students were as accommodating as you."

She laughed. "I notice you men have trouble with this part of the ritual."

"As well we should," he murmured. "When the Goddess sees fit to let us deliver babes into the world as women do, then we will bleed, too."

"You're jealous!" she laughed.

He couldn't keep the smile from his face. He loved her as much as any father would. He'd seen her birth, but only from a distance. That sight remained hidden to men, even druids. "Yes, I'm jealous, but only when the child pops forth. A more wondrous sight than your wrinkled red face I never beheld. I regret the Goddess permits only driads like you the honor of being a mother's hands in these matters."

She hugged him. "A driad, like me."

"It seems only a moment ago you were a child riding on my knee," Orlan said. "The initiation marks the beginning of a druid's life for you. From that moment on, everything will be altered."

"Aye," she said with a soft smile, "even my rank will change."

He studied his niece quizzically. "Your rank? You're the daughter of a respected driad. Your father was a chief. You needn't worry about such things. Besides, your studies aren't over."

She cleared her throat, as if uneasy about what she had to say. Orlan nodded encouragement.

"I thought it might be wise to invite the local Roman officials to the ceremony. They seem interested, and it might help relations between us if they knew more about our ways."

Orlan frowned. Her attention to Roman ways had increased since her last meeting with Sertorius five years earlier. The years hadn't removed the geas from her any more than it had removed her affection for the man she'd sworn to kill. Rhonwen's initiation meant she had attained an age at which the geas for death must be carried out.

"As commander here, Sertorius knows as much about us as he wishes, I think." Orlan gripped her hands. "Your initiation is a profound and holy achievement, but it means nothing to the Romans. More importantly, you mustn't delude yourself into thinking he would be welcome by everyone."

"You mean Mother?"

He nodded. "Baia rarely speaks of your vow to avenge Telo's death, but I can see her think it whenever a Roman soldier walks by. Don't invite Sertorius. It honors the man you've sworn to kill. That's hardly an auspicious start for a new druid." He smiled to take some of the sting from his words.

"I'm a healer," she said. "What do I know of killing?"

"As a druid, you know more about it than most," he said. Memories of old lessons in ritual death rose unbidden. "Besides, you made your vow before you became a healer."

Rhonwen rubbed her hands. "I know. I've thought about it often. He's never alone, you know."

Orlan respected Sertorius, both for his cunning and for the loyalty he engendered in his men. If Sertorius lived, Orlan had no doubt the man would be a great leader.

"He's a worthy man, hard but just, and quick to mete out punishments if they're deserved."

Rhonwen nodded, her sweet face marred only by the pale crescent moon scar on her cheek where a mercenary had struck her and paid the ultimate price at Sertorius' hand. She touched it with her forefinger. "He did nothing to harm us. Mother is more responsible for Telo's death than Sertorius."

"Nevertheless, you made a blood vow. Only Baia or the gods can relieve you of it."

Her amber eyes darkened. "Then I'll seek the Goddess' answer during my ceremony. For no one is as stubborn as my mother."

They sat silent for a long time. Orlan gazed into the fire while Rhonwen wrapped strands of sinew thread around the quill-tips of feathers and secured them to the edge of her new drum. When she finished, Orlan turned his gaze from the fire and studied her. Her tattoos, nearly a dozen denoting her achievements, seemed foreign on her.

She blushed and patted him on the knee. "You stare, Uncle." She swept a palm across her forehead to catch the errant locks that escaped the pile of curls balanced with combs atop her head.

He shook his head. "I marvel every day at how you've grown."

She gave him the fragment of a smile but caught his mood in an instant. "What is it?"

"You don't look much like an Iberian these days. I wonder if you haven't spent too much time with the Romans." She stiffened, and he decided not to pursue it further. Instead of giving her the lecture he intended, he smiled. "In the past five years, you've changed your hair style a dozen times, and it's been nearly that long since you took to wearing a *stola* rather than a tunic."

She smoothed the belted waist of the green-dyed garment. "My Roman patients are more comfortable if I wear clothing they're accustomed to."

He leaned over and kissed her, careful to tickle her with the scratchy ends of his beard. "No matter. Your initiation requires only the clothes you were born in."

⽊ ⽊ ⽊

Sertorius bent close to her face, his dark eyes intent upon her mouth, when suddenly someone shook her.

"Rhonwen! Wake up!" Baia called.

"Go away," Rhonwen muttered as she turned over, her back to the day. With eyes closed, she tried to recapture the wondrous dream, but it was gone. She rolled onto her back, enjoying the last few moments of leisure before she had to start her morning chores. She yawned and stretched. "It's well light outside."

Baia breathed a wounded sigh edged with pique. "It's more than just morning, Rhonwen. How can you have forgotten what day this is?"

Rhonwen's eyes flew open, and she sat up. She was in Healer's House, and her initiation would soon begin. "Oh, gods, I'm not ready!" she cried and threw off the sleeping furs.

Baia had placed a small pot of oats to cook on the fire. Rhonwen scooped out a ladle of the hot mash, tossed in a handful of nuts and dried dates, and ate hungrily. This would be her last meal before the ceremony. What she ate now would have to sustain her through the next day's fast.

She washed and dressed quickly, then retrieved the white linen blood cloth she had woven for the ceremony. She folded it several times and placed it in a new wicker basket. The cloth was the most sacred object of all.

"I've put a fresh edge on my knife," Baia said from the doorway. "Perhaps there'll be a bit less sting to the healer's tattoo you've earned."

Rhonwen raced to the door and kissed her.

"Your ordeal begins at noon, and it's nearly that now. Come." With a swirl of her driad's robe, Baia turned and left the house.

Rhonwen tucked the basket under her arm and followed her mother into the light.

✠ ✠ ✠

At a sacred grove, amid the holiest father oaks, those assembled for the ceremony greeted her. The druids escorted her past the gaping mouths and bulging eyes of gods and spirits that adorned the twisted limbs and trunks of the ancient trees. She had no fear, for these things were meant to frighten only the uninitiated away from this, one of the last druid holy places in Iberia.

Orlan took her right elbow while another druid stood on her left. They ushered her through an ivy-covered archway into the heart of the sacred circle, and led her from the deep shadow of the trees into a clearing lined with standing stones as tall as men. In the center stood an altar of rock covered with purple and yellow lichens older than the ancient oaks.

She stopped before the altar and placed her basket upon it. She would spend the entire day and night here, fasting, drumming, and praying, and if the gods had any pity they would release her from her vow. Orlan kissed her cheek and withdrew to a place set aside for the men, far behind the altar.

The women, tattooed driads all, wore long sun-whitened tunics. For this woman's ceremony, each also wore a flowing robe of scarlet. Sashes in the colors of a dozen clans marked their origins, while the formal vestments marked the commonality of their achievement.

Rhonwen stood. The women removed her clothing and set aside her stained blood rags. Then, armed with buckets of warm soapy water and handfuls of soft moss, they washed her.

She closed her eyes as they scrubbed, envisioning them cleaning her heart and mind as well as her body. She rocked with the vigor of their brushings.

Baia poured the last of the fresh water over Rhonwen's head to rinse away the soap. She sputtered until an attendant dried her face. Baia then bade her move toward a bed of dried moss at the foot of the altar. Baia retrieved the basket and Rhonwen took out the white linen triangle. At a nod from her mother, she laid the triangle in the center of the moss and sat upon it. Already she could feel the moisture running from between her legs to color the pristine whiteness of the cloth. A healer wore a cloak the color of newly shed blood.

The women approached her with a pot of wet, red earth soaked in wine. With quick motions beginning at her forehead, they stained her entire body. She sat before them all, made holy by the color of the Goddess' life-giving blood.

Baia held up her knife, and one of the other women set beside her a small pot of a richer red pigment, the crimson shade of heart's blood.

"O-ghe!" Baia intoned.

"O-ghe!" answered all the women and the men behind them.

Rhonwen trembled, unable to still the racing of her heart. Now it began.

Baia knelt in front of her. "Behold! Blood shed without pain," she said. "This inexplicable essence of our lives pours out freely and with great magic, given by the Great Mother as a sign of her abiding love. We praise her many names!"

"We praise her!"

Baia took the pot in her left hand and placed the tip of the knife in the mixture. "Sacred blood of the Mother," she said.

"Sacred blood of the Healer," the others replied.

"Those who heal must know pain."

Rhonwen could not close her eyes, although she wanted to. The knife tip drew close to her left breast. Baia placed the blade on the soft flesh just above Rhonwen's nipple and sketched a bloodless swirl of red pigments into the semblance of the Healer's tattoo that curved from the dark ring of her areola up toward her neck before spiraling down to her heart.

It was a design Rhonwen loved, one she had clutched at with her baby fingers while nursing, and had seen every day growing up in her mother's house: the Healer's mark.

With a satisfied grunt Baia rose and handed the knife to another woman, then retrieved a thinner, sharper blade from the altar. She washed it with red wine from a flask and, facing each direction in turn, showed it to the Mother. The women encircled Rhonwen, singing the holy names of the great goddess with each step in their moon-wise circuit of the circle.

The women chanted, and Rhonwen's eyelids closed. No sound existed save the driads' voices and the beat of druid drums. Something stung her and initiated a sharp throbbing pain that ran up and down her chest.

An owl came to her mind's eye but didn't speak. Instead he lowered himself to her, and she, suddenly small, climbed upon his back. He flew, silent and low over the pink-blooming comfrey. He flowed like water over the meadows, stopping for neither food nor drink. Together they sailed across a sea-blue sky until at last he stopped to let her rest. A white deer approached. Its brown eyes fixed on hers without fear and bid her follow. She pushed through bracken as high as her hips without seeing another living thing. The bracken closed around her, and she felt imprisoned, unable to breathe. A child cried in the distance, and she wanted to go to it, but the hind prevented her.

The voices faded, and she heard the drums as if they ringed her head. When the seven beats of the return signal came, the singing stopped.

"Rhonwen," Baia called.

"I hear," she answered, although her own voice sounded distant in her ears.

Baia rang a bell. "By the Mother's many names we call you to our ranks."

"I follow," Rhonwen said.

Baia put a water skin to Rhonwen's lips, and she drank.

"The sun will soon give way to Mother Moon, my child. Here you will remain until we come for you tomorrow."

Rhonwen could only nod. She did not want to open her eyes. She wanted only to ride the owl's back again and follow the path it had shown her.

⚜ ⚜ ⚜

Something tickled Rhonwen's foot, and she jerked her knees up close, rolled to her side, and winced. Her shoulder ached, the skin taut. She gingerly traced the hard scab line from her breast to her neck.

She wiggled upright and hugged herself for warmth. Though still dark, night was nearly done, and the eastern horizon held a pale promise of dawn. She yawned and rubbed her eyes. The night had been long, and she hadn't slept.

With only the night's creatures for company, she noted any who showed themselves to her, hoping to glean some meaning from their appearance. All such signs were beneficial to the healer's art. A grass snake slipped past her, the full moon reflecting off its back, a sure sign both the Mother and Aesculapius, the Roman's healing god, approved of her calling. And although she'd prayed most of the night for the dissolution of her vow to kill Sertorius, her appeal went unanswered. Worse, she could not make sense of the spirit journey she'd taken with the owl.

The thistle-pink sky brightened with the rising sun. The moment Lugh crested the distant hills with his flaming burden, two driads joined her. They helped her retrieve her stained linen, folding it and returning it to the basket. They presented her with a cloak of undyed linen and bid her follow them from the oak grove, its faces more terrible in the half light than they had appeared in the darkness. She stumbled more than once, but the driads stayed well away to leave her untouched during her sanctification.

She approached the altar in the heart of the village. Garlands of flowers bedecked the pathway, and well-wishers placed baskets of fruits and bread nearby to receive her blessings. A girl no more than four came as close as she dared and held up a rawhide bundle of her most secret things. Rhonwen smiled and dipped her finger beneath her tongue. She wiped a drop of saliva on the bundle, and the little girl's face broke into a smile. A healer's spittle held great worth.

Rhonwen scanned the crowd, pleased to see the faces of many friends. Nearly everyone in the village came for the celebration, and red-cloaked women from all over Iberia clustered near the altar. Baia stood in the center with Orlan and the other druids to one side. Unlike healer initiations of men, this one confirmed on Rhonwen the added honor of Midwife. Though mostly a formality, many attended this final and public part of the initiation. The promise of feasting later assured a sizeable crowd.

Near the back of the crowd, the flash of a dozen short red cloaks startled her, and Rhonwen pulled her garment more securely around her. Romans rarely attended Iberian celebrations, and the people nearest them made plenty of room. No one could miss seeing the Roman commander standing among his men in the place reserved for outlanders.

Quintus Sertorius, as handsome as ever, watched the proceedings. When the eyes of the villagers turned to her, his lingering gaze followed. She met his stare directly, as she always had, and saw something different in how he looked at her. Something inside her tilted. She looked away, determined to put him from her mind.

Baia motioned Rhonwen to kneel in front of the altar and face the east. Three bards sang the Healer's Song, their voices in a harmony accompanied only by the tinkling of a trio of brass bells. After Orlan pronounced the druid words that would bring her officially into the enclave, Baia embraced her.

"Daughter of the Mother, Daughter of Lugh, rise with the sun."

Rhonwen stood before them, her cloak falling to the ground. Brown blood mixed with the paled red stain of the previous days' ritual made her new tattoo hard to see. Her legs, too, bore dark red stains still wet with fresh moon blood. She turned, with arms upheld and eyes closed, and embraced the crowd, the village, and the sky. Then the women led her to a sheltered bower of laurel branches behind the altar and washed her again. With gentle strokes they wiped the stains away, careful not to rub the crust covering the tattoo's wounds. Then they dressed her in new white robes cinched in the middle with a belt of fine chain from which dangled three brass bells.

Cleaned and ready for the final ritual, she followed the women back into the sunlight.

The crowd cheered.

Baia gestured to the center of the altar and Rhonwen resumed her place. Baia put an empty sack in Rhonwen's hands before reaching into her own and drawing out herbs, one after the other, as symbols of Rhonwen's mastery of healing.

She raised a gray-green twig adorned with white berries. "By the power of druidswort, most sacred herb, I welcome you to our ranks."

Rhonwen grasped the mistletoe in her right hand, pressing it between her breasts.

A second driad approached. "By the good omens of vervain, I welcome you to our ranks."

Each woman in turn adorned Rhonwen with a bouquet or garland of flowers and herbs sacred to the Great Mother, symbols of a healer's obligation and trust and the tools of her trade. Bedecked finally with fragrant wreaths of interwoven feverwort, moonwort, and wormwood, she faced the villagers. The women encircled her, and Baia laid a new red cloak over her shoulders, the mark of her rank as a healer.

"O-ghe!" Baia cried. "Behold the healer, Driad Rhonwen, given to us by the grace of our Great Mother. She is worthy!"

"O-ghe," replied the crowd. "She is worthy."

The druids who had withdrawn returned. Orlan led them with a willow garland twisted about with lionsfoot and rue. "I welcome you, Driad Rhonwen, to the ways of Mystery." He signaled to one of the younger men who strode forward, a staff of polished ash in his hand.

Orlan's tree symbol on the staff was unmistakable, carved and then stained dark blue. The young man placed it in her outstretched hands. She wrapped her fingers around the smooth wood and squeezed. She recognized the staff as Orlan's own.

The druid faced the crowd. "O-ghe! She is worthy!"

The crowd cheered, repeating the ritual response: "She is worthy!"

Flower petals thrown by the swarming villagers rained down on her. Everyone offered some token of the day: a straw doll made by a child, a dried mushroom in the shape of a deer, a coin. She gathered each memento as tears of joy glittered on her cheeks.

Their gifts bestowed, the villagers dispersed toward the feasting hall. Sertorius stood on the path, magnificent in a grand toga of startling white. He stood like a god, tall and serene. Holding out a small figurine and a bundle of flowers, he bowed.

"My Queen, I would be remiss if I failed to attend one of the most significant events of the village in all the years I've been here. How delighted I am to discover you are the object of this great ceremony."

She smiled and accepted his gifts, her heart beating even faster. The statue of Mars surprised her. "You'll forgive me if I don't see what your god of war has to do with healing."

"Long before he accepted the role as father of warfare, he was Maris, the father of my people. His sacred plant is rue." He thrust a bouquet at her, and its fragrance, strong with rue and other wormwoods, nearly overpowered her. The collection included every major Roman plant of healing, including several even Orlan would have envied.

Rhonwen felt the blood rush to her cheeks at the compliment. Sertorius laughed.

"You've grown into a fine woman," he said. "Perhaps you'd sup with me in a week's time, to celebrate your achievement?"

The invitation came as a complete surprise. Though she'd often thought of him in a wistful, girlish manner, the notion of being alone with him startled her. Sertorius occasionally invited local chiefs, wandering bards, and even druids to his home, yet he maintained a reputation of moderation. He was never known to be drunk.

"I'm honored." She spotted Baia standing near the altar. Baia's scowl said more than any words. "But I can't." Rhonwen said.

He raised an eyebrow and gave no indication that he had seen Baia, and then he flashed a regretful smile. "Say no more, though should you change your mind, the invitation remains open." He bowed again and swept past her to disappear into the crowd.

She watched him go, smiling openly despite Baia's disapproval. Under any other circumstances, she decided, she would not hesitate to follow him.

6

On the morning of the summer solstice, the serving woman's son was restored to human form. Jaslon recalled that the false god had been transformed at the spring equinox. He rewarded the woman with a goat and instructed her to bring her son to the enclave for schooling when he came of age. The boy asked whether the gods had demanded his return. Jaslon looked upon him in amazement, astounded that the boy could now hear and speak.

After the healers had examined the child, Jaslon concluded the gods had shown the boy a rare kindness. With such a clear signal of divine sanction, Jaslon became even more determined to observe the fall equinox at Eban, and he designed a new tattoo to commemorate the event.

— Stave Six of Jaslon, 18th Master of Mount Eban Enclave

Belgica 91 B.C.

A fortnight of nonstop spring rain had turned the Eburone practice field into a swamp. Young warriors had trodden every plant in the arena to a pulp, and ankle-deep mud sucked at their feet. The wet Belgican terrain reinforced a lesson they experienced every day: a warrior fights regardless of time, place, or weather. Only after all the would-be warriors lay panting in the mud did Dorlas, the arms instructor, signal a cessation.

As he heaved himself upright to sit cross-legged, Mallec stifled a moan. The grizzled old warrior seemed driven to torment everyone on the field. Any show of discomfort, inattention, or dissatisfaction drew a swift and painful response. No one, especially Mallec, wished to become the object of the man's wrath.

Though free from the beatings once administered by Galan, Mallec gained no respite. Since the harvest fest accident five years earlier, Galan's friends took his place. Except for the rare occasions when Mallec was allowed to use his staff, the thrashings under the guise of combat practice continued. Since Talorec depended on Mallec to care for Galan, however, Dorlas made certain no one hurt Mallec seriously. Dorlas did not consider bruised ribs and blackened eyes serious.

Mallec closed his eyes to the rain and envisioned Galan's face, now a slack-jawed mockery of the vital young warrior he'd once been. Why the gods allowed him to live perplexed the young druid. Surely they must have intended Galan's survival more for punishment than mercy, although whom it truly punished he couldn't say. Galan had little notion of his loss, although Talorec suffered daily. Mallec wiped at the rain on his face. Surely the gods meant Galan's misshapen skull and his feeble attempts to walk, talk, or feed himself as a warning to others. Galan had paid a terrible price for ignoring them.

Mallec flexed his hand and stretched the brown skin across his knuckles. Finally healed, the burn had itched incessantly once it stopped hurting. That injury came from Galan, who still tormented Mallec although now in a different way. Some bits of the old Galan remained, in addition to his size and strength, and Mallec had to watch him carefully to make sure he injured no one, including himself. Galan had caught and nearly killed a barn kitten by pressing it down into the fire pit. The cat yowled with pain, too weak to escape Galan's grip. Without thinking, Mallec grabbed the kitten and wrestled it away. As he pulled it free, he burned himself on the coals, and the animal's fur caught fire. He doused both hand and kitten in a nearby water bucket. Galan smiled like an infant. "Again," he said, the word slurred in a way no one but Mallec understood.

Galan's diminished intellect bothered Mallec more than his physical limitations. Among the Eburones, battle-born disabilities were common, and the clan always sought to find a place for those who could no longer fight. Galan's injuries left him without the wits to fight, but his strength dictated a life of menial labor. Mallec shuddered, unable to conceive of a fate more horrible.

Only knowing he would eventually leave Belgica made his waiting bearable, and he regularly thanked the gods for making his journey to sacred Mona possible. Without the dream the gods had sent, the clan would never have agreed to support him. Soon he'd be a part of the celebrated druid enclave on the distant isle, learning from those whose knowledge spanned centuries and the worlds of both the dead and the living.

Tired enough to be dead himself, Mallec raised a grateful hand in prayer to Lugh. The god had seen him through each agonizing day on the field, sustaining his mind when his body told him no hope remained.

Rivulets of rain water washed some of the muck from his torso. He wiped at the mud covering the dark student tattoos that marked him as a future druid. He gazed at the intricate pattern decorating his left forearm, the first of many such marks. There was one tattoo for each achievement, from mastery of clan history to knowledge of festival chants. He wore ten tattoos thus far, many of which obscured scars he'd received on the training field.

The voice of Dorlas tore Mallec from his reverie. "Weakness breeds weakness," the arms instructor said, his hawkish glare drifting from face to face. "Eburones fight. When the Gauls and the Germanii lay down their arms and weep from exhaustion, we'll still be fighting. Let them have their soft beds and their Roman wine. We'll have clear heads and strong arms. We'll see who's still standing when the battle's done."

He scowled at Mallec, who met his gaze without flinching. "One last match," the grizzled veteran announced.

Mallec sensed the fear the others also felt at the prospect of being called to fight. It pleased him to know they, too, stifled groans. Of all the matches in a day, the last fight taxed combatants the most. Dorlas allowed any tactic, trick or blow. The victor often staggered away. The vanquished usually relied on the supporting arms of his friends.

"Mallec will face Danix."

No one cheered, but Mallec imagined he heard their silent rejoicing. Danix inherited Galan's title as best among the unblooded, and Mallec had little hope of beating him. He prayed Lugh would give him the strength to fight well. Without saying a word, he dragged himself to his feet. As First Called, he claimed the right to specify arms and retrieved his staff from the weapon rack. Though he'd practiced with sword, spear, and sling, his skills were unremarkable. The hefty yew staff, however, felt comfortable in his hand. He twirled the long pole above his head before grounding it at his feet. Gods willing, he'd acquit himself well in this battle. He held the staff at his side and waited for Danix to face him.

No one moved until Ambioris called to Mallec from his place among the younger boys seated at the edge of the field. "Watch his eyes, Mallec!"

Danix sneered. "You take instruction from a child?"

Ambioris threw a rock at Danix, but the young warrior dodged, and the stone struck Mallec's knee.

Danix laughed. "Help him again!"

The onlookers howled, and Ambioris shrugged an apology. The boy's willingness to help seemed proof of Mallec's dreams about his future.

Suddenly, Mallec wanted more than merely giving a good account of himself. He wanted to win this match. Without waiting for Danix to offer the first blow, he struck with all the energy he could summon, landing a two-handed jab to Danix's sternum.

The warrior toppled backward, his staff and his rump making dual splashes in the mud. Swearing, he hauled himself to his feet. Hoping to catch him before he steadied himself, Mallec attacked again, swinging his staff in a wide arc.

Danix parried the blow, turned sharply and struck down on Mallec's staff. The rod broke in two, and the force of it drove Mallec to his knees. With a wild backhand, Mallec cracked Danix on the shin, sending the warrior hopping about on one leg and spewing a torrent of curses. Mallec stood and faced his enraged opponent. Of the two pieces of his staff, one had shattered along the grain. He dropped it and gripped the remaining length with two hands, swinging it like a club.

Danix attacked. Mallec warded off the first two blows, but Danix connected with the third, smashing Mallec's wrists and forcing the broken staff from his numb fingers. Feigning worse pain, Mallec waited for the final blow while straining to hear the telltale whoosh of Danix's staff. When it came, Mallec shifted sideways. The hardwood staff smacked into the mud, and Mallec grabbed it with both hands. When Danix pulled, Mallec pushed, sending the shocked and empty-handed warrior tumbling backward. Mallec stood over him, the staff raised above his head. Danix said nothing, but his eyes betrayed his fear. He cringed as he awaited Mallec's final swing.

It never came. The arms instructor gripped Mallec's staff with both hands. "That's enough for one day," he said.

Oddly quiet, the warriors struggled to their feet and ambled from the field, comrades. Mallec expected no such company. Druids were makers of magic and purveyors of prayer, men and women to be obeyed in ritual and in law. These young men, although he'd played with them as children, now treated him as one apart. So had the arms instructor, and all the other veterans, until today.

Dorlas watched the young warriors depart. Shaggy brows and thick drooping mustaches couldn't conceal the deep lines time had carved in his face. A thousand stories lay amid those lines. With luck, one or two might be captured by a bard.

"You stopped the fight," said Mallec.

The aging warrior turned toward the young druid. "True."

"Why? I wouldn't have hit him as hard as I've been struck."

"What would you have learned from it?"

Mallec frowned. "Nothing, but I would have proven I could deliver the blow. I could have shown the others—"

"What? That you can make someone bleed? We knew that already." The man's expression softened. "Talorec bade me watch you. At the first sign of weakness I was to let the others pound you senseless. I knew you wouldn't have given Danix the hardest blow you could muster. Tell me, would that have been a sign of weakness?"

Mallec grunted. "Perhaps."

"What passes for weakness in a warrior is often wisdom in a druid. We had to know what you're made of, especially since Galan's accident."

"I tried to stop that."

"There are some who'd blame you for it," the warrior said, "but you earned the respect of others. Talorec, for one."

"Talorec?"

"An emissary of the Eburones must be more than just a warrior or a druid. You represent us all. To those who don't know us, you are the Eburones. We couldn't entrust such a responsibility to just anyone."

"And that's why you stopped the fight?"

The warrior finally smiled. "It wouldn't do for the emissary of our clan to arrive at Mona all bloody and bruised, now would it? Even if the blood belonged to someone else."

✠ ✠ ✠

The late afternoon air, thick with the tang of rotting seaweed, tickled Mallec's nose. Driad Seva rode beside him on a small horse. She seemed unaffected by the smell. Tall reeds dotted the shallows where fresh water mixed with brackish. In spots bathed only in salt water, the residue of sea plants, shells, and driftwood covered the sands.

Every bend in the road to the land of the Nervii brought new delights. He searched for more positive omens. Already he'd had the good fortune to see, nose forward, the first spring lamb of the village. When the Great Mother appeared in the morning's dream and smiled, he knew success awaited him.

The road followed the main channel as it meandered through marshland. On the higher ground south of the marsh, the Nervii town of Ryno offered a buyer's delight in merchant's wares of every imaginable kind: flats of tin by the wagonload, weapons, fine textiles, and pottery jugs full of oils and wines.

Several ships bobbed in their moorings along two narrow docks extending into the estuary. Seva pointed out the emblem decorating a Roman ship and the Numidian design of a second with its black-skinned sailors in colorful tunics. Mallec strained to see what cargo they carried down a narrow plank to the dock.

In all his life, Mallec had not known a town could be so busy. It surpassed Atuatuca's biggest market day, the day preceding the Beltane fair that brought Eburones from the whole countryside to camp in the fields beside the river. He estimated several thousand people must live in the city before him, and more nearby.

He wondered whether Mona, a hub of intellect and learning rather than commerce, would be as active.

The sun lay low on the western horizon by the time Mallec and Seva reached the bay. A small Nervii merchant ship, red banners flying, heeled with the wind and tugged at its anchor well away from the docks.

Of all the people of his clan, Mallec would miss Seva the most. A skillful healer, she had endeavored to teach him her art, even though his path lay in another direction. He'd also learned all the chronologies of his people, the laws and major rituals. Seva's tutoring had helped him earn a white druid's robe and the consent of Mona's High Ollamh to study there. But more than that, it had been Seva who forced him to believe in himself and to trust what the gods told him.

Dry, clean, and with a bag containing his few possessions, Mallec waited at the edge of the dock for the boat that would ferry him to the Nervii ship anchored in the deep water.

"Your father would have been proud of you," Seva said.

Her words surprised him. His father had been a warrior. Both his parents had died fighting Ubii raiders from north of the Great River.

She did not look at him as she spoke. "Unlike those whom Talorec leads, your parents did not live for war. Your father knew honor walks many paths, not just the one he chose. He could have slain you at the last moment to ensure you a new life far from the reach of our enemy. Instead, he hid you away in safety. He knew your destiny was not his, that you weren't to be a warrior. He saw only one path for someone like you, and you are now on it." She hugged him briefly and stepped back, her eyes bright with tears.

Mallec kissed her cheek. Mona. How the magical name played on his mind with every waking moment. There all the secrets of the Celtic people were saved, memorized, and sung. There he would learn the law and take his place among the seers and judges.

A shout from the ship caught their attention. Two men lowered a small round craft into the water. It bobbed on the surface like a phalarope hunting for water bugs, turning in circles until one man seated himself in the center and paddled toward the dock.

When he reached the spot where Mallec waited, the sailor grabbed a thick coil of rope that dangled from an iron clasp secured to the dock and held the vessel steady.

Mallec embraced Seva.

"Return to us wise and well, Mallec," she said. "The Eburones need you."

He stepped into the waiting coracle, squeezing himself between the leather sides and the paddler. With his knees raised and his bag hugged to his chest, he barely had a moment to wave to her before the little craft turned into the gentle waves. He did not look back.

✠ ✠ ✠

After six days, the rising swells barely made Mallec's stomach lurch and his head spin. He'd long ago lost to the sea his first meager supper of dried fish and bread.

They hugged the Briton coast, close enough for Mallec to marvel at cliffs, first white then black. According to the captain, they'd paid for safe passage, but Mallec never understood how the arrangement worked. He'd heard various pirate bands plied the coastal waters, and he doubted the captain could pay them all and still show a profit, yet the voyage went uninterrupted while the coastline remained in view. After the cliffs disappeared, nearly a day passed with nothing but open water to greet his weary gaze.

The ocean grew rougher as the vessel passed rugged Cernew and turned northward. At the captain's command, the helmsman kept them several miles out to avoid the treacherous waters pounding the black rocks of Land's End.

By midday the wind came straight off Cernew, and the ship plowed more easily through the waves past the headland of Rhos Penfro and straight for the Island of Currents. Mona still lay more than a day away.

Mallec rested on deck, or tried to. By early evening, the swells calmed enough for him to stretch out on the rough oak planking. With the bow of the ship turned into the swells, his stomach settled and his mind wandered. He thought of the girl who visited his dreams. Though he'd pursued her during many a night's phantom race, he had yet to see other than her back. Her face remained a mystery.

He prayed for the day her countenance would be revealed to him, a sign the gods wanted him to find her. The belief had comforted him on Beltane nights when none of the Eburone girls came near. Whether they feared him or merely found him strange didn't matter. He'd always spent those nights alone. From the wildness of her wind-blown tresses, he felt certain his dark-haired phantom lass would have no such qualms. He drifted smiling to sleep.

He followed her across an open meadow. She moved as gracefully as a hind, the wind catching her dark hair and tossing it around her head, obscuring her face as always. He wondered whether she lived at the enclave on Mona. All too soon she disappeared in the mists that swirled before him. Warriors stood in loose ranks, watching, and although they opened their mouths as if screaming war cries, he heard no sound. He ventured into the thinning strands of fog until he saw the body of a man stretched prostrate before him.

The mist faded, and his heart beat more rapidly. The body was that of a druid. A nicked and bloody sword lay on one side of him, a broken staff on the other.

Mallec's eyes sprang open, and he pressed his hand to his chest to slow his racing heart. He looked around to reassure himself he'd left the dream behind. The surface of the water offered only traces of reflected moonlight, and the ship's lantern burned low. Mallec shivered, for he'd seen more than he wanted.

He leaned against the mast. Once he calmed himself he drifted into an uneasy sleep. If he dreamt further, he remembered none of it, and for that he gave thanks.

The next morning came warm and windy, the breeze still blowing steadily from the south as if the gods themselves wanted to speed his arrival. They sailed northeast along the green Lleyn, where they followed the peninsula's spiny back all the way to the Narrows.

Mallec remained on deck all day, his gaze captured by the rising majesty of Yr Eyri, the Eagle Nest, a star-shaped union of five mountain peaks. Mallec had never seen such mountains. The setting sun shone on the crest of Yr Eyri, turning the snow that capped the highest peak a brilliant pink. Like a salmon, Mallec thought, and smiled at the sign of promised wisdom.

The ship cruised through the Narrows, the mouth of the strait calm and wide without sandbars or treacherous rocks. Once into the lee of the land off their port side, they headed into North Bay where the dock at the town of Bryn Celli burst into life with lamps and torches at their approach. The ship nudged against the wooden dock like a calf nuzzling its mother.

The first to step ashore, Mallec turned this way and that in an effort to see everything before the last sunlight disappeared. He wanted to fall to his knees and kiss the ground, in part because he stood on the sacred soil of Mona, and in part because he hadn't stood on solid land in over a week.

"Ho, Belgican!" someone shouted.

A group of young men approached, one of whom carried a torch. All but one wore the unbleached garb of students. The exception came attired in a druid's robe, although he showed only one tattoo. Mallec wondered how a man could become a druid without receiving at least a dozen such marks of achievement.

Mallec slung his bag over his shoulder, slipped a silver coin into the captain's hand, and stepped forward to meet the representatives of the enclave.

None of the young men smiled, and the druid himself bore an expression Mallec knew all too well, for he'd often seen it on Galan's face and then on Danix's. The greeting party stopped in front of him, the druid foremost.

Mallec bowed and then straightened, pushing his shoulders back.

"I'm Druid Mallec, of the Eburone clan in Belgica. Can you show me the way to the enclave?"

The young druid sneered. "You'll have to remove that robe first. Everyone who lands here is considered a student until the High Ollamh says otherwise." He tossed him a tattered brown robe.

Mallec let it fall to the ground and squinted at the druid. Though about the same age as Mallec and similarly lean, he was nearly a head shorter. The three who ringed him were all larger but obviously danced to his tune.

"Who are you?" Mallec asked, careful to keep disdain from his voice. Brusque talk had never worked on Galan or his friends.

"I'm Brucc of Cernew, and I will be the one who tells you what to do while you're here. You'll be one of my students."

Mallec felt his stomach tighten. He'd been a pupil of bullies long enough. "I'd rather discuss this with someone in authority," he said.

"I'm the only authority you need. The High Ollamh sent me to fetch you. Now, strip out of that robe and put on student clothes."

Mallec appreciated the heavy warmth of his robe, already keeping the chill damp air at bay. The thin garment at his feet would not protect him nearly as well.

He stepped past Brucc, intent on finding someone else who could point him in the direction of the enclave.

Brucc grabbed his elbow and whirled him around. "I ordered you to take off that robe!"

Mallec pushed Brucc's hand away with a rough slap, prepared for the worst. "I've had enough of the likes of you. If you won't show me the way to the enclave, I'll find it myself."

He turned his back on them and walked toward the ship, hoping to obtain directions from the captain. Those behind him snickered, but he continued to walk, his head high.

He smelled burning wool and heard laughter. A few steps later flames consumed the back of his robe.

Crying out, he ran toward the water's edge, feeling the flames feather out behind him. With the stench of burning hair in his nostrils and the sting of fire on his skin, he jumped into the bay.

One of the ship's crew threw him a rope. He clung to it as they dragged him back to the dock and hauled him up onto the rough planking. He lay on his stomach, shivering from fright as much as from the cold water.

"Here, lad," someone said, helping him stand. His robe ruined, and the hair on the back of his head singed short, he gingerly slipped out of his white garment and let it fall. He flexed his back muscles and winced. The skin stung and would soon blister.

"Is the burn bad?" he asked, afraid of the answer.

"Nay," the sailor said. "Ye'll bubble a bit, but that's all."

"Are you ready to dress appropriately now?" Brucc said. "Take this as a sign the gods expect obedience to the rules of Mona Enclave."

Mallec took it as a sign he must be more careful with Brucc and his followers.

Brucc tossed him the student's garb and walked away.

Mallec slipped the robe over his head. He retrieved his bag and grudgingly followed the others. As darkness closed in on him, he followed their torch into the night, wondering what plan the gods really had in store for him.

7

On the eve of the fall equinox, Jaslon assembled the enclave in the Cavern of the Ancients to demonstrate his mastery of the gods' power. Several druids suspected trickery, even as Jaslon disappeared in front of them. He left naught behind but a plain wooden branch, no larger than a man's leg, which we bore to the great stones at the base of the mountain as he had instructed. The following morning, the gods restored Jaslon and humbled the other druids.
— *Stave One of Harnef, 9th Master of Mount Eban Enclave*

Iberia 90 B.C.

"That does it!" Baia muttered as she struggled with the warp thread on her hand loom. She threw it on the ground in frustration and finger-signed a curse over it. For the past five days, Rhonwen had expected an outburst, but Baia maintained a brooding silence punctuated by glares, frowns, and scowls, all timed so that Rhonwen saw them only long enough to feel a twinge of guilt. She knew the source of Baia's anger but had hoped her new rank might offer some measure of protection.

Baia reclined beneath a wide-spread oak, eyes closed, her back against the bark. Her gray puppy, Tesla, twitched in its sleep nearby. Baia opened her eyes when Rhonwen knelt beside her and pointed to Rhonwen's new tattoo. "Does it still hurt?"

Rhonwen traced the scab line formed over the cuts. "Every time I move my arm it pulls the skin. It hurts much worse than the last one."

"It's the red we use in making the healer's mark, a special soil mixed with squid's blood. I'm glad it's healing slowly. After what you've done, you deserve a painful reminder."

Baia's remark made Rhonwen's mouth go dry and turned the breakfast in her stomach to stone. She feigned puzzlement. "What do you mean?"

Baia did not look at her, but retrieved her hand loom and concentrated on knotting her threads. "I'd hoped your initiation would be something worthy of bards and boasting. Instead I saw a debacle."

"How can you say that? It was perfect."

Baia paused her labor long enough to stare into Rhonwen's eyes. "I might have overlooked the presence of that Roman murderer for the sake of the ritual." She spat into the dust. "But you weren't content with that. You allowed him to speak with you."

"Sertorius merely offered his congratulations."

"I'm ashamed to think my daughter would grant him a conversation on the day of her most sacred rite."

"I didn't ask him to come."

"Enough!" Baia pushed her away. "I saw your smile as you accepted his gifts. My own daughter, sister to the man he killed. Have you relinquished your vow? Would you break an oath?"

Rhonwen's ears pounded with anger. She leaped up to stand over Baia, fists on her hips. "How can you absolve yourself of responsibility for Telo's death? You sent him to train with Tarax who filled his head with talk of killing Romans. Had you not encouraged that folly, he'd live still."

"Lies!" Baia cried. "Telo made his own choice. I'm proud of him."

"Telo's been dead for five years. Can't you let him rest?"

Baia glared back. "Five years is a long time to wait for vengeance. Keep your oath."

"I was too young. You forced it upon me."

"You took it, now keep it!"

"But—"

"You have a duty, an honor-debt. Kill the man who killed your brother!"

How could she kill Sertorius, a man who'd saved her not once, but twice? She hadn't forgotten the hated vow. She'd spent the last five years hoping this day would never come, that Baia would someday release her, and that someday she could be the woman Sertorius wanted. She had dreamed of it, imagined it, even prayed to the Great Mother for it.

"I can't kill him," she said.

Baia turned her back. "Then you're as dead to me as Telo."

"Mother! Surely you don't mean that."

"Kill him or die. That's the meaning of a blood oath."

Rhonwen sank to the ground weeping. "No. I will not."

Baia slapped Rhonwen, then grabbed her hair and yanked her head back. "How can I live after the child I've given everything turns on me? There is nothing lower than an oath breaker."

Baia tugged her hair again, and Rhonwen gasped. Her mother's eyes, once soft and welcoming, stared out of her hollow face like chips of obsidian.

"Mother, please stop," Rhonwen whispered.

"Kill him as you vowed," Baia said, sobbing. "Telo, my son..."

Rhonwen pried her mother's fingers from her hair and pulled free. Baia rocked back and forth in an agony of renewed grief.

Rhonwen moved away. The dog whined at Baia's knee, licking at the hands with which Baia covered her face. Unable to speak, Rhonwen wrapped herself tightly in her cloak.

She placed a palm on Baia's forehead, but her mother ignored the touch, lost in her bereavement. Baia had never before raised a hand to her. The stinging blow on her cheek served as a painful reminder of Baia's devotion to Telo. If Sertorius remained here alive, it would drive Baia mad. Rhonwen could not allow that to happen. Wiping her tears away, she took a deep breath.

She must keep this vow, although it meant her own death. She would accept Sertorius' invitation to sup, and do whatever she must to kill him.

✠ ✠ ✠

Rhonwen rose with the cock crow, weary from another night without sleep since her decision to meet with Sertorius. Alone in the hut, she gazed at the coals in the firepit: ash-gray and cold. Sitting on her sleeping pallet, she rubbed her palms across her cheeks, sticky with the night's dried tears. She had lain awake planning the tragedy she had vowed to effect. Yet every time she thought of Sertorius, and of how close she would have to be to carry out her covenant, her mind wandered. She could not follow the knife into his heart because her hand always wandered to his face. Her fingers inevitably traced the line of his jaw past his ear and ended tangled in his dark hair.

When she thought of his eyes widening in shock at the sharp kiss of her dagger, they invariably softened, the lids drooping as he took her lips against his own. Then he would close his eyes and press himself closer, his hands gentle, firm, insistent, eager, unstoppable—until Baia's agonized face intruded, her jaws clenched on words of revenge as she thrust blade after blade into Rhonwen's hand, each accompanied by the relentless command that she hack to death the man Rhonwen... loved?

"Oh, Sweet Mother," she cried, her arms crossed over her chest, her head tilted upward, eyes shut. "Don't make me do this."

"Rhonwen?" Orlan's voice cut through her emotions like a scythe. "Are you awake? I've come to say goodbye."

Goodbye? The thought came like a slap across her face. She shrugged into a tunic and scrambled to her feet. "Goodbye, Uncle? Where are you going?"

"Mona," he said.

The name of the greatest druid enclave in the world hung in the air like the fading tones of a brass bell. Sacred beyond her understanding, the name evoked dozens of images. The best of everything was there or came from there. Mona-trained bards had no peers. Ovates and druids from Mona earned the esteem of every clan because of their longer years of training in all the magics and laws of the gods and people. Mona, the ultimate storehouse of knowledge. For years Orlan had spoken wistfully of going there.

Orlan smiled. "At last I've decided to go, and I leave tomorrow. I stayed only to see you earn your robes and bear the healer's mark."

Rhonwen had no heart to lose her uncle. About to fulfill her blood vow and likely die in the process, she wanted Orlan here, to preside over the ceremony that would send her spirit properly into the Otherworld. Who would care for Baia when Rhonwen was dead?

"Why now? Why not next week or next year?"

Orlan appraised her and the smile eased from his face, replaced with a worried frown. He brushed her face to free a strand of dark hair stuck to her cheek. "I expected a tear after I announced my departure, not before. You're a woman now, a driad and a healer. You've accomplished so much. What have you to weep about?"

Rhonwen forced a smile. "We'll miss you."

She would not endanger him nor force him to stop his journey just to bury her. Knowing the Romans, he would be better off far away from her. Perhaps, if she survived her encounter with Sertorius, Mona might just be the best place for her, too.

✠ ✠ ✠

The walk from the house Rhonwen shared with Baia to the building where Sertorius lived would end all too quickly. The warmth of late afternoon did little to ease her nerves as she paced through the narrow streets of the Romanized areas of Castulo. Much had changed. Indeed, it looked like every Roman settlement she and her mother had traveled through in the five years since she last visited here. Stone slabs now covered many of the streets, although some remained as muddy and rutted as the day the Romans arrived. Roman carts and riders claimed the widest portions, leaving only narrow pathways of uncertain footing through the muck for pedestrians.

Most of the Castulans she passed glared at her. Dressed in her best stola and without her healer's cloak, she knew what she must look like to the townspeople. Women who sold themselves to the Romans garnered sneers if lucky but curses or flying offal if not. She felt for the dagger at her side. They couldn't know her true purpose. Not that it mattered, for within a few hours she would be on her way to Mona with Orlan or dead.

A rat scuttled away and vanished into a crack in the wall of a Roman storage building. She wrinkled her nose at the thought of where Sertorius obtained the food she'd eat that evening. Romans needed more cats in their granaries, she thought. She picked her way through deep muddy tracks across the street and stopped at the junction of two lanes.

The street remained unpaved, although stone lay stacked in preparation. Sertorius lived in the square two-story building nearest the corner. It frightened her to think of living so high off the ground, and she wondered if the building shuddered in a storm wind.

She stopped in front of a wooden door and roused the Roman guard lounging there. He stood as she approached, his gaze roving from her sandaled feet to her uncovered head.

Rhonwen spoke quickly to mask her nervousness. "Is this the home of Quintus Sertorius?"

The guard scowled. "Who asks?"

"I'm Rhonwen, driad and healer."

She heard the clatter of a horse-drawn cart before she saw it. Even without looking she knew it moved too fast to turn down the street where she stood. A flicker of fear crossed the guard's eyes. Rhonwen turned in time to see a cart careen around the corner, its driver struggling to control the unmatched horses that strained against the traces. The soldier pulled Rhonwen to one side as the cart rumbled past and threw up a screen of mud that splattered them both.

Rhonwen stepped back, sputtering. Gray-black muck, reeking of animal waste and rotting garbage, coated her left side and dripped from her hair and chin. The guard fared no better. He shook his fist, cursed, and spat at the retreating cart.

Rhonwen waited for him to calm down. "Sertorius—"

"Yes, yes, he lives here. You're expected." He peered at her closely. "You don't look old enough to be a healer." He sniffed. "And you're anything but presentable."

Rhonwen glared. "No thanks to Roman drivers."

The guard shrugged and opened the door, but stepped in front of her before she could enter. "Delphina!" he called. "Come out here." He turned to Rhonwen and shook his head in disgust. "I don't know why Sertorius puts up with that old woman. With his money he could have half a dozen slaves who've seen fewer years combined than that old hag."

A ferret-eyed woman with frown lines as deep as wagon ruts thrust her head through the door. "What d'you want?" she croaked.

The guard nodded at Rhonwen. "The Legate's guest has arrived."

The old woman held her nose and stared.

"Would you prefer a beating, Delphina?" the guard asked. "Help her clean up!"

Delphina backed away from the door and motioned for Rhonwen to follow. Late afternoon sunshine poured through arched doorways leading to a central courtyard and bathed the building's sparsely furnished interior with warm light. The smell of roast chicken spiced with rue and silphium cut through the rank odor of the street filth on her clothing.

"You'll find little to steal in here," the old woman said, her voice as brittle as dead leaves. "Come along now." She turned and walked away, muttering. "As if I don't have enough to do already, now I've got to clean barbarians."

"What's this?" Sertorius asked, stepping into the corridor. Spotting Rhonwen, he smiled and bowed modestly, his eyes not moving from hers. "The queen of Iberia arrives at last. You honor me with your presence."

Rhonwen turned her less-muddied side to the Roman and felt her cheeks flush hot. She gave up trying to hide the mud and spread her hands wide showing him her spattered clothing. "I'm not— I mean, this cart—"

"Delphina," Sertorius said, "delay the evening meal and assist my guest."

The old woman nodded.

"I regret the lack of paving out front. I want you to be refreshed and comfortable." He smiled. "When I served in Cisalpina, I learned to enjoy the custom of bathing with soap, and I've continued the practice here, though with certain modifications. I think you'll find it invigorating. I'll arrange to have clean clothing delivered for you."

Rhonwen blushed and held out her stola. "Don't bother. I can rinse this in no time."

"I insist," he said. "Delphina will help you. I'll check your progress shortly."

"But you must have other guests who need your attention?"

He smiled again. "I had hoped my own company would suffice. If you'd prefer, I can arrange for others to—"

"No! I mean, certainly, if that's what you'd like," Rhonwen said, wincing at her eagerness.

"I've looked forward to dinner with you," he said. "I'd rather not share my last night in Iberia with anyone else." After another modest bow, he turned and walked away.

Rhonwen stared at the door through which he'd passed until Delphina tapped her on the shoulder. "Are you coming or not?"

As if entranced, Rhonwen followed the old woman.

✠ ✠ ✠

Delphina helped her undress and produced a jar of olive oil. After rubbing the oil into the mud all over Rhonwen's body, the old woman scraped off the resulting mixture with a long curved *strigil*. The process left Rhonwen wishing for the stream that ran near Healer's House where she could rinse herself.

"Follow me," Delphina said, leading Rhonwen to a room with a sloping tiled floor. The servant pointed to a ceramic pan containing a familiar mixture of oil, tallow, and ashes. Rhonwen scooped out a bit of the mixture and rubbed it into a lather. Meanwhile, Delphina stoked a small boiler and heated water.

"Stand near the edge," the servant said as she poured warm water over Rhonwen's head. The runoff drained away through holes in the wall. Repeated rinsing finally left Rhonwen feeling clean.

Delphina patted her dry with soft cloths and made clucking noises all the while.

"What's the matter?" Rhonwen asked.

"Look at your legs," the crone said. "I've seen goats with less hair. How can you stand it?"

Rhonwen stared down at her legs. Pink and clean, they appeared perfectly normal. "I don't understand."

"In Rome, a lady with hairy legs would never venture out in public." Delphina sniffed and lowered her eyelids. "Civilized women have their legs shaved." She lowered her voice, although no one else could hear her. "It may seem troublesome, but men love it, and you will, too. When a man touches you, you'll both enjoy it." Delphina chuckled.

Rhonwen had never heard of such a thing. She blushed at the old woman's insinuation that she and Sertorius would be close enough to touch, although it loomed as an important part of her mission. She considered Delphina's words. The Iberian men she knew often scraped off or plucked out portions of their beards, but only to make the remaining hair more striking. She had never considered shaving herself.

"The trick is to use hot water and a very sharp blade," Delphina said. "Or would you rather remain a barbarian?"

"Does it hurt?"

The old woman shook her head. "Not unless you get a cut. It's too late to call the barber who shaves Sertorius. He's gone for the day and won't return until morning, when Sertorius usually calls for him. But, when I lived in Nursia with the family of Sertorius, I regularly shaved his mother's legs. I can do yours."

Rhonwen looked at the woman's wrinkled hands and swollen knuckles. She'd noticed a slight tremor too, and weighed the value of risking a cut or two. But, if it would help her gain access to Sertorius' bed, then she must consider it. "This appeals to Roman men?"

Delphina nodded emphatically.

"Then do it," Rhonwen said. "What I've seen of Roman customs thus far has been agreeable."

Delphina grinned and left the room. She returned a short while later with two large bowls of steaming water and a short, sharp dagger. At Delphina's direction, Rhonwen wrapped a dry cloth around her torso and sat in a chair with her legs extended. Delphina knelt at her feet. She worked up a lather with soapy water from the first bowl and spread it over Rhonwen's leg. Rhonwen held her breath as the old woman applied the knife.

Moments later, Rhonwen suffered her first cut. She flinched but said nothing until the third cut, then let out a short yelp. She grimaced at the pink-tinged soap on her leg.

Sertorius poked his head through the open door and frowned at Delphina. "I imagine my guest would prefer to keep her blood inside her body." As he entered the room and watched Delphina's efforts, Rhonwen pulled the cloth around her a little tighter.

"I'm sorry, I don't know what's wrong," Delphina said. "Perhaps I'm out of practice using a *novacula*."

The more deeply he frowned, the more noticeable Delphina's tremor became. She applied the dagger to Rhonwen's leg again and almost immediately drew more blood.

"Enough," Sertorius said, plucking the instrument from the old woman's hand. "Go prepare dinner before you bleed her to death."

Delphina straightened slowly and left muttering.

Sertorius watched her leave before saying anything.

Rhonwen looked up at the tall Roman.

"Do you want to finish on your own?" he asked.

She shook her head. "I doubt I'd do any better than Delphina. I've never used one of those blades before."

Sertorius knelt in front of her. "Then I suppose it's up to me." Without waiting for a response, he rinsed the cuts with warm water from the second bowl, added more lather, and finished her lower leg.

Rhonwen's face grew hot as he worked above her knees. His strong hands caressed her thigh as he rubbed the warm soapy water into a thick lather. He removed his hands, reluctantly she thought, and stroked the blade carefully down the length of her leg. Reaching her knee, he slowed and repeated the action with another stroke beside the previous one.

"You'll have to give me a little more room to work," he said, resting a flame-hot palm on her leg.

Rhonwen squirmed with embarrassment and adjusted her towel as she allowed Sertorius to shave the inside of her thigh. Between the kiss of the *novacula* and the pressure of his hands, her heart raced.

Sertorius rinsed her leg and started on the other, his movements slow and deliberate. While he worked, Rhonwen stared down at the tops of his ears and the back of his neck. His smoothly shaven cheek looked inviting, and she wondered how delicious it would feel to have his face pressed against her leg.

"You'll have to stand," he said.

"What?"

"I can't reach the backs of your legs unless you stand."

Rhonwen shook herself back to reality and pulled the towel as tight around her as she could. When she stood the cloth barely covered her buttocks. Her face burned, although with excitement or embarrassment, she couldn't tell. She forced herself to breathe steadily as Sertorius finished his work, then rinsed off her legs and dried them. He handed her a small jar of lotion. "Rub this on your legs. It smells nice and will keep them from itching."

He rose effortlessly and stood close enough for her to feel his warmth. "Give me a moment," he said, "and I'll fetch your garment."

She had to force the words out. "You treat me too well."

"My duty as a host, especially after what Delphina has done. If I had any sense, I'd have arranged for your travel here instead of leaving you at the mercy of madmen in the streets." He touched the tip of her nose. "Stay here."

Giddy, Rhonwen slid back to the chair to catch her breath. She wanted to look composed when Sertorius returned. She dabbed a little of the lotion on each knee and its heady aroma made her smile. She splashed its contents more liberally, rubbing the scented oil into her skin.

Delphina returned with a soft, pale blue gown. "Sertorius bade me help you dress for dinner."

The loose gown Delphina held out seemed to float. Rhonwen raised her arms and let it slide over her head. As it dropped down over her legs, the fabric felt smooth and luxurious against her shaved skin.

The gown fit well enough but seemed a little long. Delphina clucked. "There's no time to hem it, but at least let me do something with that unruly mass of hair."

Rhonwen turned to her in alarm and protested, but Delphina overruled her. After drying, combing and fussing with her hair for what seemed like a lifetime, the old woman finally pronounced it "civilized." Rhonwen felt only relief.

"Sertorius waits in the courtyard," Delphina said, pointing toward the door.

Rhonwen retrieved her food knife from her mud-spattered dress but then wondered where she would carry it.

Delphina sniffed as she plucked it from Rhonwen's hand. "We have enough knives for guests. I'll leave this with your clothes once they're cleaned."

Rhonwen drifted in the direction Delphina indicated, her mind in turmoil as her thoughts warred with her emotions. Bathing had been a delicious distraction. Like every other moment she spent in this house, it pulled her farther from her task. The closer she got to Sertorius, the more she wanted to throw herself into his arms. How did she ever think she could kill him? What would she tell Baia if she didn't? Each step closer to him carried her farther from a solution.

The sun had deserted the sky while Rhonwen bathed, and the corridor leading to the courtyard was dark. She walked slowly, peering into the shadows, until she spied lights beyond one of the archways and stepped through it. Alone, she gazed at her surroundings, at a low table flanked by lounging chairs, and at a dozen lamps burning scented oils and casting their pale light on slender tree trunks. Two stone pedestals stood at the garden's focal point, although only one bore a statue, a female figure.

"I shall miss this garden," Sertorius said from behind her, "now especially, since you're here to make it complete."

She pivoted slowly, her heart racing as it had when he touched her thighs. She felt the cloth of her gown like a whisper on her skin as tiny bumps tickled into life on her arms. She was drawn to his voice, a poet's voice, and his words, poet words. They warmed her, and she wanted more.

"Your garden's lovely and doesn't need me to make it so." She gestured at the empty pedestal. "I should have brought your statue of Mars back. He belongs here with his wife."

He smiled. "Such a shrew as his wife Bellona would never be welcome in my garden." He retrieved the statue from the second pedestal and placed it on the table. "This is Nerio, Mars' true consort."

She admired the slender figure. "I would have expected Mars to choose someone more robust. Isn't that what warriors look for in a woman?"

"Not all men value a woman solely for the fullness of her breasts," Sertorius said. He waved her toward the divans while Delphina brought out a tray loaded with roast chicken, diced melon baked in honey, spiced pears, boiled eggs, and hard bread. She made a second trip bearing a decanter of wine, a half-filled pitcher of water, and two heavy goblets.

Rhonwen stared at the feast, amazed. "Does Delphina bring you this much food at every meal?"

"Rarely," he said, mixing the wine with the water. "I'm usually much hungrier."

It took her a moment to catch his joke. She sat on the couch but reclined only when he did. The divans pressed together at the head, so they could speak easily to each other. A flimsy table with folding legs supported the food in front of them. Sertorius lay close to her, and she could smell the lotions he had used on himself.

He poured a libation of watered wine on the floor in honor of his gods, spoke a brief offering, and then filled their goblets.

She laughed and watched him eat, careful to emulate the way he peeled eggs and handled the hot melon. He offered her a pear and held it close to her mouth. She kept her eyes on his as she bit into it and felt a trickle of juice run down her chin. She reached to wipe it away, but his hand arrived first. He caught the juice on his fingertip and licked it off. His actions startled her. She had planned his seduction, yet it was she who was being seduced.

"You were telling me what men value in a woman," Rhonwen said. "Please continue."

"I won't speak for other men, but I look for many things— wit, spirit, and intellect to name a few." He leaned back on his couch and put his hands behind his head.

She glanced at the statue and compared the modest rise of her own breasts to those of Nerio. "A woman's physical charms don't interest you?"

He smiled and held her gaze. "I can admire a woman for many things at once, as I admired you the day we met."

"I was but a child."

"Young yes, but no child even then. Otherwise, I doubt you'd have drawn the attention of those mercenaries."

Rhonwen shivered at the memory.

"Such men lack discipline. Old comrades or not, I won't suffer disobedience from anyone in my command. You must agree, conditions in the province have improved."

She nodded. Sertorius' firm hand had kept both soldiers and mercenaries in line.

"I doubt the new legate will change anything."

She nearly choked on a pear. "New legate? You're leaving Castulo?"

"I depart for Rome in the morning."

She sipped at her wine to calm herself. "When will you return?"

His gaze focused on something far away. "Probably never. My life is forever tied to Rome. Whatever future I have lies there."

Rhonwen knew she would only have one opportunity to fulfill her vow. She rose from the table and walked to the vacant pedestal of the god, thinking how much she'd like to be more like Neria than vengeful Bellona. "I'll miss you."

Sertorius stood and held her by the shoulders, his strong hands gripping her gently. "With your attainment of high rank, you'll be too busy to think of me." He tilted her chin upward with his index finger and kissed her on the forehead, then led her back to the couches. They resumed their meal.

She ate until she could eat no more. The wine made her head swim in a way ale never did, and she laughed too easily at his amusing tales. Delphina appeared now and again to bring more wine, to take away the remains of food eaten, or bring new delights like figs soaked in honey and mashed oranges. At last, in spite of how slowly she ate, the meal ended and her eyelids grew heavy.

Sertorius yawned and stretched. "My queen," he said finally, "it grows late. I'll have one of my men see that you arrive home safely." He helped her to her feet.

He stood deliciously close, and she laid a hand on his chest. "There's no need."

He frowned slightly. "I never make the same mistake twice. I won't allow you to travel alone between your home and mine, especially at night."

"I meant there's no need for me to go home."

Sertorius raised his eyebrows.

"In any event, I can't return dressed in this," she said, flouncing the light fabric around her legs, "and my clothing is too soiled to wear."

"Delphina took care of your things. They're over there," he said pointing to a neat pile of clothing near the door. Rhonwen's food knife, a dagger, sat atop the pile.

She started at the sight of the knife, her purpose for coming clear once more. She had to stay. "Are you sending me away?" she asked.

"Only if you wish to go." He brushed the back of his hand across her cheek, and her skin tingled as he trailed his fingers down her neck.

Rhonwen slid her hands inside his toga. His well-muscled flesh felt smooth and warm, and she reached her arms completely around him, clasped her hands together, and pressed his chest against her own.

His kiss came hard and searching, and she slipped free of the blue gown, letting it fall to the floor around her ankles. She gestured toward the statue of Nerio. "We seem to share some attributes you find worthwhile. Perhaps there are others."

Sertorius gazed at her appreciatively. "My dreams did not do you justice."

Unlike any Beltane lover she'd ever had, this man compelled her with every look and every word. He swept her into his arms and carried her to his sleeping chamber as easily as he had carried the statue of Nerio to the dinner table.

It's happening, she thought, and just as the image of Baia had disturbed her sleep, so now it invaded her thoughts as Sertorius settled her gently on his bed. To forestall her panic, she concentrated on the shadowed figure removing his clothes a few feet away.

How could she possibly go through with her insane vow? She didn't want his death. She wanted him.

"I'm not forcing you to do this," he said.

She reached for him with trembling hands. "That's true," she said, "you're not."

"I won't have you—"

"Oh, yes, you will," she said as she pressed herself against him.

"I didn't plan it this way," he said.

She kissed him. "I did."

As he traced her jaw line with gentle kisses of his own, she surrendered herself to instinct and abandoned all thoughts of meting out Baia's revenge. When he bent his head to her breast and teased her swollen nipple with his tongue, she abandoned thoughts of everything else.

Much later, as she lay beside the sleeping Sertorius and felt the warmth of his body against hers, thoughts of Baia crept back. She could easily find her dagger in the dark, and she certainly knew where to find him. As she eased slowly from the bed she realized that she carried the smell of him with her, a smell she liked.

In moments she had the dagger in her hand and lay again beside the man who had driven her passion to ecstasy.

He turned his head away, as if offering his throat for her blade, as if daring her to continue.

She placed her hand on his chest, and he smiled in his sleep. A tear trailed down her face beside her nose as she gripped the dagger firmly. "I love you," she whispered.

8

In the weeks that followed, Jaslon fell ill with the wasting disease. He taught us the woadsleep ceremony and told us where to find baneweed. On the eve of the winter solstice, we performed the ceremony and once again transformed the Master to wood. The gods restored him the following morning, and he appeared not to have suffered for his piety, although he succumbed to his disease before the spring equinox.
— *Stave Two of Harnef, 9th Master of Mount Eban Enclave*

Isle of Mona 90 B.C.

Mallec shivered as he stared out over the high stone wall of the enclave, all too aware of the perpetual dampness of his cloak. He wondered whether the sheep that gave the wool ever knew a day of warmth and sunshine. The excitement of arriving in Mona had lasted only until he'd stepped onto the shore and been deprived of his well-made Belgae cloak. Even now, a year later, he had nothing but a plain student's garb to show for his work with Seva. He couldn't even protest. All newcomers were alike in the eyes of the High Ollamh. All remained students until tested by the High Druids.

He wrapped his cloak tighter. Too short, it let the wind whip up past his calves and chill his thighs. Welcome to Mona, he thought, an island within an island. The enclave, a gray isle of stone, rose amid sodden greenery on a speck of soil as aloof from the mainland as it was from mild weather. Yet the isolation he felt from the place only shadowed what he felt from the other druids.

"You there, novice. Wake up!"

Mallec turned toward the voice and recognized the pinched face of Brucc. As officious with the local druids as he was ruthlessly disagreeable with strangers, Brucc oversaw the studies of all newcomers not yet assigned to one master, newcomers like Mallec.

"Yes?"

Brucc straightened the folds of his white robe. "Have you nothing to do this morning?"

"I was up late."

"I didn't ask about last night."

Mallec sucked his lips between his teeth. "I thought I—"

"Yes or no will suffice," Brucc said.

Mallec fell silent. He knew that "no" would yield punishment for idleness, while "yes" would earn him the same for shirking his duties. Brucc took great pleasure in harassing those not yet allowed to wear formal vestments.

Brucc clucked. "You're wasting my time, boy."

Mallec stood straight, weary of the sham his education had become. The months of inactivity had chafed at him in a way he never expected. He'd survived greater threats on the muddy practice fields at home. Brucc could do no worse.

"What's it to be then?" the druid demanded. "Is my question so difficult?"

"The answer is yes." Mallec forced a tight smile. "And no."

Brucc's eyebrows drew close in suspicion.

"Before you came along," Mallec said, "I had nothing to do."

"And now?" Brucc rocked on his heels, an air of smugness sharpening his badger-like features.

"Now I'm busy restraining myself from throwing you off this wall."

"You threaten me?" he snarled.

Mallec prepared for Brucc's assault. No warrior he knew would accept such an insult without action. "It appears so."

"I could have you dismissed and sent back to your dirt hut."

Mallec looked over the parapet. "Assuming you survived the fall."

Brucc stepped away. "Your kind shouldn't be allowed here."

"I had the same thought about you," Mallec said.

The druid's countenance darkened. "You dare mock me?"

"It takes no courage to face a fool, nor intellect to mock one."

Brucc hiked up his robe and backed further away. "Don't think such insolence will go unpunished. You're a marked man."

"Better a marked man than an imitation of one," Mallec muttered as the druid hurried out of sight. He took a deep breath and noted with satisfaction his heartbeat remained slow and steady. He stepped away from the wall and nearly bumped into a stranger in the green-sleeved robe of an ovate.

"Pleased with yourself?" the man asked. Though lean, like Mallec, the other appeared thrice his age. His thin beard matched the thinning spot on his head, and piercing dark eyes gave him the look of a wild man. His Iberian accent identified him.

"You're Orlan, aren't you?" Mallec asked.

Orlan nodded. "And you're the scholar from Belgica?" He gestured down the path and Mallec fell into step beside him.

"Scholar?" Mallec shook his head. "I've been here nearly a year, and in that time I've been allowed in the library exactly once."

"The road to wisdom is neither short nor straight," Orlan said.

Mallec groaned at the maxim he'd heard all too often. "I'm not saying I haven't learned anything. I know how these ingrates like their meals prepared, their clothing washed, their livestock tended, and their crops harvested."

Orlan chuckled.

"I'm no slave," Mallec said.

"Nor will you be a student here much longer if you continue to point out the shortcomings of people like Brucc."

"He's an ass."

"That's why he's still here. The High Ollamh has more sense than to send him out among the clans."

Mallec didn't respond, but the thought of Brucc facing Talorec amused him.

"How long do you think the people would stand for a druid with an attitude like his? How long did you stand for it?"

"Too long. A year."

"My point exactly. You let him live, but most of the clan chiefs I know would've taken his head for a decoration."

For the first time since he reached Mona, Mallec laughed.

"You may as well enjoy the moment," Orlan said. "You haven't seen the last of Brucc or his friends."

"I thought it might end after a few weeks," Mallec said, "but Brucc enjoys making me miserable."

"There's nothing to stop him, as long as you have no rank." Orlan shrugged. "That'll change once you've earned your white robe."

"I already earned it in Belgica, but I wasn't allowed to keep it."

"In that respect, they treat everyone the same way. Did you turn it over willingly?"

Mallec soured at the memory. "The moment I stepped off the boat they demanded it. When I refused, they set it on fire. I salvaged only the scrap of my clan colors." He displayed his sleeve where he'd sewn the Eburones plaid into place. "Did they treat you that way?"

Orlan shook his head sympathetically. "The High Ollamh came to the dock to meet me."

Mallec looked at the Iberian with new found respect. "Benecin himself?"

"He greets anyone who knows the healing arts. I relieved his stomach pains, and he awarded me my robe on the spot." Orlan blew on his hands and rubbed them. "Do you mind if we move a little faster? I feel as though I've been here forever, but I'm still not used to this cold."

As they strolled down the length of the wall, Mona's perpetual blanket of fog thinned.

"How long do you suppose it will take me to earn my robe back?" Mallec asked.

"Most novices wait four or five years," Orlan said. "It depends on your primary instructor." He paused. "Who's yours?"

"I'm unassigned, though a graybeard named Kenan checks on me now and then," Mallec said. "I've only seen him a few times since I arrived and not at all in the past three months."

"Look at Kenan," Orlan said, "and you'll see Brucc forty years from now. Kenan's lived here most of his life. He wears druid white, but I've never heard him offer a prophecy that made sense or came true, and he wouldn't recognize good advice if he tripped over it."

"Why is he still here if he hasn't learned anything? What happened to Mona, the great center of learning?"

"It lives on, but not always as great as it could be."

Mallec frowned and Orlan continued. "Mona is home to a few people with great minds, a few more who think they have great minds, and still more who don't care about anything but the learning. You'd do well to find a teacher among that last group."

Mallec wondered how he would tell the difference.

Orlan held his cloak around his shoulders as a stiff wind cleared the nearby fields of mist and carried it over the wall.

Mallec followed Orlan down moss-slick stone steps to a courtyard where they escaped the wind. "I would gladly study under you."

Orlan laughed. "Why would you want me for a teacher? You're a druid novice. Surely you care little for plants and healing."

What Mallec knew about plants and healing he could list on the fingers of one hand, in spite of Driad Seva's influence. "I've always wanted to be a druid, but I fear Kenan knows little I want to learn. I often have dreams and visions. Some I understand easily, others baffle me. I must assume they're messages from the gods, so I must learn to interpret them. Beyond that, I wish to serve the people."

"And you think an old herbalist like me can teach you law, philosophy, and divination?" Orlan shook his head. "My last dream involved weather without rain and a woman without clothing."

Mallec laughed. "I trust you needed no help interpreting that."

"None," Orlan said. "I presume you can read?"

"I read and speak Greek and Latin, and know a smattering of three other tongues. Seva, the driad I studied under before I came here, taught me what she could, but the Eburones have little use for any written word. Seva loved the healing arts."

"You learned all that without a library?"

Unused to praise, Mallec felt embarrassment warm his face.

"Driad Seva must be quite extraordinary."

"She is," Mallec said.

"An exceptional student often brings out the best in a teacher," the Iberian said.

"I need a teacher, Master Orlan. Will you take me as your pupil?"

Orlan looked down at his hands and spread his fingers. "I don't know. You're not much like my last student."

Disappointment gathered in Mallec's stomach. "I'm not as worthy?"

"I don't know about worthiness, but she was a quick learner." Orlan peered at him from beneath his bushy eyebrows. "And you're certainly not as pretty."

"Does it matter?" Mallec asked with a grin, knowing Orlan toyed with him. He didn't hide his joy at the realization Orlan would accept him.

"It might. Ask me again after we've had to look at each other for a week or two." He reached into a pouch suspended on a leather thong around his neck and produced a shiny round token. "Take this with you when you go to the library. If anyone asks, tell them I sent you and show it to them. That should give you access to anything you want to see."

"But what shall I study? There's so much there, I don't even know where to begin."

Still smiling, Orlan took Mallec's elbow. "I want you to spend the next three months determining that. In the meantime I'll speak to the High Ollamh. I know a druid or two who might help you understand your visions. Of course, we'll still need Benecin's approval."

Mallec's heart beat hard enough to burst from his chest. "How can I thank you?"

"You can start by staying clear of Brucc and his ilk, though they may make that difficult."

Mallec looked toward the main enclave building into which Brucc had disappeared. "I'm not worried."

Orlan pursed his lips. "A little worry wouldn't hurt. It can keep you safe. Now, you'd best get started."

Mallec turned toward the low stone building that housed the enclave's library.

"One more thing, Mallec." Orlan grinned. "I like my food hot, with plenty of spice, and my laundry done at least once a week."

✠ ✠ ✠

The following months sped by. Mallec claimed a secluded corner of the library and moved in, storing his sleeping furs under a table during the day. His initial forays into the written treasures of the enclave were frantic, unplanned episodes that left him unsatisfied. Once he forced himself to take a more disciplined approach, what had appeared hopelessly disorganized at first slowly began to make sense. Documents of importance were arranged not by discipline, topic, or even language, but by the name of the most senior druid in that calling.

Mallec made notes of the names and disciplines of everyone who entered the building as well as the location of the collections they used. He became so engrossed in the process he left the building only when necessary. He saw few druids, and although Orlan stopped by daily for a brief visit, the rest of his time he spent alone.

At the end of the first season under Orlan, the elder druid ordered Mallec to leave the building and join him for dinner in the main hall. Over a meal of steaming hot vegetables, cider, and fresh bread, Mallec spoke of his discoveries.

"I never imagined there could be so much knowledge in one place. Poetry, architecture, math, astronomy, logic, medicine, agriculture, mining, sailing, building, history—"

Orlan laughed. "And you read them all?"

"Oh no," Mallec said, "though I would like to, I still need to sleep. I've read much, but there are languages I don't know, concepts I've never heard before, and subjects I know nothing about."

"You must have found something of special interest."

Mallec picked a morsel of food from his beard and popped it into his mouth. "I found many such things."

"And which intrigues you the most?"

Mallec paused before responding. He had to trust Orlan completely. "That which isn't there."

Orlan raised his eyebrows.

Mallec rushed on, afraid to stop. "I read about Greek theater and Roman construction, about warriors from Carthage and the pharaohs of Egypt. The history, art, and literature of all those places are recorded here, yet there's almost nothing about our own people."

"It's here," Orlan said. He tapped his forehead. "We just record it another way."

"But if our way is superior, why wouldn't others do as we do? If I wish to learn about the great orators of Gaul, I must consult a bard who knows them. What if I can't find one? What if his memory fails before I extract the information I need? What if—"

"What if cows could fly? Things don't change because we wish them to. I agree that more of our own knowledge should be recorded, especially knowledge of herbs and medicines, but that doesn't mean it's going to happen."

"But it's got to be recorded!"

Orlan shook his head. "Not all of it. Writing down our sacred knowledge would only destroy its magic. Sacred ideas must be spoken and repeated so they will sustain and nurture us. Writing diminishes the power of the words to affect the people."

"But so much might be lost!"

"Maybe if you replaced Benecin as High Ollamh you could order it, but even then most druids would stand opposed. You might find some support among the ovates, but the bards would drown them out. What need would we have for bards if everything they know is written?"

Mallec rubbed his eyes in defeat. "I suppose you're right."

"Cheer up, my young friend. Just because they don't think the way we do doesn't mean we can't make our own written records."

Mallec scanned the room to see if anyone had overheard them. "Are you serious?"

"I've already begun. I've made extensive notes on what I know about the plants of Iberia. As I learn more, I'll add to those notes. There's no point in my knowledge dying when I do. In many enclaves, the bards themselves record rare old tales on poet staves. Even they write things when they must." He finished the last of the bread. "Have you made any progress with your visions?"

"Some, but I fear the druids I've spoken to have no better grasp of their meaning than I."

"Perhaps the gods intended it that way." Orlan yawned and stood. "I must go, but I urge you to think about what we've discussed."

"How could I do otherwise?"

Mallec watched Orlan stroll across the room. No sooner had the druid passed through the doorway when Brucc and two of his toughs entered. Mallec averted his eyes, but not before Brucc spotted him. Grinning, the druid signaled his companions to follow as he walked toward Mallec.

☩ ☩ ☩

Orlan returned to his quarters among the ovates, most of whom served as teachers to a select number of novices. Orlan's windowless room occupied the least desirable niche in a row of similar dark, stone dwellings. His lack of students and seniority rated him no better lodgings. He longed for the white-washed walls and airy buildings of Iberia and the smell of burning olive oil rather than the heavy odor of animal fat that the burning tallow gave to the cold stone here. He longed for sunlit mountains to blot out the gray expanse of rain-filled sky. He longed for a single autumn of hills covered with something besides Mona's ever-present green mosses. The thrill of seeing so many new plants diminished with every dark day.

He palmed the rough wall until he felt the candle sitting on a length of exposed rock that served as the room's only shelf. Heavy and familiar, the lopsided candle squatted like a misshapen toad. Orlan tugged it free and carried it into the central corridor where he ignited the wick from a common lamp.

Returning to his room, he shut the wooden door and replaced the candle on the shelf. Sitting cross-legged on his sleeping pallet, he opened the low wooden chest he'd brought from Iberia. Though made of plain fir, the inside lid bore the same tree design as his druid tokens. He traced the outline with his index finger, his thoughts drifting to the magnificent Iberian hills and wide-open plains, past the mountains and warm sand beaches with sunny days and scented nights, to Baia and Rhonwen.

"Orlan?"

The whispered voice seemed familiar, but he couldn't identify it. "Who's there?" he asked.

The door sagged inward, straining the leather latch. Orlan went to the door. He had to lean hard against it to free the latch. The moment he did, the door crashed inward, propelled by the weight of Mallec's unconscious body. The student sprawled on the floor, his face, arms, and clothing covered with dirt and blood.

Orlan held the candle close to Mallec. One eye had swollen completely shut, and the other had become a mere slit. Mallec looked more like a tuber than a human, yet Orlan knew it would get worse unless he applied cold compresses and managed to keep the cuts from festering. He ran to the well and filled a wash basin from it, then returned.

Mallec moaned as Orlan cleaned his wounds, but he didn't gain consciousness until after Orlan made a poultice of shepherd's bag for the deeper cuts to stop the bleeding.

Orlan looked closely at a particularly deep gash across Mallec's chin. "That one should scar nicely. How did this happen?"

"Brucc," Mallec muttered, spitting blood.

"I'm glad to hear that."

Mallec's purpled eye opened in surprise.

"A warrior would never admit to being beaten by a peer. I'm glad you're not too vain to tell me the truth."

"He had help," Mallec said.

"Two of them? One tall, and blond like Brucc, and the other short, with dark hair and a red face?"

Mallec nodded.

Orlan rinsed his cloth in the wash basin and squeezed out the blood-pinked water before starting on Mallec's neck and arms. "Whatever possessed you to take on all three at once?"

Mallec winced as Orlan dabbed at his wounds. "I didn't!"

"You'd have done better to jump them in the dark, one at a time."

"I didn't jump anyone," Mallec mumbled, his lower lip swelling where it had split on his teeth.

That the young man still had teeth seemed miraculous. "What did they hit you with?"

Mallec grimaced. "Furniture, I think."

Such a cowardly attack so outraged Orlan he could barely restrain himself. "Brucc should be thrashed, and soundly. I'll report it to the High Ollamh."

"No." Mallec held a cloth to his chin. "It's not your battle."

"You expect me to stand by while a fool beats my only student half dead?"

Mallec tried to smile, but the effort brought him only a wince of pain. "I've earned the right to claim revenge."

Orlan thought of Baia and sighed. "It's not as sweet as you think."

"Maybe not, but it's my right to find out."

"Mona's not the place for someone who'd rather be a warrior than a druid."

"Tell that to Brucc," Mallec said, as he probed the inside of his cheek with his tongue.

Orlan turned away before Mallec could see him smile. If the lad proved as tough as he was smart, he'd likely make a fine druid.

✠ ✠ ✠

Throughout the next four seasons Mallec assisted Orlan in recording and cataloging his knowledge of plants in exchange for the Iberian's patronage and influence. Mallec distinguished himself among the other students for his comprehension both of law and the details of sacred lore. Mallec stayed alert on every visit to the library for any volumes that mentioned a plant Orlan had not already added to his notes. With each new addition, Orlan evaluated his knowledge against that of the Greeks, Romans, or Carthaginians. Quite often he reached a conclusion different from the one recorded.

"It seems to me," Orlan said after examining the translation of a Persian scroll on purgatives, "that most of these documents are written by people who never actually used the items they describe."

Mallec, his gaze intent on a scroll from Egypt, remained silent, knowing Orlan would provide him with a barrage of weary details if he showed interest.

"In this case, I can't help but wonder if what I'm reading came about as the product of a purgative."

"I didn't think it possible to pass vellum like that." Mallec said.

Orlan flashed him a grin. "The vellum is fine. It's the content that concerns me." He returned the scroll and its translation to a leather storage sheath. "I won't be needing this anymore. You may return it to Master Brynd."

Mallec leaned forward to accept it. As he did, Orlan reached for his chin and examined it briefly.

"I was right about that scar," he said, "it's as lop-sided as Brucc's smile."

Orlan released Mallec's chin. "Might I hope you've exchanged thoughts of revenge for something more worthy?"

Mallec tapped the scroll lightly on his palm. "You may hope, indeed." He'd learned another thing from Galan: justice from the gods came sooner or later, but it always came. Brucc's disregard for law and learning would be his undoing.

"You say one thing and mean another," Orlan said, staring hard at Mallec. "Have I not yet earned your confidence?"

Orlan had been his guide and friend and made proper study possible. Without him, Mallec would not have survived the taunts and beatings. All the while Orlan had been a man of steady humor and wit. "But I am through with thoughts of revenge," Mallec said. "I've moved on to greater things."

"Like what? Forgiveness?"

"More like savoring victory."

Orlan scowled at him with impatience. "If you want to be a druid, you must act like one."

"In Iberia, do the druids not pass before the warriors on the eve of battle in search of omens? Do they not distribute blessings and offer assurances of rebirth to those who will fall?"

"Of course," Orlan said.

"I did something similar for Brucc."

"You prepared him for battle?"

"In a way. I learned that for two years he made a younger student do his Greek translations for him."

"Brucc studied Greek?"

"He claimed to study oratory. Edar, the bardic Ollamh, allows his students to recite Homer in any language, provided they donate a transcription to the library."

Orlan shook his head. "I suppose Brucc couldn't be bothered to do the work himself."

"He gave me the unfinished work and said if I didn't complete it for him, he'd see that I got another beating."

"You refused?"

"Not after the weeks I spent recovering from the last one." Mallec rubbed his jaw as if it still pained him. "All that remained were the final scenes where Odysseus battles the suitors in his home. The translation didn't take long."

"I can't believe you did it," Orlan said.

"In my version," Mallec said laughing, "the suitors won. Brucc learned it well, and I'm told he recited the death scene of Odysseus with great passion. Edar was not amused and demanded that Brucc translate as he read from the original. When he couldn't, Edar asked him to explain the difference in the two texts. Brucc failed again, so Edar stripped him of his robe and banished him from the enclave."

Orlan sighed. "He got better than he deserved, but how can you say you prepared him for battle?"

Grim, Mallec said, "I prepared him to lose."

✠ ✠ ✠

Another year passed before Mallec earned his white robe. At the conclusion of a day-long ceremony officiated by the High Ollamh, Orlan draped the white garment over Mallec's shoulders and secured it with a bronze pin. The last step required his teacher present him with a druid staff.

Orlan pulled the staff from its hiding place behind the altar.

Carved from yew with bold Ogham lines marking it end to end, the staff bore the message of Mallec's passage into the ranks of the Wise. Elaborate hand-carved knots spiraled away from the grip in a design that matched the new druid tattoo on his wrist. When he held the staff, there would be no separation between the man and his authority. At the staff's tip, inlaid into the center of a spiral, rested one of Orlan's tokens.

After the ceremony, they made their way to the great feasting hall to celebrate. Mallec drew Orlan aside, unable to contain his joy. He slipped his fingers across the smooth polished surface of the staff. "It's magnificent," he said.

"Your work has been my gain." Orlan patted him on the shoulder. "I only wish that our efforts together could continue."

Mallec had grown so accustomed to the Iberian that he had forgotten his initiation also meant the cessation of his studies.

One day soon he'd have to leave Mona, and he realized he had no idea where he wanted to go.

"Do you know where Benecin will send me?"

Orlan smiled. "I wouldn't even venture a guess, my friend, but it could be anywhere. He assigned me to an enclave in Armorica."

Mallec knew of the Armoricans. The Veneti plied the Western coast with their fast and maneuverable ships. They transported all manner of goods back and forth between Gaul and Britain, as well as around the southern tip of Iberia into the Mediterranean. A half dozen other tribes lived in the region.

"You're going to the Veneti?"

"No. It's an enclave near the towns of Gillac and Trochu, in the heart of lands settled by the Suetoni clan near the base of Mount Eban."

"I've never heard of it," Mallec said. "I thought you and Master Benecin were on good terms. Why would he condemn you to such an obscure post?"

"Benecin studied under Fyrsil, the master of Mount Eban enclave. He speaks highly of him."

"But why send you? Why not an Armorican, or at least another Gaul?"

Orlan laughed. "You've missed the point. I see this appointment as an honor. Besides, it halves the distance between here and home."

Mallec could not imagine taking a placement merely because it lay closer to Belgica. He did not long for anything there, except Seva and Ambioris.

"I've stayed here too long," said Orlan. "In Armorica I'll have the freedom to pursue my herbal work without the demands of tending to a huge clan."

Mallec looked deeply into Orlan's dark eyes and at the web of wrinkles at each corner. "I'll miss you."

Orlan embraced him like a son. "You make it sound as if I'm off to live with Rhiannon. By the Wheel, Mallec, I'm not dead yet!"

Mallec returned Orlan's smile, but could not shake the feeling of loss.

✠ ✠ ✠

The following day Mallec accompanied Orlan to the dock at Bryn Celli and watched him board a ship bound for Gaul. The vessel, its thin leather sails stained with the bright red and dark green squares of the Veneti clan, slipped away from the dock with the quiet ease of a seal. Mallec took comfort in the large number of warriors who lounged on the deck. Orlan would be safe from pirates. Mallec's feelings of loss grew as the boat dwindled into the distance, and when it turned into the wind at the tip of land that guarded the harbor, he felt lonely.

The walk back to the enclave seemed longer than ever before, and Mallec rarely lifted his head. When he reached his room, he went straight to bed.

Sleep came quickly, and he dreamed of his friend on the deck of the ship.

> The images in his mind became vivid with details of his own voyage to Mona, but new features crept in. Instead of the mist-heavy wind so prevalent off the coasts of Mona and Cernew, a hot sun beat down on a blue sea. The size of the waves diminished, the sails billowing in the wind showed blue and white, and although all looked serene, Mallec felt a growing sense of apprehension.

> On the deck lay a druid writhing in pain. Mallec called to him, but he didn't respond. Fog tumbled over the side of the boat and obscured the druid's body.

> The fog bank grew, eclipsing both the boat and the sea, but before he could content himself with any understanding, the fog thinned again to reveal a vast field.

> He recognized the place from a previous vision. Looking to left and right, he hoped to spot the dark-haired girl he'd seen before, but this time there were only warriors. Just as he remembered, they surrounded the field with their weapons raised and with their mouths open in silent rage.

> Mallec looked down, expecting to find the body of the dead druid he'd seen before. His fears for Orlan grew as the body became visible in the mist. Mallec shivered as he knelt beside the dead man to roll him over. He gripped a limp arm as the mists cleared above the shoulders of the corpse.

> It had no head.

9

The gods often veil their wishes in dreams, and it is a wise man indeed who can understand them. We bore the woad-marked stick of the false god back to the mountain. We slept beside the Sentinel Stones where the servant woman had erected a shelter and fasted three days before the midsummer festival. On the morning of that longest of days, a stranger scrambled away as we awoke. Where he went, we did not discover. Once again the gods have left their intent unclear.
— Stave Three of Harnef, 9th Master of Mount Eban Enclave

Armorica, Western Gaul 87 B.C.

Though small, with rich pelts scattered about, Master Fyrsil's house at Eban Enclave in Armorica welcomed Orlan more than the stern look on the Master's aged face. Orlan sat quietly in response to Master Fyrsil's summons. The old man had run Eban enclave with calm quiet since Orlan's childhood. He wondered whether the man ever hurried to do anything.

Orlan studied Fyrsil's quarters, hoping to learn something of his habits, but the room proved as enigmatic as the man. Nothing stood out. Yet that seemed all the more mysterious, for Fyrsil had been master of the unpretentious little enclave while remaining a confidant of the High Ollamh himself. Fyrsil stood among the First at any gathering. He counseled druids who counseled kings, and he had fostered students from many of the great northern clans.

Yet Orlan would have known none of this had he not learned it at Mona from Benecin. A year had passed since Orlan's arrival in Armorica and this first private meeting with the ancient druid.

"You please me, Orlan," Fyrsil said at last. "You're the first Iberian to come here, and I didn't know how well you'd fit in."

"Thank you," Orlan said.

"Mostly, I appreciate that you can keep your mouth shut," Fyrsil said. "Too many young people don't do that. They want too much, and they work too little."

Fyrsil put his hands on his knees and pushed himself to a standing position. He moves like a heron in shallow water, Orlan thought. The old man's skin seemed nearly transparent.

"I asked the High Ollamh to send someone to take over for me. I suppose he told you as much."

Orlan nodded, thankful he'd resisted the urge to mention Benecin's words.

"I could have chosen Dierdre. She's been studying here for years. She knows the rituals, and she understands the ceremonies. Some, I suspect, better than you."

Orlan swallowed but did not interrupt.

"Though she would gladly accept the responsibility, there are two things I don't like about her, and therefore I believe it wiser to name you as my successor."

Fyrsil's unexpected candor about Dierdre suddenly made the reasoning behind Benecin's decision to send him to Armorica clear.

"Your confidence in me is gratifying," he said, "but I'd always thought I'd go home. Why me?"

"I'm not going to live forever, and I wanted someone trustworthy to follow me. Benecin, in a rare moment of wisdom, chose you. If you want to go home, you will have to find your own successor."

"If I'm to lead, I'd like to understand your hesitancy about Dierdre."

Fyrsil twisted his lips in a parody of a smile. "First of all, she has a son in whom she can see naught but flaws."

Orlan laughed. "Since most mothers are all too eager to overlook the faults of their children, I should think her attitude refreshing."

"It's anything but that," Fyrsil said. "Dierdre's not raising a son, she's raising a weapon."

Orlan had heard her tale from several in the enclave. She had once been a great beauty, sought by warriors from clans as distant as the Parisii, but she would have none of them. In time, her youth faded as did the number of her suitors, and the villagers in nearby Gillac clucked that she would have no children to care for her in her dotage.

Some still whispered about how, after a particularly fallow winter solstice, she made plans for the next Beltane celebration. It had been fourteen years since that night, yet many remembered it because Dierdre failed to charm any men, although she offered her Beltane cup to an even dozen.

Willa, the chief's wife, felt pity for Dierdre and told her husband, Gar, to lie with her. Gods willing, Gar would give her a child to provide for the winter of her life.

Dierdre gave birth to a strapping boy and presented him to his father on the child's naming day. Gar called him Caradowc, for as an infant the boy cried as lustily as a warrior. When Dierdre bid Gar live with her and help raise the child, he refused. Angered, she swore vengeance and had not spoken to the chief since that day.

"It makes no sense for the leader of this enclave and the chief of the nearest clan to be at odds," Fyrsil said.

"Perhaps that's a reason to put her in charge. It would give her something to think about besides revenge." Orlan thought back to Rhonwen and her vow.

Fyrsil shook his head, and a thin strand of white hair floated free across his eyes. "Revenge isn't the only reason she has for wanting my place. Benecin trusts you and sent you here." He walked across the hut and opened a heavy chest sitting amid a pile of sleeping furs. He extracted a poet's stave and handed it to Orlan. "Dierdre doesn't care about the enclave. She cares for the status of being its master. She wants the enclave's secrets and knows they all have them."

"Secrets?" Orlan examined Fyrsil's offering. A leather cord joined a stack of thin wooden strips at one end. Tiny lines of druid script known as Ogham covered both sides of each strip.

"That's but one of many which recount the history of this enclave," Fyrsil said. "Now that I have a successor, I no longer need to hide them. A man of learning will surely appreciate the wisdom of those who've gone before."

Orlan bent closer to the central fire so he could read the text. Anticipation made his fingers quiver. Since first hearing whispered rumors about Mount Eban, Orlan had wanted to investigate. He never dreamed documents existed. He looked up at Fyrsil. "You've read these, of course."

"Yes," Fyrsil said, "it was my duty, though I prefer to put my faith in gods and worthy men, not words. Oh, I know well their strength, especially for prayer and council, but recording them imparts no greater power. A thing worth remembering is worth the time it takes to be stored here." He tapped a gnarled finger at his temple. "I've looked after these records as the masters of this enclave have done for generations, and even added my own, but I did so only out of respect for tradition. I seek no ancient knowledge."

Unable to suppress his excitement, Orlan opened the chest. Stacked neatly inside were dozens of poet's staves like the one in his hand. He spoke, dumbfounded. "These are messages from the past! Who knows how much good could come from such knowledge?"

Fyrsil stood with his hands behind his back, rocking on his heels. "Benecin and I chose you to lead this enclave because we believe you have the wisdom to answer that question. But you must quickly pick the one to come after you, as well. Dierdre hungers for such knowledge, and while I don't fear what she'd do to get it, I do fear what she might do with it. She must never be allowed to read them."

Fyrsil's caution overshadowed Orlan's joy at the window to the past. He held up a double handful of the staves. "I will guard these with my life."

Fyrsil bobbed his head. "Yes, you will."

✠ ✠ ✠

The following day Fyrsil called a formal gathering of the enclave. Three dozen attended, half of them students sitting around their master like brown chicks. The rest were white-robed druids, blue-cloaked bards, craftsmen and servants in multicolored tunics and breeches. They gathered under sacred oaks in twos and threes, their heads bent close and whispering.

Fyrsil sat on a three-legged willow branch stool and waited until they all settled. He carried his Staff of Authority, a rod of yew a hand span taller than he and decorated at the top with the skull of a boar, two bronze bells, and three squirrel tails. He leaned on the staff to stand, then tapped it three times on the ground to signal his readiness to speak. All conversations died.

"I'm becoming as ancient as a Father Oak, and as unbending in my ways," he said, "but unlike the trees that bless and guard us, my time here among you is short. In consultation with the gods I've decided to pass on the mastery of this enclave to a younger person."

Cries of surprise erupted from the mixed gathering. One of the younger servants started to cry. Fyrsil called the girl to him, embraced her and stroked her head.

"I'm not dead yet," he whispered, tickling her under the chin. The girl smiled and Fyrsil guided her back toward her mother standing behind the students.

He turned to the druids and bards sitting at his feet. "I've considered all the candidates carefully. You each have much to offer."

One druid, a senior bard who had recently returned to the enclave, laughed and thumped his round belly. "I have more than most to offer, Fyrsil, yet I decline."

Fyrsil chuckled. "Aye, Leuw, somehow I thought you might."

The woman beside Leuw snorted at him. "Shut up, you fat fool. Must you make light of everything?"

Leuw grinned at her. "Yes, Dierdre, I must. My task as a bard is simple. I remember everything and make a song of it at my leisure. With a word I can make the world praise or revile anyone. I desire no other power."

"You're an idiot." She scowled, but as her gaze met Fyrsil's she smoothed her features. Orlan shivered. She masked her thoughts too easily.

The old man continued. "I've sought a worthy replacement for a long time, even soliciting the opinion of my old friend, Benecin, the High Ollamh, in Mona." He rattled the boar's head staff. Several students giggled at the reminder of Benecin's Boar. Fyrsil smiled, needing only one cautionary raised finger to stifle the laughter. "Now I can happily tell you I have made my decision, and it is blessed by the High Ollamh, himself."

It surprised Orlan that his heart fluttered a little. He had not expected to be nervous. Dierdre sat rigidly upright, her face serene, and hands clasped, although one thumb pressed nervously into her palm.

Fyrsil motioned Orlan to stand beside him with a wave of his staff. Orlan knew about plants and healing, but he knew little about running a schooling enclave. Being the center of attention bothered him.

Dierdre's eyes narrowed. Leuw's face crinkled in a wide grin, and he applauded as Orlan stepped toward the Master. The students and servants cheered.

"Here is your new leader," Fyrsil said. "Master Orlan, lately from Mona and originally from Iberia. He is the High Ollamh's choice, and mine."

Cheers accompanied Orlan as he stepped toward Fyrsil's outstretched hand.

Dierdre jumped to her feet, anger clouding her face. Leuw grasped the hem of her tunic and jerked firmly enough to return her to the floor. She sat down hard, sputtering in fury. As one, every voice in the room fell silent and every eye turned to her.

"I would speak," she said, her expression as fierce as the carving on an altar tree.

"You have the right, Driad Dierdre."

"I protest Orlan's naming as your successor. I have studied faithfully here my whole life. I have excelled at every task set for me. The honor to follow you as Master is rightly mine."

Fyrsil eyed her carefully before speaking, then glanced toward the servants and dismissed them with a weary wave. When the students did not venture to move away, he nodded at them. "You leave, too. This is for druids and bards alone."

Their grumbles of protest died away as they dispersed. Orlan suspected he could soon find a few of them hiding in nearby bushes, straining to hear how Fyrsil would answer her.

Fyrsil sat wearily on his stool, but the gaze he fixed on her retained a trace of something strong and vibrant. "Driad, this enclave has been mine for over forty years. I know what's best for it. Your rightful path lies among the lawgivers and decision-makers of the villages."

Dierdre opened her mouth to speak, but Fyrsil waved her to silence. "Your tongue's too sharp, and your inner fire burns too hot and too fast to train the young minds here. They're seedlings, Dierdre, not kindling."

He spat into his hand, then clasped both palms together and rubbed. "'Tis done." He rose and stared hard at her. "I will hear no more about it."

He walked to the door leaning heavily on Leuw's arm, and Orlan thought him more frail than ever. Within minutes, everyone had followed the old man except Orlan and Dierdre. He turned to leave.

"One moment," she called.

He paused. Though well past the balance point of her life, Dierdre retained more than a hint of her beauty. Her bright blue eyes, golden hair still unstreaked with gray, and comely although haughty face, suggested she had presented a charming image as a youth. Had he not been warned against her by Fyrsil and others at the enclave, she could have easily called him to her bed.

He forced a light smile to his lips. "Yes?"

"What did Fyrsil tell you?"

He shrugged. "He's told me many things."

Her smile tightened. "What did he tell you about me?"

He met her gaze without hesitation. "Very little, but I would keep such things in confidence in any case. Unless you're suggesting there's something that needs to be said." He looked deep into her eyes. "What should he have told me?"

She laughed. "Your words are circumspect. They wander and turn, their meaning hidden. Shall I expect them to leap out with their intent thrust forward like a blade?" Her laughter faded. "Is that it, then? Are your words weapons? Must we be enemies?"

"Certainly not," he said, "but let us understand each other. The High Ollamh sent me here, and Fyrsil has seen fit to name me his successor. When Fyrsil steps down, or dies, I will take his place and you will be my subordinate."

A flicker of emotion flared briefly in her eyes before disappearing under a mask of control. "But we remain equals until then, correct?"

He nodded, intrigued by her game. "Of course."

"Then, try to understand how I feel," she said. "I've spent years here, toiling to follow Fyrsil's example. It's only natural I should feel disappointment knowing he found someone else more worthy than I."

"I don't think he believes that."

"No?" She blinked innocently. "Why else would he select an outlander instead of me?"

"I don't know," Orlan lied, hoping the White Lady would forgive him. "He said my knowledge, of plants especially, favored me."

"Oh, I'm sure that weighed heavily in his decision," she said, her voice edged with sarcasm. She raised a questioning eyebrow. "Isn't it odd we share a common interest."

"Herbs?" he asked.

"Power, Druid Orlan. I'm interested in the power of living things. If plants can enhance one's power or health, then certainly they intrigue me. Of course, not all plants are beneficent."

"Quite true," Orlan said, growing wary. "Some are unfit even as fodder, much less as medicine."

"And some are clearly dangerous." Dierdre appeared wolfish in the waning light. "Have you never wondered who first discovered poisonous plants? Who tested them, and why?" She waved her hands. "The bards say that past masters of Eban Enclave have recorded all that's known about the vegetation near here, but only other masters of the enclave may share in the knowledge. Is that true?"

"I don't know." He met her gaze without flinching. The hope of new and potent medicines among the plants of Eban enticed him, but he forced a look of disinterest. "But if so, how would that make your life any different?"

"Like you, I'm a scholar. I would study such material, if available."

"But if not?"

She smiled, and her blue eyes sparkled. "Then I'd be no worse off than I am right now." She reached for his brow and brushed a strand of hair from his eyes, then lightly stroked his beard. "Add a bit of color to this and you'd appear much younger. I know of ways."

Orlan brushed her hand away. "Wisdom and age travel together."

Dierdre laughed. "But the young travel farther." She let her hands fall to her sides. "As for poisons, have you discovered any?"

"No, but I care naught for them. I seek plants that heal."
He thought back to his work with Baia and Rhonwen. "It helps
to have someone who can test to see whether an herb or
medicine works. In Iberia, we found some of our best testers
among the Romans."

She raised one eyebrow in disbelief. "The Romans administered your potions?"

"No, our healers did. The Romans took the medicine."

She laughed. "I appreciate the wisdom of such an arrangement, but if I had to do it, I wouldn't know where to begin."

Orlan shrugged. "Be your own test subject."

She shook her head. "I think not. My work would likely
require a different kind of subject."

"If you'll tell me what you wish to do, perhaps I can help."

She smiled. "I want to read the poet staves. I know Fyrsil
has them, and I can't understand why he won't let me see
them."

Orlan suddenly wanted to be far away from her. "I don't
know either, but that's his wish, and I must honor it."

"So be it, then." She patted his cheek, and he drew back
at the slight. "I shall seek my knowledge elsewhere. I already
know more than everyone here."

"Including Fyrsil?"

She smiled. "Oh yes."

"Then I can't see why you'd wish to stay here any longer.
Perhaps, as Fyrsil says, your path follows a course different
from the enclave's."

"No doubt," she said, and her smile chilled him. "I've
decided I'll spend some time in Trochu. They've always had
a need for a good druid." She turned and walked regally away.

"Maybe that's why Fyrsil chose someone else to succeed
him," Orlan muttered to himself. "He needed a good druid
here, as well." He walked quickly to his quarters, intent on
reading everything the master of the enclave had given him.

✠ ✠ ✠

Dierdre shivered while standing under rain-heavy branches
of an elm tree near Fyrsil's dwelling. The steady morning
shower had let up long enough for her to traverse the muddy
grounds separating her own lodgings from the tree that shaded
the enclave master's. Despite the damp and the chill, she
welcomed the bad weather since it would encourage people
to stay indoors, making it less likely anyone would see her.

The door to the hut stood but a wagon-length away, and
Dierdre strained to hear the sounds of any servants who might
be working inside. She couldn't afford discovery, but had to

know what secrets Fyrsil denied her. If caught taking anything from Fyrsil, let alone something as sacred as a scroll or poet stave, the consequences would surely include loss of rank and banishment. She shuddered at the idea of the most likely punishment: the destruction of her driad's mark. A burn scar would obliterate its power completely.

Pulling her cloak tight around her shoulders, she imagined issuing such a sentence to someone like Orlan. The prospect pleased her, and she suddenly wondered if she had made a mistake in her plans. Would it be possible to arrange things so that Orlan would appear the thief? She shook her head. He had no need to steal. As Fyrsil's successor, he could have any of the old man's things that weren't buried with him. Staves and other such relics were never interred with a master, no matter how great his stature. She bit her lip, infuriated that Fyrsil had ignored her to appoint a newcomer to succeed him. Not only a newcomer, but a foreigner! She stepped on a mound of mud, and it flattened with a soft hiss beneath her foot. The old man would regret his decision.

A noise from Fyrsil's house made her shrink back behind the tree. The sound of footsteps squishing in the mud dwindled as a servant scuttled toward the kitchen. Dierdre smiled. Once again, patience prevailed. With a last furtive look around, she crept inside.

A bed of coals kept the simple room warm but afforded little light. She picked a straw from a bundle near the fire pit and used it to carry a flame from the coals to an oil lamp hanging near the sleeping pallet.

She looked around, surprised at how few possessions the old man had accumulated. What a fool! As soon as she obtained his position, she'd have anything she wanted. She sniffed at the primitive hut with disdain. The first thing she'd have would be suitable quarters.

It took but a moment to find the trunk in a corner under a pile of sleeping furs. It wasn't even locked! She added that shortcoming to her mental list of changes she'd institute as soon as she replaced the old fool.

She dragged a three-legged stool close, put the lamp on it, and opened the chest. Flickering light illuminated the contents—layer upon layer of thin wooden slats, each covered with Ogham script. Poet staves.

She pulled the lamp and the stool even closer. The staves were larger than she expected. Several stretched as long as her forearm. She strained to lift the trunk. The confounded things weighed too much. She had no hope of taking the trunk without being seen or leaving a trail through the mud any child could follow.

Whispering curses, she sorted through the staves to find a set she could hide under her robe. She avoided the oldest as either too brittle or simply illegible. She had just added a set signed by Master Cullinor to her stack when she heard the sound of whistling outside. She froze.

The whistling grew louder, and she blew out the lamp.

Footsteps accompanied the monotonous trill. Dierdre ground her teeth.

Silence.

Her knees ached from squatting on the cold dirt floor. With no place to hide, she grabbed a fur and sat down.

Someone stood at the door and drew back the leather covering. Had the servant returned? Dierdre held her breath.

She stared at the silhouette that eased into the opening. Small. Short.

Dierdre felt for the long brass pin she kept in her cloak. She had nothing else to use as a weapon. She pulled it free and held it butted in her palm with the point toward the door.

"Is anyone here?" asked a timid voice.

Dierdre relaxed. Students she could handle, especially the younger ones. "Who's there, and what do you want?"

The shape backed away from the opening with a gasp.

"Idiot! Come in out of the rain," she snapped.

A boy of ten or eleven ducked under the door flap. Dierdre re-lit the oil lamp and tossed the remains of the lighting straw on top of the coals.

The boy stood with his head bowed and his hands behind his back.

"Well?" Dierdre asked. "Answer me. Who are you, and what do you want?"

"I'm Budec," the boy said. "Master Fyrsil sent me to fetch his cloak."

She stepped closer to him, her chin level with the top of his head, and held the lamp close to his face. "Do you know who I am?"

He swallowed and nodded. "You're Driad Dierdre."

She noticed a scattering of crumbs on the front of his tunic. A gob of something reflected the light from her lamp and twinkled from his chest like a tiny star.

"What's that," she asked stabbing her finger toward his chest to scoop up the offending material. She held it to her nose and sniffed. The sweet scent of honey triggered an idea, and she licked it from her finger.

"So, Druid Fyrsil sent you on an errand but you decided to stop somewhere along the way. Stealing honey cakes is more important than doing the master's bidding?"

Eyes downcast, Budec shuffled his feet and said nothing.

Dierdre grabbed his jaw and yanked his head upward. "Answer me!"

Budec shook his head, clearly terrified.

The tears rapidly forming in his eyes gave Dierdre all the encouragement she needed. "Thief," she said, pushing his jaw away.

"I didn't steal anything. Cook gave it to me!"

Dierdre crossed her arms and scowled him back into silence. "Stealing food from the enclave is bad enough, but you interrupted me as I prepared a surprise for Master Fyrsil." She shook her head. "What am I going to do with you?"

"I won't tell anyone," he said. "I swear it on the Cauldron!"

She frowned. "Now you make oaths, too?"

The boy's sliver of defiance dissolved as quickly as it had come. "No."

Fyrsil's rain cloak hung from a peg on the wall and Dierdre pointed to it. "Wipe your hands on your tunic, then you may touch the Master's cloak."

Budec leaped toward the garment and pulled it from the wall, but made no move to return to Dierdre's side. He cradled the garment protectively.

Dierdre put her pin away. "When was the last time you had a beating?"

Budec cringed, eyes wide with disbelief. "Never."

She picked up a hazelwood switch from the woodpile. "Then perhaps it's time I gave you one. I'd hate to think you'd missed one of the joys of childhood." She slapped the stick across her palm, the sound echoing with a sharp crack. "Maybe it'll help you remember not to spoil any other surprises I plan for Fyrsil."

"I won't tell anyone. I promise," Budec said, wiping tears from his cheeks.

"Then how else will you explain why you've been crying?"

He sniffed. "I'll say I fell."

Dierdre tapped her foot. "You know, the gods have little use for liars. Did you come to the enclave because you think you might become a druid?"

Budec, his back pressed against the wall, nodded. Dierdre lunged at him and again gripped his tender jaw. She pulled his face close enough to smell the honeycake on his breath.

"If you spoil my surprise, I'll have you beaten every day for a fortnight. Understood?"

He bobbed his head up and down.

"Go!" she commanded, and the boy fled as if pursued by angry spirits. It generated the best laugh she'd had in months. Pathetically stupid as children, it came as no surprise most students grew into pathetically stupid adults.

She returned to the chest and repacked all but the half dozen staves of Cullinor, doing it in such a way that the collection appeared not to have been disturbed. She closed the lid, restored the sleeping furs, then walked to the door and looked out. No Budec.

Unwilling to chance being seen with the staves, Dierdre wrapped them in the hem of her tunic and secured them with the long pin before venturing outside. The rain kept most people indoors, and she didn't see another soul. She reached her quarters unchallenged.

Safe in her own hut, she tossed a few sticks of hazelwood into the firepit, coaxed them to bright flames and sat down to examine the stolen staves.

Out of practice with scholarly work, she found translating the Ogham script slow and difficult. It took her nearly the entire afternoon to work her way through the first of the ancient commentaries.

> *We are but men. High-born or low, we share the fragility of life, the inevitability of death, and the allure of transcendence in the Otherworld. Temptations assail us in that guise we each find most difficult to withstand. Yet face them we must. Jaslon's lie wore the face of history. That which he wrote was untrue, nor did events happen the way he recorded them.*
>
> *Two hundred, one score, and three years have passed since Jaslon's death. How then do I, Cullinor, now know Jaslon failed his test? A witness from that time still lives, and I spoke with him.*

She recalled both names, Cullinor and Jaslon, from the Master's Chant, a recitation of the names and deeds of the enclave's leaders, which she'd been required to commit to memory as a student. Two things intrigued her: Cullinor's assertion that an enclave master had lied, and that a witness could have survived for over two centuries. Doubtless, one of them had lied, but Cullinor's assertions seemed impossible. How could a man live for over two hundred years? No doubt Jaslon spoke the truth.

She continued reading, her eyes growing larger with each new discovery, especially when she read the fourth stave.

Some of our wealthy students bring servants who are accorded no greater share in the labor of the enclave, nor are their rewards any less. Amrec's claim that Jaslon enslaved him seemed unlikely, yet what reason did the ancient man have to lie? He claims Jaslon was attempting to commune with the spirits near a mound of the Ancients that the villagers call the tomb of the giant. Jaslon had just completed a prayer when Amrec appeared, as if in answer to it. Perhaps Jaslon thought the gods had sent him a servant.

The tomb of the giant? Impossible! She reread the stave. She'd made no mistakes and pressed her hand to her chest. Her heart pounded as if she'd just run from the enclave all the way to Trochu. She certainly wanted to. Her father's land, taken forty years ago and now held by a neighboring tribe, the Lemarii, should have been hers—the land and everything on it, including the Giant's Tomb.

The words of Cullinor swirled in her head along with something her father had told her the day he died. "Hold this land no matter what, for it bears a treasure of immeasurable worth."

At long last, she began to understand what he meant.

✠ ✠ ✠

Between the candle at his elbow and the hazelwood blaze crackling in the central fire pit, Orlan had ample light by which to read. Fyrsil had allowed him to take four of the staves, and he handled them carefully—all were brittle with age. A webwork of cracks as dainty as the veins of an insect's wing checkered the ancient strips of wood, and the etched Ogham lines had merged with the cracks such that Orlan had to squint to determine where a line began and a crack ended.

He examined the text carefully, lamenting that the Ogham characters were so cumbersome. Had it been done in Greek or Latin, languages meant for written poetry and commerce, the message of an entire stave would have fit on a single strip of wood. Instead, the words came slowly:

A god walked among us today. He came disguised as a length of wood from the cavern in the mount. Because it came from such a sacred place, we brought it into the open and left it near the sentinel stones of the Ancients where we might examine it when Lugh's great chariot hauled the sun into the sky. At first light the wood changed. As we watched, it took the shape of a man. We knew it must be Lugh himself, transformed by the power of the fiery orb.

He paused. He had heard the tale once in Mona but dismissed it as something meant to entertain children. Now he wasn't so sure. He worked through to the end of the first set of bound strips.

We fell down before him in supplication, offering prayers and praise, but he answered us not and looked upon us with fear as if we were the gods and he the mortal, nor could he speak to us in any tongue we knew.

An inscription on the final strip read "Jaslon," followed by the Greek numeral one. Orlan knew the names of all the druids and students living in Fyrsil's domain, but he had left memorization of the enclave's lineage of masters to the students. No doubt Fyrsil would know if Jaslon had achieved any notoriety, and Orlan determined to ask him about it in the morning. For now, the tale beckoned, and he read on.

He learned of the enclave's growing anger at the one they venerated as Lugh when he failed to speak their language. When it became clear they had resurrected a man and not a god, the enclave clamored for his head, but Jaslon intervened and won his freedom. The druid followed him back to the sacred mountain where he marked himself with woad, recited an incantation, and inhaled the fumes of burning baneweed. While Jaslon watched, the man turned back into a length of wood.

Could such a tale be true? Druids had long ago recognized shapeshifters and change magic. Everyone knew a man could assume the shape of an animal or bird. Yet Orlan also knew most public demonstrations were mere tricks designed to assure the masses that the druids had the ear of the gods. Had he not designed his own tokens for that very purpose? He read on, his heart beating faster as he realized the long-dead Jaslon must have come to the same conclusion. Jaslon succeeded in duplicating half of the false god's feat, but did he also effect a resurrection? The fourth stave did not say.

✠ ✠ ✠

The steady rain pounded on the thatch roof of Fyrsil's house. An occasional clap of thunder echoed, and Orlan thought the Greeks may have been right about arguing gods.

Fyrsil, oblivious to the weather, sat cross-legged facing Orlan from the far side of the fire. He blew a few experimental notes on a wooden flute then tapped the instrument carefully on his palm. He cleared his throat, sat up straight, and began to play a tune Orlan recognized immediately. He played the verse several times before he paused for breath.

"Excellent!" Orlan said. "It's 'Benecin's Boar.' I heard it often on Mona. The Ollamh wrote it himself."

The old druid gave a snort of derision. "I taught it to Benecin long before he became High Ollamh. I should've guessed the weasel would take credit for it." He jerked his head toward his druid's staff. "Just as he wanted to take that boar's head!"

Orlan winced at the thought of anyone maligning the High Ollamh. Fyrsil's irreverence caught him by surprise. "I never knew you went to Mona."

Fyrsil shook his head. "Benecin came to me. I thought him a dullard at first because he rarely spoke. It turns out he listened. The little sponge remembers everything, even that which should be forgotten." He licked his lips and began another tune, this one slower and with a hint of melancholy. The fire seemed to respond, its flames burning low, and when it dimmed to no more than glowing embers he met Orlan's questioning gaze.

"Like what?" Orlan asked, wondering if the time were right to ask about the author of the first four poet staves.

"Stoke the fire while I decide if I should give you an answer."

Orlan reached for more wood. Fyrsil still amazed him. How could a druid from a tiny region like Armorica have risen to such prominence that Ollamhs came to him?

Before he could ask, an aging warrior entered Fyrsil's hut. He shook the rain from his long cloak and hung it on a willow peg fastened to the wall. His lean face glistened with raindrops and water pooled under the hem of his well-soaked breeches.

"It's too dark and cold in here, Fyrsil. You're as bad as a Belgae—no heat, no light and worse yet, no wine!"

Orlan recognized Gar, chief of the nearby Suetoni clan, and moved to make room for him near the fire.

Fyrsil glanced at Gar. "So, Willa finally let you out?"

Gar made a sour face. "I'm not chained down."

"Of course not," Fyrsil said, his voice somber, but his eyes alight with amusement.

Gar nodded emphatically, the ends of his long mustache wobbling as he settled on the fur.

"Still, we missed you when Leuw arrived for the Fall Equinox ceremony," Fyrsil said. "He brought two amphorae this year. He wanted to be sure the wine wouldn't run out."

"I'm more than sorry I missed it. How fares Leuw?" Gar asked.

"He's still breathing."

Orlan squinted at Fyrsil. "Do you mean the Bard Leuw?" Though round as a cart wheel, the man seemed healthy the last time Orlan saw him.

"Sick with disappointment, he was," Fyrsil said.

"Cursed clanhold business kept me away," Gar said.

Fyrsil clucked. "Orlan, Leuw and Gar have a standing wager on which of them can drink the most wine and still carry a tune. Leuw's won the past five years."

"Four," Gar said. "This year doesn't count."

Fyrsil winked at Orlan. "Gar's wife doesn't think much of the competition."

"You can leave Willa out of this," the warrior muttered. He waved his arms expansively. "Women just don't understand tradition."

Fyrsil grinned at Orlan. "They entertained the entire clanhold at the top of their lungs until Gar could no longer stand."

"I could stand," Gar said. "It was walking that gave me trouble, that and the words. They became slippery."

"Of course, you had Leuw to help you."

"Aye. He still stood, though I don't know how." Gar chuckled, looked at Orlan, and wiped his forehead. "By the gods that man can drink! I've greeted the dawn from the middle of the commons the past couple of years. Last time Willa sent our daughter, Arie, to fetch me. The girl dragged me all the way home."

"At least she knew where to find you," Fyrsil said.

"Arie doesn't think I should drink any more, and now she's got Willa believing it," Gar said. "The child's too sensitive. It comes from being born to an old woman."

Fyrsil blew a low note on his flute. "I wouldn't say that too loudly around Willa."

"Well, it's true. We're too old to be raising children." He glanced around Fyrsil's modest home. "I don't suppose Leuw left any of that wine here, did he?"

"No. He feared it might turn sour, so he took it with him."

Gar raised his hands to the fire. "Pity."

"So now it's little Arie ordering you about?"

Gar puffed up his cheeks and let the air out in a rush.

"Keep an eye out for that one, Orlan," Fyrsil said.

"She wants to be a driad," Gar said.

"Would that be so bad?" Orlan asked.

"I'm not ready to think of her all grown. She's just a child." Gar's eyes softened. "And as sweet as a nightingale's tune. I might be willing to foster her here someday." He squinted at the old druid. "But not while Dierdre's nearby. You aren't going to name her your successor, are you?"

"No," Fyrsil said. "That position falls to Orlan."

Gar clapped Orlan on the shoulder. "If you come with Fyrsil's blessing, you must be a worthy man. I wish you well." The warrior slapped his hands on his knees and stood abruptly. "Such an announcement deserves a celebration. Are you sure you haven't any wine around here, Fyrsil?"

"I'll check the larder," Orlan said, shifting to stand.

Gar pressed him down, his strength surprising. "I'll go. If I find Leuw, maybe I'll find something to eat, too." The chief retrieved his cloak and stepped once more into the wet night.

Orlan held his words until the door flap fell back into place. "For a clan chief, he doesn't seem very full of himself."

"He's not," Fyrsil said. "He's one of the few who think before he acts. It's why the Suetoni prosper."

Orlan retrieved his kit from a peg near the entrance and removed the poet staves. "I've come for more, and to ask you about Jaslon, the man who wrote them."

"The enclave's master's chant is long, but Jaslon's place in it is secure. I'm surprised you don't know it."

"I can recite that of the enclave where I studied," Orlan said apologetically, "and I know the older verses of the master's chant of Mona, but—"

"How will you correct your students here if you don't know it?"

Orlan lowered his head. "You're right, of course. I'll begin immediately."

"Good." Fyrsil collected the staves and put them back in the chest. He studied the contents carefully, picked up a loose stave and gazed at the pile for a long moment. He raised an eyebrow at Orlan. "Have you been digging around in here?"

"Not without your blessing. Why?"

Fyrsil pressed his lips together. "I haven't reviewed the staves in years, but I know I left a different set on top, and now they aren't there. The knowledge contained in the staves was not meant for everyone, else the bards would know and recite it like any other account." He closed the chest. "Woe be unto he who reads them without permission."

"Wait," Orlan said. "I want to read more of Master Jaslon's words."

"They'll keep. Memorize the master's chant, and you'll know the history of the enclave. Come back when you can recite it." Fyrsil fixed Orlan with a stern look. "I'm too old to do your work for you. Learn the names of the dead before you speak with them."

10

Jaslon's witness arrived at the enclave in need of sustenance. He spoke none of our language, nor did we recognize his. Tendal, a young bard with knowledge of many tongues, was quick to learn what he could.

The man calls himself Amrec and proved as adept as Tendal. He wintered with us, and when the first flowers pinked the meadows he could speak as well as we. That is when we learned he has lived for eight hundred years.

— *Stave Two of Cullinor, 28th Master of Mount Eban Enclave*

Armorica 87 B.C.

Caradowc kicked at the leaves filling the wheel ruts in the road. Horses and carts crowded the lane, and twice he had to dodge some careless fool also headed to Trochu's market. Banners flapping in the wind crowned the tops of the wide battle wall surrounding the clanhold. In these times of peace, the wall needed repair, and the gates stood wide open.

Caradowc's mother walked ahead of him, knowing he would follow like a faithful dog. He bristled at the thought and held his head higher. The fall wind caught his long hair and whipped it into his face, stinging his eye. He slowed to rub it.

"Have you gone lame, boy?" Dierdre called. "Why must you always lag behind?."

She continued without waiting for his answer, as usual. Nothing he had to say interested her.

"I'm hungry," he called back. "I haven't eaten since yesterday."

At the gate she stopped walking, her hands fisted on her hips—a stance he knew well. When he was a child she acted as if waiting for him were painful, and although he now neared manhood, she treated him the same way. He brushed quickly at his eye. "I'm coming."

She began walking again, her steps sure as she approached the market's center. Makeshift stalls of vendors crowded the clanhold commons. Somewhat smaller than Gillac and farther from the enclave, Dierdre still preferred Trochu on market day.

Gillac was Gar's clanhold, and his mother made it clear she had no intention of going there. Gar was a weakling who had abandoned him and his mother to live without support of kin. Who could respect such a man?

She passed three stalls without interest, although Caradowc had difficulty ignoring anything in the tumult of the market. The vendors and buyers, mostly women, bickered and whined, prattled and cooed, laughed and complained over nothing. He hauled his attention away to keep up with his mother as she weaved through the crowd. He saw only the top of her head as she left him behind. She flowed through the ranks of the common folk like a serpent in high grass.

He paused beside an enclosure formed by stacked wicker cages. The clamor of hens and ducks all but drowned out the vendor's voice. Not that he cared, for only the fair-haired girl working with the merchant interested him.

The bored expression on her face fled when she noted Caradowc's interest. She seemed to stand a little taller, her chest rising slightly under his gaze. He nodded a greeting and let his eyes roam over her gentle curves.

"Could I interest you in a young hen?" She gestured toward the cages. "I can produce one sweet as a fig and tender as a kiss."

He returned her smile. "How young? I've no use for one that's learned to cluck but not to scratch."

"A cock, then?" She smiled invitingly.

Claws dug into his shoulder, followed by Dierdre's shrill voice. "Didn't I tell you to keep up with me?"

"I—" She silenced him with a glare before inspecting the girl. "Sometimes I forget how easily men are distracted."

Caradowc turned, hoping to draw Dierdre away from the stall.

She brushed past him, and Caradowc hastened to stay with her, his eyes focused on the back of her head. One day, he promised himself, he would set the pace and others would follow, including his mother. No one, druid or not, would tell him what to do.

As they pushed through the noisy throng, he contented himself with examining the few things that interested him: arm bands, cloak pins, and leather goods in one stall, knives, shields, and war horns in another. His mother concentrated on a small but varied collection of spices, wine, and clothing. As she haggled with a crone over the price of some foul-smelling unguent,

Caradowc glanced beyond the stalls to a crowd of men gathered in a circle less than half the size of the market oval.

He could see them laughing and yelling, their attention directed toward a pair of unarmed combatants.

"I'm going to watch the wrestling." He winced, hating the timid lilt of a question in his voice.

She exhaled wearily. "Go. I'll meet you near the well at midday. I have plans for us this afternoon, but I need some information first."

"I still haven't eaten."

Her smile carried a winter chill. "I'll be eating soon. Too bad you aren't interested in staying with me, or you could have a bite as well."

Yet another test, he realized. She never gave anything away. If he wanted an hour of freedom, he'd pay for it with hunger. "Enjoy your meal," he said, stalking away.

He joined the men, as was his right. He wanted no woman to provide for him and hated that he still depended on his mother for every morsel.

The jeers of the crowd watching the wrestlers grew as he approached. He paused briefly beside a stout man eating an eel from a wooden skewer. Grease dripped down the man's face and caked in his mustache. Caradowc realized the space around the man was given in respect to his smell and not his station. Caradowc paced the crowd's perimeter before finding a vantage point. He turned his attention to the combatants.

Two men circled each other within an arena formed by spectators. The taller one appeared to have taken the worst of the fighting. Swaying slightly and gasping, he wiped at a layer of mud formed from the sweat and dirt covering his naked body. Less winded and with less dirt on his body, the shorter man offered an open hand to his foe.

"More?" he asked.

"I've had enough, Gwair," the big man said, puffing. "I prefer to face men who'll stand and fight. You're too slippery for me." He gripped the offered hand.

Gwair bowed his head briefly and grinned. "Then go wrestle a cow, Bren. Anything smarter than that will know to get out of the way of those great fists of yours."

Bren waved a brawny fist at Gwair. "You wouldn't grin so much if I ever greeted you with one."

"That's true, which is why I took pains to avoid them."

"You took pains?" Bren rubbed his jaw. "What about mine?"

"I gave them as best I could," Gwair said. "Would you care for another helping?"

"Not today," the big man said as he splashed water on himself from a horse trough. "All I want now is an ale and a place to rest. I don't fancy starting the harvest tomorrow with all the bruises you've given me."

"Buy me an ale and I'll join you in the fields," Gwair said. "You don't want to be too weary to celebrate Samhain."

The two men walked away from the circle as another pair prepared to battle in their place. Caradowc followed.

Although one had soundly thrashed the other, neither showed any sign of animosity. It made no sense that they would go off drinking together. If an opponent had bested him so soundly, Caradowc would not want such fellowship. The two men stopped outside a tent set up between the market area and the livestock pens. At the entrance they handed a few coins to someone before disappearing inside.

Caradowc knew without checking that no coins nestled in his own pouch. He glanced at the sun to judge how much time he had left. If he ran he might catch one more wrestling bout.

☩ ☩ ☩

"Came then Farnestal, the Remi, to add to the work of Tilgan who repaired the sacred well." Orlan stopped pacing and let his voice trail off as Leuw shook his head for what must have been the thousandth time.

"Tilgan was the Remi." Leuw never opened his eyes. He leaned against a rough-barked beech tree and listened to Orlan's pained recitation.

Orlan continued. "Came then Farnestal, the..."

"Of the Carnutes," Leuw said. "Let the rhythm roll the words from your tongue."

Orlan sighed. His tongue worked well enough for most things, but this lyric chronology of dead masters could not hold his interest. It was exactly why he'd become a scholar and not a bard. "Of the Carnutes, to add to the work of Tilgan, who repaired the sacred well."

Leuw shook his head again.

Orlan stopped. "What is it this time?"

"You should start at the beginning," Leuw said.

"How will I ever reach the end?" In his own voice, he heard that of every student he'd ever taught. He sank to the ground beside Leuw with a weak smile.

"Some never do." Leuw kept his eyes closed and swatted idly at an insect buzzing near his face. "Those who survive we call warriors."

Orlan grimaced. "I'd like to practice some of the later verses. I can't tolerate the same stanzas day after day."

"Very well, but don't expect me to make any excuses for you when you stand before the enclave and mumble through it. If you think I'm difficult, wait until you make a mistake in front of the students."

Orlan groaned. Leuw was right, and they both knew it. "From the beginning?"

"It's a short journey from what you know to what you don't."

"How long did it take you to learn this?"

Leuw scratched his ample girth. "A few days. These things come easily to me."

It would take Orlan more than a month. Fortunately, he didn't have a dozen other things to memorize at the same time, like most students. "Do you suppose anyone would notice if I just moved my mouth while you recited the verses? Or better yet, I could feign a toothache and bandage my jaw."

"There's one who'd spot such a counterfeit instantly."

"Fyrsil?" Orlan asked.

"Me."

Orlan forced a frown. "I don't know what Gar sees in you." He stood and resumed pacing.

"Gar sees a fine drinking companion! Now, once again Master Orlan. 'In the days before time, when the Father Oaks were but acorns...'"

Orlan took up the chant and continued through several generations of those who led the enclave near Mount Eban and who had served as druids for both the towns of Gillac and Trochu. He sang of great teachers, brilliant seers, wise judges, steadfast leaders, and confidants to famed warriors, and he never stumbled until the superlatives began to repeat.

"How is it that so many can bear the title of 'greatest teacher' or 'unequaled seer?' These titles make no sense."

Leuw nodded. "They were all great, otherwise they'd never have become Masters here. These verses were composed by lesser men and women while grieving the loss of their leader. The stanzas may be flawed, but the people they commemorate weren't." Leuw opened his eyes. "Fyrsil isn't asking much. When the time comes, you may be the one to write his verse. How can you do that if you don't know what's been said of the others?"

"I know, I know," he said. He paused, gauging whether to mention the poet staves. "I'm more interested in something else."

Leuw raised an eyebrow. "Male or female?"

"Neither, you old reprobate." Orlan laughed. "Fyrsil has information about this enclave written long ago."

"I thought you weren't interested in the history of the enclave."

"Oh, but I am. I'm especially eager to learn more of Jaslon's work."

Leuw looked at Orlan suspiciously. "What about Jaslon fascinates you?"

Orlan tried to keep his excitement from showing. "He speaks of something called 'woadsleep.' Do you know what it is?"

Leuw sat upright. "I've heard tales."

"What tales? What do they say?"

"I didn't say I could remember them."

Orlan quickly sat beside him. "That's nonsense! You just told me you memorize such things with ease. Now, what do you know about woadsleep?"

Leuw pulled him close, his voice low and ominous. "I know it's dangerous. I know it's a way for men to wield the power of the gods, and I know that Jaslon was the first druid to do it. What do you have in mind?"

"Nothing," Orlan said. "I'm just curious. I want to read more about it before I decide if it's worth pursuing."

"It's not," Leuw said.

"How can you say that?"

"If it were a good thing, we'd still be doing it." The bard shifted his bulk forward and stood. "But there's no tradition of it."

"Perhaps it never had a chance to become a tradition," Orlan said. When it became obvious Leuw would not discuss it further, Orlan turned his attention to the Samhain rituals they'd soon perform. "Anyway, we have other traditions to observe, like the one in Gillac. By the way, when are we leaving?"

"As soon as Fyrsil's ready, I suppose."

Orlan shook his head. "Fyrsil's staying here. He says his hip pains him too much to travel. He wants us to lead the celebration in Gillac."

Leuw whistled. "As long as I've known him, Master Fyrsil's never missed Gillac's Feast of the Dead."

"You know there will be a call for divination," Orlan said. "I'm not very good at it, even on Ancestor Night when spirits are plentiful. Will you scry the future for them?"

"On two conditions. First, make sure I have plenty of wine, and second, see that I'm seated among the unmarried women."

✠ ✠ ✠

"There it is," Dierdre said, pointing from the cool shade of the trees that flanked the river. Fallen leaves muffled their footsteps. They'd left the horses they borrowed from the enclave tethered out of sight beside the river.

Caradowc scanned the area. "There's what?"

His inability to see anything not pointed out to him irked her. "The Giant's Tomb. See the high ground over there?" She gestured across the acreage once owned by her family. "The high grass, boulders, and brush confuse the eye and make the mound seem smaller. It's really a wide, flat ridge. If you stood next to it, the top would be twice your height."

"And there's a giant buried inside?"

She cuffed the back of his head. "Must you demonstrate your stupidity every chance you get? Forget giants. The peasants around here thought the mound odd and named it thus to explain the presence of high ground in a flood plain. But, there's more to it than that."

He raised an eyebrow.

"When I was a child," she said, "my father told me of a treasure in this land. I always thought he meant crops, but now I'm beginning to understand what he really believed."

Caradowc looked at the cattle grazing on the lush grass and at a rough hut nestled in a stand of trees at the opposite end of the pasture from the mound. "I don't see any crops, but there's a fortune in livestock here. Whose land is it?"

"It's mine!"

He gestured toward the house. "Then who lives there?"

"The Lemarii took this land from my family years ago. This morning I learned the Lemarii chief gave it to his son, a muscle-headed oaf named Gwair."

"I've seen him," he said. "He wrestles well, for a farmer. He looks more like a warrior."

She ignored him. "My father never allowed me near the mound, but he never said why. Now I want a closer look."

He hesitated. "You're sure there's no one buried there?"

"I said there's no giant buried there."

"But it is a holy place?"

She rubbed her eyes. "Perhaps for the Ancients who lived here long ago, but no one comes to worship now."

He eyed her skeptically. "I don't want to anger any spirits."

"We won't," she said. "I don't want anyone to know we're here, so we'll leave the horses where they are and walk the rest of the way."

Dierdre led the way, keeping to the trees and then creeping through the high grass until she reached the mound. Caradowc followed her to the side of the ridge away from the house, where they rested.

"Now what?" he asked, sitting on a boulder.

"Now we look for a way in."

"Into the mound?"

"It's a tomb of the Ancients. There'll be an entrance somewhere, though possibly buried or disguised. If they went to the trouble to build something like this, they wouldn't waste it on one grave."

"What should I look for?"

"Look to make sure no one sees us. I'll inspect the mound. Keep vigilant and stay close in case I need you to lift something."

No one appeared in the pasture, so Dierdre chanced circling toward the front of the mound. Caradowc kept a wary eye on the distant hut and remained by her side.

When they completed a full circuit, she paused. "Let's look on top."

With a boost from Caradowc, she scrambled up the steep bank. He followed. Large rocks protruded in many places on the broad flat surface. Thick shrubs and thorn bushes grew in abundance, although none attained much height. She signaled a halt near a large circular outcrop of dark stones. One place had vegetation cleared from between the stones. She prodded at the rocks and found an opening a little larger than a badger hole.

"Can you see down in there?"

He lay on his stomach and looked in. "No, and I wouldn't expect to find anything but snakes and spiders."

The boy irked her. "How did I birth such a coward?"

"I'm not afraid!"

"Good, then crawl in there and tell me what you see."

He looked like a rabbit in a snare. "It's too small! I'd never fit."

"You must. Help me move a few of these rocks." She braced herself and pulled on one of the stones lining the hole.

He put his back into the effort, but the stone wouldn't move.

She had to know what was inside. "Stop. Just wiggle in." She bundled dry grasses and twisted them together. "I'll make a torch."

"What for?"

"So that when you plug the hole with your body, you'll still have some light to see by."

"I don't think I want to do this."

Dierdre pushed past him. "I've no time to waste on cowards. I'll go in myself."

He stopped her. "I'll do it. Just give me a moment." He tried stepping into the opening but quickly discarded the approach.

"Head first," she said.

"It might be a long drop."

She glared at him. "I'm waiting."

He leaned into the opening, twisting to get his shoulders through. Bent over the edge, he still had more of his body out than in, so she grabbed his legs around the knees and lifted them into the air. With a yelp, Caradowc dropped into the hole, his feet kicking frantically. He landed in the dark with a thud and a grunt.

She stared into the hole but couldn't see a thing. "Can you hear me?"

"Yes," he gasped, "but you're blocking the light."

She shifted to let in the sun. "What do you see?"

"There are some coins," he said after a time, "but not enough to call a treasure."

"Anything else?" she asked.

The sound of horses caught her ear, and she flattened against the ground.

"Just—"

"Quiet!" she whispered fiercely. "Someone's coming." She shrank down behind the rocks and watched two riders pause beside the hut before continuing toward the hill.

Dierdre found a hiding place behind a pair of slabs sticking into the air at odd angles. A hundred generations earlier, the stones had likely formed an altar.

The riders came closer, unaware of her presence. She hoped Caradowc had the sense to keep quiet.

Squinting against the light coming from behind them, she finally made out the features of Coemgen, chief of the Lemarii. She didn't recognize the muscular young man beside him. They kept riding until they reached the foot of the ridge, and then wove their way between the rocks for the length of the mound, much as she and Caradowc had done earlier.

Coemgen seemed distressed, which pleased her.

"Listen to me, Gwair, it's just not wise, that's all," he said. "What good can come from building so close to the spirits of the Ancients?"

"You sound like an old woman," Gwair said. "I won't disturb any spirits, and if I do, they won't be those of anyone we know."

"How can you be sure?"

"Because Mother made up most of the stories we've heard about this place. You know how she likes to tell scary tales to amuse children."

"Almeda's good at that," Coemgen said, "but it doesn't change the facts. This hill was sacred to the Ancients. If you build on it, you're likely to anger their gods."

"Be practical," Gwair said. "Look around. Do you see any other high ground? The river has flooded twice since we built the caretaker's hut. Do you want your grandchildren washed away?"

"I don't have any grandchildren. Besides, Almeda and I want you to build in Trochu."

"And waste this magnificent land?" Gwair laughed again. "No thank you. I'll make my home here."

"Not while I still lead the clan," Coemgen said.

Gwair paused before answering. "I'm in no hurry."

The two men rode back across the field. They reached the far end without looking back, and Dierdre ventured once again toward the hole. She seethed with anger at the thought they would build on top of the Tomb.

She heard Caradowc muttering and peered over the edge. "They're gone. Now, what do you see down there?"

"Other than a big stick and a handful of coins, nothing."

There had to be something else. She expected to find bones at least. Hadn't Cullinor mentioned an Ageless Man? Where did he hide, if not here? "Are you certain? Have you looked everywhere?"

"It's a small space," Caradowc said. "May I come up now?"

She suddenly had an inspiration. "What do you see on the walls?"

"Nothing."

"No writing or pictures?"

"I doubt it," he said, "but, it's too dark to be sure."

She squinted at the sun hovering near the horizon, and then glanced back at the rocks shielding the opening.

"Are you still there?" he asked.

"What is it?"

"How do I get out of here? It's getting darker," he said.

"Climb out."

"There's nothing to climb on!"

Dierdre shook her head yet again. The boy was helpless. "I wish you'd remembered to bring the rope. Now I'll have to go back and get it." She leaned out over the hole. "How many coins did you find?"

"Two dozen, more or less."

"I want to inspect them," she said.

"They're mine!"

"Do you want me to get the rope, or not?"

"Yes, of course."

"Then you'll give me the coins when I get you out." She had taken only a few steps away when she stopped and returned to the hole. "Throw me the stick you found."

"What for?"

"Just how long do you want to stay where you are?" Caradowc thrust the stick from the hole and she grabbed it. The wood prickled her hand. She pulled away from it as if stung, and it tumbled back into the hole.

"Hey!" Caradowc yelled.

She stared at her hand and flexed her fingers. The stick left no marks, only a strong unpleasant sensation. "Are you holding it now?" she asked.

"Yes."

She squinted into the darkness below, her heart racing with new excitement. "How does it feel?"

"What do you mean? It feels like a stick!"

"Hold onto it until I get back," she said and hurried toward the horses.

How strange, she thought. The secret of the Tomb remained tantalizingly close. She needed more information from Fyrsil or the staves, but she knew one thing for certain: Coemgen's son, Gwair, must not be allowed to build on the Tomb.

✠ ✠ ✠

Dierdre lashed at the cart horses, already lathered and breathing hard. The cart thumped along the deserted road to the enclave and tossed Caradowc a hand's breadth into the air.

"What's the hurry?" he asked.

"I have business at the enclave. Private business." She glanced toward the stick wrapped in an old cloak and tied securely to the inside of the wagon. It held the key to a miraculous treasure, and she didn't want it out of her sight, although the tingle she felt whenever she touched it made her queasy.

The staves Fyrsil had kept hidden from her would be unguarded tonight. She didn't fear being seen, for the enclave would be deserted because of the celebrations. Fyrsil himself always went to Gillac for Samhain.

"Then we should have left Trochu earlier," Caradowc said.

"No. I needed to be well seen in Trochu today, and again at first light tomorrow."

"But why?"

Dierdre smiled. "Because, Caradowc, timing is everything."

✠ ✠ ✠

A few men paced the defensive wall of Gillac as Orlan and Leuw reached the clanhold. A dozen warriors and a few women and children waited at the gate. Gar stood at the front of the small crowd. Baskets of new acorns and dry oak leaves, still red and orange, adorned the portal into the village. Straw dolls, made by the village children for luck, hung from the tops of each section of wall. Orlan thought they must encircle the entire clanhold.

Orlan, Leuw, and the rest of their small entourage drew to a halt in front of Gar.

"Welcome!" He looked at each member of Orlan's group. "Where's Master Fyrsil?"

"Fyrsil's hip is too sore for him to ride with us," Leuw said. "Otherwise, he's fine." The bard dismounted and made a show of rubbing his tender backside.

"I hate horses," Leuw said.

Orlan grinned. "I imagine they feel the same way about you."

"I want to add a third condition to my coming along on this venture," Leuw grumbled, "we return to the enclave in a wagon."

"Conditions?" Gar asked.

Orlan leaned close to Gar to whisper, "Plenty of wine and a place among the unmarried women."

"I'll see to it," Gar said, chuckling. "When you're ready, join us in the hall. We've butchered a cow for the feast, and the smell of it roasting is driving me mad. Don't delay."

"We won't," Orlan said. "We have some preparations to make, and then we'll be along."

Orlan and Leuw led their horses through the small crowd. Laughing children jostled them with demands for blessings, and everyone chattered with the latest gossip from the village and the surrounding areas. This part of the celebrations delighted Orlan. Being greeted like an old friend made him miss Iberia a little less. A gang of youthful warriors insisted on leading the druids' horses to the commons and hobbling them there, which gave both Orlan and Leuw more time to arrange what they'd need for the celebration.

Orlan slipped tokens into both of the hidden pockets in his robe and made sure he had his special goblet. Leuw unpacked the drums and tucked a small whistle into his pocket. If it appeared someone might be catching on to Orlan's sleight of hand, Leuw would be prepared with a distraction.

They entered the crowded hall and, as one by one people noticed their arrival, the noise diminished. They crossed the room to where Gar waited.

"Again, welcome, Druid Orlan! This is my wife, Willa," Gar said, taking the hand of an imposing blonde standing beside him. He nodded at the child standing next to her. "And that's my daughter, Arie."

Willa kissed both of Orlan's cheeks in a warm welcome, and then embraced Leuw with more familiar zeal. It surprised Orlan to see Leuw's face redden. Arie approached the druids and bowed. Her solemn demeanor would have been more at home on Fyrsil. Orlan touched her head and uttered a blessing.

Gar glanced at Leuw. "I understand you want special seating."

Leuw squinted at Orlan. "I—"

"There's no need for thanks," Gar said. "I'm only providing what you so richly deserve." The clan chief pointed to a spot along a long wall where a number of old women had gathered. "You'll sit with the widows tonight, and I'm sure you'll find them both interesting and interested."

Leuw scowled, and then laughed with Gar.

It took only moments for the feast meats to arrive. Along with the savory aroma of roasted beef, the mouth-watering promise of succulent duck, boar and pheasant filled the room. Fresh rounds of dark bread lay everywhere. Surrounded by dishes of nuts, berries and red apples, Orlan could see why Leuw so enjoyed his stays in the villages. He popped a hazelnut into his mouth. It seemed to signal the others and everyone fell to eating and talking.

When everyone had eaten their fill, servants cleared away the remains of the meal. Orlan took one last swallow of honeyed ale and forced himself to stand and walk to the front of the main hall. By the time he reached the spot traditionally reserved for chiefs, bards, and judges, the noise in the great room had dropped to a hum occasionally marked by a cough, a belch, or the harsh bark of a parent at an unruly child. He took a deep breath and began.

"Master Fyrsil's sore hip makes him unable to join us tonight, but he sends his blessings and his finest bard." Orlan gestured at Leuw, who appeared quite comfortable surrounded by a trio of solicitous grandmothers.

"In Iberia, we often celebrated Samhain by counting the good things that happened during the year." He produced a silver token and spun it in the air. As the shiny object caught everyone's attention, he palmed several others and caught the first disk as it fell.

"The High Ollamh himself blessed this token. It is unique. Let it be a symbol for all the children born to the clan this year." With the token between his first and second fingers he slowly moved his hand so that all could see it. "Perhaps if we can think of other worthy events, the gods will see fit to add to our treasure."

"The barley harvest will be a good one," someone said, and in response Orlan dipped his hand rapidly. When he held it up again, another token appeared between his second and third finger. A collective gasp went up from the people.

A slope-shouldered woman with deep worry lines in her face stood and held up a rough pelt. "My husband killed the wild dog that's been eating our chickens."

Orlan waved his hand again, but no new coins appeared. He frowned. "The gods must be waiting to hear something else."

The woman nodded. "Well then, they should know 'twas the same dog what attacked my daughter's babe last winter."

Orlan waved his hand again and a third token appeared. The woman gave a smile of satisfaction.

"Anyone else?" Orlan called.

"You've no more room in that hand!" cried a youngster.

"The gods are resourceful," Orlan said.

"No Suetoni died fighting the battles of others," Gar said from the back of the room. Orlan waved his other hand and a token appeared.

"My oldest daughter finally took a man," said a farmer near Orlan's feet.

"We bought our first cow," a young woman nursing an infant said.

"I built a house."

"I opened a shop."

A boy of no more than five rushed forward. "I'm learning to play the harp."

With each announcement, Orlan produced another token. When both hands were full, he made a show of emptying them into the shallow goblet on the floor in front of him. No sooner were his hands free than someone else made another claim. It continued thus for several minutes until nearly everyone in the room smiled.

"I've decided to become a druid," Gar's daughter said.

With a final wave of his hand, Orlan produced three tokens in exchange for her announcement, which seemed to cap the declarations.

"It sounds to me like this has been an excellent year," Orlan said as he leaned down and picked up the goblet. He held it aloft in both hands as the tokens in it slid through a hidden opening in the bottom and fell, out of view, into the open cuff of his robe.

He smiled. "I would ask the gods for a blessing, but it seems they've already blessed this clan." The last token slipped past his elbow, and he turned the empty goblet upside down. The crowd gasped again.

Orlan lowered his arms carefully. "A wise man does not mourn the loss of a symbol. He celebrates what it represents." He gestured toward Leuw. "Are you ready to speak with the spirits?"

"Yes," Leuw said. "I'll need someone to drum and open a path into the Otherworld for me."

The three women surrounding him volunteered.

"I wish to speak with Gar's daughter," Orlan said, "for her announcement has touched my heart."

Arie stepped forward without waiting for a sign from either parent.

Orlan followed the youngster out of the hall and into the moonlight. Though the evenings had grown colder, the bite of winter had not yet arrived. They sat on a rough log.

"What do you know of the druid's life?" Orlan asked.

Arie looked at him with wide innocent eyes. "The gods talk through them."

Orlan emptied the tokens from his robe into a pouch. Shifting his white garment aside, he slipped the strap of the pouch over his neck and let it hang under his arm.

"Sometimes the gods don't always talk to us," he said. "When that happens, we have to think of something to say for them." He opened his hand to reveal one of the shiny round tokens. "This is for you."

Arie accepted the token reverently and examined the designs on it. "It's like jewelry from the gods."

"The gods didn't make it," Orlan said. "I did."

Arie blinked. "Didn't they give you the idea?"

"I suppose so."

Arie slipped the token into her pocket. "Then, in a way, they did make it."

Orlan appraised the child. "What makes you think you should be a druid?"

"I can't imagine doing anything else."

"It takes years of training, you know. Fifteen if you're smart, twenty or thirty if you're not. Some remain students all their lives or leave the enclaves entirely."

"I'll finish," she said, her eyes sparkling with confidence. "The Great Mother told me."

"You've a year or two to grow before you're old enough to come to the enclave, but if the Great Mother bids you join us, I'll look forward to your arrival."

They re-entered the hall as the drumming slowed to the traditional seven beats that called Leuw back from his spirit journey. When he opened his eyes, worry painted his face. He looked straight at Orlan.

Orlan rushed to his side. "What is it?"

"I spoke with the Dark Lady," he said, his face pale. "She told me I must write Fyrsil's verse for the Master's Chant."

Orlan shrugged. "Someday you will. Who else could do it as well as you?"

All trace of mirth had vanished from Leuw's face. "She told me to write it tonight."

Orlan stared at Leuw until the worried whispers of the villagers caught his attention. Druids always shared the Samhain vision with the clan, so Orlan forced a smile to soothe their concerns. "Bard Leuw fusses more than usual. The Great Lady offered the old bachelor a bride!"

Laughter erupted around the room, and as the celebrants resumed their merry-making, Orlan led the bard to the door. "Well?"

Leuw wiped at his mouth. "I know visions are sometimes only shadows of possibilities, but this one felt real. Fyrsil is dying."

"He's very old. We should expect it."

Leuw shook his head. "I'd like to go back anyway."

That Leuw would leave the feast now alarmed Orlan. "I'll go with you." He motioned for young Budec to join them.

"Fetch our horses," Orlan whispered. "We must return to the enclave tonight."

Budec nodded and ran from the hall.

Before they had a chance to gather their cloaks, Gar cornered them at the door and grasped Leuw's arm. "What are you up to?"

When Leuw didn't answer, Orlan spoke. "We're concerned about Fyrsil because of a vision, but we don't want to alarm anyone. We're going back to the enclave."

"Stay 'til morning," Gar said. "If you leave now, you won't even be able to see the road."

Budec returned, leading two horses and a pony, his intention of returning with them plain.

Leuw struggled onto the stout bay that had brought him to the clanhold and groaned. "As long as the horses can see, we'll be fine."

Gar nodded and held his hand up to Orlan. "Will you send Budec back with news, whether good or ill?"

Orlan grasped Gar's proffered hand. "Of course." Then he kicked his mount to a trot.

With a sigh of resignation for the discomfort to come, Leuw did the same, and Budec followed. Once they left the torch light at the clanhold gate, night enveloped them.

Orlan glanced at the star-littered sky and the half moon, which cast enough light to see the road.

The riders spoke little for most of the night. Budec seemed content to wait for an explanation.

As they neared the enclave, Orlan's horse lurched into a fast trot. A welcoming whinny echoed from the darkness ahead, and his horse answered.

Orlan called over his shoulder at Leuw's dwindling shadow, "I'll see to Master Fyrsil. Meet me there." He cantered into the pasture in front of the enclave.

Sheltered by hardwoods at the edge of the clearing, the buildings were dark smudges against a darker background. Orlan reined in his horse near the center of the compound, jumped down from the saddle, and hurried to the entrance of Fyrsil's lodging. Brushing aside the leather door covering, he called into the blackness.

"Master Fyrsil?"

There was only silence. Orlan stepped cautiously into the humble building. The hearth lay at the center of the room, but the room lacked the odor of a recent fire.

A noise at the entrance made Orlan spin around, but it was only Leuw.

"Fyrsil sounds like a winded war horse when he sleeps," said the bard. "He's not here."

Orlan stumbled over something on the floor. He reached forward slowly to feel.

"What is it?" Leuw asked.

Orlan's hands brushed cool skin. He shivered. "A body, I think."

Leuw choked back a sob. "Fyrsil?"

"It's too dark."

"By Lugh's balls, I should have brought a lamp! I'll be right back."

Orlan knelt beside the body. His fingers met only cold flesh covered by a thin sleeping robe. He rested his hand on the flat of a man's chest but felt no hint of life.

Leuw returned with a lamp and two aging servants. He rushed to Orlan's side and held the light close to the body.

Both druids stifled sharp breaths as they stared at the fierce countenance of the dead man." His was no gentle death," Orlan whispered.

Leuw held the lamp higher. "Look at this place. You'd think someone had been wrestling in here."

What few belongings Fyrsil had were scattered about. Orlan grunted. Though old and stiff, Fyrsil had fought for his life.

Leuw turned to the women huddled near the door. "Did either of you hear anything?"

"Not a sound," said one, "though I warrant my hearing isn't what it used t'be. The others all went to the Samhain parties in the villages. We thought we were the only ones who stayed behind." She wiped at the tears spilling down her cheeks.

"Bring the lamp closer," Orlan said.

Leuw sighed. "I wish this light was Lugh's, bright enough to bring him back."

Orlan nodded. Only Lugh could restore the dead once they'd passed through the Cauldron. "I want to see his face."

Leuw handed him the lamp then spoke to the women. "You may prepare Master Fyrsil for his final journey. We'll bury him as soon as the others return and the villages can be alerted."

The women hurried away. Budec waited near the door without speaking.

"Come outside with me, lad," Leuw said, "and I'll tell you what to say to Gar. You can ride back in the morning when you're rested."

Orlan held the lamp above Fyrsil's nose and studied the old man's face. Thin lips, framed by strands of an ash-colored beard, were drawn back to expose yellowed teeth. He'd been close to his death for a long time, his face deeply etched by the years. Blue eyes, dry and dull in death, looked at nothing from beneath half open lids.

Orlan reached out to close the eyelids and noticed something odd. As a druid, he'd seen men and women dead from long years, from sicknesses, from mischance, and from war. Yet in all his life, Orlan had never seen one that wept blood.

He leaned closer and decided "weep" was too strong a word, yet there could be no doubt that a thick drop of dried blood marked the inside corner of the old man's left eye. Orlan settled the lamp and looked for an injury that might have produced the blood in the eye but found nothing.

Muscles aching from the round trip to Gillac, weary from a night without sleep, and depressed by the death of a fine man, Orlan forced himself to his feet and trudged to the door.

Outside, Leuw sat on a tree stump, and the servants loitered nearby. As Orlan stepped away from the door and nodded to them, they entered, each carrying the ointments, herbs, and cloths necessary to prepare the dead.

"It's been a long night," Leuw said. "We should both be in bed, though I doubt I'll get much sleep."

"Aye. There's nothing we can do for Fyrsil now."

Leuw yawned. "Perhaps if I dream, Rhiannon will return and suggest something I can say about him in the chant."

"I'd rather she told you who killed him."

"Don't be daft. No one would murder a druid, much less one like Fyrsil. It was his time."

"What about the mess in his quarters?"

"He may have stumbled around at the end. A heart death is painful, and pain can make a man do strange things."

Orlan agreed, but only because fatigue made him too tired to argue. He bid Leuw goodnight and walked toward his own hut, then stopped. Fyrsil was not burdened by possessions. If someone killed him to steal from him, the only things of value they'd find were the poet staves, and they would only have value for those who could read them.

Orlan turned and headed back to Fyrsil's hut, the flame from his lamp guttering against the light wind. Samhain was the night the spirits of the dead returned to visit the living. Perhaps Fyrsil himself would give the answer to his death. He entered the hut.

Inside, Fyrsil lay where Orlan had found him. The two women washed his body without speaking, their tears mixing with the soapy water they lavished on the corpse. The time for wailing would come later.

Orlan waited until they dressed Fyrsil in his finest ceremonial robe, then he set the lamp on the dirt floor and lifted Fyrsil's frail body onto the sleeping pallet. He straightened Fyrsil's legs and crossed his arms over his stomach. Though he pushed the jaw closed, it wouldn't stay shut. Orlan smiled. "Still trying for the last word?"

Satisfied with the disposition of the body, he dismissed the women and looked for the chest containing the poet staves. Other than a few pieces of clothing, some linens and personal effects, Fyrsil's house stood empty. Neither the chest nor its contents remained.

First murder, then theft! Overwhelmed by both crimes, Orlan abandoned the dead man's house and left the lamp behind, its light the only hint of warmth in the compound.

He kicked once at the ground on the way back to his quarters, too weary to do more than scatter a few loose stones in the darkness. The enclave—his enclave—emerged from darkness in the earliest traces of dawn. This was no way to begin his mastership. At the very least, he'd expected to benefit from a private word or two from Fyrsil, but that too had been stolen.

He undressed and fell into bed, but he couldn't sleep. He shifted continually, first under the furs then atop them. The sounds of morning greeted a sleepless man. Spirit-weary, he forced himself to stand and dress.

He glanced at the table by the door, wondering if he should light a fire. As he turned to the table to retrieve his flint and tinder, he saw Fyrsil's chest beside the table partially covered by Orlan's heavy winter cloak.

Heart pounding, he lifted the lid and peered inside. The staves were safe.

He slumped to the floor in relief and envisioned Fyrsil lugging the heavy chest here, perhaps in response to a premonition.

"I'll safeguard them from here, my friend," he said.

11

Neither druid nor god, Amrec called himself a traveler on time's road and claimed to have lived at this enclave long ago. When I asked him who was then Master, he mentioned Jaslon's name, but said Jaslon had not allowed him the freedom to come and go or talk with anyone else. Jaslon met with him many times and often spoke at length, as if Amrec could understand him. When he didn't, Jaslon became angry.

When asked why he didn't leave the way he had come, Amrec laughed. He said traveling in chains was difficult, and that is the way Jaslon first brought him to the enclave.

— Stave Three of Cullinor, 28th Master of Mount Eban Enclave

Iberia 87 B.C.

Three years on the road pretending to run from the Romans had left Rhonwen more weary than she imagined possible. They rode the ox cart for that first day after leaving Castulo, but walking proved considerably easier on her backside, although it did nothing to ease her conscience. No matter how often she relived the half-truths she'd given Baia the day they left, she did not believe the gods had released her from her blood oath. She'd have no respite knowing she'd failed to kill Sertorius.

She left Sertorius before he woke to avoid the escort he ordered to take her home. She had run the entire way to Healer's House where Baia met her with a wagon already loaded.

"We must leave before the *togas* come looking for you," Baia had said. "They'll expect you to leave the country with Orlan, but we'll fool them by staying in the hills."

Baia had spoken little until they'd left Castulo far behind, and the morning sun warmed their backs. "Did he die quickly?"

she had asked. "Or did he live long enough to feel some of the pain I've born all these years?"

The questions burned in Rhonwen's heart just as fiercely now as they had when Baia first asked them, yet she knew her answers would be unchanged if Baia asked them again today.

"He's gone, Mother," she had said. "He won't hurt anyone in Iberia ever again."

Baia had gripped Rhonwen's wrists and stared into her eyes. "Did he feel any pain?"

Rhonwen could not look at her. A sleeping man feels nothing. "Would it make yours ache any less?"

"Tell me!" Baia had shouted.

"No," Rhonwen had said, for once telling the truth. "He felt no pain."

The answer wasn't what Baia had wanted to hear, but to Rhonwen's relief, she accepted it in silence. For three years Rhonwen had endured their wandering as penance for her lies.

Though she and Baia had walked all over Iberia, tending the sick and injured, or settling the inevitable squabbles among the inhabitants, the women had visited fewer than half of the villages that littered the mountains. Nearly every day brought a new farm valley or a hilltop settlement built around a rocky outcrop.

Baia walked on the far side of the cart, leading the ox with one hand and resting the other on the wolfhound, Tesla, pacing beside her. Tesla's mate, Iago, roamed ahead. Both dogs stood as tall as roe deer and carried scars from boars and wild dogs that occasionally harassed the women. Baia whistled, and Iago turned and loped toward them with his tongue lolling to one side. Tesla wagged her backside and leaped to meet him, her whip-like tail slapping against her sides.

The day passed without incident until Rhonwen noticed a white butterfly near the rear wheel of the wagon. She dismissed the omen at first, but when it continued to hover she surveyed the dun-colored hills through which they traveled. She even walked near the ox to have a clearer view of the road ahead.

"I think we should set up camp," Baia said, squinting into the distance. "From what that merchant told us this morning, we're still a half day away from the Bateri village."

A meadow graced in the center by a single sycamore tree opened along the trail leading down to a shallow creek protected by thick willow bushes. The large tree offered protection from the sun and wind.

Baia pointed. "That might be just the place to spend the night. We can tether Inez to the tree and rest in the shade. I hope there won't be many mosquitoes. Last year we had to lather up with fat to keep them at bay. I'll burn more tansy this year."

Rhonwen wrinkled her nose. "I'm not sure which smells worse, rancid fat or burning tansy."

"I suppose you'd rather slap at the buzzers all night?"

"When I'm downwind from you, yes."

Baia grumbled and Rhonwen was grateful for another day during which her mother had not mentioned Rome or Romans. She maneuvered the ox and cart to the tree, using them to block the wind. They set up the tent they'd bought from a brown-skinned African in the south. The red and white panels set them apart from other itinerants, and whenever they arrived in a village too small to house them properly, the tent became a healer's house and justice hall. Both women dispensed medicines and decisions in local disputes, although Baia did more of the healing and Rhonwen more of the judging. The tent, roomy and tall, allowed them to see to the needs of the ill. Rhonwen liked it best when they performed the healing magics by the brazier at the tent's center. She especially liked erecting the tall stave that bore the symbol of traveling healers. It always brought respect from the clans, and even from the occasional Roman patrol.

After raising the tent and arranging their sleeping furs inside, Rhonwen unloaded an armful of dried bush grass to use as kindling at the fire. As she hunched over the grass and sparked her flint, she glimpsed Baia carrying a bucket toward the stream. Tesla, as always, followed. Iago settled beside Rhonwen, his large brown eyes watching her.

Rhonwen glanced at the wheel to reassure herself that the butterfly had flown away. Relieved it was no longer in sight, she concentrated on fire-making. After another few tries, the spark ignited the dry tinder. She cupped her hands around the flame, feeding larger bits into it until it burned the twigs she offered. In moments a cheery fire blazed.

"Dinner will come soon, my friend," she said to the dog.

Iago's tail thumped the ground once before something caught his attention. He stared first toward the road and then at the brush on one side of the meadow. His hackles rose and a growl formed deep in his throat. Rhonwen tensed.

Concerned, she stood up and looked for Baia, who remained out of sight.

In the distance, Tesla snarled. That and Baia's surprised cry sent Iago on a frenzied tear into the undergrowth. Rhonwen grabbed her druid's staff and plunged after him.

Tall grass and brush whipped her skin as she ran until she burst into a small clearing by the stream bank.

Baia lay on the ground, unmoving, as her bucket floated slowly downstream. Two men stood nearby, each with a sword. Tesla, bleeding from a gash in her side, crouched beside Baia's head and snarled at them. Iago paused only a moment at the edge of the little clearing, as if to distinguish his enemy clearly, then leaped at the nearest man, who half-raised his bloody sword. Iago's massive jaws closed on the man's face. He dropped his blade and fell backward, screaming and clawing at the great wolfhound.

Sword raised, the other man rushed forward to strike at Iago. Tesla jumped between them, and the man's sword came down hard on her. Rhonwen gasped at the sound of Tesla's pained howl as she crumpled.

Rhonwen grabbed a handful of sand and threw it at the second man's face. He cried out and rubbed at his eyes. Staggering slightly, he raised his sword again. She struck him on the shoulder with a double-handed blow of her staff. Something cracked and the man dropped to his knees groaning, his limp arm cradled against his chest.

"Iago, back!" Rhonwen shouted.

The dog released his hold on the other man's face, but straddled his chest, teeth bared and snarling. The man clutched at his wounds and whimpered.

"Hold him, Iago," Rhonwen said, knowing she didn't have to—the dog wouldn't let him up until she ordered it. She knelt beside Baia. Dazed, Baia sat up and gingerly felt her scalp where a small gash bled profusely. She'll heal, Rhonwen thought, although she'll have an ugly scar to show for it.

"I'm all right," Baia muttered, pushing Rhonwen away. "Tesla?" She held a hand out to the injured dog.

The animal whimpered, and Rhonwen intercepted her mother's probing fingers. "Best wait until we muzzle her. She may bite you, though she'd regret it later."

Baia nodded and unknotted one of the laces from her sandal. She tied a loop and secured it around the dog's snout with a tender pull.

One of the men moaned. "You tend to dogs first?"

"I tend to my friends first." Rhonwen rose and approached him, pleased to see that she'd dislocated his shoulder. She hoped it was also broken. "Explain yourself well and perhaps we'll tend to you, too."

The man spat at her.

Fury rose in her, and it took all her patience to resist dislocating his other shoulder. "What clan do you come from that you attack healers and druids?"

The man sneered. "What healers? I see only a merchant tent and women alone." Groaning, he struggled to his knees and reached for his sword.

Rhonwen jabbed her staff into his injured shoulder. "What courage you must have to attack lone women. I'm sure the bards will sing your praise." She retrieved their swords, and threw them as far as she could into the river.

Leaving Iago to watch them, Rhonwen knelt beside Baia and the injured dog. Tesla lay limp in Baia's arms, her eyes half open as she stared into the Otherworld. Since her puppy days, Tesla had been at Baia's side every moment, guarding against boars, bandits, and snakes. She died then, a true warrior. Rhonwen placed a hand on the dog's back and both women wept.

"We lie here injured and you mourn a dog?" said the man with the damaged shoulder.

Rhonwen turned to him slowly. "When I see you again," she said through gritted teeth, "I will curse and condemn you for all your clan to see." She looked at the man lying beneath Iago, who snarled every time he moved. Deep bite wounds would likely fester without a healer's help. Let him come to her then.

"Iago, come," she said.

She picked up Tesla and trudged back through the willows toward their tent. Baia followed slowly while Iago paced behind them. He frequently stopped, his ears cocked for danger as he turned to look back. When Rhonwen glanced back, too, the men were gone.

⌖ ⌖ ⌖

The women reached the Bateri village by mid-morning of the following day. The Bateri greeted them with respect and offered them a mud-walled house, the best the poor clan had to offer. Sleeping rugs and furs strewn on the limestone floor around a central fire made the room surprisingly comfortable. Typical of upland village dwellings cut out of the mountain itself, the plastered interior walls retained some of the original likenesses of dancers and wild animals once painted there.

It took the villagers three days to realize that, despite her youth, Rhonwen deserved her formal druid's robes. Though it had taken the better part of two months to sew, Rhonwen's handiwork pleased her. The body of the robe gleamed sun-bleached white, to symbolize the unity of all druids. The sash and left sleeve bore the colors of her parents' clan, the Cosetani. The right sleeve bore a single wide band of deepest red, the healer's color. Someday, if Rhonwen ever achieved her mother's Ollamh status, she would add an additional crimson stripe.

Baia helped her gain the clan's confidence. When the people insisted on the older woman's decisions first, Baia deferred to Rhonwen.

As for the healing, Rhonwen tended only to Baia's wound until satisfied that her mother would heal. Afterward, both women tended only those gravely ill or in severe pain. The others had to wait.

In less than a week Rhonwen settled a score of minor disputes and a dozen serious ones. Together, she and Baia officiated at the proper sending of two souls through the Cauldron to the Otherworld. Every day new arrivals with ailments or squabbles trickled in from the hills.

Those not sick wanted insights into their futures, and Rhonwen wished the gods had made her better at augury. She urged the supplicants to rely on their own common sense and let the future take care of itself. As the last one left their house, she sank down on the cool floor to catch her breath. She had much to do before tomorrow's full moon ceremony signifying the first day of planting, when she would bless the seed grains and perform a sacrifice.

She set aside midday as the time to deal with the troublesome Trepani clan and their incursions onto Bateri lands. The Bateri always ended on the losing side. She'd try to resolve the greater quarrel of a border later in the day.

She dozed off waiting for the Trepani envoy outside the healer's house. Shouts and cat-calls roused her. She faced the village's main gate and shielded her eyes from the sun's glare. A dozen riders approached from the east. Another dozen men ran beside the horses holding straps attached to the saddles. The Trepani had arrived.

"Lugh's balls," she muttered to herself. "They've brought neither druid nor bard." Settling boundary disputes without a druid the clans knew and trusted would make her task all the more difficult.

Baia appeared and tossed bloody water from a pail into the brush beside the house. A young woman, her foot wrapped in new cloths, and partially supported by a man a few years her senior, hopped from the interior on her good foot.

"She's not to walk on it until the swelling goes down, and then only when she must. No carrying anything heavy."

The man nodded with a solicitous smile.

"Including those babes of yours, Milo," Baia added.

The woman laughed, and Milo pressed a coin into Baia's palm. "Gods keep you, Driad," he said as he hoisted his wife into his arms and carried her up the path toward their home.

Baia palmed the coin with a grin at a pair of gap-toothed children. Their mouths dropped open in awe as the coin disappeared. When they ran away, she glanced toward the approaching horsemen and motioned to Rhonwen. "Are you prepared?"

Rhonwen shrugged. "I may need you to stand beside me."

"You have the authority of the gods. An old woman standing at your elbow can't improve on that."

She nodded toward a Trepani warrior who had fallen behind the rest of the riders and dismounted in the shade of some stunted oaks. "I believe we know one of these Trepani already."

Rhonwen squinted at the man. He turned his bruised and scabrous face to them, and for a moment Rhonwen thought he paled at seeing her. Without command, Iago rose from the doorway, gave a low growl, and moved to stand in front of the driads.

"I see him, Iago," Baia said as she smoothed his hackles. "The more I think on it, the more I believe he was fathered by a Roman."

"Soon enough we'll see their game. Already I'm disposed to the Bateri side," Rhonwen said.

Baia turned toward the house. "I'll clean up and join you as soon as I can." She patted Iago's great head. "I don't feel very impartial myself," she said. "Come, dog. You stay inside, this time."

Rhonwen felt self-conscious, knowing they all watched her walk across the clearing, no doubt looking for some sign of weakness. By the gods, she thought, not today as she smoothed all traces of emotion from her face. This was no time to show anything but the will of the gods. The laws were plain. She would be just.

The Trepani leader approached her without ceremony. She bristled but held her tongue. He insulted her by not waiting for the proper introductions and praises.

"Hail, Driad," the Trepani chief said with an open smile. "You asked us to come, and we obey."

She did not smile in return, for he had not honored her with the gift of his name. She struggled to remain calm. "You bring no druid to speak for you. You will therefore abide by my judgment alone?"

The chief's smile faded, and the cold glint of his eyes as he examined her suggested she might make an enemy today.

"I see you're a healer first and a druid second," he said. "How can we abide by your decisions? You're too young."

She eyed him up and down. Shorter than the others, but by his stance she imagined he thought himself a better man than most. The tight, corded muscles of his exposed chest and arms supported that notion. He wore a helmet of finely crafted bronze and iron topped by an elaborate bronze boar, although rust marred it in a few places. She wondered if he'd received it as booty in some battle. Scarred on his shoulder and arms, he wore an odd mix of Iberian and Roman gear. Black hair framed his angular face, and blue eyes of some northern clan appraised her without blinking.

She returned his gaze with a studied smile. "I have the authority of the gods behind me. That's been enough for people of honor far longer than either of us has been alive."

The smile froze on his face, and the men with him shifted uncomfortably.

Rhonwen glanced toward the man who had attacked Baia and saw his companion standing with him. She noticed with grim satisfaction the dog bites had already festered. Neither of them dared look her in the eye. Their cowardice would serve her purposes, although it would be easier if a druid represented the Trepani.

"Honor is something all men should aspire to," she said.

The Trepani chief's eyes narrowed.

One villager gasped at her words, but several others snickered. The Trepani had few friends among the Bateri.

"You come here expecting me to settle your border claims yet you behave without honor," Rhonwen said.

The Trepani chief threw his shield to the ground in anger. "Who are you to claim you know honor when you see it? I look for wisdom in grizzled old men or bearded women."

Jaws clenched, Rhonwen raised her druid's staff. She'd smoothed every bit of rough bark away from the stout yew and decorated it with sacred spirals and interlocking patterns. Orlan's tree symbol graced one side. She'd been careful to use only the finest materials—a single eagle feather, a boar's tusk and bits of fur from those animals that traveled with her in her dreams and spirit journeys. She shook the staff at him, and the deer hooves clattered.

The Trepani chief sputtered a protest, and his warriors pressed close to either side of him.

Rhonwen dropped her cloak to the ground, exposing her tattoos, the colored badges of her achievements covering her arms and shoulders. "You need only see these to know my power is real. I speak for the Bateri who have great honor, though their clan is small. What druid speaks for you? A clan without honor has no right to make a border claim."

The chief met her gaze thoughtfully. "So be it then. I'll send for one."

He motioned for two riders to join him. "Bring Hamel at a gallop."

The warriors nodded and departed. Without another word to Rhonwen, the Trepani chief directed his men to the stunted grove where they pitched their camp.

Rhonwen fumed. Turning, she nearly bumped into a man she recognized as the mate of the woman with the injured foot. He stepped close.

"I know him, Driad. Aras has a temper wilder than a wounded boar's. His men could destroy this village easily. Maybe we should just give him what he wants."

"Milo, the Bateri elected you headman because of your wisdom. How is it you trust us with your lives but not with this negotiation?"

He twisted his belt between his fingers. "We're farmers, Driad. Few of us have held to a warrior's way since the Romans defeated the men of Carthage long ago."

"Either trust me or find another druid to represent you. If you choose to give in, you dishonor the faith of your people."

Milo dropped his chin to his chest. "You shame me, Driad." He looked up. "We may be poor, but we do have honor. Please speak for us."

⌘ ⌘ ⌘

As dawn illuminated the trail, shouts came from the Bateri sentinels. They spotted rising dust from riders.

Rhonwen hurried into her robes and settled a feathered head-dress on her forehead. She would wear all her finest ceremonial garb. The soft white linen of her cloak stood in stark contrast to the red tunic she wore beneath it. It set her apart from the multi-hued clothing of the villagers. Baia stood beside Rhonwen in her common healer's robe, but with her arms bare everyone could see her druid tattoos. No one could have mistaken her for a simple merchant woman.

Villagers gathered as the Trepani advanced. An old man dressed in a time-worn white robe approached her, leaning heavily on the arm of the Trepani chief. His red-rimmed eyes watered and the flesh of his jowls seemed to hang in the same way his sparse mustache drooped past his chin. He clutched an old staff in his right hand. How they'd managed to bring the old man so soon from their village surprised her.

He bowed low and spoke with confidence, although his ancient vocal cords would not allow him to speak loudly. Villagers pressed close to hear.

"I am Hamel ap Honzec, druid to the Trepani clan for over fifty years." He motioned to the chief. "This is our leader, Aras. The gods have seen fit to allow me to answer your summons. I obey them. Rhonwen mav Baia a Senin, allow me to offer you a prayer for good fortune and for a life of peace and harmony."

That he knew her full true name startled her. She had never heard of him. "You honor me with your greeting, Druid Hamel."

"The honor is all mine, Driad."

Milo, representing the village, joined them. Rhonwen held an open palm toward him. Though his simple clothes and lack of sword showed him for a farmer rather than a warrior, he nevertheless stepped forward without hesitation and met the Trepani with a steady gaze and a firm hand.

"Welcome," he said.

She nodded to him and turned back to the Trepani druid. "Will you join me inside, away from the sun's heat, so we may discuss what we must?"

Hamel flashed a smile. It surprised her to see he still had all his teeth, white and strong. There was more to this old man than she thought. She offered him her arm, and he accepted.

They settled inside, and all the adults of the Bateri crowded in as well, hugging the perimeter. The Trepani sat with sheathed swords across their knees in front of the druids. Milo occupied the space a few feet away. Rhonwen and Hamel sat side by side on a bench and Baia stood behind them.

Once they had finished the formalities, Rhonwen began the proceedings. "We are met to resolve two matters," she said.

"Two?" Aras grumbled. "What issue is there besides the border question? We've suffered the Bateri on our pastures long enough."

Rhonwen stared him down. "We'll get to that, but first would you agree that such disputes may be settled only by those with honor?"

Aras sputtered but a small flick of Hamel's fingers silenced him. Rhonwen liked this old man more each moment, and for an instant remembered how much she missed her uncle Orlan.

Aras crossed his arms on his chest. "Yes, yes. I agree."

"As do I," Milo added.

Aras ignored Milo in favor of Rhonwen. "What is the other issue? Let's dispense with it as quickly as possible."

Rhonwen smiled. "We are. It's why I had to confirm the tradition of honor."

"You waste my time."

"Really?" Rhonwen let her smile evaporate. "How much of your time do you spend with thieves?"

Aras leaped to his feet, his hand on the hilt of his sword. Rhonwen forced herself to remain calm and all but missed the restraining hand Hamel placed on her arm.

"This is no battlefield, Aras," Hamel said, his voice soft but clear, his tone reasonable. "I suggest you keep your blade covered."

"First my honor is questioned and then I'm accused of consorting with rabble! How else should I act?" He glared at Rhonwen, shaking with restrained anger.

"Calmly," Hamel said.

Rhonwen ignored Aras' bluster and pointed to the man with the dog bites. "Do you know him?"

"Enogat? Of course I know him."

"Ask him how he received his wounds."

"He told me a wild dog attacked him, and he killed it."

"My dog is neither wild, nor dead," Rhonwen said. "And yet his teeth left those marks."

The chief stared hard at her. "Why would you set your dog upon my kinsman?"

"Because he and another attacked my mother, the Driad Baia, four days ago." Rhonwen pointed to the gash in Baia's scalp. Both villagers and warriors gasped. "When his companion attacked, I struck his shoulder. I doubt he's able to use that arm yet."

The Trepani chief, his mouth set in a grim line, turned slowly to look at the man she had pointed to. "Enogat, is this true?"

"She lies," the bandit said without looking directly at Rhonwen or his chief.

Rhonwen raised a hand to forestall any more comments. "As the gods willed it, the wounds our dog gave him fester. If he wishes to live, he must beg aid from the very woman he tried to kill."

Enogat stepped forward with a snarl. "I didn't try to kill anyone!"

"Where's your worthless brother?" Aras asked. When Enogat didn't answer, Aras turned to another warrior. "Find Aube and bring him here."

Rhonwen locked her gaze on the Trepani chief, refusing to honor the offender with a glance. Within moments, Aube arrived, a strong warrior on either side of him and his arm bandaged against his chest. He looked at Rhonwen, Baia, Aras, and finally at Enogat. "Fool! I told you we should never have come here."

"Silence!" Rhonwen said, her voice as menacing as she could make it. She looked at those assembled. "I swore the next time I met these two I would condemn them before their clan. That part of my oath is fulfilled. We will hear of their crimes from the one they injured. I will then judge them on their acts."

She pounded her staff three times into the dirt to seal her pronouncement. No one spoke. She glanced at Druid Hamel who sat silent, his fingertips drawn together in thought and pressed against his lips. When he looked up and caught her gaze, he gave her a nearly imperceptible nod.

Enogat scowled at Rhonwen, but when he caught the expression on his chief's face, traces of emotion bled away.

Rhonwen turned to her mother. "Baia, tell us how you came by the wound on your forehead, and how your dog, Tesla, died." She prayed Baia would stick to the facts and not venture into tales of Roman treachery, but her fears proved unfounded.

Baia related the story, adding nothing and leaving nothing out. From the merchant in the morning, to setting camp and seeking water, she told the whole tale simply and eloquently. Had she not chosen to heal, she could have been a bard. She laid aside her healer's cloak and acted out how she had leaned over the stream and been struck from behind, and how she had raised a tattooed arm to protect herself, although Tesla took the blow for her. Those assembled heard of the second blow that killed Tesla, and many grumbled with anger. Few men could be as loyal as a good dog. Baia finished, then sat and cried for the dog whom she'd loved like a child for eight years.

Aras sat in silence, staring at the two men kneeling in front of him. One of the Trepani warriors slapped Enogat's swollen face.

No one else moved.

Rhonwen looked at Enogat and held his gaze. "I would remind you that neither gods nor men have any use for liars. Now, answer before your judge and the gods of this land: did you and your brother attack the Driad Healer Baia?"

Horror marked the faces of everyone present. Druids were sacred. Attacking one was unthinkable.

Enogat's face contorted as if in pain. "We didn't know she was a druid."

"You think an unarmed woman bending over a stream with a bucket in hand is an honorable target?" Aras spat into the dirt at the prisoners' feet. "No warrior could do that."

"It was a mistake," Aube said.

"A grave one," Rhonwen added.

Aube shuffled forward a few inches before Aras pushed him back. "We always honor druids."

Baia scowled. "Unless they seem like easy prey?"

Aube said nothing, but dropped his gaze.

"Have you anything else to say?" Rhonwen asked Enogat.

He glowered at his brother and then at Rhonwen before turning to Aras. "We've known each other since our childhood. I've stood by you in battle. What has she ever done for you?"

Aras drew his knife and plunged it deep into Enogat's belly, then yanked the blade to one side before pulling it free. The Trepani sank to his knees, his hands clutching at the wide gash in his stomach as blood pumped freely over his arms and down his legs. White-faced, he looked up at Aras in shock, and then, whimpering, lowered himself to the ground.

Aras straddled the dying man and waved the bloody knife above his head. "He's my kinsman. I have the right." He turned and grabbed Aube by the hair.

"Hold!" Hamel said.

Aras paused, his knife at Aube's throat.

"We must hear the judgment. All have agreed to abide by the driad's pronouncement."

Aras wiped the blood from his knife on Aube's tunic and tossed him away like a dirty rag. "I await the gods' decision. Speak, law-giver."

Rhonwen glanced at Hamel. He avoided her gaze and offered no counsel. She had only heard of such judgments as she had to make. Her breath came short, and she focused on breathing evenly. It calmed her. She held her arms above her head to draw everyone's attention, although they knew the outcome before she uttered the words.

"O-ghe! Let all assembled hear the judgment of the gods and the pronouncement of the law."

Suddenly she felt sick and didn't want to say the words. She wanted to find solutions to benefit both sides of a dispute. She wanted to heal people. She wanted to see children grow strong and straight-backed with respect and dignity. She did not want to make these other choices. She looked again at Hamel. He must know these men, their lives and families, but he offered her no more encouragement than before. He had confidence in her decision and made it plain by not moving to intervene nor speak on their behalf although he had the right. The villagers gathered around her said nothing, and the Trepani warriors wore solemn faces. One crow flew overhead and cawed. The gods spoke, their meaning clear.

"There is only one penalty for attacking a druid," she said. "Death."

She glanced at Aras who met her gaze without emotion, his thoughts unspoken. The condemned man quivered in silence.

"The law requires that you have a day and a night to pray to the gods for another life. Do so, Aube of the Trepani, for the following day you will break your fast before dawn with a meal proper to the nourishment of your spirit. You will see your last sunrise as you don Rhiannon's torc and this life ends. Your body will be buried under rocks and without ceremony, and you will be left to enter the Otherworld with neither food nor weapons."

Once again Rhonwen pounded her staff on the dirt floor three times. For some time no one moved or spoke.

Aras then motioned to two warriors who led Aube away. The Trepani chief faced Rhonwen, his eyes hard and his voice clipped. "We must cleanse ourselves of the shame these two have brought upon us before we can discuss the second issue."

Hamel cleared his throat. "Such stains do not wash away easily, Aras. What acts will the Trepani perform to balance the scale?"

"Two men will pay with their lives!"

"Indeed," Hamel said. "And they are part of this clan. What will the Trepani do to balance the scale?"

Aras crossed his arms. "Any animals and goods those men owned will be given to the driads they attacked."

Rhonwen frowned. "We don't—"

Hamel held up a hand for silence but never took his eyes from Aras. "Would you have the wives and children of those men pay, too? How will they live without livestock or land? And how does that absolve the clan of its blood debt? Enogat and Aube are Trepani!"

"Hear me, then. The Trepani will withdraw from the disputed lands and stay on the north side of the river for the balance of the year."

"The whole year?" Hamel asked.

Rhonwen raised an eyebrow. Less than half a year remained.

Aras scowled at the druids. "Five years," he said.

The ancient druid merely closed his eyes and shook his head.

"Ten?" Aras' voice rose in pitch.

Hamel did nothing.

Rhonwen secretly smiled with satisfaction. Orlan had taught her that he who speaks first loses. Aras stepped forward one pace, his head high and his chest out with pride. Hamel had won, she thought, but Aras had given up more than she thought he would.

"Without Bateri permission," he proclaimed, "we will never again cross the river that separates our pastures." Aras stared at his men. "I will kill the next warrior who raids on the south side of the river."

Hamel stood and raised both arms in a gesture of supplication, first to the gods and then to Rhonwen. "O-ghe! Is this an honorable settlement?"

"It is," she said, clapping her hands together. "And it is done."

The Trepani left first, and Hamel went with them. When the Bateri villagers crowded around her to offer their thanks, she waved them away. Rhonwen needed time to cleanse and prepare herself. She had never executed a man.

✠ ✠ ✠

Every Bateri in the village as well as several dozen hill people lined the path from the druid's house to the stone altar in the center of the commons. The day started with fire in the eastern sky, bright red on the horizon beneath a layer of cloud. The dark silhouettes of Trepani tents crowded the outer edge of the commons. Many from both clans had come to witness the execution. During the previous day, people milled around and spoke in muted tones, although a few children played Chase Me, Catch Me while some adults huddled over *tabula* or other games.

Rhonwen fingered the braided leather strands attached to the winding stick she would use to wrap around Aube's neck at the first flash of the sun's rays above the horizon. Two wooden balls, the beads on Rhiannon's Torc, were spaced on the thong where they would insure an end to Aube's life as soon as Rhonwen began to apply pressure. Her stomach lurched at the prospect.

She pulled away from the door and resumed her seat beside the fire. Baia stirred the oatmeal and dried grapes Aube would eat as his last meal. She waved a hand over the concoction and muttered a binding spell. Rhonwen handed her an earthen jar of honey. Baia pulled the honey stick free, letting the golden liquid drip into the oatmeal pot where it merged with the hot grain to symbolize the cycle of life. Her lips moved in constant prayer for pity from the gods for the man meant to eat the offering. When the honey stretched into a strand too thin to see in the dim light inside the house, Baia thrust the stick back into the pot and replaced the lid. Rhonwen said her own prayers over the meal, then wrapped the leather thong and beads around the winding stick and placed it in her pouch.

Her deep sigh caught Baia's attention. "You act as if you've never killed a man."

The comment startled her, and she nearly denied it. "This is different."

"I suppose you're right," Baia said, as she touched Rhonwen's hand. "Shall I come with you to take the oatmeal to Aube? It's only a short while until the sun rises."

Rhonwen shook her head, still unsettled by guilt for letting Baia believe she'd killed Sertorius. "I'd best do this myself. I am a druid." She wished she felt more like one. She wondered whether Orlan or any of the other druids she'd met would be unmoved by the taking of a human life.

"He brought this upon himself," Baia said. "What you will do to him is right and proper. You act on behalf of us all."

She handed Rhonwen the small cauldron, a bowl, and a wooden spoon. Both bowl and spoon would be burned after the ceremony. Proper observances of procedures and rituals could not be overlooked. Otherwise, how could she expect the gods to consider Aube's death as meaningful?

As she walked toward the prisoner sitting bound beside the altar, she thanked the gods Orlan had taught her to do things the right way.

Several children had gathered near Aube, and a girl with wine-red hair and a freckled face laid a water skin against his lips. Aube ignored it. "Sit," he snarled at her. "I'll tell you when I want it."

The girl sat but neither spoke nor looked at him.

Rhonwen pitied the child, but realized Aube treated her the same way he had lived, without respect. If he held nothing sacred, how could he revere his own life?

As Rhonwen approached, the children stood and dropped their heads in deference. Both Trepani and Bateri alike joined them, if not eager for the execution, then merely curious.

She nodded an acknowledgment to them all and then addressed Aube. "Here is your last meal. It has been prepared properly, so you may, in time, be returned to this world a better man than you leave it." She put the food on the ground and prepared to feed him.

He scowled at her and struggled against his bonds. "Keep your swill. I demand my right to Walk the Altar."

Rhonwen's mouth dropped open. She had forgotten this last recourse for the condemned to prove themselves innocent. That Aube would ask for such a trial after the accusation of two druids amazed her since the tradition had grown from the customs of honorable men.

Word of Aube's demand spread quickly, and custom allowed Rhonwen no choice but to grant it. Only an altar trial left him any chance. If he suffered no ill effect, he would be judged innocent. Though she had seen it performed several times, she had never presided over it herself.

Aras strode to her, his face reddened with anger. "You'll allow this?"

"The law allows it."

"Drinking sacred water and walking nine times around the altar means nothing to him." Aras shook his head. "Aube is a man without belief. The gods will have to be very strong to take him."

Rhonwen felt her control of events slipping. "I have no choice in this. Perhaps the gods do not wish him to die today."

Hamel wormed his way between the Trepani chief and Rhonwen. "As a druid, you let the gods' will be known. Is that a problem?"

Rhonwen met his gaze steadily. "No," she said, "but I don't know the proper incantations to say over the water. I'm not sure about—"

Hamel patted her hand. "I know the words," he told her. "I'll teach you."

"Then," she said with a sigh, "let it be done." She turned to the crowd. "So be it! Aube, the Trepani, will walk the altar. I will prepare the water that tests him."

Aube grinned triumphantly. "I believe I'll have that oatmeal now."

Aras and the Trepani warriors swore in protest but returned to their tents. Milo and another Bateri villager stood guard over the prisoner, who sat and ate each mouthful of oatmeal Rhonwen spooned for him. She shivered at what would happen to the people's faith if he survived.

⚓ ⚓ ⚓

Rhonwen raised her eyes to the sky where the gods dwelt, silently praying that they help her get the words right. Hamel presented her the cup of consecrated water, and she held it close to her breast remembering the words he had taught her. She spoke loudly at times so most of the onlookers could hear her. Other times, the words were meant for the gods alone, and she whispered. She passed a palm over the water three times.

She felt energy rise from the ground to settle into the center of her back, warm and radiating outward, giving her the strength she needed to carry through the entire ritual. Her fear subsided as the feeling of power grew. She knew the gods would not let her fail.

She nodded to Aras. The Trepani chief, his face stony, stepped forward propelling Aube with one hand on the prisoner's good elbow. The crowd fell well away from the altar and from the powdered limestone Rhonwen had used to mark the path Aube must walk. He had but to circle the altar nine times to prove his innocence. No one dared enter the circle except the three druids, the Bateri headman, and the Trepani chief.

Aube had been released from his bonds and rested his injured arm against his chest. He stood on the line and scuffed it with his toe, mixing the white dust into the reddish soil. She briefly entertained the idea he might indeed be guiltless, that he merely played bystander to Enogat's attacks as he claimed. The strong presence of the Goddess at her back soothed her fears.

She offered the cup, and he took it without hesitation.

An eerie silence fell on the commons. Not even the smallest child whimpered or whined. All eyes watched as Aube drained the cup. He swallowed the last of it, making a show of its seemingly good flavor before he wiped his mouth with the back of his hand. Rhonwen took the cup and set it on the altar, then gestured toward the circle.

"Walk," she said, pointing into the afternoon sun.

"With pleasure," Aube replied. He strode in a widdershins direction, head high and with a swagger to his step despite his injured shoulder. At the end of the first circuit he stopped and grinned at her. He made two more laps, each a little faster than the one before. Nearly half way around on his fourth circle, he slowed and pushed a hand flat against his abdomen. The smile that had played maliciously around his mouth disappeared, and a worried frown drifted across his face.

He staggered forward and completed two more rounds. His forehead glistened with beads of sweat.

Rhonwen dared not say anything. Whispers from the crowd reached her, the questions they carried unanswered. She felt weak in the shadow of the gods' power. They spoke as plainly as if they addressed the world with words.

Only one and a half circuits remained before Aube fell to his knees. He bent forward with his arms folded across his belly and rocked back and forth. Whenever he tried to straighten up, a new agony etched his face and he doubled over again. With more effort than Rhonwen thought him capable, he staggered to his feet. In a swaying, staggering gait, he made his way nearly once more around. He reached out to the crowd for someone to help him finish the last half turn. The woman closest to him, her face hidden by a hood, grabbed her child's shoulders to keep the girl from offering assistance.

Aube cursed the woman. He stepped away from the nearly obscured limestone trail and reached for her. As she pressed backward away from him the crowd drew back with her, like sandpipers retreating from a wave.

His sweaty face became blotchy and pale. He turned angry eyes to Rhonwen and fell to his knees. "May crows eat your eyes before you're dead," he said and dropped groaning to the ground.

The woman who had refused to help him began to sob softly until Hamel raised a warning hand. He handed Rhiannon's torc to Rhonwen, the killing loop wide enough for everyone to see, and wide enough to pass easily over Aube's head.

Rhonwen felt vindicated. The gods had answered her prayer and shown the people not only their will but their might. Her initial judgment stood, and she would carry out the law.

She knelt beside Aube as he lay on his side. With his mottled face contorted in pain, he moaned once. She looped the thong around his neck. One turn of the winding stick tightened it. She glanced at the sky one more time, looking for a last sign that she was wrong, but the cloudless blue heavens revealed nothing. She twisted the winding stick again.

Aube's fingers dug at the cord tight around his neck as he gasped for breath. Though his face had begun to turn red, his wheezing meant he could still get some air.

She gave the stick two more complete turns, forcing the leather to bite deep into the skin on either side of his neck where the echo of his heart's rhythm was strongest. His eyes bulged and his face purpled as the veins at his temples swelled. He kicked his heels on the ground, desperate to twist free, but Rhonwen held steady. She squeezed her eyes shut to blot out the vision of Aube's last seconds of life.

After what seemed an eternity, he ceased struggling, and his hands fell limply into the dust.

She rose and stepped away from the body feeling sick and dirty. Silently, most of the Bateri filtered away from the altar in small groups.

Rhonwen heard someone weeping and looked up to see the hooded woman who had refused Aube's plea for help to finish his walk. The freckled girl Rhonwen recognized as Aube's daughter stood among the children clustered around the crying woman. The girl clung to her mother without tears. A younger child, one eye yellow and purple from some hard hand, nestled with three other little ones beside the woman. Because of Rhonwen's judgment, the woman would have to raise those five children by herself.

Hamel pulled her close to the altar and out of her reverie. "You've done a druid's hardest task. Nothing compares, not even raising wounded warriors to face their last battle."

She nodded toward the new widow. "What about them? How will they manage?"

"Better, I think, than before. I knew Aube all his life. The clan will care for them better than he ever did."

Rhonwen forced a smile. "The Trepani have honor, though he and his brother did not."

Hamel snorted. "Neither believed the gods had any power over their lives."

"The gods' power was proven today. I said the incantation properly and the gods confirmed his guilt."

"Your faith does you credit, Rhonwen. I don't regret he's dead. The entire clan would have been humiliated once more and Aras thought rash for killing Enogat." He pulled a coin seemingly from the air, rolled it over his fingers and then palmed it. With a snap of his fingers it reappeared. "Even when the gods fail to answer our every prayer, we must still show the people the right path."

Rhonwen stared at him, puzzled. "What have you done?"

Hamel shrugged. "Nothing that wasn't necessary." He took her hand, placed the coin in her palm and closed her fingers over the gold. "If he were innocent, the gods would have spared him."

Rhonwen recoiled. "You did something to the water!"

"He was guilty."

"The gods test us. We do not test them."

Aube's wife put a timid hand on Rhonwen's wrist.

She turned as the woman pushed the hood from her head. Once beautiful, her dark hair now framed bruised cheeks. She had the furtive eyes of a beaten dog. Her nose, flattened at the bridge and slightly crooked, had been broken more than once.

"Druid Hamel is right. Aube was no more innocent than his brother. Given the chance, he'd have killed you."

12

As children, we are told many tales, often by those who do not know if they are true. Such were the stories I heard of the ageless man, he who walked among men but slept among gods. Now I know Amrec is that man. He comes among us once each year, sometimes staying for a month, sometimes only a day. Always he appears the same, although the years hang heavily on me. For him, the years are but nights, and the friendship I count in decades he counts in weeks.

I always plead that he stay with us and share all he knows of the past. He always declines, saying he seeks one not yet born.
— *Stave Five of Cullinor, 28th Master of Mount Eban Enclave*

Armorica 87 B.C.

Orlan spent the week following the old Master's death orienting the enclave to his new leadership. He took pains to avoid any change while the enclave mourned Fyrsil's passing. Eventually, however, he returned to the poet staves.

Every stave had the name of a master carved upon it, and he sorted them in order of the names he'd learned in the Master's Chant. He hoped to find a stave from Fyrsil himself, despite the old druid's disdain for the written word. Many of the previous masters shared Fyrsil's preference for oral histories and gaps in the records abounded. Orlan could think of no way to tell whether any single master failed to write a stave, or whether it was simply missing. Nevertheless, he pulled the staves out of the chest and lined them up, and eventually discovered Fyrsil's handiwork. He grinned at the old man's final gift, a last surprise Orlan intended to share with Leuw. He continued his study and quickly discovered Master Cullinor's staves were discontinuous. He examined each one carefully in case Cullinor had used the backs, but there could be no doubt, at least five staves were missing.

There had been a theft in Fyrsil's house after all. Orlan vowed to gather all he could from the knowledge the staves held and hide them well afterward.

Eager to read the balance of Jaslon's staves, Orlan separated them from the others. He read with horror the account of Jaslon's experiment on an innocent child, yet when he read of the mute's recovery, he realized the gods had once again intervened. And what a marvelous intervention! He had to find the plant that made such a restoration possible: woadsleep.

Without a word to anyone, he saddled a horse and rode to Mount Eban. There he foraged around the Sentinel Stones at the base of the mountain, which, compared to the mountains of Iberia, was little more than a wooded hill. Still, he spent hours gathering specimens. Any plant he didn't recognize went into his collection sack. By late afternoon, although he had searched but a tiny portion of the mountain, he had more samples than he'd assembled since his earliest excursions as a young druid. He returned to the enclave, arriving just as a crimson sky faded to deep purple.

Leuw met him outside Orlan's quarters. "We missed you at dinner," the bard said. "I was beginning to worry."

Orlan felt a pang of shame. As the new master, he should not have left the enclave without telling anyone. "Did I miss a good meal?"

"Not particularly. I saved you some bread and a chunk of mutton, but I got hungry again waiting for you, so I ate them." He wiped his hands on his tunic and peered at the rough sack in Orlan's hand. "What have you there?"

"Weeds, mostly," Orlan said. "Let's go inside."

Leuw made himself comfortable on the thickest wolf fur nearest the fire. Orlan set the collection bag on the floor and sat on the room's only stool.

"The students want to know when we'll celebrate your investiture as master," Leuw said. "I would, too."

"I've barely given it any thought," Orlan said.

"You'll have to choose whether to do it in Gillac or Trochu," Leuw said. "The enclave is important to both. If you have no preference, I'd suggest Gillac, since Gar is—"

"Is not a factor in my decision," Orlan concluded.

Leuw whistled. "You may want to think that through again. Gar is a good friend of this enclave."

"And Coemgen in Trochu is not?"

Leuw rubbed his chin. "The Lemarii and the Suetoni have been at odds for years, though Fyrsil tried not to show any favoritism."

"A wise strategy," Orlan said, "and one I intend to adopt. Besides, there's no need for a big ceremony. I can become the master of this enclave without venturing near either clanhold."

"So, in the interest of fairness, you'll anger both clans?" He crossed himself with the Great Mother's protection sign. "I can see this enclave has a bright future with you in control. I wonder if the Veneti could use a good bard."

"Possibly," Orlan said. "Do you know any?"

Leuw grinned. "Maybe you'll survive here after all."

Orlan chuckled and reached for the Jaslon stave he'd set aside. "Do you recall when I asked you about Jaslon?"

Leuw squinted at the strip of wood. "Why?"

"Because according to these writings, the man accomplished amazing things."

"If my mother had known how to write, I'm sure she would've recorded something similar about me. That alone should prove that what is written may not always be trusted."

Orlan shook his head, refusing to be distracted. "What do you know of a plant called baneweed?"

"I've seen it on the mountain," Leuw said. "I don't believe it's used for anything."

"You know what it looks like?"

"Yes."

Orlan nearly tripped over himself in his urgency to retrieve his samples. He dumped the contents of his collection bag onto the hard-packed dirt floor. "Do you see it in there?"

Leuw picked through the specimens, discarding one after another. He stopped at one particular sample, studiously avoiding it.

"Is that it?" Orlan asked, reaching for it.

Leuw grabbed his wrist. "Keep away from that," he said, "or you'll break out in tiny red welts that'll itch for a fortnight."

"It's a little late to be concerned about that. I already plucked it, roots and all, from the ground and put it in my sack," Orlan said. "But is that it? Is that baneweed?"

"No," Leuw said, shaking his head. "But that name would be fitting."

Orlan sat back on his stool staring at the troublesome plant. It looked nothing like the welt-inducing greenery he sometimes found while hunting medicinal herbs at home. "Please keep looking."

Leuw continued to paw through the pile, stopping when he came to a scrawny growth. "There. That's baneweed."

Leaning forward, Orlan again reached out, this time stopping on his own before he touched it.

Shallow-rooted and odorless, the specimen appeared utterly common. A modest clump of short, hairy leaves at the base gave rise to a pale, foot-long stem that supported roughly two dozen tiny blooms, each the color of dried blood.

"I wouldn't even give flowers that ugly to Dierdre," Leuw said. "What's your interest in them?"

Orlan related the tale of Jaslon and how the plant allowed him to shapeshift.

"It turned Master Jaslon into wood?" Leuw asked, gazing warily at the plant. "I'd prefer to be a bird, I think, preferably one people don't find tasty."

"I want to try it," Orlan said. "Will you help me?"

Leuw stared at him as if he were mad. "Certainly not."

"But—"

"I like you as you are."

"By the gods, Leuw! Can't you take anything seriously? This is important."

"Important or insane?" No trace of humor remained on Leuw's face. "What do you really know about this plant or Jaslon's methods for using it?"

"I know more than he did the first time he used it. I know the secret of the restoration to human form."

Leuw shook his head slowly. "A handy tidbit, for sure."

"The winter solstice is but a few weeks away. I want you and Dierdre to attend me."

"You can't be serious! What if it doesn't work?"

"Then I shall be disappointed."

"And what if it works too well? What if you can't be revived?" Leuw folded his arms across his big chest. "What then?"

"Then I suppose you'd need to find a new master."

Leuw's eyes flared wide. "Not me!"

Smiling, Orlan shook his head. "Certainly not. I have another in mind."

"Surely not Dierdre?" Leuw's face betrayed his disbelief.

"No," Orlan said. "A young druid I met on Mona. He'd be perfect."

"Wonderful," Leuw said with a groan. "You'll be rootstock, this pup of yours from Mona won't be old enough to know whether to fetch or piddle, and I'll have to deal with Dierdre. You know she won't be happy."

Orlan laughed. "I'm not dead yet."

Leuw shuddered. "True, but then, Dierdre hasn't heard your plans yet either."

✠ ✠ ✠

On the eve of the Winter Solstice, Orlan, Leuw, and Dierdre sat near the sentinel stones eating a light meal of bread, dried fruit, and watered wine.

"It'll be dark soon," Leuw said, rubbing his hands. "If we're going into the Cavern of the Ancients, I'd rather climb over those rocks in the daylight."

"Let's get started then," Orlan said, rising. "I'll help you carry your things."

Dierdre frowned. "I wish you'd tell me more about this mysterious ceremony."

"I don't want to give you all the details because I want to hear an account of your observations," said Orlan, "and I don't want Leuw's wit to color it."

She glowered at the bard. "I can't imagine that being a problem."

Leuw struggled to his feet and offered Dierdre his hand. She ignored it, rising with the supple ease of one half her years.

"I'd love to be able to do that," Leuw muttered.

Dierdre smiled sweetly. "It's easier when one doesn't have quite so much druid to move."

Orlan ignored them. When he had realized some of the staves were missing, he couldn't help but link their disappearance to Fyrsil's death. Since only Dierdre and Leuw knew the staves existed, he knew that one or both were involved.

Leuw's complicity he discounted instantly. Even if they hadn't been together in Gillac the night the enclave master died, Orlan wouldn't have suspected Leuw. Not only had he and Fyrsil been close friends but the bard had no interest in the staves.

Dierdre, however, had asked to see them. Orlan also recalled her bitterness at not being named Fyrsil's successor. Yet when Orlan inquired of those who attended the Samhaim festivities in Trochu, they said Dierdre and her son, Caradowc, had been seen by many, especially in the market. Better at law than ritual, no one expected Dierdre to participate in the ceremonies, although she and Caradowc returned to the enclave with everyone else the following day.

Orlan resigned himself to Leuw's explanation that Fyrsil died of heart failure, possibly brought on by his delivery of the staves to Orlan's quarters, and the missing ones had likely been misplaced long ago by one of Fyrsil's predecessors.

The pink granites of Armorica, covered with moss made bright green by the frequent winter rains, formed a rugged barrier at the steepest part of the path. Recent rains made the footing treacherous and the druids often had to scramble on all fours. Despite Leuw's grumbled curses, he kept up with his companions.

They made their way across the last boulder and slipped down to a low tunnel. Leuw muttered an old tune about how the mountain rumbled with the play of the gods, and Orlan prayed he would not have the opportunity to hear that song made true. A single spiral carved deeply into a flat stone marked the entrance.

Orlan hesitated long enough for Leuw to catch his breath before leading them inside. They crawled single file to the end of the corridor where they encountered a space large enough for all three to stand. Orlan took a torch from a dry pile left by generations of druids who had stopped in the same place. Using a flint and tinder, he brought his torch to light. He used its flame to ignite two more for the others. "Would one of you like to lead from here?"

Dierdre stepped forward. "Follow me," she said, "if you can keep up." She continued into the dark passage without waiting.

Orlan had no regrets about letting Dierdre set the course, although he'd have been content to move at a slower pace. Leuw wasted no breath on words. He examined every side passage and intersection. Orlan felt certain Dierdre would maintain her own safety and hence theirs.

Eventually they reached the great Cavern of the Ancients, whose walls bore their handprints and artwork. Magnificent animals graced every flat surface. Later visitors had whittled faces and forms like those found in sacred groves into many of the graceful spires and columns joining floor to ceiling.

The place gave Orlan a feeling of great serenity. The gods certainly knew the meaning of peace, for no sound or light penetrated from outside.

"Put your things down," Orlan said, handing them spare torches, "then join me." He turned toward an altar carved from rock and began to prepare for his transformation.

By the light of his torch, he dabbed the fermented leaves of woad to blue his face, hands, and chest. He dragged a fingertip across his thighs and inscribed scrolls. He arranged sprigs of mistletoe, new marigold, and laurel around himself and offset his sacred space with an offering of snake skin gathered by the full moon. When he felt ready, he knelt in prayer to Dagda, Lugh, and the Great Mother. Finally, he prayed to gentle Rhiannon, imploring her to protect him while he underwent the mysterious change. Dierdre and Leuw sat quietly and watched.

At last he stood ready. He'd shredded the leaves, stem, and flowers of the baneweed into a censer and left it on the altar beside the torch. He lay down on the altar. "Leuw," he said, "you may began."

Leuw grasped the light chain attached to the open metalwork containing the baneweed, and swung the plant toward the torch.

"I still don't think this is a good idea," he said.

Orlan smiled confidently. "I'll see you in the morning, my friend."

Leuw turned his head from the smoldering weed and took a deep breath, then held the censer close to Orlan. The pungent odor brought tears to his eyes. The baneweed glowed, and subtle eddies in the dark fumes curled around his face.

Orlan inhaled deeply. For a split second he felt dizzy, and his mind clouded. After that, everything went black.

✠ ✠ ✠

A strong odor wasn't the only reason Dierdre held her breath as Leuw waved the burning plant in Orlan's face. Though she had no idea what the Iberian had in mind, she didn't intend to participate involuntarily. Besides, Leuw made no effort to hide the fact that he wasn't going to breathe the fumes.

Accompanied by sounds normally associated with burning wood, Orlan shriveled and shrank while she watched. Her stomach writhed like a nest of serpents as she observed the hideous transformation. In a few short moments, Orlan disappeared completely. In his place lay a stick no larger than Dierdre's arm. She and Leuw bumped shoulders as they both reached for it.

Leuw eased away. "After you. But once you've examined it, let me have it for safekeeping."

Dierdre's fingers closed on the bare wood, but something in it stung her as surely as if she'd shoved her hand into a hive. She dropped the stick and backed away.

Seeing Orlan's transformation was frightening. Allowing oneself to be so utterly vulnerable appalled her. Yet the power to do such a thing left her reeling. This was no trick, no mere sleight of hand. Orlan had discovered how to tap the power of the gods.

The sensation she'd felt when she touched the stick was the same as when she touched the stick from the Giant's Tomb. She sat back on her heels, mouth agape. What she'd carried away from the mound *lived*. If she believed the staves, it could only be one thing: the ageless man, Amrec. Cullinor had called him the keeper of a great treasure.

It had been weeks since she'd even looked at the stick, and all that time it lay in plain sight in her quarters. What if a servant threw it in with the kindling?

She gave a sharp shriek, grabbed a torch, and scrambled to exit the cavern.

"Where are you going?" Leuw yelled after her.

"I can't stay," she said without looking back.

"But—"

"I can't explain just now."

The darkness seemed doubly impenetrable as she hurried through it, tripping over unseen seams of rock and brushing against the sides of the corridor when it narrowed. Somehow she made it out of the mountain and over the protective boulders. Stars dotted the blackened sky as she reached the horses and struggled to saddle the beast that brought her. It shied away.

"Stand still!" she cried, "or I'll butcher you myself and feed you to the pigs."

Eventually she managed to saddle and mount the animal. She kicked the horse into a run and left Mount Eban behind. If someone had already burned the stick, no punishment would be great enough. As her thoughts wandered, her horse stumbled.

Dierdre rolled out of the saddle and hit the ground in the dark while the cursed nag kept running.

"Come back here!" she screamed into the dark, her voice drowning out the receding clatter of hooves.

⌘ ⌘ ⌘

The world came into focus slowly.

Unlike the moment in which Orlan lost consciousness, his recovery took much longer. Things gradually became real as feeling returned to his limbs, arriving with the sounds of birds, the chill of the unexpected breeze, and the smell of Leuw's unwashed body.

Orlan stared up into bright sunlight, desperate to clear his throat and wanting to speak, but too numb to do either.

"You have no idea how happy I am to see you," Leuw said. The bard's round face hovered into view above him. "If you hadn't recovered, I would've had to tell the enclave they'd lost another master. That's not the sort of message one wants to deliver at the celebration of the winter solstice."

Orlan's tongue felt thick, and he wanted water.

Leuw frowned. "Can you hear me? Speak up. Blink, fart, do something!"

Orlan found the strength to smile, although every other motion felt stiff, like running in a dream. "I'm thirsty," he said, surprised at the hoarseness of his voice. "And cold."

Leuw fetched Orlan's wool cloak. He covered the druid and pressed the mouth of a water skin to his lips. "I hope you'll be ready to leave soon. We've a long way to travel if we're to reach Gillac for the celebration. Drink up."

Orlan reveled in the feel of the water running down his throat. Though it bore a stale flavor from the leather bag, it soothed his cottony mouth and throat. Leuw helped him sit. When his head stopped spinning, Orlan looked all around, and especially at the stone altar known as Cad Cerrig.

"Where's Dierdre?" he asked.

"She left last night," said Leuw, "about two heartbeats after you turned into a length of firewood. She touched you with a fingertip and ran shrieking from the cavern."

Orlan's heart raced. "Without a torch?"

"She's not that stupid."

"True." Orlan flexed his fingers and toes, and lay back pillowing his head on his arm.

"Hungry?" Leuw asked.

"No," Orlan closed his eyes and imagined Dierdre running through the dark, her long hair flapping like bat's wings with her cloak flailing behind her. He would have gladly paid to see the usually tightly poised woman at such a loss. "I never thought she'd be so frightened, but it's given me an idea. If true transformation frightens her, suppose I decree that whoever succeeds me as master of the enclave must experience this woadsleep."

"That would take me out of the race, not that I want the job anyway."

Orlan grinned wickedly. "And how do you think Dierdre would react to the idea?"

After a pause, Leuw grinned back. "What's the name of that student of yours from Mona?"

"Mallec," Orlan said, beginning to feel quite satisfied. "He's a fine lad, an Eburone."

"A Belgae?" Leuw asked. "I've always thought of the enclave as a place of reason, a place to train young minds, a place to have a spot of wine to soothe an anguished soul."

"And you've heard the Eburones don't drink."

"It's worse than that," Leuw said. "I've heard they crave combat and absolutely worship war. Their tiniest babes can thrust and parry before they've left the nipple. How could you select someone like that to lead the enclave?"

"Mallec isn't like that." He stretched and heard his stomach growl. "You know, I think I could use something to eat."

"I'll fix something," said Leuw.

Orlan closed his eyes and let his mind drift. Jaslon had been right about woadsleep. He felt sympathy for the man Jaslon had called a false god, for he was surely one of the Ancients. Orlan wondered whether he would have acted differently had he been in Jaslon's place. He certainly would have reacted differently to the healing of the mute.

If woadsleep worked, he felt certain the healing would, too. If anything, the staves had been more specific about that than anything else. He imagined how like a god it would feel to be able to cure anything. How many times had he seen wounds that never healed? How many people had he seen the healers weep for because they could do nothing?

A somber thought crowded the joy from his mind. What would happen if the whole world learned of the marvelous healing power of baneweed? He felt grateful Jaslon never made much of it, for if he had, the world's sick would have marched to the mountain and ripped every growing thing from its surface in hopes of salvation.

Orlan knew it had to be handled differently. The source of baneweed must remain a secret, at least until he could cultivate it elsewhere. If he could, and if he could teach the world to grow their own, just imagine how much suffering he could alleviate.

✠ ✠ ✠

Back in her hut at the enclave, Dierdre washed the scrapes she'd suffered when she fell from the horse. The cool water soothed her sweaty skin, but nothing calmed her as much as the discovery that the stick from the Giant's Tomb was safe, precisely where she'd left it.

Surely the gods favored her. It would have been simple for them to invoke disaster, but they hadn't, and now she knew the secret of woadsleep. Nothing stood in her way. That fool Orlan could—

She stopped cold. Orlan had not named a replacement in the event anything happened to him. That meant he expected to be revived, but how? She screamed in sudden, comprehending rage. She had left the mountain too soon, and now only Orlan and Leuw knew how the revival process worked.

"Driad Dierdre, are you all right?" called a timid voice from the doorway. She recognized Budec, one of Orlan's darlings.

"Yes, yes, I'm fine," she said.

"You returned in such a great hurry with neither Druid Leuw nor Master Orlan. I thought—"

"The others will be along soon."

"Will you be riding with us to Gillac?" he asked.

Dierdre threw back the door flap and glared at him. "Have you nothing better to do than annoy me with your questions?"

She smiled as Budec fled. So far, the boy had kept silent about seeing her the night she'd taken the staves. She wished now she'd gone back for more. If so, perhaps she would be privy to the secrets of the gods, not Orlan. Now the staves were gone forever. Fyrsil, the great fool, had confessed to burning them. With that, she lost what little inclination she'd had to let the old man live.

The stick she had rushed back to see stood taunting and useless in the corner. The more she thought about it, the more convinced she became that Orlan would never share his secrets. Perhaps others would. The city of Vannes' had a larger and older enclave. It might have information useful to her. Failing that, she knew other ways to extract the knowledge from Orlan.

✠ ✠ ✠

A light wind from Quiberon Bay ensured that the steady smell of rot blew inland. Caradowc pressed his hand to his mouth.

"How do people stand the stench?" he asked as Dierdre led him through the fishermen's stalls that lined the thoroughfare to the docks of Vannes. As new odors assailed him, he wondered which smelled worse, the old-dead of the ocean or the near-dead of the fish crowded into tubs of sea brine.

As usual, Dierdre didn't respond. He never quite knew whether she heard him or ignored him. She had yet to explain her interest in the enclave at Vannes or her claim that the Veneti could give him better training as a warrior than anyone in either Trochu or Gillac. He hoped she was right.

Most villages set aside one morning a week for market. Vannes' market stayed busy every day. Merchants arose at dawn to lay out their wares and at night threw rugs over them and posted slaves or servants to stand watch. Unlike Trochu's market, there seemed no end to the volume or variety of the goods offered.

An open space separated the merchants from the docks, and Caradowc gladly left them behind. Fir trees, permanently bent by the constant wind, lined the road. He noticed a handful of ragged peasants resting in the afternoon shade of the scrawny trees as they combed through each other's hair. Once in a while someone would pick something from a strand of hair and squish it with a grimy fingernail. Caradowc scratched his own head. He'd been told the limewash he used on his hair would make it almost impossible for a louse to survive. He hoped so.

Dierdre came to a stop, cursing. "What's wrong?" said Caradowc.

"I've been robbed," she said as she felt for the pouch missing from her belt. She looked up, her forehead creased in concentration. "Do you remember when that crowd of urchins pressed close to avoid a passing wagon?"

"Which one?" he asked. There had been several such incidents.

Dierdre scowled. "Do you recall the one-eyed boy who squeezed between us?"

Caradowc remembered the boy's companion much better, especially the way she'd pressed herself against him as the wagon passed.

"Stay here," Dierdre said, "I'll be back soon."

He felt a momentary pang for the boy, then dismissed it, glad that someone else had earned Dierdre's wrath for a change.

A group of men standing beside a foreigner caught his eye. The man wore a colorful robe unlike anything he had ever seen. In front of the man stood a rickety table bearing three halves of some large nut shells. Caradowc marveled at how skillfully the man moved the shells around the table top. One of the bystanders pointed to a shell. The foreigner lifted it to show nothing lay beneath, and then he raised the shell's neighbor to reveal a dried pea. The foreigner shrugged as the other man swore and surrendered a coin. Several others tried their luck, but it seemed no matter which shell they picked, the pea appeared elsewhere.

Caradowc watched as the exotic foreigner won bet after bet. Eventually the crowd grew surly, and several made pointed remarks about the foreigner's great luck. Just as they began to get unruly, a young man approached the table. Though he wore the checkered breeches of the Veneti, his complexion suggested origins closer to those of the foreigner himself. He pointed with confidence to the middle shell and grabbed the wrist of the gambler just before he touched it.

"May I?" he asked.

The foreigner complained, but the crowd pressed close, their thoughts on the matter clear.

He withdrew his hand. "If you insist."

The young man lifted the shell, and the crowd cheered to see the pea under it.

"Satisfied?" the foreigner asked. "Now, go away."

"But I want to try again."

Grudgingly, the gambler agreed and shuffled the shells. As before, the younger man caught his wrist, lifted the shell himself, and exposed the pea.

"Again," the young man said, clicking his coins in his palm.

"I must go now," the foreigner said, but a solid wall of locals blocked his way. One of them shouldered the young winner aside and slapped his own coin on the table, a broad smile creasing his face.

Caradowc watched the foreigner rearrange the shells, expecting his hands to become a blur. Instead, he moved at the same speed as before, which was quick enough, but not so fast that anyone could question the whereabouts of the pea.

The new player pointed to his choice, a selection the onlookers also approved, and the foreigner reached for the shell. Just as the previous player had done, the new one grabbed the gambler's wrist. "Perhaps some of my friends would also like to bet," he said.

"I would urge them not to," the foreigner said.

The crowd responded with howls and catcalls, and a small shower of coins rained down on the little table. The foreigner merely shook his head.

Caradowc smiled at the spectacle, wishing he'd been close enough to add his own coin to the pile. He watched as the new player slowly raised the nutshell to reveal only bare wood beneath it. The foreigner lifted another shell and exposed the pea, then scooped his winnings from the table as the shocked crowd looked on in silence.

"Let's go," Dierdre said jostling Caradowc's arm as she inserted her elongated cloak pin into a fold of her robe. It left a tiny blood stain on the stark white fabric. He glanced at the pouch restored to her waist.

"What did you do to him?"

Dierdre stared at him. "Does it matter?"

"I'm only curious. I thought a girl traveled with him."

"She's caring for him," Dierdre said. "He'll need someone to lead him home."

Caradowc reached involuntarily for his own eye. Dierdre smiled.

The smell of salt water grew stronger and the calls of the sea birds more raucous as she pulled Caradowc along. He caught sight of the squatting hulk of a Roman merchantman, its canvasses flattened and tied securely to wooden crosspieces, moored to the end of a long pier in the deeper water of the vast harbor. It surprised him the vessel could maneuver so close to shore. Normally Dierdre hated ships, but she made for this one like a bear to honey.

She thrust a coin into his hand. "Can you amuse yourself for the rest of the afternoon?"

It took all his will to restrain a grin. "If you wish."

"What I have to do will take a few hours. Meet me here at sunset." She walked toward a stubby Roman merchant conversing with three Veneti men at the end of the dock.

"Scotus!" she called and the merchant turned to her, a smile of recognition on his face.

Caradowc appraised the richly dressed merchant and his dark, muscular companion. Shirtless, the latter wore only a pair of leather trews and a stout iron collar, something like the bronze torc Caradowc wore. Unlike a torc, the iron collar had a ring in it similar to those put into bulls' noses. Slave, he thought. There seemed to be many in Vannes. He idly wondered what a slave girl would cost.

He left the docks and retraced his steps toward the market. The crowd that had gathered in response to the foreigner's game had dispersed, but Caradowc noticed the gambler lounging outside a wagon pulled behind the trees. Caradowc wanted to ask him about the shells when he saw the young man who had beaten the gambler exit the wagon and join him by the fire. The two conversed like old friends, and Caradowc realized what they'd done. He smiled in appreciation of the way they'd tricked a crowd of fools into throwing away their money. He gripped the coin Dierdre had given him, pleased that he'd not contributed to their scheme. He wondered if there might be a reward for turning the thieves in but decided such cleverness legitimized the deception.

"Can I interest you in some of our finer wares, young warrior?"

Caradowc turned slowly at the sweetness of a young woman's greeting. He expected to see the usual lone girl, minding her family's fruits and vegetables. He turned with a smile and his jaw dropped. Instead of one, three Veneti girls smiled at him, all quite pretty and as alike as the gambler's walnut shells.

Thoughts of the slave market and the gambler vanished. He would have no trouble finding something with which to occupy himself until sunset.

✠ ✠ ✠

Orlan watched with amusement as the bay pony carrying Gar's daughter, Arie, walked toward the enclave. It tossed its head and whinnied to the horses in the nearby paddock. Those horses leaned against the wooden fence, joined by a half dozen students all no less eager than Orlan to see the newcomer.

Arie sat stiff-backed with her chin high and a relaxed hand on the pony's reins. Orlan had the impression that, although her gaze never wandered, her young eyes saw everything. Even from this distance he could see her broad smile. She leaned back against two large sacks piled behind her and flowing over both flanks of the pony.

By both coloring and demeanor, she reminded him of a young Rhonwen, although she wore her dark brown hair pulled into one tidy braid at the back of her head rather than in the unruly mass his niece wore. The Suetoni cloak draped over her shoulders looked new, the squares of red, yellow and green vivid in the morning sun. The garment appeared too big for her, but he had no doubt she would grow into it.

He raised a hand in greeting, and she directed the pony toward him. As the animal's hooves thudded on the hard-packed dirt of the enclave's inner yard, six servants and the enclave's two dozen students gathered to greet her.

She drew the pony to a halt and slid lightly to the ground. She took a deep bow and, before Orlan could say anything, she pulled an armload of scrolls and folded vellum sheets from one of the sacks, hugged them to her chest and grinned.

"Arie, daughter of Gar and Willa of Gillac, greets you, Master Orlan. I have come to begin my formal studies."

13

I grow old and must soon entrust the enclave to another. That I could do so under the eye of the Ageless One and thus present him to the new master is my fondest wish. With the summer solstice near, I hoped that day had come, yet when Amrec arrived, he lay bleeding in the back of a cart, the victim of bandits. Our healers could do nothing for his wounds.

He bid me take him to the Giant's Tomb and leave him nearby with water and baneweed. This I did, and when a fortnight had passed, and I felt sure he must be dead, I sent Tendal to fetch his bones back to us for burial. Tendal found no trace of him.
— Stave Six of Cullinor, 28th Master of Mount Eban Enclave

Armorica 83 B.C.

Caradowc's stay in Vannes was short. Within a year his mother had sent him back to stay in Trochu. Couldn't the woman make up her mind? First he should study with the warriors in Vannes, and now he had to settle for the second-rate fools of a country tribe. Dierdre said he needed to stop first at the enclave, although her reasons remained her own. He stayed only as long as politeness demanded and left without a backward glance.

The new master, an Iberian, had welcomed him poorly, although with decent food and drink, and told him his half-sister, Arie, had been fostered there to study only a few weeks earlier. He made a point of visiting her. It seemed wise to have something nice to say about her to their father.

He'd met the child twice before and had come away gagging on her wide-eyed sweetness. After meeting her again, he concluded she hadn't changed. Women had one purpose, his mother notwithstanding.

He walked toward Gillac instead of Trochu and took a little-used path to avoid meeting anyone. Lacking a mount, he felt vulnerable. Mount Eban should have been visible in the distance behind him, yet nothing in any direction rose above the height of the trees growing close to the track. When he realized the path had become little more than a deer trail, his concern grew.

A distant clearing with a farmhouse seemed to beckon, and he left the trail to cut through the woods surrounding the pasture in front of the house. No sooner had he pushed into the thick brush than he spotted half a dozen riders wearing the red and yellow breeches of Redoni warriors approaching the building from the opposite direction. The Redoni had quarreled with the Lemarii for generations, but this was the first time he'd seen them in Suetoni territory. He stayed behind the concealing foliage to watch.

A Suetoni farmer left the house and approached the horsemen. He carried an iron pitchfork under his arm like a lance and said something to the leader of the riders.

Caradowc couldn't make out their words and wormed through the bracken to get closer. The farmer shouted an alarm, but as he turned to run, the leader struck him down with a single sword blow. The farmer lay in a crumpled heap while his attacker watched his companions ride into the pasture and drive the small herd of cattle away.

Caradowc stared at the raider's chief. An iron war helmet obscured the man's features, but nothing disguised the unbleached white druid's robe he wore. No strip of cloth on the arms gave any hint of his rank, achievement, or even clan. Only a single tattoo decorated the man's wrist. Caradowc fingered the knife at his waist and wished he carried a sword. With fewer of them about, he might have risked a counter-attack. If successful, he could claim a horse at least. Such a trophy would raise him in the eyes of Gillac's warriors.

As the raiders drove the herd through the gap they'd torn in the fence, a boy of about ten ran toward them from the house. Bearing a length of firewood for a weapon, the youngster charged like a hero, straight for the warrior-druid, who wheeled his horse to face him.

The warrior kicked his mount and rode straight into the boy, crushing him to the ground. Caradowc expected the druid to follow his men and the cattle, but he merely paused until the boy stood unsteadily.

The druid raised his sword and brought it down in a wide arc that sliced deeply into the boy's shoulder. Caradowc heard the bones break. The boy's scream ripped the still air. The druid dismounted, wrenched his weapon free and took two more swings to silence the whimpering child. With sword still bloody, he entered the house. A woman shrieked, but her cries, too, were soon cut short.

Caradowc remained hidden. The druid reappeared with a small pouch that he tucked into the larger purse hanging at his waist. Without a second look at either the boy or his dead father, the druid rode away.

Caradowc turned away from the house, confident whatever money they had went into the pouch the druid found. He walked back the way he had come until he found the path that had led him to the farm. By the time he reached the turn he'd taken earlier by mistake, he had put the morning's events into perspective.

Warrior-druids were rare, although he had heard of them, and while he knew druids from wealthy enclaves often traveled with armed escorts, he had never heard of one who preyed on farmers like a common bandit. There had to be some reason. Perhaps he only retook stolen cattle.

Satisfied the farmers suffered what they probably deserved, Caradowc continued his journey on the road to Gillac. He found the clanhold and passed through the main gate unchallenged.

He climbed to a higher vantage point on the wall near the gate to await Gar. From his perch he watched the people of Gillac: peasants, utterly lacking the sophistication he'd acquired during his year in the great port of Vannes. His mother had directed him to Trochu rather than Gillac. She felt he might better fit in with the locals and continue his warrior training. Caradowc had other ideas.

The people he'd met in Trochu seemed reasonable, if pedestrian, but they all believed Gwair No-scar, son of the Lemarii chief, Coemgen, would one day lead the clan. No one in Trochu challenged that belief, and that left nothing for Caradowc.

Though his mother had never spared two good words for Gar, the Suetoni chief might still be useful. What harm could come from gaining his father's confidence? Look what such a relationship had done for Gwair.

A girl walked toward the well at the center of the clanhold, reminding him of the fire-lit beach at last Beltane and a green-eyed lass whose name he never bothered to learn.

"Have you been waiting long, Caradowc?"

The boy looked up at the sound of his name.

"Father! It's good to see you." He held up a hand in greeting, letting the wide smile at the sight of the girl spill over into something that might look like joy in seeing Gar.

Gar sat easily atop a nervous bay, its ears half laid back in warning to anyone who might venture too close. Gar jumped down and handed the reins to a man at the gate. "I'll be back soon." He stepped closer to his son. "Welcome! Come let me look at you."

Caradowc eased off the wall and dropped to the ground. He pulled his shoulders back and lifted his chin, pleased to note he stood a good hand taller than Gar.

"When I heard you were coming," Gar said, "all I could think of was the lad I last saw in tow behind Dierdre. You've certainly grown." His smile faded and he looked around. "She's not with you?"

Caradowc smiled. "No. She stayed in Vannes. I hope to find a place here."

Gar slapped him on the back, a contact Caradowc disliked. "Even better. You can stay with us."

This was just what he wanted to hear. Years of disguising his emotions for his mother enabled him to hide them from his father. "I've just come from the druid enclave. Its master and my sister both send their greetings."

"My Arie! How does she fare?"

"Druid Orlan says she's a marvel. She told me herself she fares well, though she misses her mother."

"As I would myself. Willa is the best of women." Gar paused. "Speaking of mothers, has Dierdre heard the news?"

Caradowc frowned. "What news?"

"Surely they told you at the enclave," Gar said.

"You know Mother. I doubt she'd be interested in hearing about Arie."

Gar smiled tightly. "I'm sure you're right, but I was talking about Master Orlan's announcement. He plans to return to Iberia."

Caradowc struggled to disguise his dismay that Dierdre might return just when he had begun to make progress on his own. He had no desire to live with her again. "I didn't know, so I doubt Mother knows either."

"How is she, by the way?" asked Gar.

Caradowc waved the question off. "I didn't see her much. I spent most of my time on the practice field."

"I thought the Veneti preferred to do their fighting at sea," Gar said.

"That hasn't changed. I learned what I could, but I want to be a warrior, not a sailor. That's why I'm here."

Gar put his arm around the boy's shoulders. "Then you've made a wise choice. We may not be the biggest clan in Armorica, but we're strong."

Caradowc had heard unflattering remarks about the Seutoni from the warriors of Trochu, whose fighters had distinguished themselves on many battlefields, some as mercenaries for the Romans in Iberia. While Gar had been chief, the men of Gillac had never ventured beyond their own borders. "I'm eager to learn," Caradowc said.

Gar chuckled. "I'm eager to find out what you already know. If you're ready, we can go to the practice field now."

"I'm ready," Caradowc said. More ready than you can imagine, he thought.

✠ ✠ ✠

Orlan hunched over a fire and rubbed his palms together in a vain attempt to warm them. He hated these cold Gaulish winters. Why the gods delivered such annual torment to those born north of Iberia he couldn't guess, but the prospect of escaping it and returning home delighted him. Only Mallec's installation as master of the enclave and the preparation of a few baneweed plants for transport remained.

He'd given much thought to what he might tell the young druid when he arrived. Even without Dierdre around, Mallec would have his hands full running the enclave and continuing to record the achievements of their race, a task he'd begun on Mona.

A clattering of hooves distracted him, and he hurried outside. Two riders charged through the opening in the fence surrounding the front pasture. He recognized Mallec even though the hood of his druid's cloak obscured his face. Still lean, the Eburone sat with long legs dangling down the sides of a horse a little too short for him.

Mallec's arrival made Orlan's departure for Iberia suddenly attainable. He raised a prayer of thanks to Ollamh Benecin for allowing Mallec to take Orlan's place.

"Welcome," Orlan said.

Mallec slipped from his horse and hugged his old teacher fiercely, then bowed to the student bard who had accompanied him from the docks at Vannes. "I'm in your debt, Budec."

"It was worth it to hear your rendition of 'Benecin's Boar' and tales of Mona."

Orlan's eyebrow inched upward. "Tales of Mona?"

"Aye. The greatest center of learning in the world!"

"Do you mean the Mona where we met?"

Mallec laughed. "Indeed."

"Then it's changed much since I was there," Orlan muttered. He remembered bad winters, unthinking scholars, and consistently bland food.

"Our enclave is blessed," Budec said. "Two of the finest druids ever to study on Mona have come to teach here."

Orlan nearly choked and had to pause to clear his throat. He motioned to two of the older students. "Take this boy some place warm and dry and feed him. Then discover what lies this young druid has told him about me." He winked at Arie, who stood behind the bigger boys.

Arie smiled and grabbed Budec's hand to drag him away. Happy in the girl's tight hold, he let himself be pulled away.

Once he had pulled Mallec inside, Orlan settled him by the fire. Mallec shrugged off his cloak and spread it near the hearth. "What prompts your decision to leave this place? Your message was vague on that point, and the High Ollamh offered me no information either." Mallec studied the rough building and its sparse furnishings. He frowned slightly. "On second thought, I may have an idea already."

"It's not what you think," Orlan said. "This is an old enclave, and the students here are sincere, if not remarkable."

Mallec nodded. "Not unlike Mona. Except for one or two like Brucc, most of the students recognized their good fortune in being there. Thanks to you, I got over my disappointment with most of the senior druids and managed to accomplish something." He smiled. "I owe you more than I can repay."

"That assumption may prove hasty," Orlan said, laughing. "You haven't heard everything."

"And I look forward to it, as I look forward to continuing my work here. You were right about how the others on Mona would react. As long as you were there I made progress, though there is so much to record, I know I have a lifetime of work still to do. After you left it became more difficult. The bards, especially, resented my efforts. I tried to explain they could only benefit by it, that a written record of the accomplishments of our people would mean they'd have even more knowledge to draw from when relating their stories." He shook his head. "They just couldn't understand."

Orlan patted his shoulder. "Don't be too disappointed. Remember that most of them have trained since childhood to use their memories. Such work doesn't exercise the muscles of original thought. Here you'll have the opportunity to change that, to begin new traditions."

"New traditions?" Mallec said. "That would require extraordinary students."

"Or an extraordinary teacher," Orlan said. "Actually, there is one student here who shows remarkable promise, but she's young. I'll expect you to look after her."

Mallec appeared not to have heard him. "New traditions," he mused. "I don't know that I'm the right one to—"

"Of course you are!" Orlan said. "Such a thing requires a man of deep convictions, a man who trusts his own ability, a man who can think for himself. How many such men did you meet on Mona?"

"Only one," Mallec said, smiling. "And he moved to a tiny enclave in a damp corner of the world no one's heard of."

"I've made a discovery here in this damp corner of the world, one that could be important. It's the real reason I needed you here."

A servant knocked once and Orlan grunted. The boy fumbled with the door and entered with a tray bearing bowls of steaming soup and chunks of dark bread. He set the food between the men and exited with a smile. Orlan offered a bowl to Mallec.

Mallec tilted his head. "You've discovered a new plant of some kind?"

"Rediscovered," Orlan said. "It makes shapeshifting possible."

Mallec sat still, the bowl half-way to his lips, staring at his old mentor. Skepticism covered his face.

"It works."

Mallec broke a long silence with a torrent of questions.

Orlan answered each in turn. "There are some aspects of woadsleep I haven't worked out yet, and I intend to lean heavily on you to help me do so. It'll be much easier once you've done it yourself."

For the second time that evening, Mallec became speechless.

"Oh, yes," Orlan said, slurping the last of the soup. "I want woadsleep to be an integral part of the tradition here. In fact, I've already told Leuw that only those who've experienced it will be eligible to become master of this enclave."

"And how many have done it so far?" Mallec asked.

"You'll be the second."

☩ ☩ ☩

Mallec followed Orlan and Leuw up Mount Eban's rocky slope. In places the mount reeked of brimstone, and twice they crossed warm streams that wove interconnected rivulets down the mountainside. A village of house-sized boulders lay at the base of the steepest side.

Each boulder they climbed elicited a grumble from the bard. More than once Mallec had to push the big fellow while Orlan pulled. Leuw barely caught his breath and then used it to bemoan the rigors of the climb.

Mallec enjoyed Leuw's company, although it was the first time he'd ever seen anyone so unwilling to exert himself. Among the Eburones such a man was fined silver for every inch of flesh the war chief deemed over trim. Mallec chuckled, glad to be in a place where being a warrior of the body was less important than being a warrior of the mind or spirit. He'd never met a more lively wit than Leuw's.

Leuw leaned against a boulder to rest, wiping sweat from his forehead with the edge of his sleeve. "I regret the suggestion that I come along. A nice honey-ale drawn from a cool cellar would suit me well right now."

Orlan grinned and slapped the bard on the shoulder. "While you're wishing, wish one for me, too. Come, my friend, we're nearly there. I can see the entrance from here."

Now, facing a ceremony more mysterious than anything Mallec might have imagined, he felt light-headed.

"You dawdle more than I, Mallec," Leuw called over his shoulder. "I suppose I'll have to wish you an ale, too?"

This camaraderie was a new thing, too. "I'm an Eburone. We do not drink strong spirits."

Leuw sputtered. "Oh, my poor lad! How much you've missed. I make a solemn oath, here on the sacred mountain, that I shall remedy this dreadful failing in your upbringing immediately upon our return." He shook his head in exaggerated sadness. "Next you'll tell me you've never accepted a Beltane ale from a willing woman."

Mallec's face flamed and Leuw roared with laughter. "That, too, is something we must remedy!"

Orlan stopped at the entrance to the cave. "Perhaps Mallec's worldly education can wait?" He slipped a wine skin from his shoulder and handed it to Leuw, who took a deep swallow and wrinkled his nose.

"Bah! It's water." He took another long draught and handed the pouch to Mallec.

Mallec managed two swallows for the sake of his throat. He returned the pouch to Orlan.

Orlan clasped his shoulder. "Something extraordinary happened here, my friend. Before my own transformation, I doubt this ritual had been performed in over two hundred years."

Orlan lit one of the torches left inside the opening and bent into the passage. He'd warned Mallec that they'd have to crawl a distance in the dark, a prospect Mallec did not relish. As he made his way on hands and knees, he imagined the weight of the mountain pressing down on him. The dank smell added to his sense of foreboding, unrelieved by the meager light of Orlan's torch.

When they finally traversed the maze of dark corridors, low-ceilinged rooms, and twisting trails to the inner chamber, Mallec breathed more easily. As they walked, their footfalls populated the space with invisible others. Mallec shivered, knowing this place must be the home of many gods. Orlan lit five additional torches to illuminate a room vast enough to swallow a village. Lit by flickering torchlight, the great central cavern overwhelmed Mallec's senses. Giant rock fingers and curtains of stone hung from the ceiling, and in some places the shattered remains of stone columns from someplace far above lay crumbled on the cave floor. Some worshipers had even carved faces into the rocks. Such grim visages lent even more solemnity to the surroundings.

"This is the Great Cavern described by Jaslon, the eighth Master of Eban," Orlan said softly, and even his whispers came back like exhalations of the gods.

The torches revealed scores of drawings on the walls, some in black charcoal, others in rich ironstone and ochre. Some of the animals depicted Mallec had never seen before, but others he knew well—bears, boars, and deer.

"Magnificent," he whispered.

Orlan pointed to a stone circle in the center of the Cavern. "Those stones have been here for eons, and the ceremony you're about to undergo may be nearly as ancient. We are truly blessed, Mallec. While all druids know transformation of the spirit, only we will know true transformation of the body." He pointed to the nearest stones. "Let's start there. I'll build a fire and prepare the baneweed while you two ready yourselves."

Mallec had fasted all night and all morning in preparation for the ceremony. The following day was Imbolc, the pregnant time when the sun reclaimed the year and seeds stirred in the belly of the Earth Mother. He enjoyed this woman's festival that marked the half time between the winter solstice and the spring equinox. As a boy he'd looked forward to the new lambs and fresh ewe's milk.

The druids mimicked the holy preparations of the women to ready themselves for today's special rite. Mallec prayed to The Great Mother that the goddess wouldn't mind them using her festival time.

"Lie beside the fire, Mallec," Orlan said. His words echoed around the cavern.

Mallec slipped out of his robe and tunic and left his leather shoes and breeches beside them. The cavern's cool air made the hairs on his arms stand on end.

Leuw spread Mallec's woolen cloak on the ground beside the fire. "That should keep you from freezing," he said.

"If all goes well," said Orlan, "he won't be in here long enough to worry about the chill."

In spite of reassurances from both druids, Mallec shivered with anticipation. Would he remember anything of his experience, or would he, like Orlan, simply sleep as deep as death?

Orlan knelt to prepare the baneweed. He began the ritual by hailing all within hearing of his prayers, be they men, spirits, or gods. Leuw chanted in harmony, his rich baritone punctuated by the rhythmic stamping of his foot. The echoes of Leuw's beat flowed over Mallec like an incoming tide. With eyes closed, he begged Rhiannon to embrace and protect him. The druids' chanting, as entrancing as a drum, lulled him. He felt the energy of the Goddess enter him.

"O-ghe, Mallec," Orlan whispered. "Have you made your peace with the gods?"

He nodded, feeling the tendrils of a trance. "I prayed that if this is death I may live again."

"Good," Orlan said.

Mallec relaxed to the echoed rhythms of Leuw's drum, until something sharp pricked him.

"I give you a remembrance of this sleep," intoned Orlan. "I draw Jaslon's mark in blood and stain it with woad."

Pain danced a pattern across Mallec's chest.

"Bear the mark as a sign of enlightenment. Breathe deep, my friend, and sleep."

Mallec obeyed. His nose wrinkled at the acrid fumes. Not entirely unpleasant, it reminded him of burning yew.

Blackness spiraled around him and he heard pops, like hard grain kernels thrown on a fire. The last thing he knew was intense and burning pain.

⌘ ⌘ ⌘

Mallec felt a bone-numbing cold that skipped past the searing pain in his right foot to wrap itself around his shoulders. It made him shiver so hard he knocked his elbows on his bed. Then he remembered. Not his bed. He lay on the sacred stone slab of Cad Cerrig. He was alive, although whether in the world of people or in the Otherworld he couldn't yet say.

"By the grace of Rhiannon, Lugh, and all the gods, you're back!" Leuw's voice quavered with fear and awe. "Oh, no. Orlan, look what I've done!"

Mallec forced an eye open. Only the bright morning sky greeted him until he shifted his gaze around and saw two figures bent near his painful foot.

He groaned.

Orlan straightened. His eyes held concern and fear. "Welcome back. How do you feel?"

Mallec dragged a dry tongue across parched lips, his eyelids heavy. He clutched at Orlan, barely able to croak out words. "What happened?"

Leuw moved to Mallec's side. His puffy eyes had the dark underscoring of one who had suffered a sleepless night.

Mallec grabbed Orlan's shoulders and hauled himself partially upright. "What's happened?"

Leuw bit at his lip and did not speak. Orlan touched Mallec's hand. "We accidentally burned you last night," Orlan said.

Mallec turned his eyes to the blistered flesh of his right foot. The burn stretched from his heel along the outer calf to his knee. It looked as though someone had laid a hot iron down the length of his leg.

"It's my fault," Leuw said with a grief-tinged voice. "Last night, after we'd left the cavern and prepared our evening meal, I tripped over your cloak and dropped you into the fire. I didn't know which of the sticks you'd become! If Orlan hadn't been near, you might have burned up."

"We doused the fire as quickly as we could and placed all the wood there." He gestured to a line of partially burnt sticks spread out on the broad surface of Cad Cerrig.

Leuw covered his face with his hands.

Orlan pursed his lips. "It's my fault, Leuw. I should have taken better precautions. I made the fire too close." He closed his eyes and bowed his head to Mallec. "Please forgive me."

Though he had no great desire to smile, Mallec forced one anyway. "So, a student can instruct a teacher. My first day at Mona left me with burns, too. I have to tell you, this isn't a lesson I'd care to repeat a third time."

"Perhaps the ceremony should be abandoned."

"There's nothing wrong with the ceremony," Mallec said. "I'll take my miracles where I can get them." He smiled again, this time at Leuw. "But next time, let's put someone else in charge of the cooking."

The jest met with approval from Orlan and a sheepish smile from Leuw.

They helped Mallec back into his tunic and robe. Leuw gave him a short cord, which Mallec tied around his waist. He pulled the robe up above his knee on one side and tucked it into the cord. Better to keep the burn exposed to the air, he thought.

Orlan brought the pony cart close. Mallec nearly made the move from stone to cart unassisted until he put weight on the injured leg and the burned skin stretched. Leuw caught him and helped him into the cart. Orlan led the pony toward Gillac, where the women gathered for Imbolc. Mallec hoped a healer lived among them.

✠ ✠ ✠

Mallec traced his new woad tattoo. In spite of the pain of his burned foot, he had no recollection of pain from the tattoo. This was no ordinary tattoo. The gods had marked him in a way he never thought possible. They accepted the sign and rejected the wound. What a marvel! It made him light-headed to think the gods found him worthy. He stretched, and the tender skin on his leg pulled, reminding him the gods also saw fit not to reject his burn, although it already seemed better. It was ever thus with the gods. They always let men accept the burdens of their own carelessness. If accepted to lead this enclave, he would ensure ceremonies always proceeded in the proper manner.

He fondled the bits of sacred leaf and stem Orlan had given him. Orlan said baneweed grew sparsely on Mount Eban, and Mallec had no doubt the proximity of the great cavern caused it to grow. No wonder Jaslon had kept it secret. To have every druid in Gaul seeking entrance to the cave would be madness. He envisioned camps of worshippers destroying the sanctity of Cad Cerrig. Such places should be guarded. An extraordinary rite like woadsleep must be kept from everyone outside the enclave.

He felt comfortable for the first time in his life and knew all his struggles to find his place had come to fruition.

"Mallec?" Orlan called before stepping into the hut. He set his staff against the wall by the door and joined Mallec near his bed. "How's the burn?"

"Healing, though it still pains me," Mallec said. "It's been nearly two weeks, and new skin is starting to grow."

After a long pause, Orlan pointed to Mallec's chest. "And the mark?"

Mallec pulled his tunic aside to show the tattoo, as perfect as if he'd been born with it.

Orlan nodded with satisfaction. "I marvel at that, though I wonder about your burn."

Mallec laughed. "You look for the healing potential in everything. Leave something for the gods."

Orlan chuckled. "What would you do, my friend, if you found a potion that always healed with or without the will of the gods?"

Mallec laughed. "If I knew of such a thing, I'd hide it immediately! My life and peaceful home would be forfeit to every trader and invalid from here to the other side of the sunrise."

"My thoughts exactly," Orlan said with a slow smile. "By the way, have you decided what you will do about the baneweed ceremony?"

Leuw and Orlan made the perfect pair to help him devise a ritual in which no participant could ever be injured again. "I've decided we should use only small amounts of the baneweed to make sure no one inhales what is not meant for him. I also intend to make this the most significant ritual of initiation a druid can have at this enclave and one that marks the highest level of achievement. The master of Mount Eban enclave should not be the only one to know first-hand such a potent similitude of death."

Orlan's rapt attention gratified him. Like the deference the students showed him, he'd come to enjoy it. "Besides," he said with a smile, "I like the idea of doing something that requires neither skill with a sword nor wrestling in the mud."

"Speaking of mud, the damp around this place is beginning to make my bones ache," Orlan said. "Are you ready to accept this enclave?"

Startled, Mallec said, "Isn't this too soon? Don't we need the approval of the Ollamh council in Carnute?"

The Iberian slapped his thigh for emphasis. "Benecin sent you with that decision already made. I asked him to send you only if he agreed to your suitability." He spread his hands. "You're here."

Mallec sat speechless.

"Well?" Orlan asked. "If you accept, Leuw will stay for a while to aid you."

Mallec found his voice. "I'm honored to accept." Then he frowned. "But what of you? Shall I lose my old master again so soon?"

"Don't worry," Orlan said. "I'll stay until this cursed weather improves. It's a difficult enough trip through the mountains in summer."

"Such a long journey! What if something happens? This enclave is too poor to send an armed guard with you. There are bandits to consider, and Romans. Iberia's overrun with them, isn't it? You could be slain."

"Aye," Orlan said. "I might. But I can think of nothing better than to spend my last moments on this side of the Cauldron on the warm plains of Iberia. Even death is better than being incessantly wet and cold."

"You sound like Leuw!"

"Which reminds me, he expects you to drink much ale at the feast before my leave-taking."

"I'll try," Mallec said, "but there's no assurance I can keep the stuff down."

"No fears, there. If Leuw and Gar cannot teach you to drink, no one can."

Mallec's thoughts drifted to the old days when the young warriors left him alone in the practice field and went off, arm in arm, to drink cider and jest about the day's activities. He never thought to know such friendships. Now, here in Armorica, he'd found comrades with wits keener than any weapon.

He would like it here.

✠ ✠ ✠

Mallec didn't think anything could throb as painfully as his head. Even thinking hurt. The student who woke him well after sunrise hadn't shouted, but Mallec winced just the same. He'd spent a miserable night after Orlan's farewell feast and at last fell dead asleep. He finally comprehended why his clan and several others in Belgica forswore ale or wine. He promised himself, and the gods, he would never do such a foolish thing again.

With the advent of good weather, Orlan had said his farewells and left the enclave with little fuss. He'd allowed the students to feast and drink his departure long into the night. Finally he took Mallec aside, wished him well, and left the enclave whistling a tune from Iberia.

Mallec walked to the main hall where he waved away the boiled oat breakfast Arie offered him. He accepted a cup of hot cider and took it outside to drink.

His head still pounded, and he sat on a stool, striving to remain motionless. The cider, its tart flavor smoothed with a little honey, warmed him. He stared southward in hopes of catching a glimpse of Orlan in the distance, but even the dust on the road had long settled.

Someone rang the bell and half a dozen older boys trudged from their chores in the barn to the practice field. Each dragged a heavy wooden sword. Three others laughed and pushed each other in happy anticipation of their morning practice. Once a week a warrior from Gillac arrived to train them, and every other morning the boys practiced. Mallec recalled his own days on the practice field, then grinned.

"Arie!"

The girl came running. "Master Mallec?"

He smiled, his headache almost forgotten. It was the first time anyone had called him "Master," and it felt good. "Assemble the students."

"Even the boys in the practice field?" she asked.

"Especially them."

Arie poked two fingers between her lips and whistled. She then clanged the great brass bell outside the main hall twice, signaling everyone to come at once. It took only another few moments for the rest of the students, the other druids, and the servants to find places to sit before the master.

Mallec took a sip of his cider and turned a solemn face to them.

"Many changes have come to Eban enclave in the last few years. Your old Master, Fyrsil, gave the enclave to Master Orlan, and he in turn entrusted it to me. I assure you little will change. Most of you will continue exactly as you have. I do have one small change to make, and it will be implemented immediately.

"Daily activity is essential for a healthy body. Most of you work hard here in the enclave in addition to your studies. Not all of you wish to learn how to wield a sword as your fathers did. I understand that. I was raised among the Eburones, where everyone trains. That upbringing had a profound effect on me, and I want you all to benefit from what I learned as a boy, all sweat soaked and exhausted in the muddy fields of Belgica."

Two of the boys, always reluctant at battle play, groaned loudly, and Mallec could no longer hide his smile.

"We'll all continue in our pursuit of skill with knives, spears, and slings, for your life on some battlefield one day may depend upon it. As druids, your staff, wielded with authority, is your best defense. Those of you who wish to learn sword skills may spend two days a week in Gillac practicing with the young men there. From this day forward, and for as long as I am the Master of this enclave, no student will be required to practice swordsmanship every morning."

Complete silence enveloped the students while they digested his words. Then, one thin boy whom Mallec recognized as a bardic student, raised a tentative hand.

Mallec nodded to him. "Yes, Budec?"

"Does this mean we still have to meet with the warrior from Gillac?"

"Yes, some training is essential, but you need not practice the sword every morning."

The boy whooped with delight and a host of others flooded Mallec with questions. At the end of the session, each student left happier than before. The three boys who loved swordplay would have more, and those who detested it would have less. Their enthusiasm remained even when he sent them back to their chores.

In a moment he was again alone in the morning sunlight, and unaccountably lonely. He wondered how often future decisions would leave him sitting by himself. As his thoughts drifted to the woman from his dreams, his loneliness faded.

14

The Ageless One has returned. He missed the funeral of Cullinor but offered an ancient prayer, called our dead master friend, and wept with us. He then asked my help to prevent the death of future friends. He laughed when I asked what magic could prevent such a thing and explained that he only intended to stop having friends.

He will remember us to the gods if we remember him with an offering of silver from time to time. There is an opening atop the Giant's Tomb, and he has asked that we drop our offerings into it. I find it strange the gods would have any use for our poor coins.

— Stave One of Tendal, 29th Master of Mount Eban Enclave

Iberia 80 B.C.

Rhonwen's stomach grumbled, since she'd forgotten to eat. No matter. She pulled herself deeper into the tree hollow that sheltered her, drew her knees close, and hugged them, delighting in the solitude after a long night of tending an ill child. Soon she'd fetch a late breakfast. A white butterfly danced from blossom to blossom, and she waited to see whether the creature signaled some important change. It could be lucky or not, depending on how long it flew around her. The butterfly rested on a leaf, its wings fluttering silently until a bird descended and plucked the hapless insect from its perch. Its death boded something important, she thought, although not necessarily bad.

The bird flew into the tree above, and the cheeps of its hungry young ones blended with the laughter of children playing in the nearby commons. She brushed away the wistful regret none of them belonged to her. Time enough for that later. Until then, she had other families to attend.

Her thoughts drifted to Orlan as they often did of late. Almost twelve years had passed since she'd last seen her uncle. Apart from Baia, only Orlan remained of her family. She recalled their joy three months ago when a message arrived with one of the itinerant bards. Orlan would leave his Armorican enclave as soon as the Ollamh sent a replacement and would meet them right here in Castulo.

Rhonwen turned her gaze to the busy east-west Roman road. If Orlan remained permanently, his help would lighten Baia's burden, and perhaps they could at last find a peaceful place in which to settle. With Orlan gone, Rhonwen had little respite from her mother's demands. Years of tending the sick or wounded had not softened Baia's disdain for Romans. Lately, her bitterness extended to Rhonwen, for the old woman often complained that her hopes of being cared for in her crone-years had died with Telo.

In Castulo, Healer's House offered a welcome change from their life on the road. She and Baia had spent most of the past years traveling from village to village, offering healing potions, setting bones, pulling abscessed teeth, and seeing to the needs of people without healers of their own. Every fall they returned to harvest the medicinal herbs that grew in the river valley an hour's walk south of Castulo. Baia often talked about how much she wanted a place to settle, but something always drew her away. She tired more easily each year. Living out of a horse cart and a tent grew tiresome and dangerous, with nothing to protect them but their druids' staves and an old dog. For every few hours they spent healing, they spent many more bumping along dirt tracks between hill towns and grain fields.

Baia called from the hut, and Rhonwen hurried to join her. "I fixed some porridge to end your fast." Dark smudges of fatigue beneath her eyes made her look even older than she was.

"A tinker gave me a bit of cardamom spice yesterday," Rhonwen said. "He was pleased with the way we set his daughter's broken arm. I left his gift with the fresh herbs near your kit."

Baia nodded. "I'll add some of that, too. Come along."

Rhonwen's mouth watered at the thought of the rare treat, but she wasn't ready to face another work day. "Not just yet. There'll be time enough for me to eat later."

Baia retreated to their quarters, muttering.

Rhonwen faced the door to the healing house, now expanded to include a sick room. She took a deep breath and swept aside the woolen blanket draping the doorway. A blanket, rather than a door, kept most of the flies out but not the fresh air required by those in the sick room. She stooped to fuss with the charms at the threshold. A palm-sized willow basket held the talismans she had assembled, prayed over and blessed for the healing of those within. All was correct. Knowing Baia had already looked in on their patients, she closed the blanket behind her.

She stepped back into the yard and bumped into a raggedy figure leading a road-weary donkey that pulled a cart so old it should have been discarded before Rhonwen was born. She gazed for a long moment at the man under the dust. Road filth covered his travel cloak, his thin-soled leather sandals were frayed, and his once black hair and beard were frosted with gray, yet the grimy face was one she knew and loved.

"Uncle Orlan!" she cried, flinging her arms around him, causing the donkey to bray. She guided him away from the house with a finger to her lips.

"Thank the gods, you've returned safe," she said once they'd moved away from Healer's House. She hugged him again. "Welcome home!"

She let go of him in a rush. "What am I thinking? I've got to tell Mother!"

"No, wait," he said as a handful of curious well-wishers gathered around. Orlan asked them to care for his donkey while he spoke with Rhonwen. He took her by the elbow and guided her away from the others. His face grew somber. "Happy times come entwined with sadder ones. I met a Lusitanian rider in a village east of here. He and scores like him are traveling throughout Iberia seeking men and supplies to use against the Romans."

Rhonwen frowned, trying to make sense of his words. "What makes the Lusitanians think they can defeat the Romans when no one else has?"

"They've found a general, a man with an army of Africans and disaffected Romans who fled Rome after Marius' defeat in the civil war. By joining forces they think they have a chance."

"Disaffected Romans?" Rhonwen laughed. "I didn't know there were such people."

"Have you heard nothing of what's gone on in Rome?"

Rhonwen shook her head. "The less Mother hears about Rome, the better. Besides, what goes on so far away means little here. They take what we give them and then take more. That'll never change."

Orlan wiped his forehead. "There's been a great civil war in Rome, and a man named Sulla has emerged the victor over Marius. Those loyal to Marius have fled or died. The one the Lusitanians have chosen to lead them is a Roman, but among Sulla's bitterest enemies."

"I thought the Lusitanians hated all Romans," Rhonwen said. "Who could possibly lead such a group of disparate souls?"

"A man who understands the Romans and their tactics," said Orlan. "A man who understands the people of Iberia."

"He's an African, you say?"

"He's a Roman, but he defeated Ascalis in Mauritania even though Sulla had sent Ascalis an army of reinforcements. Those who didn't die in the battle joined him! That's the kind of general he is."

Rhonwen exhaled wearily. "Castulo has had enough war. Why should we care?"

"Because this man intends to unite all of Iberia," Orlan said, "and because you know him."

She squinted at him. "I do?"

"Have you forgotten the name Quintus Sertorius?"

An iron hand clutched Rhonwen's heart. She leaned against Orlan, speechless.

"He and his army march even now to the great crossroads," Orlan said. "Those who intend to join him will gather here in three days." He looked at her with deep concern. "As the Lusitanian rider said, 'the name Sertorius will soon be on the lips of every man, woman, and child in Iberia.'"

Rhonwen released Orlan's arm. She glanced skyward and spied a crow playing on the wind. She shivered. At last, Baia would know the truth.

✠ ✠ ✠

Rhonwen sat cross-legged in front of the fire, idly poking at the brands with a crooked stick. She had only the amount of time it would take Orlan to bathe and eat to tell Baia the truth. She'd been content to let her mother believe the man responsible for Telo's death was dead when he'd only left the country. Shunning news of Romans, they'd heard no reports of him in all this time.

Now Sertorius had returned to fight against the power of Rome itself. It boded ill that Rome used Iberia to wage their civil war. That he'd come back did not surprise her, but it astonished her he could raise an army and threaten the very walls of Rome. She wondered if he would remember her.

She tossed the stick into the fire, grateful its glow covered up the red-faced shame she knew burned on her cheeks.

"Stop fiddling with the fire." Baia spoke from the doorway behind her. "I'm surprised at you. Orlan returns as we've prayed he would, and you do nothing to prepare for a celebration. Whatever ails you?"

Rhonwen remained silent. Her mother gazed at her with such a rare display of affection she had no desire to evoke the woman's reproach.

"That which eats your heart," Baia whispered, a hand clutching Rhonwen's shoulder, "will consume you if you don't let it out. Or have the gods forbidden you to speak of it?"

"If only that were the case," Rhonwen said, "I might rest easy." Unable to look Baia in the eye, she sighed and bit her lip.

Baia moved closer, her angular features etched with worry. "What is it?"

Where to begin? Not with Telo's death from Roman arrows, nor at her own vow of vengeance, and not with that last night when she'd slipped from Sertorius' bed to escape a murder she could not commit. Besides, there could be no honor in killing a man asleep, even to fulfill a blood vow. "Sertorius has returned to Iberia."

"Sertorius?" Baia said without comprehension.

Rhonwen rubbed the back of her neck.

"I hoped him dead." In truth, she'd hoped the gods had done her task for her.

Recognition clouded Baia's face.

Rhonwen wanted desperately to look away, but dared not.

Baia's brow wrinkled. "How did he survive his wounds?" Her voice trailed off and she straightened, pulling away.

"I misled you when I said he'd never bother us again. I knew he planned to leave Iberia the next day. I thought that was enough."

"Oath breaker!" Baia whispered the word as if sullied by the sound of it.

Everything Rhonwen felt boiled out in a rush of weak, stupid excuses. "I couldn't kill him in his sleep! I would have been dishonored."

Baia shrieked like a hare in the talons of an owl. "Dishonor? You can say that word while Telo's death goes unavenged?" She grasped Rhonwen's tunic, gathering handfuls of fabric into tightly balled fists. "You and the Roman both still live?"

Rhonwen said nothing.

"Oh!" Baia cried, thrusting her away. She dropped to the floor rocking back and forth with her eyes squeezed closed and her face contorted in anguish and rage.

Her wails brought Orlan at a run. He knelt beside her. "Baia, what's happened?"

She shoved him away and shrieked again. She lunged at Rhonwen, grasping and slapping. "Oath breaker!"

Rhonwen flinched from her mother's blows, weeping in shame at the truth of Baia's accusations. Orlan squeezed between them, pulling Baia away. She sobbed with fury. When he looked to Rhonwen, she only shook her head in despair.

He grabbed Rhonwen's hands and gripped them hard. "Tell me what this is about."

The flow of tears blinded her. "I told her the truth."

His lips, pursed tight and grim, revealed his distress. As a druid he would be forced to curse her for failing to fulfill her vow. She would be refused the favor of the gods, forbidden to participate in any ceremony offered by a druid, and forever denied the honor and prestige of a healer.

In exchange for failing her blood vow, she would lose everything but her life. She collapsed beside him, unable to face his decree.

"Look at me," he said, not unkindly.

With effort, she knuckled away her tears, sat up, and met his eyes. She would accept his judgment with what dignity she had left.

"What punishment would you pronounce for yourself?" he asked.

Exclusion from ritual, she thought. She wondered if Orlan would brand her as she had seen other outcasts marked. If so, the mark would surely cross through her druid's tattoo, and he would certainly break her staff.

She grieved for her mother, too. Baia rocked back and forth hugging herself in silent agony. Rhonwen's expulsion would leave the healer with no one to look after her in her old age. She was as trapped as Rhonwen, caught between the honor of vengeance and the need to be cared for by her family. Without Rhonwen to sing her song properly, there would be none left to do it when Baia died.

"Answer me," he said.

Rhonwen wished she could take it all back. She gazed at Orlan, ready for his judgment and knowing what it would be. "It is not for me to say."

He stared hard at her. "If Sertorius stood before you right now, could you kill him?"

She knew she couldn't. She had never believed him responsible for Telo's death, and so she'd never believed he should die for it.

She shook her head, and Orlan slapped her hard across the cheek.

She heeled backward in surprise and brought a hand up to soothe the sting. She felt the scar left long ago by mercenaries, the very ones Sertorius had killed for attacking her. Here came yet another attack, this time from Orlan. Her heart raced. He'd never struck her, not even when she was a headstrong girl.

"Speak!" he commanded. "You're not a child."

She drew herself erect, summoning all her pride. "The penalties for oath breaking are death or banishment."

Baia sobbed loudly, then muffled her cries with her hands.

"And what is the penalty for a child's oath breaking?"

The question puzzled Rhonwen. Children rarely made serious vows, but if they broke one, each was judged independently. In this case, it didn't seem to matter.

"As a woman, I failed to keep my vow," she said.

"You were a child when you made it."

Baia looked up. "That alters nothing!"

He reached for her, but she shoved him away.

"I've seen many strange things," he told her, softly. "The gods have plans for Rhonwen, for had she killed Sertorius, she would surely have been slain. Later, the gods removed any other chances she might have had to fulfill her vow by sending Sertorius out from Iberia. I believe they have other plans for both of them."

Rhonwen covered her face. "It is a blood oath, Uncle. Not even the gods may overlook that."

"No," he said pulling her to her feet, "normally they would not, but in this matter it seems the will of the gods is for you to continue living. Had they wished to punish you, they would have done so long before now. Therefore, you are absolved of this crime. You're no oath breaker, and you never were."

Baia shook her fist at him. "You shame your nephew's memory!"

He knelt beside her. "You must put this aside, sister! The gods chose to give you a daughter for the rest of your days! Accept their boon and do their will. The vow is no more."

"I cannot forgive the Romans," she whispered. "My husband and son are both dead at their hand."

"Then that is the burden the gods have chosen for you. Forgive your daughter."

Baia sobbed, her eyes puffy from tears as she pulled away. "Not today. Today I mourn my unavenged son."

Rhonwen nodded once, although her mother did not see it as she shuffled like an old woman across the room to the door. When Baia had left, Orlan sighed deeply, as if he were suddenly older, too.

Rhonwen shivered. No matter who or what caused it, a broken oath meant someone, somewhere, would still pay the blood price.

✠ ✠ ✠

"Baia?" Orlan leaned through the door of a small hut beside Healer's House in search of his sister. Not a single lamp lit the interior, nor could he detect any sound. She had remained out of sight since the previous morning.

"What do you want?" she asked.

"You're speaking to me again. Excellent!" he said, forcing cheer into his voice in hopes of raising her spirits.

"I once dropped a heavy stone on my foot. I said many things to it, too, though it hurt me less than you have."

Orlan left the door flap open for light and walked in. "I see Healer's House is nearly empty. That should please you."

She scowled. "The gods have given me time to think about my daughter's treachery and the shameless manner in which my brother thinks he can invalidate an oath of blood."

Orlan forced a smile. "It's nice to know I've been missed."

"I missed you every day, but if I'd known your return meant you'd tell me this, I think I'd rather have talked to the stone. Better you had stayed in Armorica."

He grimaced. "Don't be so hard on me. I've traveled many days just to be here. I've seen and heard and learned so much." He leaned close. "There are miracles within our grasp."

"I suppose I'd need one to make you disappear."

"Yes, you would," he said. "I have something to show you." He reached for her hand to help her to her feet, but she pulled away.

"Be gone! I don't wish to see you now."

"I intend to go away," Orlan said. "So if you're going to see me at all, you'd better do it now."

Baia looked at him in surprise. "You just got here."

"But why should I stay? My niece claims she's an outcast, and my sister, who hasn't seen me in a dozen years, won't speak to me."

She grunted. "You conveniently overlook the circumstances."

"It's better than letting them blot out everything else."

Baia sighed and shifted to her feet. "You can't stand not to have your way, can you? You were the same as a child."

He kissed her cheek and pulled her outside. "I have something for you to see."

Stumbling along behind him, Baia maintained a look of pained resignation. Orlan ignored it and pulled her around the front of Healer's House where he'd last seen Rhonwen eating her breakfast. He grabbed her hand, too, and pulled her upright.

"What is it?" she asked.

"I've a wonder to share," Orlan said, towing them both to a table he'd set up beside his donkey cart. A half dozen plants growing in terracotta pots occupied the table, their thin stems bent under bedraggled flowers.

He released the women and waved his hand at the plants with a flourish. "Feast your eyes on this!"

Smiling, he turned first to Baia, then Rhonwen. Neither woman showed the slightest interest in the plants, and gazed straight at him.

"It's baneweed," he said.

Baia turned away, muttering. "We have enough weeds already. We don't need Gaul's."

"It has amazing properties."

"Name one."

Orlan glanced over his shoulder quickly to ensure no one else could hear him. "It can heal," he whispered.

She paused, still doubtful. "What can it heal?"

Orlan motioned for her to come closer. He reached for Rhonwen's hand and drew her in, too. "I believe it can cure anything," he said, his voice barely audible.

Baia continued to stare and Rhonwen's brow dipped skeptically. "Anything?" Baia asked.

He nodded.

"Broken bones?" she asked. "Blood fever? The wasting disease?" Her voice grew harsh and clipped as she named one malady after another.

He smiled and nodded again.

"Only the gods could do that," she said. "You've seen such miracles?"

Orlan pursed his lips. "In a manner of speaking."

"Prove it," Baia said. She looked at Rhonwen and bobbed her head toward Healer's House. "Do we have anyone inside who needs a miracle? Your uncle seems to have found a way to put us all out of work forever."

Orlan stared at her in surprise. "You see a universal cure as a threat, rather than a marvel?"

"You've shown me nothing but weeds," she said. "Rhonwen, fetch the miller's boy, the one who lost a finger between the stones."

Orlan put a restraining hand on Rhonwen's shoulder. "It's not that simple. We can initiate a cure at any time, but it can take weeks or months to complete, and it has to be planned around an equinox and the standing stones of the Ancients."

"I thought so," Baia said, waving her hands. "Call me when you're through telling children's tales." She walked back toward the hut.

"Baia, please wait," he called, but she ignored him.

"You can explain it to me," Rhonwen said. "Sometimes it's hard for people to give up old methods when new ones appear."

"Baia isn't angry about old methods."

"Are you so sure?" Rhonwen smiled sadly. "What else does she have left?"

Orlan remained silent, staring at the corner of the building behind which Baia had disappeared.

Rhonwen lifted one of the baneweed plants. "Do you make a poultice from it, or does it bear seeds? What do the standing stones have to do with it?"

Orlan chuckled. "I'll tell you what I know, which isn't much." He looked into Rhonwen's dark eyes and reached out to touch her wild hair. "The questions you ask me now are the kind Baia would ask, back before I left. I'm glad to know her passion for healing lives on in you."

"I still have much to learn."

"As do we all. Now, let me tell you about this plant and a strange little mountain in Armorica."

✠ ✠ ✠

Rhonwen had never seen Orlan as excited as he was about his unusual plants. The man went to extraordinary lengths to prepare the soil where he planted them, and he took pains to see that they received neither too little nor too much sun. He described in detail the climate of Armorica where he'd found them. He feared the warmer, drier weather in Castulo would prevent the plants from thriving.

"Once I know if they'll grow well, I'll locate the nearest standing stones of the ancients," Orlan declared as he brushed dirt from the knees of his breeches.

Though he'd only been home a few days, Rhonwen felt even more comfortable with him than she had as a child despite all that had happened since those carefree days.

"I've heard the cursed *togas* have been using the stones for their roads and buildings," Orlan said.

Rhonwen blinked, realizing she'd been daydreaming. "What roads and buildings?"

"I don't know which ones specifically," he said, his tone betraying a touch of impatience. "What's important is which stones are still standing."

Rhonwen stared uncertainly at the Roman road that connected Healer's House with Castulo and the rest of Iberia.

"Stones," Orlan said. "I need to visit the standing stones."

"Oh, yes, of course," Rhonwen said. "The closest stones still standing are at least a day's journey from here. I doubt the Romans would bother with them, for they fear the spirits living there. Mother insisted we visit them wherever we traveled."

Orlan smiled. "I'll ask Baia. I'm sure she knows what I'm looking for."

"How would I know that?" Baia asked as she joined the two near Orlan's neat garden plot.

Orlan explained.

Baia reached down to pet Iago, who rarely left her side these days. "It would be easier to lead you than tell you how to get there."

"Excellent!" Orlan said. "How about tomorrow?"

"That won't be possible. I'm leaving Castulo."

"What?" Rhonwen couldn't believe her ears.

"Where are you going?" Orlan asked.

"I'm joining the Lusitanian fight against Rome. I figure they'll welcome any healers they can get, even worn out old women like me."

"You're not serious," Rhonwen said.

Baia scowled at her. "One should never question a driad, especially one who's forgotten more than you've learned. I'm leaving this afternoon. I just thought you should know."

"In case we wanted to join you?" Orlan asked. "You know I can't." He gestured toward the baneweed plants. "I have a far more important mission than binding the wounds of fools."

Baia grimaced. "Before you disparage others, perhaps you should look to yourself."

"It's too dangerous for you to go alone," Rhonwen said.

"You have nothing to say in the matter."

"Rhonwen's right," Orlan said. "The Romans will be looking for every opportunity to attack. They have never shown mercy to those who rise against them. Do you honestly believe they'll let you live if they think you support rebellion?"

Baia waved his objection away. "I may get a chance to get close to the man who killed Telo, and kill him myself. I must go." She glared at Rhonwen. "And even if I don't, what could be better than watching Romans killing Romans?"

Her mother's anger and grief had not abated in all the years since Telo's death. Alone, she might do something foolish. Rhonwen had always come after Telo in her mother's heart. Nevertheless, Rhonwen's path was clear. "I'm going with you," she said.

"I won't stop you," Baia said, "but I'm not inviting you, either."

"You're acting like children!" With a kick, Orlan raised a small dusty cloud. "Do you think I traveled all this way just to live by myself?"

"I can't help that," Baia said. "I'm leaving."

"And I have to go with her," Rhonwen added.

Orlan shook his head. "You mustn't do this. It's dangerous and unnecessary."

"I must finish packing," Baia said as she walked away.

"Listen to me—" Orlan began.

"I don't want to leave you behind," Rhonwen said, "but I can't let her go alone."

"I know. May the gods watch over you." He bowed his head in sadness. "Baia's not the same woman I left behind twelve years ago."

Rhonwen embraced him fiercely and then stepped back without looking at him. She did not want him to see the brightness of her tear-filled eyes. "Neither am I," she said, and followed Baia into the house.

⑆ ⑆ ⑆

Much to Baia's annoyance, the women remained at Healer's House until the following morning because it took so long to load all the supplies Rhonwen and Orlan insisted they take. Not only would they need food, personal belongings, and medicines, they'd have to take the tools to make other supplies. Caring for battle wounds meant being ready for anything. Their goodbyes had been short and pain-filled for both Rhonwen and her uncle. In spite of Baia's long separation from her brother, she seemed driven to leave him and shed no tears as she turned away.

As usual, Rhonwen walked beside the cart with Iago walking ahead like a scout. Baia rode in silence, speaking to Rhonwen only when necessary. The ox that had served them so well in their travels north moved too slowly to please Baia.

They abandoned the Roman road on the second day, choosing instead to follow the trail left by the mass of men they sought. By the end of the week such signs seemed fresher, and a few of the campfires still smoldered.

On the ninth day they crossed a ridge and looked down into a valley choked with Iberian warriors. A sentinel challenged them but let them pass when he saw their druid robes.

Rhonwen put Iago in the cart with Baia and led the way into the encampment. It looked nothing like the villages they once visited. Men sharpened weapons, cooked meals, or engaged in mock combat. There were few women and no children. Warriors tended to stay with their own clans.

A guard dressed in breeches of fur, his upper body sun-stained a dark bronze, stepped in front of them. The ox's nose pressed into the man's hard midsection, but the warrior held his ground, and the animal halted.

"We are driads," Rhonwen said. "Let us pass."

The warrior pointed at Baia's cloak. "She's a healer?"

"We both are."

"Then come with me. You're needed." Saying no more, the warrior angled away, walking briskly.

Baia waved impatiently at Rhonwen to follow him. Pulling on the ox's halter she urged the great plodding animal into motion once again. She looked up to see the warrior standing with his hands on his hips, a crevice-like frown cleaving his jaw from the rest of his craggy face.

"You'd move faster on foot," he said, ignoring Rhonwen and speaking to Baia. "Leave the wagon. I'll have someone bring it to you."

Baia laughed. "You want me to surrender everything I own to someone I've never met?" She shook her head.

The man bellowed a name and within moments a youth appeared beside the warrior. He seized the boy's shoulder. "Drive this wagon to the council tent, and let no one but these driads near it."

The boy darted toward the wagon and leaped into the seat beside Baia. Iago snarled at him and would have lunged had Baia not held him.

"Quiet!" she ordered. The dog settled beside her, his hackles raised and a low growl in his throat. Baia patted his head.

"Come, Mother," Rhonwen said. "Let the boy drive the cart. Iago will look after our things."

The boy nodded as Iago drew near and sniffed him. Satisfied, Iago wagged his tail.

Baia grunted her assent and climbed down. After bending and stretching to ease the cramps of travel, she approached the warrior. "Lead on."

The three walked a serpentine route between camps and campfires, knots of men, racks of weapons, and hobbled mounts. Rhonwen quickly realized the wagon would be an hour or more just passing through the camp, and if the destination lay much further, it wouldn't arrive until nightfall. Meanwhile, the warrior guided them to a large tent set apart from the rest. Scores of armed men garbed in the colors of a dozen clans lounged outside.

"This way," the warrior said, plowing aside any who failed to move out of his way. The women followed in his wake, entering a crowded tent without challenge.

At one end of the tent they saw a warrior chief propped in a sitting position atop a bed of furs. His leg had been hastily bandaged, but the dressings were soaked red and the man's face was so pale Rhonwen didn't recognize him.

"Driad Rhonwen," he said, his voice calm despite the apparent severity of his injury. "I'm happier to see you this time than last."

With the voice came recognition, although it had been years since Rhonwen had last seen him at the execution of his countryman. "Aras," she said, "I had no idea you'd be the one needing our help."

He smiled tightly. "Cesada, the man who brought you here, isn't used to talking. We Trepani are much better at war than conversation."

"What happened?" Baia asked, "and what are all these men doing in here?"

"I was on my way here after meeting with the Lusitanian chiefs. The Roman, Sertorius, called us together to discuss his plans." The tone of his voice suggested nothing but respect for the man the Lusitanians had put in charge.

"A wagon startled my horse," he said, "and I was thrown beneath its wheels. I thought I had rolled out of the way."

Baia deftly cut away the material covering the wound and clucked at it. "Did anyone think to rinse off the dirt and inspect your injury before they wrapped it?"

"We're warriors," he said stiffly. "I ordered my men to bind the limb and bring me here. I have much to tell them." He gestured toward the others in the room, all of whom wore the trappings of leadership.

"Dead warriors win few battles," Baia commented. "And that's what you'll be if you treat all your wounds this way."

Some of the others in the room shrank back from her. Two or three made warding signs.

"I need hot, clean water and better light," she said, then looked at the men all around them. "And more space. Your meeting can wait."

"No, it can't," Aras said. "These men must return to their warriors, but we've certain deliberations to conclude first. You can work while we talk. No one will object to your presence."

A chorus of agreement went up.

"You'll have to clean it, Rhonwen," Baia said. "My eyes aren't good enough to work in this poor light. I'll find what you'll need."

Aras continued in spite of the interruption. "The war has begun with a victory. The Lusitanians have found a man who can win again. Just look at what Sertorius did to Cotta off the coast near Mellaria. He has more men at the end of his battles than at the beginning. The ships he took when he put Ascalis back on the throne in Mauritania made up the fleet he brought against Cotta. He's defeated both Cilician pirates and the galleys of Sulla's general, Paccianus."

Aras scanned the faces before him, staring into the eyes of each. "Now the Romans are massing a huge army under Metellus, a host greater than anything seen in Iberia since the days of Hannibal."

"Just how big an army?" asked a man of middle years, his helmet splotched with rust.

"Sertorius claims they number over twenty legions of five thousand swords each."

The older chief whistled. "And how many are we?"

"Twenty clans have joined his banner thus far."

"How many men?"

"Eight thousand," Aras said.

"He's mad to think we'd face such numbers!" the older chief exclaimed. Many of the others echoed his dismay.

Aras held up a hand. "That may be true, but I trust his confidence. From the way he talks, you'd think the battle is all but over and the Roman army is in disarray."

Aras grunted as Rhonwen bathed away the blood-stained dirt to reveal the mangled limb. "If you decide to fight," he said, "I'll heal in time to join you."

"You'll be lucky if this heals at all," Rhonwen said. "The bones aren't broken, but the muscles are torn, and it'll take more stitches than I've ever put into one man. If you can avoid the blood fever, you'll still come away with a limp."

"I'll heal," Aras said. "And a limp means nothing to a man on horseback."

Rhonwen forced a smile. "I hope you're right."

Aras looked back at the others. "No one can command you to stay, but Sertorius has asked that you and all your men attend a council with him."

"All our men?" The older chief looked incredulous. "He's mad! One doesn't discuss strategy with an entire army."

Aras smiled. "Don't take my word for it. Go listen to what he has to say. If you still think this is the wrong time to stand against Rome, you're free to leave. Indeed, he wouldn't want you to stay."

Several of the chiefs cocked their heads in suspicion. Whispers filled the air like fall leaves in a wind.

"I don't mean that as an insult," Aras said. "Sertorius demands loyalty above all else." He shook his head in wonder. "With a handful of such men and a few pirates, he stood against two armies in Africa, and defeated them both! It's no wonder the Lusitanians want him."

He crossed his arms and surveyed his listeners. "Will you hear the man before you make your decision?"

After some hasty and grumbled discussions, the chiefs agreed and filed out of the tent. Baia hurried them along. "There's no healing with so much hot air all about," she said, motioning for Rhonwen to join her outside.

"You've seen his wound. Will it fester?"

Rhonwen shrugged. "Let's offer an additional prayer for him. He seems a good man."

Baia nodded, a rare smile on her lips. "My thoughts exactly. According to his men, he has no wife."

Her smile made Rhonwen suspicious. "I'm sure there'll be someone to mourn him if he dies."

"It's not mourning I had in mind," Baia said. "I'm thinking of my old age, and how I'll need someone to look after me. The Trepani are honorable people who live far from the Romans. You could do worse than Aras for a husband."

Speechless, it took a moment before Rhonwen realized her mouth had fallen open.

"I'm not too old to bounce a grandchild on my knee," Baia said. "After everything I've done for you, I should think you owe me that much."

"We've a patient to care for," Rhonwen said, but thoughts of a father for her children didn't bring the image of Aras to mind. As soon as she'd finished with him, she'd tell Baia of the decision she'd just made to attend the strategy meeting with Sertorius.

15

I thought I saw the Ageless One in the market, but perhaps my eyes play tricks on me. Though it has been years since he last visited the enclave, both his face and his voice seemed familiar. Sadly, he drifted away at my approach, and I lost sight of him in the crowd. My days in this world dwindle, and I hope he returns soon. How else will he know to whom I pass the enclave?

— *Stave Two of Tendal, 29th Master of Mount Eban Enclave*

Iberia

Sertorius had forbidden those responding to his call to make camp in the same place. As a result, when he summoned them to explain his strategy, it took all morning for them to assemble.

The appointed spot, the low central portion of a great bowl-shaped valley, had already been marked. Armed Lusitanians surrounded and guarded a platform erected for the occasion. They permitted no one near.

Rhonwen and Baia, more fortunate than most, occupied a spot of high shaded ground secured by several score of Trepani warriors under the watchful eye of Cesada, Aras' second-in-command. They settled in at mid-morning and observed warriors, proudly displaying their clan colors, arriving from all directions.

Rhonwen noted how young many of the warriors were. She doubted even as many as one in ten had ever seen a battle. Their youth likely accounted for their high spirits despite the outrageous size of the army soon to be arrayed against them.

Sertorius arrived when the sun had reached its highest point. He spent a significant portion of the day walking among the warriors, talking to those who would soon be following him. His blue cloak and shiny helmet stood out amid the reds and coppers of his Roman-clad guard. By contrast, the Iberians generally bore odd assortments of arms, and except for helms and shields, wore little or no armor.

As Sertorius passed among them, he towered above the Romans and stood at eye-level to all but the tallest of the Iberians. He laughed often, and although she was too far away to make out what anyone said, Rhonwen could tell the Iberians received him warmly.

The sight of him still brought back a rush of emotions and physical reactions she'd experienced with no other men. She forced herself to think of Sertorius as a leader rather than a lover.

When spoken to from the left, he turned his entire head. Moments later she understood why. A long heavy scar cut straight across his left eye. She felt a sharp twinge of regret for the disfiguring mark on his handsome features, then chided herself for being more concerned with the man's appearance than with the man himself. Though blind in one eye, it seemed no handicap. On the contrary, it enhanced his status among his warriors.

Finally he made his way toward the center of the valley. The masses parted for him, and he reached the wooden stand without incident. Climbing it easily, he stood and raised his arms above his head. All conversation ceased.

Rhonwen had doubted that anyone would be able to hear him, but when he began to speak in the common tongue of the Iberians, his voice carried to everyone in the valley. He thanked them all for coming and called off the names of every clan represented. With each name thus recited, warriors in the crowd responded whether they numbered in the hundreds or fewer than a dozen. Their war cries rang proud and vibrant. Rhonwen rubbed at the chill bumps on her arms.

"Most of you have heard about the size of the army we must face, and many of you are worried," Sertorius said.

A rumble of agreement met his statement.

"Any fool can see that an army of six or eight thousand stands little chance against a host twenty times as large."

A collective gasp went up among the crowd. Though few among them had the skill to calculate the size of the Roman army just described, they all recognized it had to be vastly greater than they expected.

"Only a fool would lead such a small army into open battle against such a large one." He paused and waited for the crowd to settle. "I promise you, no man still alive ever called me a fool."

The crowd went silent.

"I will defeat Metellus."

"How?" cried someone nearby.

"I know more about them than they'll ever know about us. Metellus is a doddering old man who should have left the field years ago. He knows nothing about the land here, nothing about the proud people here, and nothing about how to wage war here!"

The crowd followed his every word, as eager as Rhonwen to find some scrap of hope for the campaign ahead.

"I will not tell you where and how we'll fight Metellus. I will show you." He raised his blue-caped arm and pointed toward the east. "Clear the way for those two warriors and their mounts."

Two men, one tall and heavily muscled, the other old and stooped, led two horses toward the central clearing. The big man led a sorry nag in no better condition than the old man. In contrast, the old man clung precariously to the halter of a fine stallion.

"Let them through!" Sertorius commanded as the Iberians laughed at the struggles of the decrepit old man and the ease with which the younger one pulled the swayback behind him.

The crowd noise swelled as the two reached the space set aside for them. Sertorius, still atop the stand, raised his hands again for silence.

"I've given both of these men the same task," Sertorius said, his voice booming across the valley. "But each has a different method for accomplishing it."

Would they kill the horses? Rhonwen wondered. Without benefit of a priest or druid, most Iberians would consider such an act sacrilege. Sertorius motioned to the two men before him. "You may begin."

Both stepped to the back sides of their respective horses. The younger man grabbed the tail of the old nag with both hands and began to yank and pull on it. The horse, clearly annoyed with the man, dragged him around the circle. The crowd's laughter soon drowned out the sounds of the younger man's curses.

Nearby, the older man remained calm and patted the flank of the magnificent horse as he plucked hairs from its tail one by one. The stallion lowered its head and munched on the lush grass at its feet.

Before long, the younger man released the old horse and sat down, exhausted. The old horse pranced like a colt and shook its proud, full tail. Meanwhile, a patch on the stallion's tail had been plucked nearly bald, and most in the crowd smiled knowingly.

"Our task in the days ahead is not so different from the one I set for these two men," Sertorius said. "I have no desire to yank out the tail of Metellus all at once." He paused just long enough to give his next words more importance. "We will pluck it out one hair at a time. When we're done, we'll have enough Roman hairs to weave a thousand blankets!"

While the crowd roared its approval, Rhonwen looked at Baia. Like those all around them, she nodded until she caught Rhonwen's eye. Instantly, she looked away, and the blank face she'd worn since Rhonwen's confession once again cloaked her features.

"Our work is well under way," Sertorius said. "We've already met Cotta, the first of Metellus' four generals." He grinned broadly enough for even the most distant ranks to see. "Cotta and his army were last seen swimming back to Rome. I can only imagine what they'll report to Sulla when they get there!"

Cheers and war whoops rang through the valley, punctuated by loud cries of clan names from the lips of thousands of eager warriors. Rhonwen shivered with excitement as the clans signaled their approval. When their voices grew hoarse, they pounded their shields with their swords, and the racket echoed from the distant hills.

"Chiefs, come to my tent, and I will outline my plans for the campaign. Everyone else, return to your camps," Sertorius said. He stepped down from his dais and disappeared in the crowd.

Rhonwen thought he'd have to repeat the command for the rowdy young men, but they dispersed as he'd ordered. As they left the valley behind, they displayed even higher spirits than when they'd arrived. She prayed their confidence would prove justified. She remembered all too well how pleased with himself Telo had been the night before he died.

"Well, look who's here," said a familiar voice, "it's the Queen of Iberia."

Rhonwen's breath caught, and she bowed to Sertorius who stood among a knot of his officers just below the shady rise where she'd spent the day.

"You're every bit as beautiful as the last time I saw you," he said, returning her bow. "I'm honored you would attend my humble demonstration."

She blushed deeper, wishing the gods had built a wall to shield Baia from the conversation. "I've never seen better."

"I would stay and talk, but I must meet with these men." He frowned briefly, then brightened, almost enough to eclipse the scar across his eye. "Would you visit my camp?" He smiled broadly. "I'll send an escort this time."

Unused to being the focus of so much attention, Rhonwen stammered. "We're camped—"

"With the Trepani," he said, nodding to Cesada. "You keep excellent company. I'll send for you this evening." He waved and allowed the press of his officers and the swarms of men all around them to push him along.

Rhonwen glanced at the nearby Trepani warriors, who regarded her with greater respect than before. Rhonwen decided she liked it.

"The queen of Iberia?" Baia asked, her eyes hard and cold.

Rhonwen turned away, mortified at how terrible Baia made Sertorius' nickname sound yet eager to hear him say it again.

⌘ ⌘ ⌘

The escort from Sertorius arrived in the Trepani camp just before sunset. A dozen hard-edged men drawn from African, Roman, and Lusitanian stock waited for Rhonwen as she prepared to accompany them.

Baia railed against the idea. "Why does he want to speak with you? There are other druids, and other healers for that matter."

"I've little choice in the matter," Rhonwen said as she wiped at a stain on her ceremonial robe.

Baia grunted and poked her. "He didn't ask you to perform any rites, did he? Why honor him with sacred clothing?"

Rhonwen discarded the stained garment. She'd wear something less official. "The rites are sacred, not the garb. You've told me that often enough." She selected a light blue gown that looked good against her hair and resembled the one Sertorius had given her so long ago.

"The way you primp for this man is a disgrace. I'm surprised you haven't colored your lips like the whores who spread their legs for the legionaries."

Knowing a reply would only fuel Baia's anger, Rhonwen made no comment.

Baia grabbed her shoulder and spun her around. "There's a fine man, one of our kind, lying hurt not two dozen paces away. Why can't you attend to him instead of this Roman?"

"Because Sertorius summoned me," Rhonwen said, trying to keep the exasperation from her voice. "Or didn't you notice those men he sent? Perhaps you'd like to tell them I'm not going with them."

"Gladly." Baia straightened and stepped toward the waiting warriors. Rhonwen rushed past her, and one of the men steadied a horse for her while she mounted.

"When will you be back?" Baia asked.

"I don't know."

Baia whirled around and walked briskly toward Aras' tent. Her attitude so angered Rhonwen she kicked her horse into a run. The Trepani camp lay near the edge of the general encampment, and Rhonwen soon outdistanced her escort.

She let the horse run for a time, enjoying the rush of excitement such speed gave her. When she at last paid attention to the shouts of the men behind her, she reined the animal in.

The escort rapidly surrounded her, and its leader, a scowling, dark-eyed Roman, grabbed the halter of her horse jerking the animal to a stop.

"What are you doing?" he demanded.

Rhonwen shook her head, still angry. "Riding."

"That's obvious," the soldier said. "But our camp lies that way." He thrust a well-muscled arm in the direction from which they'd come.

Rhonwen groaned.

The soldier released her horse and turned his own around. Without looking back, he urged his mount to a trot. Rhonwen followed obediently.

Eventually the escort slowed to a walk, and Rhonwen was grateful to remain in the saddle instead of bouncing up and down. They reached an estate more grand than any Rhonwen had ever seen. Camped warriors jammed the grounds. Their general wasn't likely to be taken by surprise.

Sertorius stepped into the fading sunshine as the escort arrived. He bowed as he approached.

"Ah, Rhonwen. How many men are privileged to welcome a queen to their homes twice?"

She laughed, suddenly at ease. "You must stop calling me that! What will people think?"

"Whatever suits them," he said. "In your presence, I have nothing but you in mind." He helped her dismount, nodded his thanks to the captain of the escort, then took her arm and led her inside the largest building.

Inside she found wide airy rooms filled with rich furnishings from lands on every coast of the Mediterranean. Heavy cedar chairs and lounges lined the elaborately painted walls. Tiled mosaics of dancers and goddesses, dogs and game peppered the floors. A statue, the base stained with blood, caught her eye. She looked to Sertorius for an explanation.

"This was once the home of Fufidius, governor of this province and one of Metellus' generals. When we arrived, he called me a traitor to Rome and ordered my surrender."

Rhonwen glanced around the room, suddenly aware of other bloodstains on the walls, floor and furniture. "What happened?"

"I offered him the opportunity to leave unhindered. He ordered his men to attack." He shook his head wearily. "He's lucky to still draw breath."

"Is that how you lost your eye?" she asked, knowing the wound was an old one. She'd tried without success to avoid staring at the scar bisecting his left eyebrow and cheek. The lid remained shut, the eyeball removed, a common outcome of such an injury.

He smiled. "Does the mark discomfit you?"

"No," she said, too quickly. "How did it happen?"

"I ran into a Gaul who was quicker than I." He laughed. "I'm fond of it, actually. The man who gave it to me is an able warrior who later served under me."

He poured her a cup of watered wine and placed it gently in her hands, his touch lingering long enough to rekindle the thrill she'd felt years before.

"Many have asked why I don't keep it covered," he said, smiling. "To be honest, it's the only bragging I allow myself. It's one thing to say one's been in battle and quite another to wear the proof of it."

He turned at the sound of someone's approach. "Spanus! Come in, come in," he said.

Rhonwen, too, looked toward the new arrival, his name familiar. She squinted at the humble man who stood in the open portal, trying to place him.

"I brought the hind, as you requested," the man said.

"Excellent. Let me see her."

The man left briefly then returned carrying a dainty white fawn. His gentle touch and sad expression made her remember him as the stableman who cared for the prized mare of Fufidius.

"Set her down," Sertorius said, reaching for a knife and a bowl of fruit.

Spanus released the animal, a tiny roe deer whose faint spots were the only distinguishing marks on its clear white coat.

"It's magnificent," Rhonwen said. "Such a creature is among the most sacred."

"So I've heard." Sertorius sliced off a piece of apple and offered it to the deer.

With tentative, soundless steps, the animal approached, then stretched its long neck and nibbled at the fruit.

"What do you intend to do with it?" Rhonwen asked.

He waved her to a soft cushion and then sat beside her, the deer following hesitantly as he provided additional slices of apple. "I need your help with that," he said.

"With what?" Rhonwen asked. She leaned back, conscious of the soft luxury of the furniture.

"Between his various generals, Metellus has a considerable force in the field," he said. "As you know, I've tried to convince the Iberians we still have a chance against them, though their numbers are far greater than ours."

He ate a slice of the apple himself. "As soon as I've dealt with Fufidius, who prepares for battle even now, I need to convince more Iberians to support us."

"What does that have to do with the hind? Or me?"

Sertorius shrugged. "I thought a sacrifice might be in order." He gestured toward the deer. "Knowing how special such animals are to your people, I hoped it might appear as a good omen and convince those still looking for a sign that they should join me."

Alarmed at the blasphemous notion, Rhonwen stood, and the fawn backed away fearfully. "You speak of a sacrifice as if it were merely a tool."

The contemplative look on his face gave way to a rueful smile. "I've always known my people were dreadfully superstitious. I didn't realize you were, too."

Rhonwen bristled. "That which is sacred must be treated with respect."

Sertorius raised his hands in mock surrender. "I meant no offense." He offered the fawn another slice of apple, which it munched contentedly. Leaning forward, he stroked the animal's long ears and half-whispered, "If you talk to the gods, my little friend, please tell them I hold them in the highest regard."

Rhonwen smiled despite herself. "I would caution you against being too familiar with an animal you intend to sacrifice."

Sertorius cocked an ear toward the deer, listening to it. He blinked, then looked at Rhonwen. "She says the gods approve."

"Are you mocking me?" she asked.

His contemplative expression returned. "Not at all, and if you felt that way, I apologize." He gazed at the deer nuzzling his palm. "I understand what you mean about getting to know a creature too well." He stroked its soft chin and the deer extended a long pink tongue and licked his wrist.

"You'll perform the sacrifice for me?" he asked.

"Perhaps. If there is no other way to seek the gods' approval for all to see. An offering of such an exquisite creature is fitting." She couldn't escape the feeling his motive would taint the offering.

"Thank you," he said. "I've no qualms about killing a pompous fool like Fufidius, but this little one..." He scratched the deer's chin. "I doubt I could do it myself."

☣ ☣ ☣

Rhonwen had never seen so many Iberian warriors in one place. Added to the expatriate Roman soldiers and foreign mercenaries, Sertorius' army looked formidable, although the odds against him remained enormous. Yet, his ability to make meager resources adequate impressed her. As he laughed, cajoled, and encouraged his ragtag army into fighting for him, her admiration for him soared. She thanked the gods Baia had chosen to follow Aras. Somewhere in the horde of fighting men, near the Trepani contingent, Baia readied herself for the work to come. Here in the midst of Sertorius' camp, Rhonwen knew it was better if Baia stayed away.

Sertorius waved her aside as she guided her wagon into the second position in the baggage train. "I don't want you near the fighting. The wounded will be brought to the rear."

"Then I presume you'll offer condolences to the families of those who die because I couldn't reach them in time."

Sertorius grinned, then leaned forward and patted the neck of his horse. A low cloud of dust swirled about his hand.

"You find that funny?"

"No. It's just your attitude is so refreshing after what I hear from Roman physicians."

She straightened and pulled a double handful of unruly curls past her ears and tied them behind her head with a strip of cloth. "I can't speak for the healers of Rome."

"A wise decision. I'd guess they kill more than they save," he said. "And none want to be anywhere near a battle."

Rhonwen smiled sweetly and nudged her team forward. "Then you're in luck. I'm not Roman. I'll be where I can do some good."

He exhaled in mock defeat. "As you wish, but I'll put a guard detail at your disposal."

"What for? I won't be involved in the fighting."

"You could be if Fufidius escapes my trap."

She bit at her lower lip. This man counted on having his way about things. Why didn't he see she needed to be close to the wounded? If she arrived in time to stanch a blood flow, a man could be saved. "But—"

He held up his hand to silence objection, then dropped his head toward her in a modest bow. "I couldn't concentrate on the battle if I thought I'd left my queen in jeopardy."

Rhonwen turned her head so he might not see her blush. She hated the effect his flattery had on her. He had only to look at her, his gaze soft and warm, and she obeyed. She stared out at the level green flood plain they had crossed, and the path through high grasses beaten down by the columns of warriors ahead of them.

"I must go," he said, "but I'll send someone I trust to accompany you." He spurred his mount away.

She watched him canter into the distance, finally obscured by the dust kicked up by all the horses around him. "If you insist," she said, although only the wind heard her.

Later, as the sun neared the center of the sky, a lone rider approached. Rhonwen assumed it would be some hoary veteran of a hundred campaigns, yet a very young man approached her, his cheeks as smooth as Telo's. What first appeared to be a shadow on his neck and jaw turned out on closer inspection to be a dark birth-mark. The gods sometimes marked those babes who'd done something outstanding in a previous life. Here, she thought, was a lad with destiny both behind and ahead of him.

He reined his horse to a stop and saluted her with a closed fist. "My general commands me to stay with you." He eyed with uncertainty the pair of draft horses Sertorius had insisted she use instead of her slow but even-tempered ox. "Do you need help with your wagon?"

She couldn't help smiling at the seriousness of the young Roman. "I think I can manage."

He seemed both eager to do something and unsure of exactly what. "Then I'll ride ahead and survey the trail. If this were a proper road there'd be no problem, but a hidden rut could—" His voice faded under her gentle laughter.

"If you're my guardian," she said, stifling her amusement, "wouldn't I be safer with you closer?"

The question left him red-faced and speechless, so Rhonwen followed it with others he'd find easier to answer. "What's your name, and how long have you served under Sertorius?"

"I'm Lucius Aemelius," he said, straightening, "and I've marched with Sertorius for two years."

He barely looked old enough to be away from his parents so long. "You seem a bit young for soldiering."

He leveled his shoulders. "Our families have known each other for generations. My father sent me to Sertorius after the troubles in Rome began." He stopped abruptly.

"Go on," she said.

"Sulla had my father arrested. I don't know if he's alive."

"These are difficult times," she said. "For your sake, I hope he fares well, but he has fostered you to an able man."

"Fostered?" Aemelius preened. "I'm his aide and personal messenger. I sit in on all the important councils. If he needs anything or anyone, he sends me." He looked in both directions before crossing one leg over the other and letting the reins fall to the horse's neck. The animal kept pace with those pulling the wagon.

"That's quite an honor," Rhonwen said.

"It's part of my education. One day I'll lead legions of my own, and the name Lucius Aemelius will fall from the trembling lips of barbarians everywhere."

Rhonwen struggled not to laugh. "I feel a little tremble even now."

The blush on the boy's face crept past his cheeks and tinged his ears. "I— I meant no disrespect."

"I can take it," Rhonwen said. "We barbarians are hardy."

Aemelius chewed his lip. "It's just that I don't often have the chance to speak to women." He shrugged. "I don't often have the chance to speak to anyone."

"You stay that busy fighting?"

"Oh no, Sertorius never lets me near the fighting, but I do hear his plans." He gave her a confidential smile. "For instance, I know exactly how he intends to defeat Fufidius."

Rhonwen turned in her seat and reached into the wagon to retrieve a pair of apples. She tossed one to Aemelius who almost dropped it in surprise. "Everyone in the province of Baetica has seen Fufidius leading his legion. Sertorius has fewer than half as many men. What makes him think he can win?"

"Sertorius says we're fortunate the governor is a fool." The lad took a huge bite of apple and chewed it for a moment as he surveyed the warriors ahead of them. "Did you notice we have almost no mounted men with us?"

The question surprised her, for she'd wondered about that very thing. "Why is that?"

"A contingent of Lusitanians rides even now to Fufidius' camp. A quarter of them will attack and then retreat, but slowly enough to lure the enemy into following. When they are far from Fufidius and any hope of rescue, the rest of our riders will counter-attack."

"This will work?"

Aemelius' eyes brightened. "I know it will. Sertorius has done it before. The tactic worked in Africa against a real general. Besides, Sertorius knows how many mounted men Fufidius has, and they're no match for the Lusitanians."

Rhonwen raised an eyebrow in surprise at the mention of Lusitanian horsemen. She knew few could match their expertise. "That's quite a statement for a Roman to make."

He smiled self-deprecatingly. "Sertorius says pride should never blind a man to the truth. On foot, none can compare with a well-trained Roman legion, but when it comes to horseman-ship, the Lusitanians have few peers."

"And Fufidius isn't aware of this?" She tossed her apple core aside.

Aemelius sent his apple core flying after hers. "He suffers the kind of pride Sertorius warns against."

The two fell silent and continued that way until the column halted and word came to make camp. Aemelius promised to return with any news, then rode toward the front of the column.

As Rhonwen prepared her evening meal with the others who'd spent the day following the army, Aemelius returned. She stared at her pot of boiled oats and wondered if she had enough for both of them.

"Magistra Driad," he called, "Sertorius sends his regards and bids you a pleasant night."

She smiled at being singled out by Sertorius, if only via his messenger.

Aemelius motioned to the others at nearby campfires. "Gather 'round," he said. "I have news!"

The men and women crowded closer, and Aemelius waited for them to quiet before he spoke.

"Fufidius dispatched all his horsemen to catch ours," he said. "They obliged us by riding straight into our trap. Fufidius no longer has any mounted men, and we have many new horses!"

A cheer went up accompanied by considerable back-slapping. More than one container of wine appeared and passed among the celebrants.

Aemelius glowed until he saw the wine. He lowered his voice as he addressed Rhonwen. "For their sake, I hope Sertorius doesn't know they've been drinking. He forbids it during a campaign."

"Then don't tell him," Rhonwen said, motioning toward her fire. "Have you eaten? I can make more."

"There's no time," he said, turning to the others. He shouted over the laughter and celebration. "Sertorius commands the baggage train to remain here for the night, though the troops are moving out. A rider will return tomorrow to escort you the rest of the way."

One of the men waved a wineskin. "That suits me!" Others joined his laughter.

As the people wandered back to their own campfires, Aemelius turned to Rhonwen. "You're to move tonight, and I'm commanded to assist you."

The order came as a puzzle. "I thought Sertorius didn't want me near the battle."

"He wants you near it, but not in it," Aemelius said. "I'm to make sure you don't get too close. We'll leave as soon as you're ready."

Rhonwen sat beside her fire and motioned him to sit beside her. He did so reluctantly. "I intend to rest and eat my supper before I go anywhere. What's the hurry?" she asked.

"We've had news that Fufidius is anxious to defeat Sertorius before Lucius Domitius arrives from the north with his legion."

"This means we rush into battle?" She ate her meager portion of oats as Aemelius scuffed dirt over the campfire, then moved to harness the horses.

"Fufidius bragged that the Senate will reward him handsomely when he sends Sertorius to them in chains. He also declared he has no intention of sharing his triumph with Domitius."

Rhonwen threw the rest of her camp gear into the wagon and climbed aboard as he ran the traces and handed the lines to her. He pulled his horse alongside the wagon and took up the position he'd occupied all afternoon.

"Better still," he said as he mounted, "Sertorius has let it be known that we have split our forces, and sent half to the coast while the rest are camped on low ground beside the Baetis River near Nebrissa."

Rhonwen frowned. "Split our forces? Who'd be foolish enough to believe Sertorius would do that?"

"Fufidius!" Aemelius laughed. "We'll catch him shortly after he leaves the road. There's a valley where our archers and slingers will make quick work of the legion. His men have no discipline and will collapse without leadership."

She clucked at the horses and slapped the lines lightly on their haunches to make them step out. Defeating the provincial governor would send a powerful message throughout Iberia. Those who'd suffered under the Roman heel would flock to Sertorius. "What happens when Domitius arrives?" she asked, still surprised at the depth of the lad's knowledge of his general's plans.

He shrugged. "If I know Sertorius, he'll have troops on the way to meet Domitius as soon as we're finished here."

✠ ✠ ✠

Rhonwen and Aemelius hid the wagon and horses in a stand of trees a considerable distance from the ambush site. The army had marched all night to be in place by the time Fufidius and his legion arrived. The need for healers would be dire, and Rhonwen bristled at not being allowed nearer the battle, but Aemelius forbade it.

"Then help me prepare for the wounded," she said as she unloaded tables and tools, rolled bandages, and set out her supply of herbs and medicines. Aemelius made himself as useful as possible for one who had no idea what she intended. He fetched when she asked and hauled whatever needed moving. When satisfied with their readiness, Rhonwen gathered nearby deadfall to make a fire.

"What are you doing?" he asked and laid a restraining hand on her as she reached for a dried branch.

She arched a brow in annoyance. "I'm about to give birth," she said and brought out her tinder and flint.

He stared at her without comprehension.

"What does it look like I'm doing?" she asked.

"Please don't be angry with me," he said. "I'm only doing as I've been ordered." He put his hand over hers. "That means no fires. Fufidius might see the smoke, or worse."

"Worse?"

He nodded. "Sertorius might see it. He gave me orders to stay hidden. The price he exacts for disobedience is more than I wish to pay."

The boy's words instantly brought an image to Rhonwen of the two men who had tried to rape her. Out of habit she touched the scar on her cheek. One mental picture quickly faded to another as she recalled the chained Gyrisoenians who watched Sertorius burn their clanhold to the ground. She slipped the flint back into her pocket.

They waited all day, sometimes dozing, sometimes straining to hear the sounds of battle. The blare of a war horn could carry a great distance, yet they heard nothing. By late afternoon they began to wonder whether Fufidius had ignored the bait. The sun sank low on the horizon before they saw anyone. A dust cloud whirled along the track toward them.

"Wait here!" said Aemelius, and he ran, hiding near the edge of the wooded space for a better look.

Moments later Rhonwen heard him hail the riders. Iberians! They would be carrying the injured. She prayed for strength to care for an onslaught of wounded, and smoke or no, now she would light the fire.

The men, dirt-streaked and weary, rode past her. From the proud way they sat their horses, none doubted their victory. Those who helped the wounded rode toward her wagon, the healer's red standard a guide. Only a few men arrived and Rhonwen was surprised to see no more.

The first man cradled his left arm against his chest. A gaping wound separated the muscles at his shoulder. He was pale from loss of blood and leaned heavily on his companion.

She rinsed the wound, which bled freely, with clean water. Such bleeding was a good sign. She only needed a needle to sew the cut closed and a poultice to prevent the blackening of the tissue. "What happened in the battle?"

"We attacked from the hills and cut them to pieces," the warrior said. "We charged. They panicked. It was easy."

She finished with him just as warriors arrived with more wounded. She determined which would benefit most from her assistance and concentrated on them. Those who could wait, she ordered to sit in the shade beside the wagon. A few were too badly injured for anyone but the gods to save, and she asked Aemelius to make them as comfortable as he could beneath the trees. She wished she had a supply of Orlan's pain-reducing white powder, but she and Baia had run out long before Orlan returned from Gaul and had never been able to get more.

By nightfall, she had seen to all her patients. As she washed blood from her hands and stripped off her gore-stained tunic, two more warriors hobbled in. She slipped into a clean garment and dried her hands, then turned to face them.

Sertorius stood beside Cesada, the big warrior who had originally taken her to Aras. The general supported the Trepani, who put no weight on his foot. The look on Cesada's face puzzled her. He appeared embarrassed as Sertorius helped him sit.

"This big fellow decided to capture Fufidius all by himself," Sertorius said.

Rhonwen regarded the Trepani with respect.

"He hacked his way through a half dozen legionnaires to get to him," Sertorius said, "and just as he was about to drag the fat old fool from his saddle, the horse stepped on Cesada's foot."

Cesada closed his eyes. His breathing remained even, but frustration colored his cheeks. She called for Aemelius to help her strip off Cesada's leggings and sandals. When she pressed on the middle of his foot, he winced. It had already swollen to twice normal size, and the deep bruising suggested broken bones.

"Lie down." She pushed him back and shoved a pile of furs beneath his calf and foot. "Stay here and don't move."

Cesada nodded and lay back with a deep sigh.

"How badly is he hurt?" Sertorius asked.

"His foot's broken."

Cesada groaned, not from the pain, she suspected, but from what he knew would be a long recovery.

"Fufidius got away?" she asked.

Sertorius shook his head. "No. Cesada slowed him down enough for others to reach him. We won the day. By my count, we killed over two thousand of his men."

That many Roman deaths had to mean thousands of Iberians killed and wounded as well. "How many did we lose?"

"Fewer than a hundred dead on the battlefield. I don't know how many more we'll lose here." He looked around at the wounded and gestured to Aemelius. "I trust my mottled young friend has taken good care of you?"

Rhonwen frowned at his jest about the lad's birthmark. "One must never make light of the gods' handiwork. Young Aemelius bears their stamp. He should be proud of it."

"He hates it," Sertorius said. "I tease him because he's convinced himself it's the reason young women won't talk to him." He rubbed absentmindedly at the scar crossing his face, then watched the lad scramble to feed several of the wounded. "How many are here?"

"About three dozen," she said. "Fortunately, most will live." She touched two purpled toes on Cesada's left foot. "Including you," she said to him. "Aras will be pleased to hear that."

"So am I," Sertorius said. "Have you any word about Aras' leg? Can he travel?"

"Probably," she said.

Cesada grunted. "Where he goes, I go."

Sertorius clapped him on the shoulder. "You'll need each other. I want Aras to stay close to Quintus Aespis, my lieutenant. I'm giving Aespis command of enough men to dispatch Domitius, and I want Aras to learn everything he can from him."

Cesada acknowledged the command as Rhonwen tried to straighten his damaged toes. If they didn't heal properly, he would always limp. For now, she could only ask the gods to consider him worthy of being healed.

Sertorius leaned close to Cesada. "I expect another victory, and when it comes, make sure word of it reaches me privately." Cesada agreed and Sertorius looked up at Rhonwen. "When you're through here, come with me. There's something I'd like to show you."

She nodded, although uncertain what he had in mind. "What is it?"

"Do you recall the white hind I asked you to sacrifice? I want you to see what the little scamp has learned to do."

"You brought it here?" she asked, incredulous.

"Yes." Sertorius shrugged and grinned. "She's a clever thing and comes when I whistle. She'll lick my ear and kicks up her heels when I offer her a bit of apple. She will even lie down when I command it."

Rhonwen stared at him. "She's to be sacrificed and you made her a pet?"

"How could I do otherwise? She makes only the simplest of demands on me, and I enjoy her company."

"You're serious?"

"I am always serious."

✠ ✠ ✠

Following the victory over Fufidius, Rhonwen returned to the general encampment to prepare for the sacrifice of the sacred hind. Baia arrived a few days later and added the usual turmoil. She gave Rhonwen no respite to get ready for the ceremony, although she knew more than a hundred clan chiefs would attend. Instead of helping, Baia railed against her for not going with Aras and the rest of the warriors to face Domitius.

"Don't they need a healer as badly as your precious Roman?" Baia had asked.

Rhonwen's answer, that Sertorius had ordered her to stay behind, felt hollow.

Now, when she needed to clear her mind of such thoughts, Baia's words intruded, as did her renewed efforts to push Rhonwen into Aras' arms. Under other circumstances she might have wanted his attentions. The man had attributes Rhonwen certainly found appealing, both physical and social, but when compared to Sertorius, he fared poorly. Aras sought his destiny as if he could command it, that he need say only, "Here I am. Treat me like a king," for the wish to become true. Sertorius allowed his destiny to find him, and he wore it as comfortably as an old cloak.

Rhonwen slipped her killing knife into the belt of her robe and inspected the blood bowl, although she had scrubbed it earlier. It wouldn't do to let some impurity affect the results of scrying the hind's blood. Indeed, the gods might choose to reveal in it the future of the entire war, but she doubted it. She'd never had a useful scry in her life, one of the reasons she'd chosen the healer's path.

Satisfied she could do no more, Rhonwen signaled her readiness to Aemelius, and he accompanied her to the place Sertorius had chosen for the ceremony.

The site, a sheltered clearing beside the River Baetis, would afterward serve as a meeting place for the clan chiefs. Surrounding hardwoods softened the harsh summer sun just as thick grasses cushioned the ground.

Rhonwen approached the makeshift altar Sertorius had provided. Built by Roman hands to Roman standards, it stood too square. Unadorned and unblooded, the thing felt unnatural, more an affront to the gods than something with which to honor them. Yet, she supposed, it was better than nothing.

"Good morning," Sertorius said from behind her.

Rhonwen turned quickly at the sound of his voice. "I didn't hear you approach."

"I've been here all morning, back behind the trees. It's quite restful."

She saw someone limping away from the shelter of the trees: Cesada, judging from his great size. What had happened in the fight against Domitius that he would leave Aras to return?

Sertorius smiled, took her hand, and bent to kiss her fingers. Her heart beat faster despite her efforts to will it calm, and all thoughts of the battle, the Trepani warrior, and his chief evaporated. She wanted desperately to speak, to say something memorable, but the words wouldn't come.

"I must ask another favor of you," he said. "It's about the hind. I've grown overly fond of her."

Rhonwen responded quickly, relieved to be on firmer ground. "Didn't I caution you about that?"

He nodded, looking away.

"My knife is sharp," she said. "The killing stroke will be quick and clean. She will feel no pain."

He looked up, his eye moving slowly from her hands to her face. "There are worse deaths."

"Rhiannon is gentle," Rhonwen said. "Those who stay with her in the Otherworld, whether man or beast, receive the peace to which they are entitled. You needn't mourn for this creature. If the gods had not intended it to die this way, they wouldn't have allowed you to have it."

"We worship different gods," Sertorius said. "Since the hind came to me, does it mean my gods sent her? Perhaps she was a gift from Diana."

Rhonwen shrugged. "Perhaps. Does it matter?"

"The hind trusts me," he said. ""More than that. She depends on me like a child."

"Then it's the perfect sacrifice!" Rhonwen followed the exclamation with a frown. "If what we give to the gods means nothing to us, how can we expect it to mean anything to them?"

Sertorius remained silent for a time before he spoke, his voice low and his disappointment undisguised. "I suppose you're right."

She patted his hand. "I'm a druid as well as a healer. I read the signs the gods leave. Thus they've made their will known for generations beyond time." She gave his fingers a light squeeze. "I've no choice in the matter."

"We always have choices," Sertorius said after a moment. "We may not like any of them, but they still exist." He turned his attention to the clan chiefs gathering in front of the altar. Most talked, ate, or made plans with subordinates.

Rhonwen's thoughts drifted back to Sertorius' words. She did have a choice, just as she had the night she came to his home, ate his food, and shared his bed. She chose not to kill him.

Sertorius silenced the crowd and bade them sit, and then he motioned for her to begin. A few of Sertorius' nearby Romans whispered their surprise that an Iberian led the ceremony.

She stepped in front of the altar and raised both arms. "O-ghe!" she cried, her voice silencing all others. "We are met here today to beseech the gods to show us the path to freedom."

Still bothered by conflicting emotions, Rhonwen kept the opening rituals brief. Several of the chiefs moved restlessly, indicating their discomfort with ceremonies so loosely observed.

Curiosity replaced their initial hesitation. Sertorius strode to the altar, his blue cloak bright and luxurious in the sunlight.

He thanked Rhonwen with a deep bow and then leaned back against the altar facing the clan chiefs.

Many of those watching him were fearless, men taught since birth to disdain armor as something no true hero needed, yet they cringed at the Roman's casual familiarity with the furniture of the gods.

Sertorius' rich voice filled the farthest shaded nook of the clearing. He spoke to them in their own language, oddly accented with the guttural tones of Transalpine Gaul, but plain enough for all to understand.

"Metellus commanded four generals," he said, pacing in front of the altar, "and we've defeated two of them. Even now Iberian heroes face the legion of Domitius, whom you know as the governor of Tarraconensis. I have complete faith in these men and in the officers I picked to lead them." He waved to Aemelius, who directed several men to open chests of gold and silver coins at Sertorius' feet.

"Such wealth as this, wrested from Fufidius, I will distribute among those who fought with me then. By their valor they have earned it."

Most of the chiefs nodded. The sharing of spoils was a wise and long-standing custom. Men should not be expected to risk their lives without reward.

"One thing more," Sertorius said, "I've made arrangements to provide them with uniforms, and shields of a common size and shape. When we face the remaining legions, I want Metellus to know he deals with a united foe."

He swept his arms in a broad gesture. "Can there be any doubt the gods favor us? We have already defeated two armies of superior size. Imagine how much we can accomplish if all the clans of Iberia join under a single banner."

Sertorius raised a fist, the sign for Spanus to release the hind. Rhonwen removed the knife from her belt. Sertorius whistled softly and knelt as the deer took fragile steps through the men, who shrank away from it.

When the hind saw Sertorius, she made straight for him, leaping gracefully over obstacles and touching the ground so lightly she left no track. The chiefs looked awestruck. When the deer paused in front of Sertorius and allowed him to pet it, they gasped.

"Behold this tiny deer," Sertorius said, "a gift to me from the goddess Diana. Have you ever seen such bravery? What deer walks among hunters?" He gestured to Rhonwen standing at the altar with her sacrificial knife. "What creature approaches its own sacrifice unafraid?" He stared hard into their faces, one by one. "How many of you could do the same?"

He gathered the long-limbed animal in his arms and lifted it gently from the ground. The deer remained calm. "See for yourselves!" he said. "This white hind, sent to me by the gods, must surely be a sign."

He rubbed the deer with his cheek and the animal responded, nuzzling his ear. He closed his eye, suddenly intense.

"Silence," he whispered, and every man in the glade fell quiet. The deer continued to press its soft lips against his ear. Moments later, vast relief and joy spread across the Roman's face.

"My friends," he said, making no effort to hide the tremble in his voice, "the hind has spoken to me."

He surveyed his audience, and even Rhonwen felt herself caught within the spell of his words. "Domitius has fallen." His voice rose, and he stroked the deer to keep it calm. "Domitius has fallen! His army has fled into the hills."

All the chiefs stood.

Sertorius turned to Rhonwen, the hind still in his arms, and shook his head. "This creature is a gift too sacred for sacrifice."

The chiefs murmured agreement, and Rhonwen realized what message Cesada had brought earlier. Sertorius played the crowd like a master bard stroking a harp. The hind had never been at risk. She sheathed her blade.

"Metellus has but one general left, and then he must face us himself." Sertorius stared out at them, turning slowly so that each could see the deer in his arms, its long white ears twitching in the breeze, and its narrow pink tongue curling out.

"Will you join me? Will you help me drive Metellus from these lands? Together we can push him into the sea!"

To a man, the chiefs swept forward, surrounding Sertorius with cheers and vows of allegiance. They crowded so close that Rhonwen was pushed away.

Sertorius smiled at her as the gap between them widened. Whether or not the hind had spoken to him, it had surely spoken to the others.

16

A man appeared today and asked why the enclave no longer remembers the Ageless One. Were it not for the staves of my predecessors, I would not have understood his question. These are difficult times, I said, and we must mind our coins.

Do you offer prayer in such a meager fashion? he asked.

We are moderate in all things, I said.

Then how would I have the gods measure out their bless-ings, he wished to know.

Abundantly, said I.

Then remember the Ageless One that way, he said.

— The poet stave of Blaiset, 33rd Master of Mount Eban Enclave

Iberia

Aemelius had brought orders from Sertorius about where they should be stationed during the next attack, this time on Metellus. As Sertorius escalated his campaign, such skirmishes had become frequent. Baia had consented to stay with Rhonwen as they worked well together, although she'd invited the Trepani to camp nearby.

"Don't you think Aras looks handsome in his new helmet and tunic?" Baia asked as she and Rhonwen prepared their wagon for another move.

Rhonwen scratched at a rust spot on a pair of shears with her fingernail. "Yes, he does," she said, hoping Baia would drop the subject.

"It's gold," Baia said.

"What's gold?"

"Don't you notice anything?" Baia snapped. "The bear on his helm is gold."

"It must make the helmet heavy," Rhonwen said. "I suppose he thinks it makes him look as tall as his men." She regretted her words the moment she said them. Aras deserved better.

"But he'll never be as tall as that Roman, will he?" Baia threw one of the parcels into the wagon hard enough for it to bounce out.

"Mother, please don't start again."

Baia retrieved the parcel from the dust and hauled herself into the seat of the wagon as Rhonwen readied the hitch for the horses. "If you had any sense, you'd march straight into Aras' camp and offer to handfast with him before he dies trying to prove himself worthy of you."

"Aras doesn't care about me."

Baia huffed. "Have you seen another woman in any of these camps who's caught his eye?"

"Honestly, Mother, I don't care."

"Why can't this Roman of yours finish his campaign? It's obvious I won't be having any grandchildren while the fighting drags on."

Rhonwen stared at her in surprise. "I thought you wanted to see the Romans driven from Iberia."

"Of course I do, but I never thought we'd need another Roman to help us do it. This man will bring ruin to us all."

"Haven't you seen the way our people hold up their heads? Winning against extraordinary odds gives us a pride we haven't enjoyed for generations. Besides, who do you think paid for that bear on Aras' helmet?"

An approaching horse and rider caught their attention. Aemelius sent up an enormous dust cloud as he pulled his mount to a halt beside the wagon. "There's been a change in plan," he announced breathlessly. "Metellus prepares to besiege Langos and—"

"The Trepani clanhold?" Baia asked.

He nodded.

Rhonwen nudged his leg to get his attention. "Why Langos?"

"There's but one well inside the city walls," Aemelius said. "Besides, the Trepani have supported Sertorius almost from the start, and Metellus wants to punish them as a warning to the other clans."

"How can we help?" Rhonwen asked.

"Can you sew a water skin? My lord Sertorius has ordered two thousand such skins to be filled with water and will pay for every one delivered into Langos before Metellus arrives. You'd be amazed at how many clamor to perform the task. Sertorius and your friend, Aras, are selecting from the volunteers even now. None will be chosen who aren't also willing to escort non-combatants out of the town when they leave."

"Is Aras going with them?" Rhonwen asked.

"He could," Baia said, "his leg is all but healed."

Aemelius shrugged. "All I know is we need several hundred more water skins immediately."

"Most of the warriors in his camp carry such skins," Rhonwen said. "Why can't he use theirs?"

"He will if he has to, but those men have to remain ready to march. Armies don't move far without water."

Baia grimaced. "It appears we're in for a busy night."

Aemelius gestured toward the encampment. "Extra hides are available at the Trepani tents. Make or borrow as many water bags as you can and bring them to our compound." He turned his horse and spurred it back to Sertorius' camp.

The women visited every wagon in the baggage train to secure one of every two such skins the drivers owned. By the time they reached Sertorius' camp, their cart laden with donated water skins and new ones they had sewn during the night, the pre-dawn sky had turned ashen. They hoped the afternoon would remain as overcast and cool as the morning, for the water bearers would need any advantage they could get.

Aemelius helped them unload. "There's been another change in plans."

Baia began muttering even before Aemelius finished speaking. "I suppose now he wants us to fill the skins with wine!"

Aemelius smiled, but his face and eyes told the tale of a night without rest. "A captured courier revealed that Metellus is so confident of victory, that he brought only enough water for a five-day siege. As some of those supplies have already been consumed, he's sent one of his lieutenants to fetch more."

How Metellus became a general astonished Rhonwen. The man made one colossal error after another, and a tactician like Sertorius seized the advantage from such mistakes. "I'm sure Sertorius will intercept them," she said.

"Stopping a courier or a caravan is one thing," Aemelius said. "Stopping an entire legion is another."

Baia squinted. "He sends a legion to bring him water?"

"At least five thousand men, maybe six. Sertorius has already chosen the spot from which we'll attack them, and he wants all the healers stationed nearby."

Baia yawned and rubbed her eyes. "I didn't want to sleep anyway."

"I'll drive," Rhonwen said. "You can curl up in the back of the wagon." For a moment the hardness on her mother's face lifted, but then her brief smile faded, and Baia climbed into the cart and settled down to rest.

Rhonwen turned to Aemelius. "Will you be joining us?"

He shook his head. "Today I ride with the Lusitanians." He sat up straighter, and the weariness he'd shown earlier dissipated. "My first battle!"

Rhonwen felt a pang of sorrow. Never had Aemelius looked so much like Telo.

✠ ✠ ✠

The three men assigned to escort Rhonwen, Baia, and another healer to their place near the ambush site were all recovering from wounds received in previous battles. The men, two Celtiberians and a Roman expatriate who had been with Sertorius since his days in Gaul, exchanged few words as they directed the wagons to high ground and wedged rocks in front of the wheels to keep them from rolling down the steep grade.

Baia wasted little time striking up a conversation with the other healer, a thin, aging Mauretanian named Mohan whose eyes sparkled with a ready wit. His speech was so measured and precise, however, that Rhonwen imagined he rehearsed every word before uttering it. At least he kept Baia interested with his talk of poultices and unguents, some unique to his home in North Africa.

"I'll unload the supplies," Rhonwen said, moving to the back of her wagon. Baia helped Mohan remove the things he needed from his wagon.

With the horses hobbled away from the wagons and the three guards lounging nearby, the healers soon had nothing to do but wait for the casualties to arrive. Rhonwen munched a fig and threw a stick for Iago to fetch. The dog brought it back, the prance long gone from his old legs. He surrendered the stick only when Rhonwen snapped her fingers and pointed to the ground. She rewarded the beast by throwing the stick again as far as she could. Eventually she let him keep it, and he happily stretched out in the shade beneath the wagon to nap.

Rhonwen slept beside the dog and dreamed of hot soapy water and the strong, steady hands of Sertorius.

Iago's barking jerked her awake. She rolled over to look for the dog and spotted dozens of Romans, their weapons drawn, trudging up the hill. Blood-spattered and dirty, they bore looks of determined anger. The three men ordered to protect them were nowhere to be seen.

"Romans!" she yelled.

"Grab a weapon!"

While Baia and Mohan struggled with something in the back of the other wagon, Rhonwen scrambled from her resting place.

The horses were too far away to reach, and the only weapon at hand was a scythe they kept to cut tall grasses for bedding. Rhonwen grabbed it and raced to the front of the wagon.

"I'm ready," Baia said, brandishing a knife Rhonwen had last seen her use to gut a chicken. Mohan spilled an armload of arrows at his feet and bent to string a bow.

"Mother, run!" Rhonwen said, realizing Baia intended to make a stand.

"Let them come," Baia yelled back. "I'm too old to run." Iago had taken a position by her side and continued to bark.

Rhonwen raised the tongue of the wagon and pushed it back against the seat to get it out of her way. The sound of the battle grew nearer, and the Romans closed rapidly. She needed another idea.

Using the scythe handle to push away one of the large stones wedged in front of the wagon wheels, she ran to another wheel and pushed the next stone away. Then the third. She looked up in time to see the nearest Roman, barely two paces from her, fall backward with an arrow in his chest. Mohan slowed their advance but couldn't end it. Iago attacked the Roman closest to Baia, leaping at his chest and bearing him to the ground. The next man in the advance raised his sword, but the dog darted out of the way, barking and snarling. She threw the scythe at the Roman, and another arrow finished him.

Though only one stone remained beneath a wheel, the weight of the wagon held it firmly in place. Rhonwen gripped the spokes with both hands and shoved against it. The wagon rocked slightly then settled back against the stone.

Mohan sent arrow after arrow into the midst of the attackers. In response, the soldiers overlapped their shields and formed a protective wall. Though it sheltered them from the arrows, it slowed them. Iago rushed in to bite at exposed ankles.

Rhonwen clawed at the stone in front of the wheel, but realizing it was futile, she abandoned her efforts. Instead, she dug under it, using the weight of the wagon to press it down. If she could dig deep enough, the wheel might roll over the rock.

Finally, the wagon lurched forward and crushed the stone into the depression she'd carved.

Rhonwen jumped to her feet and clambered into the front of the wagon as it gained speed. She looked downhill at the Romans, whose shield wall wavered as the men behind it realized the wagon was headed straight for them. Iago singled out a victim and drove him away from the others.

Rhonwen gripped the wagon tongue with both hands, although she knew she lacked the strength to steer the wagon with it. She heard Baia's voice in the distance, still cursing. The wagon's speed increased, and with each bounce its passage grew louder.

Mohan's arrows continued to land among the Roman shields and spread fear on the Roman faces. Some of them turned to meet a group of Iberians moving up from below.

Rhonwen screamed, part anger, part fear, and part blood lust for the worthless men who attacked healers. Moments before the wagon's impact, the Romans scattered, their shields forgotten in their panic to elude the runaway wagon. They screamed and cursed as the heavy cart crushed bone against rock.

Suddenly the wagon passed them, still gaining speed. Rhonwen looked back at the mayhem she'd wrought when the wagon bounced again, hard, and threw her into the air.

The world spun around her. She landed on her back, and the impact forced the air from her lungs, cutting off her war cry in mid-scream.

The wagon slammed into a cluster of boulders halfway down the hillside. Straining to draw a breath, Rhonwen raised herself on an elbow and glanced at the wreckage.

The sounds of battle drew her dazed attention uphill.

A dozen Romans fell upon the hilltop position held by Baia and Mohan. The soldiers stopped only long enough to hack the healers down before disappearing over the top of the rise.

Rhonwen dragged herself to her feet and struggled up the hill even as an avenging tide of Iberian warriors swept past her. Near the back of the horde trudged Cesada, his great chest heaving as he worked to keep up with the men ahead of him.

When one of the wounded Romans raised a feeble hand for aid he stopped. Arrows protruded from the man's chest and side. They were painful wounds, and likely fatal over time.

Cesada brought his heavy sword down on the Roman's neck, hard enough to sever it just below the jaw and bend the iron. "Tend to Driad Baia," he said, straightening the blade. "I'll deal with any here who still breathe."

Rhonwen stumbled up the hill with the sounds of pursuit ahead and the sounds of execution behind. She found Baia lying next to the dead African, her hands pressed against a wound in her chest. Iago, bleeding from a dozen cuts, lay close beside her.

"Rest easy," Rhonwen said through her tears as she fell to her knees and cradled Baia's head in her lap.

Baia tried to speak. She formed the words but had too little breath to voice them. Rhonwen pressed her ear close to Baia's mouth and strained to hear.

"A blood price for a blood oath," the old woman said.

Rhonwen jerked her head back with an anguished protest. Would not even death bring her mother's forgiveness? Before she could voice a defense, Baia died.

Cesada approached softly, his curved Iberian blade dripping gore. He looked down at the dead healers, his usually flinty face twisted by emotion.

Cesada touched her hand as if he'd received a blessing. "I'll see that both Aras and Sertorius know what happened here. There are many praises to be sung. If I were a bard, I'd have much work to do."

Rhonwen would sing only of death.

✠ ✠ ✠

Rhonwen sat in the shade of Mohan's wagon. Though smaller than the one she'd wrecked, it would suffice for her needs. Cesada had loaded it with tools, supplies, and personal belongings salvaged from the wreckage and left her to sort through it. The task required several days, but she was glad to have something to take her mind off Baia.

Iago sat beside her, and Rhonwen stroked the loyal animal's neck. None of his wounds proved serious, for which she thanked the gods repeatedly. "You're better at this than I am," she said, as the dog leaned into her hand.

Baia's funeral signaled a period of mourning. Rhonwen wore dark ribbons in her hair and marked her cheeks with ashes, blending the traditional signs expected of unmarried daughters and fellow healers. She kept her head bowed and her voice low, but none of these things gave her comfort for the sense of loss or freedom from the guilt of her relief at her mother's death.

One bright moment shone when a message from Orlan arrived while she worked on the wagon. She read the Latin eagerly but then regretted her haste. She should have refused to read it until she'd finished her mourning penance.

She settled under the shade of a tree to reread the missive. Typically brief, Orlan focused on his failure to cultivate the baneweed. Despite the care he lavished on them, only two plants survived, and neither prospered. She read with delight that he considered moving to the north where the climate might be more like Armorica's. Best of all, she might get to see him.

A man approached, his wobbling gait unmistakable. She folded the vellum and waved. Aras had escaped the blood fever, but would forever carry a reminder of the accident. His days of walking on his toes to make himself appear taller were over. The thought made her smile, and when he saw it, he brightened.

He greeted her with his usual bravado but soon grew more serious. "I'm sorry to hear Baia has passed through to the Otherworld," he said. "There are few like her."

Rhonwen agreed. Aras was more right than he realized. "I'd be honored to become half as good a healer as she was."

Aras looked at her with open admiration. "You have other qualities, such as a noble bloodline. Your children will be wise and brave."

"Brave?"

"Everyone knows how you attacked the *togas*, running them down with a wagon. Amazing! Cesada said—"

"Enough." She held out her hands, and Aras pulled her to her feet. "You told me Cesada was a fighter, not a talker." She dusted her skirt. "Now it seems he can't keep his mouth shut."

Aras looked at her in bewilderment. "Such an act of bravery should be sung by the bards."

She shook her head. "Such an act of stupidity should be used as an example of how not to treat a wagon."

"You've earned a place of honor at a thousand tables," he said. "I've come to ask you to accept that place at mine." He reached for her hand. "Baia said we were meant for each other."

Rhonwen withdrew her hand. "Cesada isn't the only one who talked too much."

"Think of the children we could have," Aras said. "I have cattle and land."

She stopped him with a hand to his lips. "Aras, this should wait until I'm no longer in mourning."

"Of course," he said as he forced a gold armband from his biceps, slipped it down his arm, and wrapped her fingers around it. "Just remember, I lead the Trepani in war, and soon I will lead them in everything else. I would have you by my side."

Rhonwen looked into his eyes and saw a simple, honorable man, one in whom guile would never replace tradition or loyalty. "I'm flattered."

Aras straightened. "Good! Then—"

"And I'll think about it."

He seemed not to have heard her. "I'll have your wagon moved to my camp. You'll be safer."

She held the gold armband out to him, but he refused to take it.

The sound of a rider made them both turn toward the road. A young man, dust covered, slid from his horse.

"Aemelius!" Rhonwen hurried toward him. "I'm so glad to see you. No one I asked could tell me what happened to you."

"You didn't ask me," Aras muttered, following close behind.

Aemelius smiled wearily. "I've been with Sertorius."

Aras clasped the young man's hand in welcome. Rhonwen embraced him. "I feared you were dead."

Aras blinked at Aemelius. "Sertorius let you join the fighting?" He turned to Rhonwen. "He doesn't even have his first beard."

"Please pardon the interruption, Magistra," Aemelius said, "but my lord Sertorius bade me invite you to dine with him this evening."

Though she'd seen him at Baia's funeral, Sertorius had been surrounded by clan chiefs. There had been no opportunity to speak with him.

"What's this about?" she asked.

Aras cleared his throat. "Kindly advise Sertorius that Driad Rhonwen has made other plans."

Rhonwen glared at Aras, thrust the gold bracelet into his hand and turned back to the young Roman. "Tell Sertorius I'll be pleased to join him."

"Excellent!" Aemelius remounted. "I'm sorry about your mother. I'll dispatch an escort as soon as I return."

"There's no need for that," Aras said. "I'll accompany her. Besides we have much to discuss."

"As you wish," Aemelius said. He kicked his horse into a run.

Rhonwen faced Aras. "We have nothing to discuss."

He looked at her with the same unflinching confidence he'd shown the day she'd met him. "Forgive my poor choice of words," he said. "We can use the time to get to know each other."

✠ ✠ ✠

Rhonwen did what she could to make herself presentable. Satisfied she could do no more, she saddled one of the horses Sertorius had given her to pull the wagon and rode out of the encampment.

Though there may have been a shorter route, she ran little risk of becoming lost if she stuck to the Roman road. Sertorius and his original band of expatriates and Africans had taken up residence in the captured estate of the provincial governor. Such a prominent structure would not be far from the road, nor difficult to find.

Rhonwen recalled the first time she'd been invited to dine with Sertorius. Memories of mud-drenchings and cantankerous old women gave way to thoughts of slippery, smooth-shaven skin, a silk gown, and the passion they'd shared. She squirmed in the saddle and wondered if he remembered that night as vividly as she did.

She laughed at her girlish response to such long-ago events. She was older now, and hopefully wiser. Still, she wondered what he expected of her. Without warning, two heavily armed Lusitanians appeared on either side of her.

"State your business," demanded the senior of the two.

She fixed him with a stare. "Since when are the movements of a driad questioned?"

"No one's movements go unquestioned," he replied. He held the horse's bridle with his left hand and kept his right on the hilt of his sword.

"I'm on my way to dine with General Sertorius," she said.

He scowled. "You travel alone?"

"Yes."

"We aren't the only ones who patrol this road," he said. "There are those who have no respect for healers."

She jerked the reins to free the bridle from the warrior's hand. "I'll try to remember that."

The warriors sauntered back to the trees alongside the road. How she had missed their approach troubled her. She had never been so addlebrained when traveling with Baia, and she regretted leaving Iago behind.

Soon thereafter another guard, this time an Iberian dressed as one of Sertorius' legionnaires, challenged her.

She growled at him. "Am I to be stopped by every man I see?"

His face formed a grim mask as he, too, held the horse. "State your business."

"I'm on my way to dine with General Sertorius, but if my journey continues to be interrupted every few steps, I'll be having breakfast with him instead."

The guard bowed in apology. "I was told to expect a woman with an escort."

He sheathed his sword and produced a wooden rod decorated with white and blue stripes. "Keep this in your hand as you ride," he said surrendering it to her. "You won't be challenged again."

She accepted the short wand irritably. "Why didn't the first guard give me one of these?"

The man smiled. "He probably didn't recognize the great driad who saved the lands of the humble Bateri."

Rhonwen squinted at the guard, his name and face bursting suddenly into her memory. "Milo?"

He bowed.

"What are you doing here?" she asked, amazed to see the farmer dressed like a soldier.

"I've come to fight," he said proudly, then let his shoulders slump a bit. "Though in truth, I've yet to see a battle." He brightened. "But I led two dozen water bearers through the mountains to Langos and guided twice that many women and children back down those same passes to my own village. The General himself gave me my reward and asked me to join him."

Rhonwen laughed. "It's good to know Sertorius recognizes worthy men when he sees them."

"May the gods push the stones from your path," Milo said.

She raised a hand. "May they return you safely to your family when these troubles are done." With a firm grip on the baton, she waved and rode on, saying a short prayer for the gentle man and his people.

Though her route took her through the camped ranks of thousands of men, no one else stopped her until she came within sight of the former governor's estate. Aemelius stared at her in surprise for a moment before rushing forward to help her dismount.

"Where's Aras?" he asked, craning his neck to see down the empty road behind her.

Rhonwen shrugged. "I've no idea."

"Sertorius will be furious when he discovers Aras didn't accompany you."

Rhonwen patted the young man's arm and handed him the baton. "Aras had nothing to do with it. I left without him."

Aemelius rolled his gaze skyward. "As long as you're here safely, I suppose it doesn't matter, but please, let me know when you plan to leave."

She agreed, if only to receive the baton for the return trip, and Aemelius ushered her into the sumptuous quarters. No signs of struggle with the previous resident stained these walls.

"Rhonwen!" Sertorius said, his white toga brilliant in the late afternoon sun. The purple stripe at its edge lent it an air of royalty.

Sertorius dismissed Aemelius and escorted her into a spacious courtyard where comfortable lounge chairs and tables of fruit, fresh bread, cheeses, and cooked meat had been set out.

"How many others are you expecting?" she asked as she eyed the banquet.

"I planned to feed Aras and his men before I sent them to inspect the camp. Where is he, by the way?"

Rhonwen explained, puzzled by the growing look of concern on his face.

"Promise me you'll never do that again," he said.

"I've learned not to make vows I don't intend to keep."

Sertorius laid a warm hand over hers. "I've never known a woman so intent on throwing herself in harm's way. I hold myself responsible for your mother's death. I should've known the ranks would give way where they did."

Rhonwen gently pushed his hand aside. "Only the gods know everything, and sometimes even they forget."

Sertorius watered the wine before splashing a bit on the floor for his gods and handing one of the vessels to her. She took a deep draught.

"You're not responsible for Mother's death. She chose to die. She could have gotten out of the way the moment she saw Cesada and his warriors starting up the hill. The Romans would never have taken the time to chase her. They were too busy running for their lives."

Sertorius pursed his lips. "Cesada didn't mention that. The only details he gave me were about you."

She winced that he'd heard the story. "He told you I wrecked my own wagon?"

"He sang high praises for a resourceful woman with great courage." Sertorius smiled. "You haven't changed so much from long ago."

"I'm not the child you avenged in Castulo, nor the girl who shared your bath," Rhonwen said. She willed herself to relax, to banish the maelstrom of emotions that had plagued her since Baia died.

He reached out and gently touched her hair. "You're a woman now. I'm quite aware of that."

When Aras touched her, she felt a hand, but when Sertorius touched her, she felt something primal and urgent. She reached for his arm, but he'd moved away. She turned to see Aemelius standing in the courtyard.

"What is it?" Sertorius asked, his annoyance plain.

"Aras and two dozen Trepani warriors are outside. He demands to see Magistra Rhonwen."

She sat on one of the lounges and rubbed her temples. No wonder Aras was considered such a fierce warrior, she thought. He never gives up.

"Show them in," Sertorius said.

Moments later Aras swept into the courtyard closely followed by his men. They spread out as if expecting treachery. Sertorius stood motionless until they settled down.

Aras nodded to Sertorius but walked straight to Rhonwen. "I told you to wait."

She rose and faced him, hands on her hips. "As I recall, you merely told me when you'd return." She didn't add that she'd put the information to good use.

"What kind of handfasting can we make if you keep acting this way?"

Rhonwen shrugged. "I can't think of one."

The Trepani warriors shifted in discomfort.

Sertorius greeted the men all around them open-palmed, then pointed to the tables. "Stand easy," he said, "there's no battle to be fought here. Help yourselves to some food on your way out."

Aras signaled for the men to accept Sertorius' invitation and then faced Rhonwen. "At least I know you'll be escorted back safely."

"She will have suitable protection on her return." Sertorius laid his hand on Aras' shoulder. "I thank you for your zealous attention to duty." He guided the Trepani chief toward the house. "Your next task is to ride the perimeter of the camp."

Aras met Sertorius' gaze and nodded once in assent. He signaled to his men who gathered up all the food they could carry, then left. They rode away from the house, silhouetted against the remains of a brilliant red sunset.

Sertorius surveyed the ravaged food platters, a smile dancing at the corner of his mouth where it intersected with the scar across his eye. Had she seen the scar on another man it might have put her off, but on Sertorius it seemed a mark of honor no less distinguished than her tattoos.

Rhonwen resumed her seat on the couch as servants carried away all traces of the mess the warriors had made. In their wake they left a constellation of scented oil lamps that cast an even glow throughout the courtyard. In the distance, Rhonwen saw hundreds of cook fires twinkling, the landscape a mirror of the stars. She heard singing from somewhere out there, war ballads and love songs. The names of the fallen were already being woven into the tapestry of Iberian history. She wondered whether Baia would also be remembered.

Sertorius said, "You must miss your mother."

"I miss the loving parent she once was, but that woman died a long time ago." She forced a smile. "I'm closer to my uncle than I was to her."

Sertorius refilled her wine goblet and reclined on the lounge beside her. "Do you see him often?"

She shook her head. "He's been in Gaul the past few years and returned home only three months ago. Mother and I traveled all over Iberia while he lived in the north."

"He's lucky to have family to return to. I rejoice my mother's still alive in Rome. She's the only family I have."

"No wife?" Rhonwen asked, certain the wine had made her bold. She hoped it would affect him the same way. "No lovers?"

"Warriors have little time for lovemaking," he said.

"I suppose that depends on the warrior."

He rose and began pacing. "I can't stop thinking you might've been killed because of my stupidity. I can't permit you near another battlefield."

She forced another laugh. "So, to honor my courage you're sending me home?"

"Quite the opposite, though I'd like to send you as far from the fighting as I can. Have you ever been to Osca?"

"Yes. It's in the north, in the mountains."

"I have something in mind, and I want your help." He retrieved a bowl of fruit from a nearby table and set it between their couches. "I'm going to open a school for the children of the clan chiefs. I want them to learn the languages of Rome and Greece. I want them to study law and mathematics and philosophy. When they're grown, I expect some to find their way into the Senate."

"The Roman Senate?" Rhonwen asked.

"I intend for Iberia to have a Senate of its own."

Rhonwen selected a fig from the bowl and motioned him closer with it. "I have a suspicion," she whispered, leaning forward as he bent to hear her, "that you want to turn Iberia into another Rome."

He held her hand steady, leaned even closer and took a bite of the fig. "Would that be so bad? Those children will become the future leaders of this country. And I want you to teach them."

"Why me?"

"Because you have all the qualities I want those children to have: intellect, courage, wisdom."

"You see wisdom hairs on my chin?" She rubbed playfully at her jaw. "You make me sound like an old woman!"

"You're anything but that," he said, walking behind her. He put his hands on her shoulders and massaged her neck.

Rhonwen felt her tension drain away under his firm grip. She closed her eyes.

"Will you do it?" he asked, his breath warm on her neck.

"I don't know anything about schools."

"That didn't keep you from learning other things," he said. "Besides, you understand how Iberians learn better than any Roman could."

"Thank my Uncle Orlan for that."

Sertorius paused a moment. "Do you think he'd be willing to help?"

"He might," she said, putting her hand on top of his. "Do you intend to visit this school, or will you merely open it and forget about it?"

He pressed his lips against the top of her head. "I suppose that depends on who's there."

She guided his hand to her breast. "I might consider it, but I don't like the idea of being abandoned."

"There's a war on," he said, settling beside her on the lounge, his face pressed into her hair. "I don't know how often I'd be able to come."

She pressed his free hand to her other breast. "Often enough, I hope."

"I'll see that we aren't disturbed," he said.

Rhonwen shrugged out of her healer's robe. "Good."

17

*Fearing the Ageless Man would be disturbed, the Master of
Eban Enclave forbade the Suetoni warrior Carew from building a
house on the pasture near the Giant's Tomb. Carew ignored the ban,
claiming he had won the land for his own. When Cedwyn became
chief in Gillac, Carew and his wife were slain by a kinsman of the
Lemarii chief. The land once more became the rightful holding of
the Lemarii. They do not venture near the Giant's Tomb, and thus
far our offerings to the Ageless One rest safely.*
— *Stave One of Briac, 38th Master of Mount Eban Enclave*

Armorica 79 B.C.

Dierdre returned to Eban Enclave determined to find
answers for the two questions that had haunted her
since her departure five years earlier. She'd learned
a great deal in Vannes, and by working with the Roman slaver,
Scotus, she had improved a technique she'd developed to compel
obedience. Still, such triumphs put her no closer to solving the
riddle of the Ageless Man. The library at the Veneti enclave
dwarfed that of Eban, yet nothing in it mentioned the Giant's
Tomb or the enigma of the sticks.

When study failed to yield answers, she changed tactics. Orlan
would never have divulged the secret of the stick's restoration,
but perhaps his successor would. Since Coemgen, the Lemarii
chief, remained in good health, it seemed unlikely that his willful
son had begun to build on her land. Her plan to resolve both
issues hinged on gaining the confidence of the new master of
Eban Enclave. With Mallec under her influence, it should be a
simple matter to win her case for the return of her ancestral lands.

She arrived at the enclave before dawn but waited outside,
hoping to catch Mallec alone. The time passed slowly as she sat
shivering in her cart. It seemed the years had thinned her blood
as it thinned her hair. At last she spotted a tall lanky druid, his

long hair disheveled, exiting a dwelling near the enclave's main hall. Tattoos of achievement adorned his arms and neck.

He wandered toward the field where students once practiced with common arms. She hugged herself against the chill of late winter and noted that the field had given up its martial role and now sported row upon row of early vegetables. Mallec leaned against the fence surrounding the area as she advanced toward him. He was younger than she'd realized, perhaps half her age, and far too young to be master of an enclave. That Orlan had chosen him over her rankled more than ever.

"Much has changed since I was last here," she said.

Startled, Mallec turned.

It pleased her to see him ill at ease. Men often acted that way around her.

She bowed slightly. "I once knew this enclave well. Fyrsil was too mired in the old ways to consider changing anything, and the Iberian who followed him wanted only to go home. I'm happy to see a man of action is finally master of this enclave."

Mallec returned the bow. "You praise me more than I deserve. I've been master here for only a few years. If I succeed in the shadow of men like Orlan and Fyrsil, I shall consider myself fortunate."

"With Rome at war against Iberia, Orlan may regret his decision to leave Gaul. You, on the other hand, are too modest. I see you leading much bigger enclaves, perhaps in Vannes." She pulled back her hood. "I'm Dierdre, and I've just come from there, but I'm happy to be home."

"Home?"

"Yes. Five years studying in Vannes' enclave taught me many things, but mostly that I'm not destined for city life."

"Are you truly returning, or searching for a more worthy locale?"

Dierdre studied the druid. His welcome assuaged some of her fear that Orlan had poisoned him against her.

"I want to stay nearby. My son, Caradowc, lives in Gillac, and I haven't seen him in a long time."

Mallec's countenance darkened, and she guessed he had little use for the boy.

She smiled, as any beleaguered mother might. "He hasn't always been an easy lad, but he's my only child." She put a hand on Mallec's shoulder. "Please tell me he fares well." Caradowc was essential to her plans. The oaf had better be strong, healthy, and in his father's good graces.

"Gar has taken him into his household, though I fear the young man's companions bring him no honor."

Dierdre forced a deep sigh. "I suppose I should have made him stay with me, but he was adamant about returning to learn a warrior's ways. A druid enclave, even one as large as Vannes', is no place for such a headstrong boy."

"Will you reside in one of the towns?"

"I'd hoped there would be a place for me here."

He shook his head. "There's accommodation available for the present, but I'm so busy I don't even know when the next students arrive." He shrugged and extended his hands, palms up. "Before Orlan left, he gave me the impression you wouldn't return."

"I shouldn't have left my plans in doubt. Forgive me. It's just that I've learned much in Vannes, and I want to share that knowledge with the students here."

Mallec remained silent, as if assessing her words.

She noticed ink stains on his fingers and leaned toward him intently. "You strike me as a scholar. I wonder that Eban has enough to occupy you."

"I have little time for my own pursuits, what with teaching, adjudicating in Gillac and Trochu, conducting ceremonies, and divining the future. It's more than enough to keep me busy."

"You're a seer!" she said. Another simpleton, she thought. By mentioning how busy he was, he'd betrayed a weakness. "I confess I've no such ability. I much prefer the mundane, like keeping accounts and hearing disputes, but I imagine you have several who already help you."

"No one reliable," he said. "Most of the students are too occupied with their own studies."

"I know how difficult running an enclave can be. I often assisted Fyrsil in rendering judgments and managing day-to-day affairs."

"Useful skills."

Mallec smiled, and she was quick to follow it up. "Who do you leave in charge of the enclave when you're off performing your ceremonial duties?"

Mallec put his hands behind his back and shifted uncomfortably. "The enclave prospers, though with Druid Leuw gone, we need more teachers. Those few who remain have much to do. When I'm not here, well, you see..." His voice trailed off.

Dierdre forced a frown. "Surely someone makes the day-to-day decisions in your absence."

He shrugged.

"I could attend to them," she said. "That would leave you free to pursue those things at which you excel."

"If the Master of the Veneti enclave has allowed you to return, surely we can put you to good use here." He glanced around, obviously looking for some sign from the gods, but the sky was clear and only the call of a magpie disturbed the morning air.

"The bird promises a bit of sorrow from this bargain," he said, "but I suspect it'll be yours when you see how much work you'll have to do. Are you certain this is what you want?"

"Beyond a doubt." She could barely keep the triumph from her voice. He'd made it all so pathetically easy that she would chance going one step further.

"There is one small thing I'd like to know," she said.

"Yes?"

"Before I left, Master Orlan bid me assist him with an unusual ceremony."

Mallec's face grew grave. "The power of the gods in our hands leaves me in awe."

"As it should," she said. "When I witnessed it—"

He put his hand on her arm, and she resisted the urge to pull away. "Master Orlan told me how it frightened you."

Dierdre blinked away her surprise. "I admit being startled, but frightened? No. In fact, I was quite disappointed that I had to leave for Vannes before Master Orlan was restored." She shook her head. "Since that day I've regretted I couldn't stay to help. Now I have no idea how the transformation is reversed."

"Orlan and I discussed that very issue. He made two pronouncements that I adopted when I became master."

Dierdre forced herself to stay calm. "And they are?"

"First, only those who have experienced woadsleep will be considered for the master's position at Eban Enclave."

"Druid Leuw said as much when I met him recently," she said. "What's the second?"

"Only those who've experienced woadsleep may know its secrets."

"But Leuw—"

"Learned what he knows before the pronouncements were made," Mallec said. "That can't be undone. However, he's been sworn to secrecy."

The urge to scream nearly overwhelmed her, yet she forced herself to maintain the semblance of mild interest. "That's it, then?"

"Yes," he said. "Though you must also swear you'll tell no one of what you've seen."

She nodded. The fewer people who knew of the ritual, the better. "I so swear. When will you perform another ceremony?"

"It's been a long time since we burned baneweed, and I suspect it won't happen again soon. My two oldest students are still far from ready for initiation."

She tried not to stare. "How far?"

He laughed. "Why? Would you care to join them? If so—"

"No! I merely wondered." She would never undergo such a vile transformation of her own will. The thought of losing herself like that made her ill.

Taking her elbow, he guided her toward the enclave. "May I help you with your things? You can use Master Fyrsil's old quarters until we can prepare something more suitable."

Dierdre shivered at the prospect of sleeping in the room where Fyrsil died. If only the old man hadn't struggled. Of course, she knew the technique much better now than then. She hoped his ghost had long ago left the place.

When they reached the cart bearing everything she'd brought with her from Vannes, Mallec shook his head. "I'll send a student to help you."

"You're very kind," Dierdre said, although she would have preferred no one else touch her things.

"You'll like the fellow I have in mind," Mallec said. "His name is Budec."

✠ ✠ ✠

Winter and spring passed without incident, and a familiar melody woke Mallec on the eve of Beltane. He snuggled beneath his fur and listened. It took a moment for him to place the tune, "Benecin's Boar." It took another to realize he heard his own name mentioned in the tale. He sat upright, listening to the distinctive tenor of young Budec.

Arie's clear laughter floated on the air as the young bard sang to her. Leuw claimed the boy had been moon-eyed over the girl since her arrival several years ago. Instead of moving to Vannes to further his studies, as had been his original plan, the lad wheedled his way into staying at Eban Enclave. Budec found ample opportunities to spend more time in Arie's company than in either Gillac or Trochu. Arie obviously enjoyed his attentions, although Mallec knew Gar would prefer she found a man who earned his living with cattle and land rather than with a harp, brass bells, and a drum.

Mallec slipped into his tunic and belted it at the waist. On such a warm morning he had no need for a cloak, a good sign for the morrow's Beltane celebrations.

Arie saw him first and waved from her place beneath the enclave's oldest and most venerated oak. "Druid Mallec! You must listen to Budec's new words."

Budec's cheeks flamed as he fine-tuned the strings on his instrument.

"Did I hear," Mallec asked, "something about the 'pride of Mona'?"

Arie laughed. "Yes. It's about you and Master Orlan, and how the enclave is blessed to have had you both."

Mallec waved the praise aside. "I accomplished little in Mona. Better you should sing of women who will do great things." He patted Arie on the shoulder.

"That's what Driad Dierdre said when she thought I wasn't listening," Budec said, his expression sobering. "She's annoyed at me for not singing her praises."

Arie nodded. "She's an old sour-face when she thinks no one's looking."

Budec continued, "She frightened me years ago, but then she moved away. I wish she'd stayed in Vannes. She never liked me, and for certain I never liked her. She still makes me uneasy."

Mallec raised a cautionary hand and couldn't help compare his early years among the Eburones to the easy life Budec had, even under Dierdre. "We must bear our burdens, for that is the will of the gods. A student's life isn't always easy. Ask me someday about the people who made mine interesting. And remember, speaking ill of druids can only lead to trouble. I know Dierdre may seem harsh at times, but she's been a great help to me." Sometimes he wondered how he'd managed without her for so long.

Budec bowed from the waist. "I understand, and I'd be happy to sing a song of her praises, but keeping the enclave's accounts does not evoke the same awe in listeners as hearing of your exploits, or Master Orlan's."

Mallec peered at him. "Exploits?"

Budec plucked a chord and sang. "Mallec the Belgae, great prophet and seer, in sacred Mona met Orlan the Scholar. Then gods smiled on Eban and sent them both here."

Mallec smiled. "I'm no bard, Budec, but your rhymes seem a little forced."

The young man laughed. "Aye, but it's the sentiment that counts, and that's why I love singing them near Dierdre. When she hears praise for Master Orlan, she clouds over like a winter storm."

Arie put a hand over his. "Be careful not to antagonize her. She's slow to forgive a slight."

He leaned back. "She should count herself lucky I don't sing songs about her!"

Mallec pulled both young people to their feet. "There's much to do for tomorrow's celebration. Dierdre has offered to bless our livestock, and a few students are going to Trochu this afternoon. The rest of us will enjoy the evening in Gillac. I'm hoping Leuw will be there, too. He's due back from Vannes any day now. I assume, Arie, you'll join me there?"

"How could I miss going home on such a night?" She smiled mischievously at Budec. "I'm old enough to offer an ale at the Beltane fire. Do you know any young men who might share such a cup with me?"

Budec sputtered, his cheeks reddening.

✠ ✠ ✠

His borrowed horse protested its rough treatment, but Caradowc pushed the beast harder. He'd ordered his companions to stay behind, for he had no desire for them to see the way Dierdre might treat him. Though no longer under her care, he remembered well how she dealt with him in the past and doubted anything had changed. He wondered if she'd even notice he'd grown to full manhood. Few in Gillac could match him for size, speed, or strength.

Caradowc hadn't seen her since he'd left Vannes. She did not attend the Suetoni passage rite that marked the transition of young men into the brotherhood of warriors. She missed him leading the procession as it marched through the clanhold to the commons. She wasn't there when he accepted his sword from Gar, nor did she hear his accolades for those he'd beaten on the practice field to stand First on Passage Day.

So, why hurry to respond to her summons? He hauled hard on the reins, and allowed the sweaty animal to walk, its flanks heaving. Let others dance to Dierdre's tune. He would arrive when he wished.

In spite of his anger, he held a grudging respect for his mother. Though no one else spoke of it, it seemed obvious that Druid Mallec had all but surrendered the enclave to her, and he knew why. One way or another, Dierdre compelled obedience. If Mallec left, there'd be no one to oppose her claim to leadership. Maybe then she'd be satisfied. If she became enclave master, it could only improve his chances of gathering cattle and glory for himself.

When he reached the meadow fronting the enclave, someone sounded an alarm bell. A half dozen youths came running, only to be shooed back inside by his mother. She waited for him to approach. He halted before her and dropped lightly to the ground. At her summons, a boy appeared and led the horse away.

Dierdre extended both hands as she walked toward him.

"What do you want, Mother?"

Her smile never wavered. If anything, she added more charm, much the way he'd seen her approach wary tradesmen and merchants.

"You must learn to be more circumspect, Caradowc." She touched his arm, and he flinched. "Trusting as ever, I see."

"Trust is a coin of uncertain mint," he said, quoting one of the maxims she'd often used on him in his childhood.

"I'm glad you remember." She eyed him up and down and nodded in satisfaction. It was the first time he saw approval in her gaze.

She hooked her arm through his, and although he despised her touch, he allowed her to lead him across the grounds to a stone slab under a tree. The shade was welcome after his ride in the bright sun of late spring.

"You never answered my question. What do you want?"

"I have a task for you." She paused as if to judge his receptiveness. "You remember our lands?"

He laughed. "Where I found the great family treasure, a handful of coins and a stick?" She didn't share his laughter. "I hope you don't think I'm going back into that hole for another look."

She shook her head. "I've something else in mind." She pulled her shawl up around her shoulders and adjusted the folds of her robe. Caradowc smiled at her attempt to stir his curiosity. If she never said another word, he'd be only too happy.

"Did I ever tell you how our family lost that land?"

"I thought your father stole it from the Lemarii."

Her frown turned venomous. "He took it fairly. The Lemarii hired themselves out to the Romans in Iberia, so there was no one to stop him. If none could hold it, it was his to take."

Caradowc shrugged. "Until the Lemarii returned. They killed him then, didn't they?"

She snarled at him. "They killed everyone but me. Cedwyn, the old Suetoni chief, did nothing. Neither did the druids. I came away with my life and a hatred for Cedwyn who let the Lemarii keep it all."

"Why didn't you tell me before?"

"I couldn't send one lone boy against an entire clan. I had to wait until you were man enough to command respect, and allies. Don't you see? What they stole from me, they also stole from you. When Gar became chief, I hoped he might settle it, but like Cedwyn, he did nothing."

Caradowc's anger found a new focus. Were it not for useless druids and cowards like Gar, he'd have land and cattle today and would not have to consider hiring himself to the Romans. With holdings like those lost to the Lemarii, he would have been wealthy. Instead, he was an unblooded warrior riding a borrowed horse, with nothing but a sword to call his own. "Was there no one to exact retribution?"

Dierdre's frown lightened and her eyes narrowed. "In those days we had a famine, and the druids decided it was time for a sacrifice. It was the duty of the chief to shed his blood and travel to the Otherworld to speak to the gods on our behalf. Cedwyn had that responsibility."

"It happens often enough. There's no vengeance in it."

Dierdre threw back her head and laughed. "Oh, but there was. I had a young hound I'd trained to eat sheep's offal. When Cedwyn's intestines spilled, I let the dog go. Briac, whom Fyrsil replaced, nearly choked with anger, but he could never prove I did it."

Caradowc roared with laughter. "I wish you'd told me this long ago."

"Would it have changed anything?"

"Perhaps. Who knows?"

She stared hard into his eyes. "I want my land back."

"And you expect me to take it away from Coemgen, Gwair, and an army of Lemarii warriors?" He shook his head. "You're dreaming."

"Then share the dream with me. It's your land, too."

The thought pleased him.

"What if I headed the enclave," she said, "and you led the clan. Wouldn't that improve our chances?"

"It would be a start." Caradowc frowned.

"How close have you and Gar become?"

He grew suspicious. She hated Gar. "What do you mean?"

"Have you gained his confidence?"

"He trusts me," Caradowc said. "Indeed, he's proud of me."

"Excellent! Your day will come, so plan for it. Act like a leader, and you'll be treated like one." She patted his arm. "I hear you have a following among the younger warriors."

"Some," Caradowc said, careful not to let too much pride show lest she find a way to use it against him. "I can wait until Gar surrenders the chieftainship to a younger man."

"I can't use the same tactic with Mallec," she said. "No matter. If something happened to him, who else is there?"

"Mallec has favorites. He could pick one of them."

"Leuw? He's not interested."

"I meant Budec and Arie."

Dierdre laughed. "The girl's too young, and Budec... Let's just say he's already earned a place in my plans."

✠ ✠ ✠

A pair of geese flying northward signaled the gods' readiness for the Beltane sacrifice. The chosen bull, a shaggy beast with perfectly shaped horns, stood quietly between two druids, Arie close to its side. None of the men and women assembled near the stone altar in the center of Gillac's commons spoke, although a child coughed and cried out once before its mother hushed it. Three small baskets of grain, each representing the whole seed crops of barley, oats, and rye sat on the stone, awaiting consecration.

Mallec wore an antlered headdress sacred to the god Cernnunos. Garlands of sweet spring flowers hung around his neck and across his shoulders, bedecking him like a meadow. He scattered a handful of acorns across his path as he approached the bull. Arie pressed the fingers of one hand to the animal's neck. With eyes closed she swayed slightly to a rhythm Mallec could not hear, but one he knew was the life song of the bull.

In one hand Mallec carried a willow branch, the furred pods well opened, and in the other, a length of blackthorn as long as his forearm. Both he waved at the sky.

"O-ghe! Hear our prayers," he said to the gods, once in each of the four directions. "Great Mother! Great Father! Be with us and bless us."

"Bless us," replied the villagers.

"By sacred oak and mistletoe, by willow and by blackthorn, I purify this offering." He stroked the bull with the branches. It did not flinch, and he raised a private thanks to Orlan for showing him the white powder that stilled the fearful hearts of beasts. It gave the people greater hope to see the young bull stand proudly, the way a warrior should face his death.

At Mallec's nod, Arie took up a drum and beat a heartbeat pace. Mallec's bronze knife lay on the altar. He placed the wands on either side of the blade and raised it for the crowd to see. A small bowl held salt carried from the sea near Vannes, and he scattered a pinch of it over the bull.

"Bless us."

Arie, eyes closed, struck the drum again.

Mallec pinched the skin at the bull's neck to expose the large vein pulsing beneath its jaw. With a swift motion he sliced it the length of one hand and slipped a hollow reed into the wound. Warm blood gushed in steady gouts that matched Arie's drumbeat.

In moments the bull was too weak to stand. Mallec and Arie stepped back as its legs buckled, and it slumped to the ground, its blood added to the stains left from generations of such sacrifices.

As he concentrated on the thick red pool at his feet, Mallec felt himself pulled away from the festival into the Otherworld. He had the sensation of living between drumbeats, where his senses became acute and time slowed. The dark pool coalesced into a bright light in which Dierdre's face appeared, and she wept not tears but blood.

The drum beat resumed, and its call wrenched him back to the ceremony. Sweat chilled him, and he knew something ill would happen. He feared for Dierdre.

When the bull's eyes closed, Arie's steady beat slowed and then stopped altogether. Mallec shook his head. He must finish the ceremony, regardless of the message the gods brought.

He took up his staff and pounded it three times into the dirt. "Great Goddess! Great Lugh! Thanks be!"

Blood filled the pail in which he would soon scry the clan's fertility. Villagers pressed forward, eager to gather some of the blood for their own charms and amulets.

He turned to the druids. "Set the pole."

The young people scattered without waiting for the druids. Men and women steadied the pole, as old as Gillac itself some said, and placed it in the hole dug for it. Thin strips of colored cloth, twice as long as the pole and tied firmly to the top, fluttered in the evening breeze. Men and women, laughing and shouting, jumped and grabbed at the ribbons. Good luck came the whole year to those who danced the Beltane weaving. When an eager hand clutched each strand of cloth, Mallec raised his staff.

"Fertile blessing on you all, and the last to wind shall find good luck the whole year!"

Musicians and drummers played. The dancers leaped over and under each other, weaving the ribbons as their mothers and fathers had woven them in dances past. When the people added their prayers to the weave, Mallec signaled for the fires.

The torches flared.

Mallec withdrew to the altar. He'd seen more than one occasion when reluctant cattle and sheep, penned on the commons, would not pass between the twin flames. It was always dangerous to be in the way, and he preferred to leave it for those who knew how to handle the nervous beasts. He'd watch for a while, and then make his way into the feasting hall to visit with Gar and the other villagers.

Once again, as so many others had, another Beltane passed without providing him a companion. He wished the gods would show him the face of the dark-haired one. At least now Dierdre had released him from enough chores to allow him to resume work on his history. Still, that history would be no competition for the woman he'd dreamed of for so long.

"Druid Mallec?"

He turned at the sound of Arie's voice and was struck by her worried frown. Evening shadows played across her face making her seem older.

"What makes you so solemn at such a merry time?"

"It's Budec."

Though a steady and serious student, Arie was also a bright and happy young woman. She'd mastered far more druid knowledge than he had at her age. If she heard a thing once, she remembered with few errors. If she heard it twice, she never forgot.

Mallec tried to reassure her with a smile. "I doubt he's found another's ale more appealing than yours."

She smiled briefly, but the frown returned. "I've searched Gillac from one end to the other. He's not here. He promised to follow from the enclave this morning."

Mallec took her hands in his. "I'm sure he's merely delayed. In the meantime, come to the hall with me, and we'll sit with your parents and hear the news."

Together they made their way through the laughing crowd. The cows tried to avoid going between the ceremonial bonfires while men and women tried to herd them through. The people always won, Mallec thought. Most of the sheep and cattle would eventually pass through and be blessed, even if they had to be dragged.

A disturbance at the main gate caught his attention. Arie gripped his arm in fear. They ran toward the gate as a crowd gathered around a pair of men.

"I found him like this, I tell ye," a farmer said, "wandering lost halfway between here and Eban Enclave."

Arie pushed past Mallec, and her cry brought him to her side.

The farmer led a young man by the hand. Someone held a torch high, and Mallec recognized Budec. Filthy and exhausted, the student stood beside the farmer with his head slightly bowed. Mallec gasped. Spittle hung from the boy's open lips, and his eyes held no spark of life. He had the same slack-jawed look Galan wore after the accident in Belgica.

Arie sobbed and shook him by the shoulders. "Budec! What's happened? Speak to me!"

The young bard turned to her slowly as if he knew her voice, but no recognition glimmered in his eyes, one of which dripped tears of blood.

18

Amrec, the Ageless One came again today, and I gave him food. He kept his visit brief, asking his questions as he always does before returning to his place of slumber. I wonder that we cannot find a place for him here, but he says his mission is clear, and he must wait. Therefore, so must we.

— *Stave One of Fyrsil, 39th Master of Mount Eban Enclave*

Iberia

Orlan rode through the streets of Osca looking for Rhonwen's school. Her message requesting his help had arrived months earlier, but his departure had been delayed by a lengthy bout of dysentery. Orlan still marveled at the expense of sending a rider all the way to Castulo for the sole purpose of delivering a note and returning with an answer. The courier wore the emblem of General Sertorius and appeared capable of fighting his way through a Roman legion single-handedly.

Though grieved by the news of Baia's death, Orlan had replied immediately, agreeing to help. Seven months had passed before he was well enough to travel.

Retracing his steps along the eastern coast, on the Roman's so-called Gold and Silver Road, would have taken too long, so Orlan had opted for a direct, albeit more arduous route. A local guide led him north from Castulo through the Marianus Mountains to the town of Laminium, where he took a north-bound road leading straight to Osca 300 Roman miles away.

The Roman road was a marvel. Thick slabs of stone were joined so accurately that the seams rarely allowed room for errant seeds to sprout. Seemingly impervious to weather and wear, each mile of the road bore a marker noting the distance from that spot to Rome. Assuming the Roman engineers did not err, and nothing they'd ever done made him believe otherwise, calculating distances traveled became trivial. The smooth surface provided steady footing for both his horse and the donkey bearing his possessions and the last surviving baneweed plant.

Other than a few seeds he'd harvested from the plants he brought from Armorica, he had nothing to show for his efforts. He hoped Osca would provide a better climate for them. With such ease of travel now possible, he thought often of visiting Mount Eban to replenish his supply.

Sections of Osca's clanhold walls had been painted in cheerful reds, yellows, and white, providing a pleasant variation to the unpainted Iberian buildings. The streets teemed with people, although it wasn't market day. Most of those he asked for directions knew of the school, but few offered an opinion about it. The name Sertorius, however, brought a reverent response. He gave a young urchin a copper coin, and the lad showed him a quick route to a huge building near the center of town.

The school was typical of Roman structures in Iberia. Made of brick and decorated in gaudy blues, greens, and reds, the building dwarfed native structures. Its roof tiles soaked up the brilliant afternoon sun and made the air above the building shimmer. A wooden door barred his entry into what was surely an inner courtyard. An elderly woman answered his knock. She wore a Roman tunic belted with a sash woven in the style of the mountain people.

She took one look at him, another at the dusty animals he'd tied nearby, and bellowed toward the interior.

"He's here!" She smiled and backed away from the door.

He stepped into the courtyard.

"Uncle!" Rhonwen's voice preceded her.

He'd dreamed of this joyous reunion for months. Nothing, however, prepared him for the sight of Rhonwen waddling toward him with arms outstretched. Though somewhat hidden by a voluminous healer's robe, there was no disguising her pregnant belly. She pulled him close, and sobs of joy erupted from her. He held her for a long time before pushing her an arm's length away and looking her up and down. Despite her tears, she appeared in excellent health, her smile more radiant than ever.

"By the gods, girl, I had no idea you were with child," he said. "Are you as well as your smile suggests?"

"Aye, Uncle, I am. And I can't express how happy I am to see you. I've missed you so much. Come in, come in!"

The interior was as lavish as the frugal Rhonwen would allow. He'd rarely stepped foot inside such a colossal structure. "It's magnificent."

Rhonwen's smile lit her whole face. "We have dozens of boys here, and a few girls, all from clans that have joined the fight against Rome. It's a true center of learning." She sat at a nearby bench, a gentle hand caressing the mound of her unborn child.

He sat beside her. "When will I meet your man?"

"Soon," she said, her smile faltering. "I hope."

Orlan nodded knowingly. "He's a warrior then. What else would keep a man from being with you now. How much longer till the birth?"

"Less than two months," she said.

"A hawthorn child like its mother!" Orlan exclaimed, delighted the birth would occur in the sixth of the thirteen Celtic months. "The father's month?"

Rhonwen rubbed her belly thoughtfully and said, "It doesn't matter."

"Are you worried he won't be here for the birth?"

What remained of Rhonwen's happiness disappeared entirely. "He doesn't know I bear his child."

"By the gods, Rhonwen, you sent a message to me in a matter of days, surely there are regular couriers between Osca and wherever he's encamped."

"I've sent nothing," she said, her eyes meeting his with pride. "He promised to visit, but I've not seen him since the night we coupled."

"What kind of man is he?" Orlan demanded. "Give me his name. I'll kick some sense into him!"

She hesitated, then took a deep breath. "Sertorius."

"Lugh's balls, Rhonwen, of all the men to choose. And he doesn't know you're pregnant?"

"He sent me here to run the school. I meant to tell him when he came to visit, but he never did. If he doesn't care enough to inquire about my well-being, he doesn't deserve to know he has a child. I haven't written him since I've been here."

Orlan whistled. "Of all the men in this country, he's the one I would believe if he said he was too busy. He's waging war against Rome! He's pushed Metellus into the mountains and forced those legions into eating grass to survive. And if that weren't enough, he scared away an army sent from Gaul. Do you honestly expect him to drop everything and come here to see how you fare?"

Rhonwen raised her chin defiantly, a trait he'd seen more than once when she dug in her heels. The only woman he'd ever known who could out-stubborn Rhonwen was her mother.

"He hasn't written," she said. "If he'd done that much, I might feel differently."

"You haven't written either," Orlan said. "So how is it he's the one who's wrong?"

"Men," Rhonwen muttered. "I don't expect you to understand. Now, let me show you to your quarters, and we'll continue this discussion at dinner," she said, leading him into the house.

Mule-headed woman, he mused. Like mother, like daughter.

✠ ✠ ✠

The wail of Rhonwen's newborn drew Orlan from his slumber. Of the two months he'd spent at the school, the last week was the hardest. Rhonwen's son did not sleep the entire night, so neither did anyone else. Orlan stretched his stiff joints, slowly gained his feet, and plodded to the open window. Iago stirred as Orlan stepped past him. The dog had taken to sleeping in his room since the baby's birth.

"Is it the noise you don't like, old fellow," Orlan asked as he ran a hand over the animal's wiry-haired head, "or having to give up your place to a usurper who can't even chase a stick?" The dog licked Orlan's fingers and flopped onto his side with a grunt.

Orlan looked into the dark street and listened. Only the baby's cries disturbed the night. He still hadn't adjusted to buildings with an upper floor. The thought of stumbling through the dark to find the stairs was too much for him. He glanced up at the star-carpeted sky and decided anyone skulking about in the night deserved no warning, so he relieved himself through the window onto the street below. He returned through the cool spring silence to his sleeping pallet, and waited for slumber that would not come.

Using all of his diplomatic skills, he'd finally persuaded Rhonwen to send word to Sertorius of the child's imminent birth. Five weeks had passed, and she'd received no response.

Such silence from the man made little sense. Surely he would acknowledge his own child. If Sertorius felt shame about the child's mixed parentage, why would he spend the effort to maintain a school for the offspring of the clan chiefs? He shuddered at the alternative that presented itself. The Roman guards posted for their protection could just as easily serve a more sinister purpose. The longer he thought about it, the more convinced he became that the school for which so many hailed Sertorius, was in reality just a handy place to store hostages.

He rose and dressed, then crept through the dark corridor, down the stone stairs and out to the vegetable plot behind the building. Iago walked beside him.

Orlan's single baneweed plant occupied a corner banned to non-druids for fear they would pluck the ugly thing from the ground and discard it. The space was marked by stakes and a rope strung with small bones. No one would brave the possibility of a druid's curse for disturbing the plant.

The night sky allowed him enough light to assure himself the plant was safe. He examined it daily, and lately the spindly weed seemed more vigorous. He took it as a sign the gods approved of his efforts to cultivate it.

Torch-light and voices from the stable drew him still farther from the school. While Iago waited, Orlan peeked into the building through a crack in the door.

Two servants attended the horse of a young Roman who had stripped off his clothing and bathed himself with a rag dipped in a water bucket. He shivered as he scrubbed. What Orlan at first thought to be a smudge of dirt on the young man's neck did not wash off, and Orlan realized it was a birthmark. The Roman directed the servants to dump the remains of the water over him, and then retrieved a clean garment from a leather pouch beside his saddle.

As the Roman appeared unarmed, and his attitude toward the servants seemed benign, Orlan ended his surveillance. "Good morning," he said as he entered the stable, his druid robe dragging a faint trail through yesterday's trampled straw.

The Roman looked up and smiled in response as Iago padded toward him, tail awag. He patted the dog's great head. "Good morning, Magister," he said to Orlan. "You must be the uncle Rhonwen spoke of."

"How is it you know my niece?"

"I'm Aemelius," the Roman said. "General Sertorius assigned me to watch over Rhonwen and her mother during the early days of the war."

At the mention of Baia, a rush of anger swept over Orlan. "You were among the swine who fled rather than protect my sister?"

Aemelius extended his hands, palms up. "Of course not! Those men died slowly, crucified as a lesson to anyone contemplating desertion."

Orlan allowed himself to be mollified. "I grieve for the loss of my sister. My apologies for assuming the worst of you. It would please her to know she is avenged."

Aemelius rubbed Iago behind the ears. "You needn't apologize. It was the first time I wasn't there for them, and I've regretted it daily."

The young man's sincerity and Iago's approval won Orlan over. "What brings you to Osca without Sertorius?"

"I haven't seen the general since a month after Magistra Baia's death. He sent me to fight alongside his lieutenant, Quintus Aespis." Aemelius straightened. "About a fortnight ago, I received orders to return to Rome. I came by here because it's on the way to the port at Tarraco."

"Sertorius makes war on Rome and yet sends you, alone, into Roman territory? I thought you were an aide, not a spy."

"Sertorius isn't making war on Rome, nor does Rome make war on him. Sulla drives this conflict. He fears Sertorius and the support he earned during the civil war. Sertorius sided with Marius, and though Sulla has killed many of Marius' followers since coming to power, those who rallied to Marius still number in the thousands. Sulla knows if Sertorius returns with an army of any size, the Marians would join him. He would become invincible."

Orlan tried to read the young man's face. Traces of youth remained, although the time he'd spent at war left marks unlikely to fade. "There's more to this Sulla than you're telling me, nor have you said what you're expected to accomplish in Rome."

"Sulla imprisoned my father," Aemelius said. "I've vowed to discover his fate, and free him if he yet lives. Sertorius approves and has given me money to buy his freedom. But my main purpose is to raise more troops."

"You're expected to recruit Romans to fight against Romans?"

Aemelius shrugged. "Don't Iberian clans fight among themselves?"

"Certainly, but it's rare when a clan fights against itself."

"Romans are divided. Some rally to Sulla, but many still support Marius and therefore Sertorius. Many more simply fear Sulla and oppose him for what he represents. One of these, Perpenna Vento, has pledged an army of two hundred cohorts to supplement our Iberian forces." Aemelius spoke with the fervor of a zealot. "With such an army, we can smash our way into Rome. General Pompey will fall on his knees before us, Sulla will decorate a cross for his crimes, and Sertorius will take his rightful place as leader of the greatest power ever known!"

Orlan touched his fingertips together as he contemplated the young Roman's words. "I believe you need some food. You're beginning to sound delirious."

Aemelius laughed. "I get carried away. Rhonwen teases me about it. Do you think she would be up this early? I'm eager to see her."

Orlan listened but heard no baby cries. "I doubt it. She's already been up several times tonight feeding the baby."

Aemelius stared at him, his mouth gaping. "Rhonwen has a child?" He peered into the brightening gloom that signaled the dawn. "Then I would have expected Trepani warriors on guard here, not Roman soldiers. Has Aras been gone long?"

"Aras?" Rhonwen had told Orlan about her persistent Trepani suitor. He shook his head. "Aras is a friend only."

"Then who is the father?"

Orlan inhaled deeply, unsure whether he should share Rhonwen's secret. But as the general's aide, perhaps Aemelius knew the reasons for the man's lack of concern for a new son.

"Sertorius," Orlan said, "though he's not bothered to acknowledge the boy."

Aemelius gasped. "No acknowledgment at all?" When Orlan shook his head, the young man's aspect darkened. "How old is the child?"

"A week today. Why?"

"Roman custom demands a boy's father accept him on the ninth day after his birth."

"That doesn't seem likely," Orlan said.

Aemelius bit at his lip. "But he must! In Rome, a father holds a newborn above his head for the gods to see and accepts it as his own. An infant he doesn't accept must be exposed, left for the beasts or slavers or whatever else the gods send to claim it."

"I've heard such tales," Orlan said, "though I never put any faith in them."

"It's the law," Aemelius said. He put his hand on Orlan's arm. "If Sertorius doesn't arrive in two days—"

"Then the child will be raised according to our laws," Orlan said.

"But, in Rome—"

"Look around, Aemelius. Does this look like Rome?"

✠ ✠ ✠

Rhonwen felt blessed in her motherhood despite the lack of interest from Sertorius. Now nearly two years old, Rede wiggled like a puppy on her lap. The child had grown quickly in the last two years, and daily he became more headstrong.

"Can't you be still even a moment?" Rhonwen asked.

"Your son has inherited your stubborn streak," Orlan said. "I surmise he may have more than a bit of his grandmother in him."

Rhonwen mugged a tired smile. She didn't want Baia's Roman-hating spirit in the heart of her Roman-fathered son, although Rede did seem to carry his grandmother's obstinate tenacity. Besides, such things mattered little when faced with a scrappy warrior of two who refused to eat.

Rede clamped his lips together and turned his head as Rhonwen threatened him with a wooden spoonful of mashed apple.

"You'll eat this, or nothing," she said, knowing the child would likely force her hand and make him go to bed hungry. It wouldn't be the first time.

Rede stuck out his lower lip as far as it would go.

Rhonwen gazed at her child with undisguised pride. With a snub nose and a mass of hair that defied any attempts at neatness, Rede resembled Rhonwen more than she cared to admit.

"I could pinch his nose closed," Orlan suggested.

She waved off the effort. "I considered that, but he'd probably just hold his breath until he fainted."

"Can't you bribe him?"

"What can I offer him that he doesn't already have?"

"A sore rump?" Orlan straightened. "I think I saw a willow switch lying around here somewhere."

Rede squinted at his great uncle. "No!"

"If it comes to that," Rhonwen said, "I'll use my hand. If he feels the sting, I want to feel it, too."

"You've strange ideas about child care," Orlan admonished.

Rhonwen stuck the spoon back in the bowl and wiped her hands on a rag with which she took a quick swipe at Rede's face before releasing him.

"And leave Iago alone," she called to his back as he raced away. "The dog's too old for your nonsense!" Rede often played near the stable while Iago and a reluctant trio of cats became his small army. His forays into the stalls had become legendary.

Orlan sat beside her and peeled an orange. When finished, he handed her half of it. "You've got to discipline that boy."

Rhonwen slapped her forehead. "Discipline, of course! That'll solve everything."

Before Orlan could respond, they both jumped in response to an excited scream. "Mam! Mam!" Rede yelled as he raced back into the house with utter disregard for the dirt and straw he also tracked in. "Riders! Come see!"

The child led the druids to the stable. The parents of children fostered to the school often came for visits, and Rhonwen tried to accommodate them without risking jealousy or homesickness among the other students. When such visitors arrived, Rede often raised the alarm.

"Were you expecting anyone?" Orlan asked.

Rhonwen shook her head as she opened the stable door. Inside, a tall Roman wearing a bright blue cape held her squirming son. Several other men stood behind him as the stable boys scrambled to take care of their mounts.

"Sertorius!" Rhonwen gasped.

Rede's joyful screams echoed through the stable as Sertorius swept him through the dusty air. Father and son together, she could see how like Sertorius Rede was after all.

Sertorius set Rede on the stable floor. "Charming child," he said, then bowed. "Rhonwen, I've come for a long overdue visit."

Pent up anger rose close to the surface. "Welcome to Osca," she said, forcing a polite smile.

He brushed the dust from his clothing as Rede roared off on some new adventure, then turned to a pinch-faced man standing directly behind him. "Perpenna, I'd like you to meet Magistra Driad Rhonwen, administrator of this school."

Sertorius' smile, so beguiling, nearly washed away her ill feelings, but the other Roman stared at her without expression. He let his eyes drift to her bare feet and back to her face. She felt like cheap merchandise under his scrutiny. It infuriated her.

"Driad Rhonwen, let me introduce Perpenna Vento, lately of Rome, and now my mentor in all things administrative. The man is a genius at getting things done."

She nodded curtly, then held out a hand to introduce Orlan. She used his full druid title, which brought a bow from Sertorius but no reaction from Perpenna. Perpenna epitomized everything she hated about Romans. He displayed only contempt for anything not Roman. He bore signs of a perpetually sour temperament, and even if he had bowed cordially, she decided it would have been a show for Sertorius rather than a gesture of respect for them.

"I'm here to inspect my school," Sertorius said, "and to reward the woman who's made it work so well."

"I'm honored you found the time to visit," she said. "I recall a pledge that you'd come here 'often.' I see now our interpretations of that differ."

"I have little time these days, but with Perpenna's help I intend to change that."

"Didn't you receive my letter?" she asked.

He shrugged. "Our couriers are not yet as reliable as those of Rome. I use the best of them to carry messages to and from my officers, and even then some missives go astray. Why? What was in this letter?"

Rhonwen stared hard at him, trying to gauge his sincerity.

"It must not have been important, Magistra," Perpenna said, "or you would have sent more than one. An able administrator would've seen to that."

Rhonwen eyed Perpenna with deepening suspicion.

"If you'll follow me," Orlan interjected, "I'll show you where you can refresh yourselves after your long journey."

Perpenna opened his mouth to speak, and Rhonwen expected to see pointed teeth to match his sharp face. "We won't be staying long, but we could use a hot meal."

She frowned. "We weren't expecting visitors."

"Just show my cook what's available, and he'll make something edible of it."

Perpenna snapped his fingers, and a spindly Greek slave appeared. The man's furtive eyes would've gone well in Perpenna's face, Rhonwen thought.

⌗ ⌗ ⌗

Freed from her hostess chores by Orlan, Rhonwen sought refuge in the quarters she shared with Rede. The great Roman-built structure provided a honeycomb of such small rooms. She had furnished theirs sparingly, because she hated to clutter what little space she allowed herself.

Alone on her sleeping pallet, she closed her eyes and waited for the soothing quiet of night. Why had Sertorius remained silent for so long, only to pop back into her life now? How could he play with Rede and not see himself in the child's smile? Even the odious Perpenna should have noticed the similarity.

A light tap on her door startled her. "Yes?" She sat up.

There was no response. Had it been Orlan, he would have entered by now. Had it been Rede, he never would have knocked. Rhonwen went to the door and opened it. A wary Aemelius stood outside.

"We've got to talk," he said, keeping his voice low as he brushed past her without waiting for an invitation.

Rhonwen closed the door and hugged him. "What brings you here?" she whispered. "I haven't seen you in over two years. Did you reach Rome?"

"Yes," Aemelius replied, "to assist Perpenna, that two-faced monkey's boil, in bringing his legions to Iberia." He laughed scornfully. "As if they were his legions. The men care nothing for him, and in truth, I've never known anyone less deserving of loyalty."

This disturbing news lent support for her initial misgivings about Perpenna. "I don't know anything about him, except that he scorns Iberians, and he looks like a ferret with a blocked bowel."

Aemelius smiled as he took Rhonwen's hands, then his expression grew serious. "Promise me you'll be careful around him."

"Sertorius seems taken with him."

"I wish I knew why. There's no doubt Perpenna has connections, but I wonder how good they are. He promised to deliver two hundred cohorts, one hundred sixty thousand men. That's more than Metellus had in all his legions combined."

Rhonwen pursed her lips in a silent whistle.

"He's short of his promise by three quarters."

"Still, forty thousand men is an impressive force," Rhonwen said.

"True. The day they arrived, Sertorius' army grew by half. Unfortunately, most of them were landless peasants looking for spoils. Sertorius expected battle-hardened soldiers. He's spent much of the time since they arrived training them. Meanwhile, he's left administration of the country to Perpenna and the senate-in-exile."

"What does this have to do with me or the school?" Rhonwen asked. "Before today I'd never heard of this Perpenna."

"It's my fault." Aemelius shook his head in shame. "When I first met Perpenna, I was impressed by his wealth and the powerful people who answered his most casual summons. I wanted to appear more important and bragged to him about my friendship with Sertorius." He let his head drop forward. "When that wasn't enough, I bragged to him that I knew things about Sertorius the great general didn't even know."

"Like what?"

Aemelius swallowed hard. "I told him about you and Rede. At the time, he had no reaction. Later I realized I never should've opened my mouth."

She patted his hand. "I'll be careful."

"Never trust him. He believes a Roman birth makes a person superior to all others." Aemelius scowled. "He says no barbarian is fit to rise above the lowest rank of foot soldier. That antagonized all the Iberians."

Aemelius paced. "Such words might make sense if spoken by someone with military experience, but he has none. During our journey from Rome, he constantly overruled the men who command the legions. He has no sense for how to lead men in arms, nor any grasp of geography or direction. Eventually the lieutenants told him if he didn't follow them to Sertorius, they'd leave him behind."

"They threatened to desert?"

"All but a handful of Perpenna's personal guard. The others angered him. He said only fools gave themselves into the command of any man who set a fox to guard his hens. They asked what he meant, and he told them about you and said no right-thinking Roman would leave a barbarian to guard his barbarian hostages."

"This is a school," Rhonwen said, "not a prison."

"The truth is," Aemelius said, "it's both. Why else would Sertorius keep a permanent staff of guards camped nearby?"

"We're at war. I'm sure they're for our protection," Rhonwen said. "We rarely see them."

"But they never go away, do they?" Aemelius rubbed his eyes. "I can't stay long. As soon as it turns dark I must return to my post."

"I thought you came with Sertorius."

"No, I haven't seen Sertorius since the day I left for Rome." He smiled weakly. "When I returned, Perpenna put a few men under my command and ordered me to patrol the border with Gaul. If Rome sent Pompey or anyone else into Iberia, I was to report it to him directly, not Sertorius."

"Sertorius doesn't even know you're here?" she asked.

"No, and you mustn't tell him. If he found out I'd left my post..." He closed his eyes for a moment. "Has he seen Rede yet? I felt sure he'd accept him as soon as he found out he has a son."

Rhonwen shook her head. "If he knows, he hasn't said anything."

"Perpenna again," Aemelius said, anger clear in his voice. "I begged him to tell Sertorius he has a son. Now I understand why I've been sent into the wilderness. Perpenna doesn't want me speaking about the near-mutiny of his men or about your son."

Aemelius squeezed her hands. "Talk to Sertorius. Tell him about Rede! Doesn't he have a right to know?"

She shook her head. "He's done nothing to earn it."

"You're wrong. This war has consumed his attention day and night for over three years. If he sent no word, it's because Perpenna intercepted it. Sertorius is not an evil man. He's getting bad advice. Sometimes I think Perpenna is secretly working for Sulla."

"Then there's even less reason to tell him anything. How can I confide in a man who can't distinguish friend from foe? If I tell Sertorius Rede is his son, Perpenna will find a way to turn my words against me."

"Then let me tell him," Aemelius said, squaring his shoulders. "Coming from me it won't sound like you're trying to garner favor."

Rhonwen hugged him. He was only a little younger than her brother Telo would have been. "Promise me you won't do anything foolish."

Aemelius smiled. "Sertorius and I are friends, remember?"

✠ ✠ ✠

Rhonwen surveyed the latest of Rede's destructions. In his brief life, her son proved brash, robust, and full of mischief. As he had grown, so had his ability to commit mayhem. Now over three years old, Rede had single-handedly consumed or scattered, every bite of food she'd prepared for their evening meal, the only occasion when she and Orlan could spend uncontested time with the youngster. She wondered how Perpenna and the Greek slave who cooked for him would've reacted. Not that she cared. It had been nearly a year since Sertorius brought the sour Roman to Osca, and Rhonwen hadn't seen or heard from either one since.

Rede stuck his head through the doorway and appraised his mother with mild apprehension. Traces of stew adorned the front of his tunic, bread crumbs hung like a beard from his cheeks, and bits of orange rind clung beneath his grimy fingernails.

Rhonwen plucked a scrap of bread from the wreckage and held it up. "You seem to have missed this."

"Not hungry now," he said.

"But I am, and so is your uncle Orlan."

He brightened. "I'll hunt for you!"

"I've a better idea, little warrior," Rhonwen said, smiling and moving slowly toward him, hoping to grab him before he got away. "But I don't want to say it too loud. I think this should be a secret between us."

"A secret?"

Rhonwen counted on his curiosity to hold him in place just long enough. "Aye. Just between us."

At a sound in the hallway, he turned. Rhonwen pounced like a mouser but missed as the boy scooted under her outstretched hands.

"Orlan!" screamed Rede as if he hadn't seen the aging druid in weeks rather than a single afternoon.

Orlan entered the room with the boy draped over his shoulder. "By the gods, I'm hungry," he declared as he dropped Rede onto his sleeping pallet.

"So am I," Rhonwen muttered. "But it looks like we'll have to eat with the students tonight."

Orlan raised a menacing eyebrow at Rede. "Have you any idea what happens to little boys who eat food meant for druids?"

Rede puffed out his chest. "They get big and strong!"

"Only if they survive," Orlan said, using the same growling voice he used with Rhonwen when she was an unruly child.

"Boys who eat too much druid food will have so many chores to do, they won't have time to play," Rhonwen added.

Rede crossed his arms. "I'm a hunter." He stalked toward the bearded druid and tugged on his robe. "What do you want to eat? I'll get it."

"A bear would do nicely."

"Big or small?"

Orlan smiled. "As big as a horse."

"The last thing he needs are ideas," Rhonwen said making a quick survey of anything Rede might be able to press into service as a weapon.

"I need a sword," the boy said.

"Sorry," the druid said, "you'll have to use your hands."

Rede scowled. "Against a bear?"

"The bear won't have a sword, why should you?"

"Bears have claws," Rede said, holding his tiny hands up with fingers bent like talons. "I know. I saw one."

"Where?" asked Rhonwen.

"They had one on a chain in the village some weeks ago," Orlan said. "I took him to see it."

Rhonwen raised an eyebrow. "Bears should be in the forest, not prancing around for entertainment." She followed Rede as he crept toward the door then grabbed the back of his tunic. "Where are you going?"

He stood on tiptoes and spread his arms. "To find a bear."

"Not until you help me clean up this mess."

He shuffled toward her with his lower lip protruding until Orlan reached over and pretended to grab it. "Aren't you going to punish him?"

Rhonwen looked from her uncle to her son and back again. "Does he look like he's having a good time?"

"He left nothing for us!" Orlan said. "How's he going to learn if you won't punish him?"

Rhonwen motioned him closer and whispered in his ear. "Ask me again tomorrow night, after you and I have eaten, and he's gone hungry. Some lessons are better learned on an empty stomach."

Orlan chuckled. "This could prove interesting."

Rhonwen decided Rede had played in the wreckage long enough and shooed him away so she could clean it up. No sooner had he disappeared through the doorway than he came storming back into the room, breathless.

"There's a man, and cows, and music!" he shouted, grabbing hold of Rhonwen's hand and dragging her toward the door. "Come quick. He said it was all for me and you!"

"What are you talking about?"

"A warrior," he cried, "with a gold helmet!"

From the courtyard, the rhythmic strains of mountain music drifted into the building.

"I suppose we'd better go see about this," Rhonwen said. She stopped resisting and let Rede trot to the door. "Lead on, little man."

She followed him out into the corridor and down the stairs to the courtyard. Aras, the Trepani chief, stood dressed in fine linens with his helmet and arms gleaming. Behind him stood three musicians, four warriors from the clan herding a dozen shaggy cattle, and an ox-cart loaded with wicker cages of chickens and geese.

Several students kept time with the drummer, either slapping their thighs or clapping. A girl with a flute played a sprightly tune, and the harpist strummed an accompaniment. Rhonwen had to dodge a dancing Rede to reach the grinning Trepani warrior.

"Aras! What brings you?" she asked, offering her hand in welcome. All this seemed so out of place for the tough warrior.

He bowed low to her. "I can't expect a woman of your stature to handfast with me unless I've shown how well I can care for you." He waved at the cows and chickens. "Be my wife, Rhonwen, and these fine animals are yours."

Rhonwen's mind worked frantically for a way to decline without shaming him in front of everyone. As she walked slowly around the beasts pretending to examine them, the musicians played louder, and the crowd of students grew.

"When I see your fine son," Aras continued, "I am all the more eager for you to have my children, too."

Rhonwen could only sputter.

"You've always been pleasing to the eye, but since the boy was born, you've also proven yourself a worthy breeder: good hips, a strong back, and teats to suckle a litter!"

Orlan laughed, and Rhonwen crossed her arms, speechless. Rede giggled and tried to pet the nearest cow. The animal bawled, and the musicians quickened the beat.

"Be my wife," Aras said, his voice rising to compete with the music.

Rhonwen finally found her voice. "Aras," she said, "you're most generous."

He gestured toward the cattle. "This? This is nothing!"

Rhonwen grabbed his arm. "Come," she said. "I can't talk with all this noise."

She dragged him toward the building but glimpsed an array of amused smiles on the faces of several students. Quickly changing direction, she guided him toward the quiet inner courtyard.

Once they were alone, Aras smiled confidently. "I'm camped not far from here. We could ride double. My men would ensure our privacy." He moved his hand from her waist to the small of her back and eased her toward him.

She put her palms on his chest and countered the pressure. "Hold a moment. I've given you the wrong idea."

Aras slid his hands down her back to her buttocks. "No other woman has stayed in my head the way you have. None!"

"Hold, I said!" Rhonwen pried his hands off and backed away. "You can't come after me the way you go after men in battle!"

"You're right. I must temper myself. You can't imagine—"

"Oh, I think I can," she said.

"Then let's go now!" he said. "'Tis a glorious evening. We can couple until dawn and hardly raise a sweat!" He smiled broadly. "And you can't deny the sense of testing the saddle one may be riding for years."

"Aras, stop!" Rhonwen gripped his wrists. "I'm flattered that you think of me. I'm honored that you offer me such fine gifts, but—"

"But what? It's not enough? Those cows are the scrawniest of the lot. I've an entire herd that puts them to shame."

"No, Aras." She could not hold him in her heart the way he obviously held her. "I'll not handfast with you, nor will I share your bed."

"There's another, isn't there? The boy's father! But what kind of man leaves you with his get and never returns? Tell me his name, and I'll cut his heart out!"

"There is no other, Aras. There never was." He was loyal to Sertorius, and to tell him might inhibit that loyalty.

Aras took her hands in his, this time with earnest friendship and gentleness. "Then let me be the boy's father. I'll teach him to ride, to fight, to lead men. I'd gladly call him my son."

Rhonwen smiled with genuine admiration for the man and his sense of honor and pride. "I'm more grateful for your offer than you can imagine, Aras. If anything should ever happen to me, I hope someone would bring Rede to you. I know he'd be safe, and you'd make a man of him."

Aras bowed. "It would be an honor, should the day ever come, but why wait? I'm willing to do it now." He gripped her hands. "I don't know what words you need to hear from me. I'm no bard, but I can promise you I'll stand by you all my days, and as long as I live you'll want for nothing."

His devotion wrenched at her. "You make it difficult for me to say no."

"Then don't!"

"I must," Rhonwen said. "You're generous and loyal, and I'm sure you'd do everything you could to make me happy."

"I will!"

She brushed a wisp of hair from his face. "But there's no fire in my heart for you."

"A fire may be lit," he said with sudden earnestness. "An evening under the stars..."

"A hundred such evenings won't change that, Aras. I'm sorry."

He looked away, and Rhonwen waited for him to say something. She wished she could feel more than friendship for this proud warrior, even if it were merely a shadow of what she'd felt in Sertorius' arms.

He stepped away from her. "I should have expected this." A hard look settled around his eyes. "I should have expected things to go badly. The signs from the gods have been unfavorable for Iberia ever since that skulking dog crawled into Sertorius' tent."

Rhonwen beckoned him to sit beside her on a marble bench in the courtyard. "What are you talking about? Almost weekly I hear of another battle won, or another town that's thrown down the Roman banner and replaced it with Sertorius'."

"That much is true," Aras said, "but for the Iberian clans who've been with him from the start, it's a different story. Our taxes have risen as high as they were before we threw the Romans out. Until Perpenna arrived, we prospered. Now the levy for grain and gold has doubled twice in one year!"

"What does Perpenna have to do with it?"

Aras scowled. "He administers while Sertorius wages war. Cesada represented the Trepani at Sertorius' camp. There he learned much about Perpenna from those who lead the legions he claimed to bring from Rome."

"Claimed?"

"Aye. According to his lieutenants, he made such a mess of it, they threatened to leave him behind if he didn't listen to them and march directly to Sertorius."

She wasn't surprised. Aras' story matched the one Aemelius told.

Aras put his hand over hers. "I had another reason for asking you to handfast with me. I don't know how it is here in Osca, but in Langos and many other clanholds, the people are angry. They didn't throw their lot with Sertorius to trade a Roman collar for one of his design."

"But didn't you just say Perpenna was behind it?"

"I think he is," Aras said, "but that's only because I believe Cesada. There's going to be trouble. I know clan chiefs who speak of rising up against Sertorius." He looked into her eyes. "If it comes to that, you won't be safe here."

"I still have my old wagon," Rhonwen said. "It wouldn't take long for us to pack and be on the road."

"But where would you go? Who would protect you?"

"Who would attack a healer and a druid?"

"Perpenna!"

"I'll make you a promise," Rhonwen said. "If it appears we may be in trouble, I'll pack up and leave. If you'll still have us in Langos, we'll head there."

A look of hope flickered in Aras' eyes. "You won't regret it!"

"But you must make me a promise, too," Rhonwen said. "Before you join in any rebellion, you owe it to Sertorius to talk to him directly. If he's been spending all his time on the war, he may not know what Perpenna's been up to."

"I wonder if it's not too late. No one speaks to Sertorius anymore without going through Perpenna. Your young friend Aemelius proved that." Aras shook his head. "The poor fool."

Rhonwen stiffened with apprehension. "What do you mean?"

Aras looked at her in surprise and regret. "You haven't heard? Cesada told me Aemelius came to see Sertorius some months ago, but Perpenna had him arrested for deserting his post."

The ground suddenly seemed unstable, and Rhonwen grabbed Aras for support. "Where is Aemelius now?"

Aras held her steady. "They crucified him."

19

Though I reject the written ways, this one thing I cannot entrust to any bard. When Benecin and I are both long dead, the masters who follow may wonder how such a puny man could best the Boar of Eban. The truth is thus: by wit and courage did Amrec alone succeed in saving Benecin from certain death beneath the tusks of a sow as she led her piglets through the turnip field.
— *Stave Two of Fyrsil, 39th Master of Mount Eban Enclave*

Armorica 77 B.C.

A dozen young warriors led by Caradowc jostled each other as they crossed the commons toward Gillac's feasting hall. Mallec didn't like the look of them, especially Borwyn, a Helveti who'd attached himself to the band of disaffected youths. It irked him the way Caradowc fawned on every word Gar said while berating him behind his back. Borwyn was worse. His love of the knife offended Mallec, who preferred to see disputes handled either within the law or by a good wrestling match. The days when a blood fight settled every squabble were rapidly diminishing. According to the bardic chronologies, no one had died in a local skirmish for forty years. As the young men filed into the hall, he prayed Gillac and Trochu could maintain that peace.

"Master Mallec?" Arie said.

He turned at her subdued tones. She held fast to her foster sister Klervie, a Veneti child living with Gar and Willa. Whenever Arie visited Gillac, the two were inseparable. Now they stood solemnly huddled together, eyes red-rimmed and puffy. Arie did not weep easily, and the sight of her grief distressed him. "What is it?"

"It's Budec," she said at last.

No one ever determined what caused the young bard's malady that Beltane eve two years earlier. He'd spent the time following Arie like an orphaned puppy. He'd lost his mirth as well as his poetry, and he rarely spoke. Whenever Mallec saw him, he remembered Galan.

"What about Budec?" he asked.

Grief edged her voice. "He's dead. He sat beside me as he always did. When I glanced at him, his eyes saw only Rhiannon."

"Rhiannon is a gentle goddess, Arie."

She wiped at her tears with the backs of her hands. "Aye, although why she wanted Budec when he had so much to give angers me."

Mallec could only nod.

He reached for her hand. "Send someone to the enclave to fetch Dierdre. We'll need another druid for Budec's ceremony."

Arie paled. "Is there no one else? Budec never liked her, and even after he became sick, he shivered whenever she came near."

"I understand, but tradition demands two druids for a proper ceremony, and the others are all away."

Arie bowed her head as the crowd of young warriors clattered from the hall. She stiffened at the approach of her half-brother.

Caradowc reached out to her, but she pulled away. He didn't seem to notice. "Father wants you to join us at dinner tonight when Mallec prays for your mother's return to health," he said.

Arie sniffed. "Your service to our father does you honor. Of course I'll come." Her voice caught, and Mallec knew she only wanted to be in the wailing house when night came.

"I'll tell him," Caradowc said, herding his friends away.

The druid and the two girls had barely crossed the yard when Leuw hailed them from the direction of the Chief's residence. "Mallec! We must talk."

"Leuw?" Mallec waved. "Welcome."

Leuw dropped from his pony cart with a huff, his usually jovial face grim. "If only this were a pleasant journey." He looked toward Gar's home. "We face great trouble, but I don't know what's gotten into Gar."

"His wife is gravely ill," he said. "You can't expect him to be his old self."

"Willa's illness doesn't mean he can ignore his duties. He's still clan chief, and..." His voice trailed off as he noticed Arie and Klervie. "Has someone arrived before me with the news, or has some other sadness befallen you?"

Arie took a deep breath. "Budec is dead."

The bard leaned heavily against one of the cart wheels. Tears welled in his eyes, and he brushed them away. "As long as I live, I shall never understand the gods. Why must they heap so many troubles on us all at once?"

Mallec spread his hands. "The gods choose when to take our lives. For Budec, it may have been a kindness."

"Kindness when they kill us slowly?"

Mallec said nothing.

Leuw went on angrily, "Killing Budec and Willa slowly wasn't enough. Now they send raiders to attack those least able to defend themselves."

"Raiders?" Mallec asked. "Here?"

"Not the clanhold," Leuw said. "Such swine prey on farms and settlements of two or three families—like the one they attacked yesterday."

"Does Gar know?"

"Yes. That's why I'm so angry." He hammered a fist into the side of the cart, alarming the pony. "He says it's too late to do anything."

Leuw pulled him aside beyond the hearing of the girls. "This should come as no surprise. These raiders have been in Armorica a long time, and they've come steadily closer to us each year. As Master of Eban enclave, you should've known about them and warned Gar to be ready."

"I don't have visions about everything!"

"I'm not talking about visions," Leuw snapped. "I'm talking about being aware of something other than your private projects."

The accusation embarrassed Mallec. He'd been so busy with his own pursuits that he'd paid scant attention to events beyond Suetoni and Lemarii lands. "You're right," he said. "I left such matters to Dierdre."

"Dierdre!" Leuw raged. "You let her run the enclave when Fyrsil, who knew her best, warned against her? Yet you hand it to her! Try paying less attention to your precious archives and more to your people!"

Mallec held up a hand. Leuw's words hurt him deeply. "My work is important and must be done. I saw no reason why Dierdre's talents should be wasted."

Leuw spat. "You should distrust her. She's a dark, bitter woman who treats her own son like a cur and everyone else like servants. By the gods, Mallec, she's usurped your legal power, and you don't even recognize it."

"That's absurd. Dierdre has always done her duties, and I have no quarrel with her."

The bard snorted. "Have you looked at the servants lately? Not one of those who served Fyrsil or Orlan remains. Why do you think that is?"

Mallec struggled to keep his temper. "I won't discuss this further. I know what I'm doing."

"Good. I trust you'll make Gar send men after the raiders. Maybe one of you will do what's expected."

Leuw climbed back into the cart and untwisted the reins running the length of the pony's flank.

Mallec felt a crushing sense of loss as the big man prepared to drive away. "Where are you going?"

"Somewhere I won't have to watch you surrender anything else to Dierdre."

Mallec could not let his friend leave in anger. "Leuw, wait! If you're right, then I need your help." Leuw remained silent, and Mallec prayed for the right words. "Please stay long enough to help offer cleansing prayers for Willa?"

"After what I just said to Gar, I doubt I'd be welcome in his house anytime." He clucked at the pony and slapped the lines lightly on its back.

"Wait." Mallec grabbed at the harness but missed.

Arie ran after the cart and pulled hard enough on one line to turn the pony. "Please," she cried. "You must stay! We need another druid to send Budec properly to the Otherworld."

Leuw halted the pony. "Of course," he said, looking down at her. "Forgive me, Arie. I'll stay the night."

"Thank you." She gave him a faint smile and then led the pony back to Mallec. "Do you still want me to send for Driad Dierdre?"

With Leuw staying, he had no need to summon Dierdre. He wondered if the woman would have even answered his summons. The more he thought about it, the more certain he became she would have found some reason not to come. "Budec would prefer Leuw. I know I do."

Leuw refused to look at him, but Mallec thanked him anyway. He put an arm around Arie's shoulders. "Willa needs our prayers. We'll meet for that just after dusk. Until then, take some of the women and prepare Budec."

She kissed him on the cheek and, with Klervie in tow, ran toward the wailing house. ✠ ✠ ✠

Dierdre watched the stone mason as he climbed from the depths of the enclave's collapsed well. Since the cave-in, water had to be carried by bucket from a stream beyond the pasture. The mason grunted as he rested his back against the well's undamaged upper walls.

"Can it be repaired?" Dierdre asked.

"Perhaps, but you'd do better to build a new one."

Dierdre fumed. The enclave had no funds for such a major undertaking. To raise the money, someone would have to appeal to Gillac and Trochu. She squeezed her hands into tight fists, knowing Mallec would expect her to do it.

"It's the roots from that oak," the mason said pointing to a gigantic tree. "They've grown through the side and pushed the stones out of the way." He shook his head. "Truth be known, this well wasn't built right to begin with."

That didn't surprise her. The enclave had always been poor, and few of the masters had been as good at managing affairs as she. "Surely there's something you can do."

"If this were just a farm, I'd build with local stone, but since this well serves a druid enclave, it demands something special. Think how good it'd look made from granite."

"*Buy* stone?" Dierdre laughed. "We grow it! The students can bring all you need."

The mason frowned. "The work'll go faster if I bring my own. It takes a trained eye to find the right material. Not all rock cuts the same way, and each piece must fit exactly. If the seams aren't tight, you won't be happy. What good is a well that won't hold water?"

"Why can't you re-use the stone that's already here?"

The mason paled. "And disturb the spirits?"

Dierdre pursed her lips. "What spirits?"

"In the well!" He lowered his voice. "They come at Samhain, they do. Those what don't find their way back to the Otherworld by dawn crawl into the cracks between the stones. Some of 'em never leave, 'cept at night. I've heard 'em, especially 'round spring time. I'd stay clear of 'em if I was you. To avoid any problems, build with fresh stone."

Dierdre rubbed her temples. It seemed every laborer to arrive at the enclave brought a new set of superstitions. The mason was no different, nor did it come as a surprise his stories supported his suggestion for a more expensive solution.

"Master mason," she said, "what makes you think you know the spirits better than I?"

He pushed the shapeless rag he used for a hat to the back of his head. "I don't make claims about all spirits, just the ones what affect my livelihood."

And the prices you charge, she thought. "Use the stone that's here. Replace the broken pieces if you must, but don't expect me to pay you to haul them here."

"Beggin' yer pardon, Driad, but that'd be the same mistake Coemgen's son made over in Trochu."

Dierdre stiffened. "What're you talking about?"

He knocked the dust from his breeches. "No mason around here takes chances with spirits." He lowered his voice conspiratorially. "Have ye' not heard of the Giant's Tomb? Gwair wants to put a house on it! He's daft if he thinks any stone cutter will go near it. The same goes for your well." He crossed his arms. "When spirits are involved, it's new stone or no well."

The news about Gwair stunned her. She hadn't expected him to do anything with the land until he succeeded his father as Lemarii chief, by which time she'd always thought Caradowc would have replaced Gar.

"Gwair's building on the Giant's Tomb?"

"Aye, trying to, though no one will work for him," he said, shaking his head. "He's sent all the way to the Redones in the north for workers. That house'll cost more than money."

Much more, Dierdre thought. Gwair had to be stopped.

"I suggest we put the new well a good bit farther from the tree," the mason said.

She stared at him, too busy thinking about the Giant's Tomb and the Ageless Man to respond.

The mason pointed toward an open spot. "There. I'd put it right there."

"Fine."

He bobbed his head like a rooster. "I'm a bit short-handed just now. D'ye suppose some of yer students could help with the diggin'?"

Dierdre stared at a spot somewhere above the mason's head, her thoughts far from the well. If Gwair built on the Giant's Tomb she'd be unable to find the treasure once she resolved the riddle of the sticks.

She dismissed the mason with a wave as she walked slowly back toward her quarters. "Do whatever you need to do."

⌖ ⌖ ⌖

Mallec watched Leuw angle his cart toward Bard's House, a stone building reserved for druids visiting Gillac. Of its two rooms, one was set aside for lodging, the other for preparation of the dead. Because of its second purpose, the villagers also called it the wailing house. He wondered how long it would be before Willa spent her last night there. The same question had occupied Gar's mind for months, and Mallec had watched him wither at nearly the same rate as his wife. Mallec had little stomach for burdening him further, but Leuw was right—raiders had to be stopped.

Gar met him at the door. "Leuw sent you, didn't he?"

In the sunlight Mallec could see how much Gar had faded from the robust warrior he once was, to a man desperately in need of a new purpose for living. The skin under his eyes hung like grain sacks.

"I would've come anyway. How's Willa?"

The chief paced like a tethered hound on the scent. "She's in great pain. Do you have any more of the white powder?"

"I can spare some," Mallec said, although he knew the supply dwindled.

"Thank you," Gar said. "I feel helpless when her pains come, and my prayers for her go unanswered."

Mallec rested his hand on Gar's shoulder. "When Lugh sets his burden down at dusk and can listen, we will pray for Willa."

"You must speak to all the gods," Gar said, pleading.

"We cannot halt those deaths decreed by the gods," said Mallec, "but we can address those wrought by men. You must do something about the Redone raiders."

Gar's eyes seemed empty. "I already told Leuw there's no sense in chasing shadows. Those men may wear Redone colors, but they ride for someone else."

"It makes no difference," Mallec said. "What will people think if you don't try to protect them?"

"You don't understand," Gar said, "they can't be caught."

Mallec stared at him. "Because they wear false colors?"

"Because they have some special power. What else explains how they've eluded capture for so long?"

"It doesn't matter who the raiders are or where they come from. The people expect you to protect them. You can't just sit in your house wringing your hands." He realized Leuw's words about his own failures had made him put a sharp edge on his remarks.

"I can't leave Willa."

"Then send someone else!" Mallec said, keeping his voice low, although he wanted to shout at Gar the way Leuw had shouted at him. The man's grief had beaten away the chief's power. "I saw half a dozen young warriors on the commons with nothing to do. Find horses for them and put them under the command of someone who knows what he is doing."

"Send Caradowc?"

Caradowc was the last man Mallec would have chosen. Young warriors wanted to bang on their shields, shake their spears and attack bravely. That won't even scare seasoned raiders. The Suetoni men would die and leave the village weaker than ever. "You'd be wise to send experienced men. If these raiders are as elusive as you suggest, the men who search for them won't have time to wet-nurse pups."

"You're right," Gar said. "I'll put Setaine in charge. He can lead the gate watch. That's about all the horses we have without sending to the countryside for more."

"You're making the right decision," Mallec said.

"I want Leuw to come with you tonight to pray for Willa. Will he?"

Mallec shrugged. "You're both too proud for your own good. He loves you. He'll come."

✠ ✠ ✠

Dierdre left for Gillac as soon as she'd finished with the mason. His news about Gwair forced her to reconsider her options. To stop Gwair, she'd have to make her case for return of the land much sooner than she'd planned. She had counted on doing it as Enclave Master while Caradowc represented Gillac. Now she'd have to depend on Mallec and Gar. Her chances of success would be better asking hares to chase hounds.

The guard looked unusually stern as he allowed her into the clanhold and pushed the gate shut behind her. The Suetoni had ignored such precautions for years, and Dierdre hoped there had been no renewed hostilities with the Lemarii. Her chances of regaining her land were bad enough already.

She spotted Caradowc on the commons with a number of other young men and resisted the urge to find something for them to do. Since Caradowc refused to meet her gaze, she rode toward him and waited until the conversations around him died. At last he faced her, propping his head in his hand as he lay on the ground.

"Will you not help an old woman off her horse?" she asked.

"I suppose we can be trusted for that much," he muttered as he rolled to his feet. He gripped the bridle of her horse to steady the skittish beast.

Dierdre dropped lightly to the ground. "What? I don't distrust you. I haven't even seen you in months."

"I meant Gar," he said. "He sent out a war party today but made us stay behind."

Dierdre suddenly understood the greater care at the gate. "A war party? To Trochu?"

He shook his head. "He sent them after Redone raiders. But Gar sent the wrong men! There's more fight in us than in those fat farmers who guard the gate."

His words brought cries of affirmation from his comrades, and Dierdre gave them a sympathetic nod, although she didn't care who the raiders were as long as the peace held between the Lemarii and the Suetoni. She gripped Caradowc's arm. "I must speak with you alone."

He wore a characteristically suspicious expression but steered her to the shade of an oak. "The day hasn't been a complete loss," he said. "A bard died this morning. The idiot."

"Budec." Dierdre suppressed a smile. She had wondered how long he'd last.

"So, what do you want? I'm busy," Caradowc said.

"I see, but I thought I'd ask you for a favor."

Caradowc squirmed as he always did when she asked him to do something. She had to be careful. A grown man, he could easily refuse her.

"Done properly, you might even enjoy it," she said. When he straightened with interest, she continued. "It's about our land."

He sneered. "It still isn't yours, or mine."

"But it will be. I want you to stop the Lemarii thieves from building on it."

"And start a war with Trochu?" Caradowc laughed.

She waited impatiently for him to settle down. Why couldn't he have been born with at least a shred of vision? "There needn't be any fighting. I have something else in mind."

When she finished explaining her plan, Caradowc trotted back to his friends. As she retrieved her horse and walked toward Gar's home she heard them laughing, an excellent sign.

Gar wasted his first chance to be in her good graces, and he would have only one more. If he helped her regain her land, she might ignore the past. She hated that Gar's simpering wife distracted him. Her lingering illness irked Dierdre. She patted the pouch containing the dainty narcissus bulbs she'd brought from the enclave. One had to be careful lest they be mistaken for small onions, an agonizingly fatal error.

She stopped outside Gar's house, swatted dust from her robe and tapped on the door post.

"Enter," came the reply.

She stepped inside and gagged at the stale smell of sickness. Willa lay near the fire with her head and shoulders propped up on a pile of stuffed sacks. She coughed, and the deep wrenching sound suggested she would soon need to make her peace with the gods. Gar rested beside her.

He gasped when he recognized Dierdre. "I didn't expect to see you. I suppose you think I should have sent Caradowc after the raiders."

She let concern settle over her face. "I think you made a wise choice." She paused and glanced at Gar's wife. "We have not always agreed, but I want to put that behind us. Is there anything I can do for Willa?"

Gar's startled expression faded, replaced by pathetic weakness. "A healer from Trochu visited once, but she could do nothing. The gods call, and Willa grows weaker by the day."

Gar had aged considerably since she'd last seen him. Obviously, Willa had become an undue burden. She eased a concerned smile to her lips. "Send for me if you need me."

Gar nodded curtly. "Many thanks, but surely you didn't come here just to offer condolences."

"That's true," she said. "I came to discuss a legal matter. I hate to bother you now, but as chief..."

Gar motioned to the door. "Can we talk outside?"

271

With a sense of victory, Dierdre followed him. They walked slowly toward the well in the village center. "I've come about the border land the Lemarii stole from my family," she said. "I want it back. Not for me, but for Caradowc. He needs his own place in the world."

Gar shook his head. "I can't make that decision."

"Of course you can. You are chief. With my sanction as druid, you'll have all the authority you need."

"It's not a question of authority. If I make this demand, old wounds will reopen. We've had peace with the Lemarii for forty years. I won't jeopardize it."

She narrowed her eyes. "My birthright and my parents' blood bought that peace. Without benefit of kin, I've had to scrape by on handouts all my life. My son—our son—will fare no better. He has nothing to occupy his days and spends them idly with lesser men. Is that all you want for him?"

Gar raised his hands, palms out. "I agree about Caradowc, but for you to be involved in a judgment from which you'd benefit would be wrong. The Lemarii wouldn't stand for it."

She feigned desperation and squeezed a tear from her eye. "You can't abandon Caradowc. You must help him."

He paused as she bit at her lower lip, then reached for her trembling hands. "Perhaps Mallec could approach the Lemarii," he said slowly. "Since he's neutral, they might listen to him."

"You'll convince him to plead my case?"

Gar released her hands. "I'll speak to him."

She brushed the tears away. "I trust you, Gar, and I know you won't allow this dishonor to go unavenged."

His face returned to its characteristic frown. "I can't promise that, Dierdre, but I'll try. Coemgen may be hot-tempered, but he's not unapproachable. There may be other options. I'll discuss them with Mallec."

"I knew I could count on you." She sighed. "When will you see him?"

"He's coming to pray for Willa tonight."

Dierdre pursed her lips. "Then perhaps you'd better talk to him now. Later, both of you will be too busy dealing with Willa to think about it."

Gar glanced at his house and then toward Bard's House where Mallec and Arie had left their cart. "I suppose you're right," he said. "This may take a while. Will you look in on Willa and see if she needs anything?"

"Of course." Dierdre patted his hand. "I'll fix her a bit of soup."

✠ ✠ ✠

"No fires," Caradowc said to the young men who had taken him up on his promise of a good venture. "We stay here by the river until just before sunset. By then the workers should be leaving."

They tied their mounts to trees and settled comfortably to wait in the tall grass beside the water.

"I've been thinking about that sister of yours, Caradowc," Borwyn said after a while. "She's just the sort of woman I'd want come Beltane."

"Arie?" Caradowc snorted. "She's not the woman for you. She thinks she's better than all of us."

Weasel-eyed Pugh sitting beside Borwyn laughed. "Anyone is better than Borwyn."

"I'd leave her smiling," Borwyn said. "Sore, but smiling."

Caradowc pretended outrage. "That's my sister you're talking about! Well, half of her is."

Borwyn grunted. "You can keep the half with the sharp tongue, but I'd be pleased to use the other half tonight." He grabbed at his crotch, and they all snickered.

Pugh pushed the Helveti and puffed out his chest. "A woman that beautiful wouldn't even look at you. Why should she when she can have me?"

Borwyn flashed the feral half-smile that had first drawn Caradowc to him. Borwyn was persistent. If he desired Arie, there was little anyone could do to stop him. Caradowc might enjoy letting such a thing happen if it fit in with the plan Dierdre had suggested. He liked the idea of becoming chief of the Suetoni.

Borwyn worked his tongue over his lips and pulled at the long hairs of his mustache. "It's been too long since I had a woman," he said.

"Well, you won't be getting her tonight," Caradowc said. "We've got work ahead of us. We'll begin as soon as the laborers pack up their tools and go." He turned to Pugh. "Sneak close to the mound so you can see when they start to leave, then come back here and let us know."

Pugh wrinkled his nose. "Why do I have to go? Why don't you send Borwyn?"

Caradowc narrowed his eyes. "Are you telling me you can't do this simple task?"

Pugh rose to his feet.

"Keep out of sight," Caradowc said.

"I'm not stupid." When no one replied, he walked toward the edge of the forest that marked the boundary of the mound. There he paused and looked over his shoulder. When he saw Caradowc watching him, he dropped to the ground and crawled out of sight.

He came scurrying back before the others became restless.

"They're gone. The masons were packing up when I got there, and I watched until they left."

"Good," said Caradowc. "Stay here and wait for my signal."

He picked his way through the trees to the edge of the forest to see for himself. The house at the far end of the pasture looked deserted. Caradowc waved for the others to join him and then led them in single file to the Giant's Tomb. Just as Dierdre claimed, the early stages of construction had begun on a dwelling situated near the center of the ancient mound.

Pugh looked up at Caradowc. "Why must we do the work of spirits? Why can't they deal with the laborers themselves?"

"I asked my mother the same question," Caradowc said. "According to her, the souls of the Ancients have been ghosts for so long they've grown weak."

"What does it matter to us?" Borwyn asked.

"All spirits talk," Caradowc said, taking time to make eye contact with everyone in his little band. "When our time comes to enter the Otherworld, we'll be heroes for what we do here."

During the night, they labored to undo as much of the construction as possible. Working by the light of a half moon, the men assaulted the stones stacked carefully by size, color, and shape, and threw them in a jumble. They dislodged foundation stones and tumbled them down the slope into the thick brush and thorn bushes at the perimeter of the mound.

"Give me a hand, Pugh," Caradowc said as he stacked short flat stones in two narrow columns.

Pugh twisted his face in puzzlement. "What're you doing?"

"Building a man." When the two pillars stood as tall as his thigh, Caradowc fitted a lintel stone across both columns. "Hips," he said with satisfaction.

Pugh hurried away to fetch more flat rocks.

By the time they'd finished the crude statue, Borwyn and the others had joined them.

Borwyn frowned. "It's missing something."

"Like what?"

"It'd be better if I showed you," he said, walking away.

"Borwyn!" Caradowc said. "Where are you going?"

"You'll see," he whispered back.

Caradowc made the others clear the area of anything that might suggest people rather than angry spirits caused the mayhem. They dragged branches over their footprints and inspected the ground for any other signs of their presence. By the time they finished, Borwyn returned with a freshly killed ewe.

"What's that for?" Caradowc asked.

Borwyn chuckled as he handed the carcass to two of the others and directed them to hold it, head down, over the stone statue. He cut its throat and let the blood drip down on the structure below.

"Nice touch," Caradowc said. "We'll take the carcass and greet tomorrow with roast mutton." He started to walk away but paused at a sly thought. "Leave the head on top of the rocks."

⌗ ⌗ ⌗

Arie dragged Mallec and Leuw toward her parents' house. "It's not yet dusk," Mallec said. "Why the hurry?"

Arie spoke through trembling lips. "Mother's worse."

Leuw frowned. "Has anyone sent to Trochu for the healer?"

"Old Efa doesn't travel much anymore," Mallec replied. "She came only once this year."

Inside the house, Willa lay in her bed groaning. Gar sat near her. Leuw looked from one to the other then knelt beside the bed and took Willa's hand in his. "Forgive me for bringing harsh words into your home this morning," he said.

She turned dark-rimmed eyes at him and smiled faintly, then whispered something Mallec couldn't hear. Leuw smiled and patted her hand, although a tear betrayed his anguish. "I promise," he said. "From now on, I'll drink only with Mallec."

Leuw eased away from her and settled on the floor. Arie and Klervie joined him to form three corners of a sacred square. Mallec threw fragrant herbs on the fire as the four of them joined hands and began to chant. Mallec led them through several prayers then asked Arie to see whether the sun had touched the horizon.

She went quickly to the door. "It's time," she said and then handed Leuw his great flat drum while she and Klervie each took up a pair of rhythm sticks.

Leuw chose the beat, and the girls joined in. Before Mallec closed his eyes and surrendered himself to the world of the gods, he glanced one last time at Willa. Her cough had subsided, but now she clenched her jaws and threw her head back as the muscles in her arms and legs contracted.

The two girls stared at her and Mallec cleared his throat to regain their attention. He nodded at Leuw, and all three bent to the task of keeping the beat.

Mallec closed his eyes and let the sound wash over him. Though the journey was his, the gods alone chose the path and the destination.

As the rhythm steadied, the sounds of the drum and the beating sticks blended into a steady harmonic voice. The room shrank from his awareness. He prayed Rhiannon herself would hear his plea for Willa.

He walked alone through a silent wood with no trail. The only signs he had to follow were splashes of red on the tree trunks. As he passed through the dense forest, new growth sprang up behind him to block his retreat. His world became a narrow lane of tree bark and deadfall.

He called to the gods, asking them to show themselves that he might plead for Willa's life, but they remained hidden. Finally he passed beyond the trees. Instead of squeezing between oaks and elms, he now made his way through tightly packed warriors who waved their weapons and screamed, although he could hear nothing save the distant beat of a drum. Soon he reached a point beyond which the warriors would not venture. He struggled out into a meadow that seemed familiar, and he realized with dread he'd journeyed here in spirit before.

The dark-haired woman should be here, he thought, as he looked back at the solid wall of armed men who ringed the space. He knew what else would be there and looked down hoping to tell which druid lay headless before him.

Leuw sounded the recall rhythm.

Mallec dropped to his knees beside the body as the warriors dissolved into a fog that spread across the field. Not yet, he prayed. I need more time!

The drum beat faster than before, and the sticks failed to keep up. The disharmony pulled at him until at last he opened his eyes.

Gar stared at him from his place beside Willa, who curled in a hard trembling ball.

"Did you talk to them?" the chief asked. "Did you beg the gods for Willa's life?"

Mallec felt a hideous mix of fear, shame, and sorrow. "They did not show themselves."

Gar's eyes closed in resignation. Mallec wished there had been some gentle lie he could have told, but Gar deserved better. Besides, Mallec remained in turmoil over the scene the gods had shown him. Did they expect him to know whose body it was?

He looked at Willa lying in agony as she awaited death and prayed he would have the same kind of courage to face his own. That it would occur soon seemed only too obvious.

20

Benecin's achievement is legendary, but those who know the true tale laugh. Benecin chooses not to remember when he lay face down in the muck, surrounded by half-grown piglets and served as a throne for their mother. Had Amrec not speared her with Benecin's own weapon, he would have died without glory. The clan feasted that night as the great sow took well to roasting. Esteemed throughout the world, only here in Eban is Benecin the boar and a nameless man the hero.
— *Stave Three of Fyrsil, 39th Master of Mount Eban Enclave*

Iberia

After adding the last figure in the column for the second time, Rhonwen tried to rub the stiffness from her neck. Maintaining the accounts for the school had never been easy, but the task had grown considerably more difficult each time she received a demand for more information. Though signed by Perpenna, the author was always identified as Sertorius.

She rolled the vellum documents and slid them inside protective leather sleeves. If he doesn't like the way I run the school, she thought, he should come here and tell me himself. Since when did teaching children revolve around scratch marks in a ledger? There was much to be said for bardic learning.

Gathering the ends of her cloak, she pulled them tighter and pinned them in place. Neither the threadbare fabric nor the simple pin appeared to belong to someone in a position of authority. The colored enamel on the pin had worn through in spots, and the oft-mended cloak was as thin as slave leather. Since Perpenna began handling the school's finances, Rhonwen had received no payment for her work. The school provided her with food and shelter, but any money she needed now came from students and their parents. That had been enough to buy clothing for Rede and nothing else. Not for the first time she wondered at the wisdom of turning down Aras' offer.

Though she'd resisted the idea, the time had come to sell her wagon. The money from the sale would provide a cushion for these lean times.

She decided to discuss it with Orlan after dinner. Right now, she intended to visit the Roman bath. The demands on her time made such visits infrequent, but she allowed herself the luxury as a reward for keeping the school's books. Ever since Perpenna had ordered her to make copies of the school's accounts, Rhonwen had doubled her visits to the baths.

A commotion near the stable interrupted her, and she leaned out her window to see its cause. A man flanked by four Roman guards marched toward the school entrance. She rushed into the yard outside the school's gate, adjusted her cloak, and stepped forward to meet them.

The guards halted in ragged formation with their leader in the center. He spoke to her without preamble. "You there! I seek the mistress of this school. Bring her to me immediately."

Rhonwen didn't move. She recognized him, although he did not recognize her.

Perpenna scowled. "Are you deaf?" When she did not reply, he turned to his guards. "Do any of you speak the barbarian's tongue?"

One of them nodded and translated his demands.

"I heard him," Rhonwen said in fluent Latin.

The leader of the little band scowled at her. "Then do as I command, or I'll have you beaten for your insolence."

"There will be no beatings here," she said. "Not as long as I run this school."

"You're Rhonwen? Why didn't you say so?"

"I'm not in the habit of introducing myself to men who barge into my domain unannounced." She crossed her arms.

He regarded her with the same furtive eyes as on his first visit. He wore no helmet over his short-cropped gray hair, making his already thin face cadaverous. Missing teeth hampered his speech, although she doubted he'd lost them in battle. He glowered. "You dress like a slave."

"My attire reflects my wages," she retorted.

"You should recognize your betters. I am magistrate for General Sertorius."

"How good of you to come," she said, her animosity masked only by the civility of her words. "You've saved me the trouble of finding a courier to deliver the copies of our accounts."

"Such copies won't be needed any longer."

She felt a surge of relief. "You've decided to trust me?"

"We've decided to replace you."

It took a moment for her to register the meaning of his words. At first she thought she misunderstood something, but then the pit of her stomach rolled and the realization hit her like a hammer blow.

"What's going on here?" Orlan asked as he exited the building with a trail of students in his wake.

Rhonwen said nothing. She would not shame herself in front of the students.

"I'm here to repair the damage of a regrettable decision," Perpenna said. "I've just relieved this woman of her duties."

Rhonwen took a deep breath. "You've no authority here," she said. "Sertorius himself appointed me to this post."

Perpenna wrinkled his nose as if he detected a foul odor. "It's my responsibility to oversee administrative affairs. In that capacity I have the power to dismiss anyone I please, especially Iberian trash like you."

His words elicited cries of anger from the older students and confusion and fear among the younger ones.

"Why are you doing this?" Rhonwen asked. "The school prospers, the teachers are competent, and the students are learning."

"You have been seen in the company of a traitor." Perpenna motioned for two of his guards to enter the building.

"What traitor?" Rhonwen kept her voice level. She stepped in front of the approaching guards. Orlan moved close beside her, and the students bunched up behind them.

"Do you deny consorting with the Trepani chieftain known as Aras?"

"He's no more a traitor than I am!"

"Then you admit knowing him," Perpenna said.

"Of course I do."

The Roman smirked and nodded to the soldier on his right. "Her confession is duly noted."

"Confession?" Rhonwen glanced at Orlan, but he seemed as bewildered as she was.

"You claim to be no more a traitor than Aras. I presume you're no less a traitor, either."

"This is an outrage," Rhonwen said. Orlan stepped to her side and blocked the first guard's passage. The man shoved him aside. The children, mostly boys between eight and fourteen, circled the warrior.

"Should any of these brats get in your way," Perpenna said, "kill them."

"They're children!" Rhonwen cried as the guard drew his sword.

"Then they're agile enough to get out of the way," Perpenna said.

Rhonwen waved at the students. "Let them pass." She looked at Orlan in sudden alarm. "Where's Rede?"

"I haven't seen him since lunch."

Rhonwen pushed past Perpenna to search the barn, but he grabbed her by the shoulder. "Where are you going?"

She whirled on him with fists clenched. "To find my son."

"That can wait until you've turned over all records and assets of the school."

"Consider them yours," Rhonwen said as she brushed him aside. "They're no longer my concern."

"Where are the records?" Perpenna shrieked, his voice rising as the druids moved away from him.

"In the school, of course," Rhonwen yelled back. "You'll have to ask whoever's in charge to find them for you."

Rhonwen and Orlan entered the barn and listened for the sounds of a child playing at battle. "Rede?" Rhonwen called. "Are you in here?"

A cat zipped across the stable floor. Rede followed, intent on the hunt. Rhonwen grabbed him as he went by. "There you are!"

He squealed trying to get away, but Rhonwen picked him up and held him close. He struggled briefly, but his mother's stern look settled him.

"Do you think Sertorius knows Perpenna has forced you out?" Orlan asked.

"I've no idea," she said, "nor do I care. I'm looking forward to packing up that old wagon and finding a new place to live." She hugged the boy. "Would you like that?"

"Where are we going?" Rede asked.

"I'm not sure yet," Rhonwen said, "but it will be far from here."

Rede looked at her with doleful eyes. "Can I bring the cat?"

⌘ ⌘ ⌘

Rhonwen and Orlan gathered up the belongings Perpenna's men had thrown into the road outside the school. Rhonwen was glad the rooms she and Orlan had occupied were so small, as most of the things needed for living outdoors were stored in the wagon.

The students milled aimlessly until she shooed them away, with instructions to the eldest on how to proceed until the new administrator arrived. Reluctantly the children went back inside, the youngest ones crying, and the older ones grim-faced.

"I still can't believe this," Orlan said, shoving a trunk into the back of the over-loaded wagon.

"Let it be," Rhonwen said, forcing a smile. "We should be grateful. I was weary of teaching anyway."

"You sound like Aesop's fox turning his nose at sour grapes," Orlan said.

Rhonwen chuckled softly. "Had I not been daydreaming about leaving here when Perpenna arrived, I'd confess you were right."

They spent the afternoon consolidating the contents of the wagon and everything Orlan had brought. They would take only what they needed to travel through the mountains just as she and Baia had done.

"Where shall we go?" she asked.

Orlan heaved a sack of grain appropriated from the school's larder by a concerned student into the wagon. "Anywhere we'd like. As long as there's a war, we'll be needed. As long as there's a Rome, there'll be war."

She wiped at her tears as she packed the gifts of food and a new water skin the students and servants gave them when Perpenna's guards weren't looking. She fondled the tinder and flint kit from one of the oldest boys. It had been a gift to him from his father, and he prized it greatly. She turned to hide her face from Orlan and dusted her hands. "I've had enough war for one lifetime. Let's go somewhere peaceful."

"Armorica?"

"Too cold and wet," she said. "Isn't that what you keep saying?"

"That's Mona. Armorica is warmer. Green and beautiful. Besides, I need to go back there. Now that we're free of the burdens of the school, I can resume my work with baneweed."

The thought of traveling through lush forests and rich pastures, meeting congenial people, and enjoying life without Romans appealed to her.

"If we time it right," she said, "we can arrive in the summer. After that, perhaps we could sail south."

"Not back here," Orlan said. "How about Africa?"

Rhonwen thought about it and smiled. "We'll leave for Armorica in the morning, and then on to Africa." She sat down and leaned back against the wagon. "I can't wait to see Rede's face when you tell him we're going where the elephants live."

Orlan shook his head. "Poor elephants. They have no idea what they're in for."

✠ ✠ ✠

The sun floated just above the western skyline as the druids prepared the evening meal beside their loaded wagon. Few words passed between them as they sat beneath the widespread arms of an oak standing just outside the school.

The progress they'd made and their decision to leave Iberia pleased Rhonwen. A new life in a new land! Perhaps she would have a chance to forge her own way in the world instead of constantly reacting to the demands of others.

They ate in peace and Rhonwen had just settled Rede for the night when a man approached in the gathering darkness. "Driad Rhonwen?" he called.

She looked up from the fire but saw only a shadow. "Who is it?"

An aging Roman, his hair completely gray, stepped into the light of their fire. He squinted at the druids. Rhonwen thought she recognized the face, although the man's name escaped her.

"I'm Spanus," he said. "You and Driad Baia once helped me with a foaling mare for Governor Fufidius."

The man's words brought her memories into focus. The image of a stable and a mare with a broken leg, became sharp. "Yes, I remember," Rhonwen said. She felt a sudden pang, for it was the same night she'd last seen Telo alive.

Spanus smiled in relief. "I've come to ask for your help again."

"Another suffering mare?"

He crouched by the fire and held his hands up to the warmth. "The white hind the gods gave to Sertorius."

Orlan ran his fingers through his thinning hair. "I don't like the sound of this. Will we never be done with him?"

"What's wrong with the hind?" Rhonwen asked.

"I don't know," said Spanus. "I've tried everything, but I can't get it to eat. It lies in a stall and doesn't move. I think it's waiting to die."

"Perhaps it is," Rhonwen said. "Everything dies sooner or later. Is it in pain?"

"Oh, yes." Spanus twisted his hands. "I can't explain it. There's something special about this animal, to me, to Sertorius, and to the whole army."

Rhonwen looked across the fire at her uncle. "Can't we spare the time? I hate to let an animal suffer."

"Can't it wait 'til morning?" Orlan asked. "I'm not taking this overburdened wagon anywhere in the dark."

"The hind may be dead by morning," Spanus said. "Leave the wagon. It'll be safe here. Everyone knows it belongs to the druids of Osca, and no one would dare disturb it."

Orlan stirred the fire's embers apart, dimming it. "I suppose so."

"Thank you," Spanus said, his voice trembling. "I'll help with your horses."

"I can't leave my son here all alone," Rhonwen said. "Give me time to find someone in the school to look after him."

"The gods surely smile on you," Spanus said, taking the traces from Orlan. He secured them to the wagon.

Rhonwen pressed Rede, limp and heavy in sleep, against her breast. "I hope so."

✠ ✠ ✠

The druids flanked Spanus as they rode. A fat red moon illuminated the road and the fine weather made the ride almost pleasant. Their destination, the former summer estate of the governor of Tarraconensis, was a two hour ride along the northern Roman road. Spanus thanked the druids profusely for accompanying him, after which he maintained a nervous silence.

Rhonwen wearied of watching the man open his mouth to speak only to shut it again without saying anything. "Is something wrong, Spanus?"

"I hope you won't— I mean..." He exhaled.

"Go ahead and ask your question," Orlan said. "It can't be so bad we'd kill you for it." He turned his head. "But keep up this mystery and I might consider it."

Spanus took a deep breath. "Why does the mistress of the great school live in a wagon?"

"Because I no longer hold that position," Rhonwen said.

"You quit?"

"I was dismissed." Saying it aloud made it hurt. The work had meant more to her than she thought, and its loss clawed at her while the back of her throat burned with unshed tears. Somehow she'd believed her ability, her rank, and her friendship with Sertorius had made her invulnerable to the whims of men like Perpenna.

"That rat-faced little man, Perpenna, threw us out," Orlan said.

"He's well-known," Spanus said, "but not well-liked. It wouldn't surprise me if he took old Metellus up on his offer."

"Roman generals make offers?" Rhonwen asked.

"Yes, especially when they're losing a war. He's offered a hundred talents and twenty thousand acres of land to any Roman who kills Sertorius."

"A hundred talents?" Orlan asked.

Spanus nodded.

"Preposterous!" The druid made the calculation quickly. "That's two-hundred fifty thousand pieces of gold!"

"Aye."

Rhonwen whistled. Could Sertorius be such a threat that Metellus would bankrupt himself, and possibly the Roman Senate, to be rid of him? "I knew Rome feared him, but I didn't realize how much."

"There's talk of little else among the warriors," Spanus said.

"We tried to teach by example," Rhonwen said. "If we didn't ignore rumors, we couldn't expect the same of our students."

They rode the rest of the way in silence, eventually reaching the estate. Spanus accompanied the druids past a dozen guard posts before he delivered them to an unlit stable hidden by the deep shadows of thick trees along two walls. He tethered their horses and led them quickly inside.

"The hind is in the last stall," he said as he lit a lamp. He handed it to Orlan and lit another as the druids approached the stall.

Inside, the roe deer lay on her side, motionless.

"We may already be too late," Rhonwen whispered. She knelt beside the creature and put her hand against the animal's pale coat, pleased at the warmth of life she felt. She pressed her ear to its side and listened for a heartbeat. Though much too rapid for a person, she couldn't be sure it was inappropriate for a hind.

The deer's stomach was hard and distended, a bad sign in any animal, as were her dry nose and labored breathing. "How long has she been like this?"

"Three days," Spanus said. "She's usually eager to eat, but now she won't even look at an apple or a carrot. What's wrong with her?"

Rhonwen shrugged. "It could be some sickness that only strikes animals, or it may have been something she ate. All I can tell is that she's terribly weak. I'm surprised she's still alive."

The deer shivered and rolled its eyes. Spanus, helpless to do anything more, clutched at Rhonwen. "You've got to do something!"

"If I knew what to do, I'd do it," she said. She felt for a pulse at the animal's throat. "Rhiannon calls her. I'm sorry."

"The tribes will take this as a sign the gods have abandoned Sertorius," Spanus said, and his haggard face told a vivid story of grief at the loss of a beloved creature.

Orlan stood. "We could try the baneweed. I packed what's left of the last plant in my kit."

"But that's all you have," Rhonwen said.

"I know, but we're going to Armorica." He smiled. "I'll get more. Besides, I've never seen it work on anything more serious than the cut of a tattoo."

"Will it work on an animal?"

"I don't know why it wouldn't." He walked out of the stall. "I'll be back in a moment."

Spanus watched Orlan leave. "What's he going to do?"

"Ask the gods for help."

He let his head droop. "I'd hoped for more than prayers."

"And that you'll have," Orlan said, returning. "If this works, you'll witness the true healing power of the gods, but you must swear to tell no one."

Spanus looked warily at Orlan.

Rhonwen placed her hand on his. "If you came so far to find us, then you must trust us."

The hind shivered and Spanus turned red-rimmed eyes to Rhonwen. "I swear I'll tell no one."

Orlan spread the remains of the baneweed on a metal pan and set it afire with his oil lamp. The weed smoldered. "Stay back," he said. "Whatever you do, don't breathe the fumes."

He set the smoking pan near the hind's nose and covered both with a cloth. The weak creature offered little resistance to either the smoke or the druid.

"Pray, Rhonwen," Orlan said. "Let the gods know we need them."

Accompanied by a popping sound like fresh wood in a fire, the transformation began as the hind's features became indistinct, then shriveled and shrank. In moments the little deer was transformed into an arm's length of wood, its bark nearly white.

Rhonwen gasped. Though Orlan had told her how the magic worked, she'd not truly believed him until this moment.

Awestruck, Spanus murmured, "What have you done?"

Orlan smothered the burning baneweed with the cloth to extinguish it. "We've put the hind into the hands of the gods," he said. "We'll have her back on the morning of the next equinox."

"But that's weeks away!" Spanus rolled his eyes. "What will I tell Sertorius when he asks for her?"

Rhonwen turned to Orlan, still speechless.

He shrugged. "Tell him you've taken the animal to be healed and that you'll bring her back on the day of the equinox."

Spanus nodded, although reluctance plainly set the straight line of his mouth.

Rhonwen reached for the stick and quickly pulled her fingers back. It tingled. She looked at Orlan in surprise.

"The life of the hind is held within. Some can feel it."

Spanus reached for it, and he too trembled when he touched it. "She lives?"

"Yes, and given enough time, she will heal. That's all we can do now. See that the stick remains safe until the equinox."

Spanus embraced each druid in turn, tucked the stick into his belt, and then waved a parting blessing. He disappeared into the night.

"That wasn't so bad, was it?" Orlan said sitting back on his haunches.

Rhonwen sat beside him in the straw, shaking her head at the transformation. "This is miraculous, Uncle. Truly your plant has opened a path directly to the gods."

Orlan smiled reassuringly. "Since the baneweed transformed her, I believe it will also cure her, though hard-belly is certainly more serious than a tattoo cut. We won't know until she returns to us."

Rhonwen touched the five points of her body in a gesture of supplication. "Only the gods can help us now."

The crunch of heavy sandals on the barn's dirt floor made them look up. Perpenna barred the entry to the stall. "In that you're not mistaken." He clapped his hands and a brace of guards appeared behind him.

Rhonwen scowled. "Do you usually creep around in the dark like a thief?"

Perpenna backhanded her across the mouth and sent her sprawling. Orlan dropped to her side. She raised a hand to her burning lip and drew it away bloody.

Perpenna stared at her, a sneer twisting his lips. "Sertorius bade me look in on the hind," he said. "What a surprise that instead of the deer, I find a pair of traitors. What have you done with the animal?"

Orlan spoke before Rhonwen could. "She's gone to a place of healing. She'll return safe and well on the day of the next equinox."

Perpenna's face wrinkled with false humor. "You actually expect me to believe that?"

"We don't care what you believe. That's the truth."

He turned to one of the guards. "I suspect they've taken the beast somewhere and killed it. When Sertorius calls, it won't come, and thus the barbarians will think the gods have forsaken him. It's a scheme to help incite rebellion."

Rhonwen clambered to her feet. "That's absurd." Perhaps Perpenna had caused the animal's distress for just those reasons.

"Then produce the animal."

Orlan growled. "It's not that simple."

"To return an animal from the dead? No, I suppose it isn't."

"The hind is not dead," Orlan said, "but it won't be healed for several weeks."

"I'm weary of arguing," Perpenna said. He gestured to the guards. "Arrest them."

"But we're telling the truth!" Rhonwen exclaimed.

Perpenna's smile contained venom. "Convince Sertorius of that, and he might let you live."

✠ ✠ ✠

Perpenna left Rhonwen and Orlan under guard outside the largest building on the estate. The hard-eyed Romans forced them to sit on the stone walk beside the entrance.

Orlan leaned into her. "We'll be fine," he whispered, "Don't worry."

One of the guards kicked Orlan in the side. "Silence!" he barked.

The druid doubled over, and Rhonwen could only watch in horror and frustration as he tried to roll himself into a protective ball. The Roman grabbed him by the hair, yanked him upright and shoved him back against the wall. Orlan moaned but said nothing. When she reached for him, he shook his head at her. She trembled with anger but forced herself to control her tongue. She would wait in silence and save her anger for Sertorius.

Rhonwen stared into the night sky hoping for a sign this would all be over, a mistake that would soon be corrected. The constellations burned brightly, yet the gods left her without benefit of even one falling star. Despite the late hour, the long ride, and the day's events, she remained too apprehensive to rest. Orlan sat beside her, his head tilted back against the wall and his eyes closed. She wished she had such composure.

She had faith Sertorius would believe her, even over his conniving countryman, and she counted on his fairness and sense of justice to hear her defense. She wondered why Perpenna had branded Aras a traitor. The unsophisticated Trepani chief had been a trusted warrior and staunch ally to Sertorius for years.

She looked skyward again, praying for guidance. Instead she saw only the dark silhouettes of the guards, and many more wandering the grounds, their harsh whispered conversations playing in counterpoint to the friendly night sounds she'd known all her life. Once, Sertorius had not required personal guards. Why would he fear men like the Trepani? The reward Metellus offered was meant only for Romans. She snorted. What kind of people so lacked honor that their leaders resorted to bribes and treachery to achieve what they failed to accomplish in battle? Aras, despite any other failings he may have, would rather die than live with such shame, as would Orlan. Could Perpenna make the same claim?

As she thought his name, the administrator stepped outside and breathed deeply of the honeysuckle on the night air. He paused long enough to kick Orlan, whose outstretched legs obstructed the path. As he drew back his foot to deliver a similar blow to Rhonwen, Orlan made a warding sign.

"Think first," he said, "lest that leg fail you when you need it. I've laid curses on better men than you, men who've crawled back to beg forgiveness."

"You're no threat to me," Perpenna said, but he lowered his foot anyway. He ordered the guards to bind the druids' hands behind them and bring them inside. "Sertorius wants to question you, though I advised against it."

"Good," Rhonwen said, returning the Roman's scowl. "I've much to tell him."

"If it were up to me," he said, "you'd both be dangling from crosses in the center of Osca as a warning to anyone else wishing to join your conspiracy." He turned back into the house and the guards pushed them forward.

Sertorius sat in an unadorned chair at a table supporting a pile of charts and a pair of fat, guttering candles. Lamps throughout the room cast a low but even light. The guards shoved the druids to their knees halfway across the room.

Three men wearing purple-trimmed togas occupied a distant corner. Two others in Roman-style armor conversed in low tones near their chief, and a servant huddled in discreet silence by the door. Unlike years past, no Iberians attended Sertorius.

The general stared at them without rising. For several long moments no one broke the silence and when Perpenna opened his mouth to speak, Sertorius motioned him to remain quiet. The Roman lowered his eyes and obeyed.

"Where is the hind?" Sertorius asked, his voice flat.

"She's recovering," Rhonwen said.

"Where?"

"With the gods."

Sertorius drummed his fingers on the table.

"You see?" Perpenna said, "they admit it's dead."

Sertorius silenced him with a raised finger and turned to look directly at Rhonwen. The skin on his face sagged, especially beneath his scarred eye socket. He regarded her with a chilling lack of feeling, and she drew herself a little straighter.

"I know you care deeply for the hind," she said, "and we would never do anything to harm her. She was dying. What we've done will restore her to health."

Sertorius paused a long moment before he spoke. "Once, long ago, in a town full of insurgents, I cautioned you to keep silent if you were about to lie to me. Perhaps I should give you the same warning now."

Rhonwen stared back at him fearlessly, despite the pounding in her chest. "Honor prevents me from lying, though that can't be said of everyone in this room." She glared at Perpenna. "What lies have you spread about us, or about Aras?"

"Aras speaks of rebellion," Sertorius said.

"Surely you've spoken with him yourself?"

"His actions speak for him. Now answer me. Does the hind live?"

"For now, she sleeps," Rhonwen said, "but she will walk again."

"Do not play word games with me, Rhonwen. I know you make little distinction between the worlds of the living and the dead, but I want the hind in this world. Does she live among men or spirits?"

Perpenna snorted. "I can't believe you bother with these swine."

"Will it walk among men or spirits?" Sertorius asked again, ignoring Perpenna.

"Among men," Rhonwen said.

"The hind is dead!" Perpenna exclaimed. "I—"

"You forget your place," Sertorius said without looking at him. "When will she be returned?"

"On the day of the next equinox," Rhonwen said.

Sertorius rubbed his jaw. "You test my credibility to the limit. What am I supposed to do with you in the meantime?"

"If you let them go now," Perpenna said, "the hind isn't the only thing you'll never see again."

"I have no prisons," Sertorius said, "nor men to waste guarding prisoners."

"Then kill them now," Perpenna urged. "What point is served by prolonging this?"

"Only truth and honor." Rhonwen glared at Perpenna.

Perpenna drew his sword.

"Harm us, and the hind sleeps forever," Orlan said.

Sertorius signaled Perpenna to stand down. "Seven weeks," he mused, "but I need assurances."

"You have my word of honor," Rhonwen said.

"The woman's child would make a better guarantee," Perpenna said.

Rhonwen recoiled at the thought of Rede as a prisoner." So you now make war on children?"

"Hold me as hostage," Orlan said. "Leave the boy alone."

Sertorius crossed his arms on his chest. "Hold both the child and the druid at the school. That should assure the hind is returned."

"She will be," Rhonwen said, although her eyes prickled with tears in deep gut-wrenching fear for her son. What if Orlan's magic failed?

"Alive," Sertorius added, nodding at Orlan, "or he and the boy won't be."

21

Mount Eban rumbled today. This was not unusual, except it settled a large boulder over the entryway to the Cavern, and Amrec came to us seeking help in pushing it aside. I told him I could not— the gods closed the Cave for a reason. He left in anger and stayed away for seven years. The standing stones that he inquires about each year remain as always.
— *Stave Four of Fyrsil, 39th Master of Mount Eban Enclave*

Armorica

Dierdre stood in the open doorway to Mallec's quarters. "Considering all I've done for you, why do you drag your heels when it comes to the only request I make of you?"

How many times must they have this conversation? Mallec thought. "You know it's not entirely up to me."

"What did Coemgen say?"

Mallec struggled to remain calm. "These things take time, and it has been only a month. Surely you can be patient. You've waited forty years to claim that land. Besides, knowing how hard Gar took Willa's death, you can't expect much of him so soon."

"It's not Gar I'm waiting for, it's Coemgen," she said. "The Lemarii have occupied my land long enough."

"We're negotiating a major tract of land on the border between the clans. Coemgen knows the Suetoni have a war party in the field, and he knows what it costs to keep them there, both for their support and in terms of leaving the clanhold vulnerable."

"That has nothing to do with me or my claim," she said.

Mallec pulled on his mustache. "Wouldn't you rather have Gar bargain from a position of strength? The longer we delay, the more time Setaine has to deal with the raiders. Coemgen cannot simply give up the land. It's already being settled by his son."

Dierdre scowled. "So Coemgen has a personal interest, but not me? Waiting is useless. Everyone knows that land belongs to Gar's son, not Coemgen's. Is Gwair more worthy than Caradowc?"

Mallec wanted to scream, Yes! Gwair was a hundred times more worthy than Caradowc. Gar deserved a better son than Caradowc. If Mallec had a father as loving as Gar, how different his own life might have been.

"Well?" Dierdre tapped her foot.

He wrenched his attention back to her. "I've spoken with both chiefs. Neither is willing to give as much as you ask."

"Seven acres and thirty cattle, with sheep and fowl. That's not so much."

"Though the land you ask for has been in Lemarii hands for many years, for the sake of continued peace between the clans, Coemgen offered to give up three acres across the river."

She raised a fist at him. "And I said no! I want my land, not some swamp. How can Caradowc raise cattle and sheep there?"

As if she suddenly realized how close to hysteria she appeared, Dierdre's face smoothed. "I ask only for my son."

He shuddered. Her face held all the charm of an adder, yet she was far more dangerous, something he'd refused to recognize before. He understood at last the source of both Fyrsil and Orlan's admonition that she must never control the enclave. He had given her too much power.

He returned her smile as well as he could, hiding his mistrust. "I promise to bring the chiefs together one last time, and then I'll make my decision."

She turned and tramped toward her house, her skirts flapping in the sudden wind off Mount Eban.

May the gods tell me their answer, he thought, for I already know what mine will be.

✠ ✠ ✠

Once clear of Mallec's quarters, Dierdre allowed herself a smile. Gwair's workers at the Giant's Tomb fled when they discovered the "spirits" were unhappy, but she knew it would only be a matter of time before Gwair found replacements. Nor was she happy about having to rely on Caradowc and his friends to deal with any new workers.

She knew the chiefs would never give in to her demands, nor would Mallec take a stand for her. It was all an act, but one that she had to play out before she could move on to the next phase in her plans, the elevation of Caradowc.

The arrival of the raiders had caused an unexpected delay, but it put added pressure on Gar. Willa's death had a more profound impact on him than she thought it would. The woman's lingering illness had aged Gar, but when Willa was lowered into the ground, the old chief lost what little joy he had left. Now he knew what it was like to live all alone.

He probably thinks this is as bad as his life can get, she thought.

⊞ ⊞ ⊞

Augmented by a few lamps scattered around the feasting hall in Gillac, the hazelwood fire burned brightly. Mallec surveyed the space in preparation for his judgment. The place of honor beside Gar remained vacant in memory of his dead wife. Caradowc occupied a place at Gar's left. Dierdre sat alone closest to the fire, her face void of emotion.

Arie, flanked by a pair of older students, stood at the door and held Mallec's bag of sacred objects. Few were present to hear the settlement of Dierdre's claim: Mallec and his three students, Dierdre, Caradowc, Gar, and a pair of elders from both villages. Setaine and the senior warriors, gone nearly six weeks, had not yet returned.

Mallec wielded a smoking incense pot attached to a chain and paced the perimeter of the room to create a sacred circle. Dierdre said, "Can't you just tell me your decision without all this bother?"

He shook his head. "These things must be done right, or the gods will not sanction our work." He finished the purification by smudging the air in front of Gar and then set the pot aside.

"O-ghe!" he cried, his staff in his right hand raised over his head. "Let right prevail in this judgment." He pointed his staff at Gar. "Here is the matter: Shall Dierdre, daughter of long-dead Carew and Rubana, regain those lands lost when Carew died? Those lands have stood as a marker for peace between the Suetoni and the Lemarii for forty years."

Gar looked at Dierdre only for a moment and then spoke. "I have thought long and hard. Dierdre was recompensed for her loss. This clan raised her as our own, paid for her schooling to become a druid, and welcomed her at every opportunity. We are not to be held accountable for the actions of men no longer living. Let her ask them for repayment when she sees them in the Otherworld." He folded his arms across his chest to punctuate his final word on the matter. "No."

Dierdre said nothing, but her eyes burned into Gar, and he shifted in his seat uncomfortably.

Mallec tapped his staff on the ground three times.

"O-ghe! I have the words of Coemgen, chief of the Lemarii and keeper of those lands Dierdre claims as her own. Arie, relate what Coemgen said to you."

Arie stepped forward and passed the sacred parcel to one of the young men beside her. She stood motionless in the room's center, her eyes focused on someone not there. Her memory for words was astonishing. She could mimic every nuance of voice. Mallec thought she had bardic talent.

She cleared her throat and spoke, her voice somber but as ripe with melody as a spring morning.

"Even-handed Coemgen brings this greeting to all gathered. Hail Gar, esteemed chief of the Suetoni, formidable opponent and courageous friend. Your exploits are legendary and the Lemarii sing you to long life and good health. We wish only peace between our peoples.

"Though three families now farm the land in question, we are of one mind. Dierdre's father could not hold it, and in the old ways of both clans, she may only take what she can hold. We will not strip the livelihood of the three families who now depend upon that land for their sustenance. We will give her four acres beside the smaller stream that borders our territories. We stand ready to post this area with her mark. This I, Coemgen, declare. My honor is my seal." Arie looked at Mallec. "That is his whole message."

When Dierdre spoke, she surprised Mallec with her lack of emotion. "Coemgen's son works that land, and yet he passes judgment on my claim. Why should I have expected justice from him? This whole affair is a sham."

Mallec stamped his staff again to silence her. "I have decided, Dierdre. You're a driad, and as such have wide power and deserve respect. As a driad, you receive a share of wealth from both clans, enough to buy whatever you require. Druids do not work the land, so no point is served by denying it to those who do. Here is my decision: Accept the land that Coemgen offers, a place to raise a few extra sheep for your crone years, or accept nothing at all." He raised his hands above his head and showed his staff of authority to the gods above. "I have spoken. So it will be."

Dierdre turned to Gar. "How can you do this to your own son?"

The old man straightened. "I can't favor the needs of one or two over the needs of an entire clan. You have all that you require, and Coemgen offers you even more."

"I'm the one who's been wronged," she snarled. "You would do well to remember that." She reached for Caradowc's arm and allowed him to steady her as she marched out the door.

Mallec realized he'd been holding his breath. He let it out in a rush. A quick glance around the room told him he wasn't the only one to react that way. "I expected worse."

Gar, haggard from weeks of mourning, quaffed a cup of ale before speaking. "Me, too." He rose unsteadily, and the village elders came to his aid.

"Gar?" The deep-toned bass of the warrior, Setaine, captured everyone's attention.

Mallec's stomach had barely settled. Setaine's arrival set it churning once again.

"You caught the raiders?" Gar asked.

Setaine said, "We have them trapped in a farmstead a day's ride north."

Gar frowned. "Trapped but not captured? Then why not kill them?"

"Because they're led by a warrior-druid," Setaine said, "and my men refuse to fight him. They say if they raise a blade against a druid, the Great Mother will punish them."

Setaine turned toward Mallec. "My men have no fear of outlaws, but only a druid may face another druid in battle. That would be you."

Despite growing up with daily combat practice, Mallec never believed he would have to fight anyone. He had not held a sword since the day he left Belgica. Dream memories flooded Mallec, and he once more saw the headless druid.

"You look a little pale, Mallec," Gar said. "It's a good thing you had warrior training among the Eburones."

Mallec forced dread from his voice. "What weapons does this warrior-druid carry," he asked Setaine.

"A staff and a long blade," Setaine replied. "The same as you'll carry, I imagine." He shrugged. "It's too late in the day to begin the return trip, but I don't want to leave my men alone much longer. Get some sleep tonight, Druid Mallec. We ride at dawn."

⌘ ⌘ ⌘

Dierdre walked briskly from the hall, shoulders squared. Caradowc had seen the posture often as a child. Resigned, he quickened his own steps to stay beside her. "Isn't there something we can do?" he said, watching her face for a reaction. Her tight smile came quickly.

"Of course there is. We'll have our land, and a good deal more. We need only remove two impediments. Gar and Mallec are too weak to do the right thing. Their replacements won't be."

"What replacements?" he asked.

She frowned. "Is it really so difficult to figure that out?" She swept a spider thread from their path and wound it round her finger as they walked. "Who better than you and me to watch out for our own interests?"

"But Druid Mallec is still young, and Father's said nothing about stepping aside."

She nodded. "Quite so, therefore it falls to us to facilitate such changes. I've already begun."

"And?"

Her smile grew wider. "And Gar will be first."

✠ ✠ ✠

"Where's your sword?" Setaine asked as Mallec led his horse to the clanhold gate.

Mallec pointed to a bundle secured behind his saddle. "Gar loaned me one of his."

"He must think highly of you," Setaine said as he and Mallec rode north at a brisk pace.

Mallec had not slept the night before, as the gods had chosen to torment him with fresh images of his headless corpse sprawled in a field of flowers. "Doesn't this man have a name?" he asked. "He's not the first druid to carry a sword."

"He calls himself Brucc the Bold," Setaine said with scorn. "Bold enough to kill unarmed farmers."

Surely it couldn't be the same Brucc he knew on Mona. "You've seen him? What does he look like?"

Setaine shrugged his broad shoulders. "He wears a helmet that covers his nose and casts his eyes in shadow."

"Is he tall, or short? Thin, fat, young, old, dark, fair?"

"He's of average height and average weight, near as I can tell. He doesn't move like an old man, so I assume he's not."

Mallec's spirits improved. Perhaps it was the Brucc he knew from Mona. If so, he could be defeated. Mallec had done it before.

They rode quietly for a few miles before Setaine called a halt. While the horses grazed, the men walked to loosen stiff muscles.

"How long has it been since you handled a sword?" Setaine asked.

Mallec remembered the near-beating he'd received from Danix so long ago. "Years." He twisted at the waist and stretched. "I trained hard as a boy. I'm sure it will come back to me."

Setaine unstrapped his own sword belt and handed it to him. "Cinch that on and we'll see what you can do with it."

Mallec hefted the weapon. The blade was longer than those used by the Eburones and felt heavy. He pulled it from the sheath and swung it a few times to test the balance.

"You look like an old woman swatting at crows," Setaine said, laughing. "You'll have to do better than that to put any fear in the heart of Brucc the Bold."

Mallec turned and dropped to one knee as he swung the weapon around cleaving a small tree at a spot level with Setaine's thighs.

"Not bad. Would you like some advice?"

"No," Mallec said, returning the sword. "It's too late for that. The best I can do is try not to be too tired. If the gods are smiling on me, this Brucc will be who I think he is. If so, then I have a chance."

Setaine accepted the weapon. "This man has been in the company of raiders for years. He's probably learned a thing or two about fighting."

Mallec hoped not.

They remounted and continued their journey, halting frequently, more for Mallec's benefit than for the horses. Despite the delays, they reached the Suetoni encampment before nightfall.

A sentry recognized Setaine and hailed him.

"Have they tried to escape?" Mallec asked.

"Only one has shown himself," the guard said. "He told us they were leaving tomorrow. If we didn't stand out of their way, their druid would ensure that our swords could not touch them, and they'd be free to strike us dead. Can you counter such a warding?"

"Easily," Mallec said, pleased to see the confidence his word inspired.

Setaine sent the warrior back to his post and they walked the rest of the way into camp. Mallec's arrival caused a stir among the warriors, who gathered around him and clamored for his blessing.

Setaine finally ordered them to back away and bring food. As two men hurried to obey, the rest remained close.

"Will you use magic on him?" asked a tall, thin warrior Mallec had often seen atop the wall around Gillac.

"They say he's never been beaten," said another.

"Men are blinded by his blade."

"He built a house with the heads of his enemies."

"Enough!" Mallec shouted. "Give no further voice to the man's lies, lest they grow even more." He looked at the simple men surrounding him. "Let me get some rest tonight, and I'll deal with him tomorrow."

The men scattered like chickens from a hawk as Setaine walked among them. "Leave us," he said, "and make sure you're all rested. After Mallec wins his battle, we may have one of our own."

Mallec watched the men drift away, their spirits high. He wished he felt the same.

✠ ✠ ✠

Rough hands roused Mallec from a dreamless sleep. Fog lay thick on the lowlands as he dressed and forced down a measure of hasty rations beside a smoking fire. He shivered. The gray sky above matched the foggy terrain below and his visions rose in front of him. It was happening now. Mallec forced himself to advance to the center of a meadow ringed with Suetoni warriors.

In front of him gathered a host of Redoni raiders. The warrior-druid stood in front of them, his face hidden by a war helmet.

Bearing a druid staff in one hand and a sword in the other, Brucc walked to within a half dozen steps of Mallec and jammed the staff's spiked end into the ground.

Mallec recognized the man's build and gait. "Do you know me?" Mallec asked.

"I've killed many men," Brucc said. "I knew few of their names. Why should I know yours?"

"Because I'm the last man you'll face in this life."

Brucc laughed. "Brave words, fool. Have you prepared your greeting for Rhiannon?"

"Prepare your own," Mallec said. "Try making one in Greek. As I recall, you have a gift for it."

Brucc snarled, drew his sword, and attacked. Mallec had time only to drop his staff and raise his shield. With luck he managed to deflect Brucc's blows, but others bit into his shield, sending shards of wood and hide flying.

"Draw your blade, Mallec!" Setaine screamed, his voice booming over the din of warriors from both camps.

Brucc yelled a challenge, but his war cries became more guttural with every breath.

Mallec remembered Galan raining blows down upon his shield. He remembered Brucc setting his cloak on fire. He remembered the visions of a headless body lying in the dirt, fearing it was his own. But he was no longer a boy and would not accept defeat so easily. Scuttling backward to give himself breathing room, he drew his sword. He continued to give ground, moving backward in a broad circle defined by the surrounding warriors.

Twice Brucc's sword reached his flesh, scraping and bruising rather than cutting with the dull edge on his iron weapon. He landed a vicious swing across Mallec's shield, and the resounding crack of the shield's spine echoed across the field.

Mallec threw the useless shield at his opponent. He would retreat no more and raised his sword in both hands.

"Does the rabbit have teeth?" Brucc asked as he blocked Mallec's blade with his shield and hacked at Mallec's legs.

Mallec jumped back unharmed, but wiser. "I thought they burned off your tattoos before throwing you out of Mona," he said.

Brucc's breath came in short gasps. "They couldn't catch me."

Mallec attacked again, trying to push Brucc off balance. "Anyone can dress like a druid," Mallec taunted, "but it takes more than that to be one."

"It's been enough," Brucc said, his voice carrying the same sneer Mallec had endured on Mona.

Mallec slashed at him. Brucc danced clear, and Mallec stumbled on a rock hidden by the low fog. The sword tumbled from his grip.

Brucc sliced the air and Mallec rolled away. He fell forward and landed near his staff. With staff in hand, he twisted to his side as Brucc advanced for the final blow.

"You're no druid," Mallec said. "You never were."

Brucc's eyes narrowed with hate. "I was a druid once. You stole that from me!" He raised his arms high overhead, his face a fearsome mask.

Mallec couldn't breathe. Cut now in half a dozen places, his arms too weak to raise in defense, he feared Brucc would fulfill the vision. He would not let fear defeat him. He could change the outcome of this dream. With a ragged breath, he thrust the blunt tip of his staff upward and struck Brucc's chest. He toppled backward. Mallec pushed forward and swung the staff in a wide arc.

Brucc parried the blow with his sword, breaking the staff in two. Brucc attacked again. Mallec warded off the first two blows, but Brucc connected with the third, forcing the broken staff from Mallec's grip.

He dropped to the ground frantically feeling for the remains of his weapon. Brucc cursed as he advanced, his sword high above his head.

Mallec grabbed the broken staff. He lunged forward, driving the jagged end deep into Brucc's side.

The false druid went rigid, and his face lost its fierce certainty. He groaned and let his sword fall. Setaine, looming behind him, imprisoned Brucc's wrists in his two great hands and held them high as Mallec regained his feet.

Setaine yelled for all to hear. "He says he was once a druid, but no longer!" He released Brucc's hands and retrieved his sword from the dirt.

"It's true," Mallec shouted. "He was exiled from Mona as unworthy."

"I am a druid!" Brucc cried, pressing on the wound Mallec had given him. Dark blood dripped from beneath his fingers. He glared at Setaine. "You're a dead man," he whispered and thrust at him with a knife pulled from his belt.

Setaine smacked Brucc's hand with the pommel of his sword, sending the knife spinning into the fog. A quick jab propelled Brucc to the ground where Setaine anchored him by placing his foot on the man's chest.

"Hold!" Mallec cried.

Setaine shook his head. "You are a druid, Mallec, and an honorable one." He raised Brucc's sword. "This man tried to kill you, and every man knows the penalty for attacking a druid."

Brucc stared up at him, weeping in terror.

"He should be given time to make his peace," Mallec said.

"Peace? He slew my kinsmen," Setaine said. "I have the right."

He brought the blade down on Brucc's neck but failed to sever it completely. A great spurt of blood danced up Setaine's chest and dripped from his mustaches. He rolled the body over, then took another swing and cut the head completely free.

Those few of Brucc's men who remained turned and ran.

"Let them go," Setaine called to the Suetoni who had begun to chase them. "We have the one we came for." He dumped Brucc's head out of the helmet and held it aloft by the hair.

Mallec approached as Setaine discarded Brucc's sword. It landed in the damp soil with a thud. Mallec broke Brucc's staff across his knee and dropped the pieces next to the body. "So much for Brucc the Bold."

"So much for Brucc the Short," said Setaine.

22

Amrec returned and again begged our help in moving the boulder. Favorable signs were everywhere, so I relented. With ropes and levers we moved the stone from the entrance. When we had finished, a pair of red insects landed on my sleeve, and I took this to mean the gods were pleased. Amrec rejoices that he can once more pray in the sanctuary of his long-dead people.
— *Stave Five of Fyrsil, 39th Master of Mount Eban Enclave*

Iberia

With little to keep Rhonwen occupied as she waited for the equinox, the days crawled by. The nights became interminable, and sleep was impossible.

Rhonwen spent the long days near the school. Aside from an occasional villager in need of treatment for a boil or a cut, she had nothing to do. In the third week of her vigil, her dog Iago curled up beside her, laid his chin on her knee, and died. She buried him beneath an oak and placed three charms around his grave to speed him into the Otherworld. Alone in the darkness she wept.

When the guards stopped watching her movements, she retrieved the woadslept hind from Spanus but declined his offer to stay in his house. She needed to locate the nearest standing stones where she could place the stick for its transformation back into a deer. After only a day of searching, she found a suitable place three hour's walk from the school.

She often caught sight of Orlan and Rede, but just seeing them was never enough. As the days crept by, she and Orlan silently conversed using Ogham finger signs. She told him how she survived. He spoke of watching Rede play as if nothing were different, although the guards never took their eyes from the pair. The druid taught Rede to sign "I love you," and the boy used his tiny fingers against his arm to mimic the straight lines of Ogham to speak to his mother. Rhonwen fought her tears to return his message of love.

Her only other visitor had been Cesada. She recalled his arrival late one evening a fortnight before the equinox.

"Driad," Cesada whispered from the shadows.

"Welcome! I'm surprised to see you." She offered him warm cider against the night's chill.

"Thank you. I bring tidings from Aras. There's much resentment for Sertorius these days," he said. "Aras bids you, your uncle, and your son travel to the safety of Langos." He paused. "Aras says come, even without handfasting. You are always welcome."

Aras' concern touched her. "I regret I can't, at least not yet, and after the Equinox, when we're free to travel, we'll go north, out of Iberia altogether."

"That may be the wisest course," Cesada said.

Rhonwen hugged him. "Aras is generous to send you all this way with a message for me."

"There's more to it than that." He spared her the briefest of smiles. "I'm calling upon the chiefs of the clans to stand with Aras when he speaks to Sertorius about the harsh treatment we've received."

"He's used us all badly," she said bitterly. "When his army was poor, he was quick enough to befriend Iberians. Now, as it swells with expatriate Romans, he no longer needs us."

Cesada nodded. "Aras believes as you do. We pray our words will be heard."

"I wish you well, and may the gods bless your mission."

The stern-faced warrior bowed, kissed her cheek, and departed as soundlessly as he'd arrived.

⚜ ⚜ ⚜

Rhonwen had calculated the date of the equinox many times and knew without question tomorrow would be the day. She prayed everything else would fall into place as she prepared to travel to the standing stones. She wrapped the hind-stick in a spare cloak and packed fruit, water, and bread for the journey. She planned to arrive before nightfall and rise before dawn.

If all went well, she'd have Rede back before the end of the day. She would not think about the consequences of failure. Orlan's confidence had never wavered, and that bolstered her own.

At midday Rhonwen threw her travel sack over her shoulder and stepped out of the wagon. Almost immediately, a man pushed her back inside and collapsed at her feet.

"Rhonwen," Aras gasped, "help me."

She stared at the battered and bloody warrior. "By the gods, Aras! What happened?"

"We were attacked," he said, his breath rasping as he pressed his hands against a deep gash that touched the ribs on his left side.

Rhonwen pried his hands away to inspect the wound. "Who did this?" she asked. "Cesada told me you were gathering allies." Though cut in dozens of places, only the wound in his side appeared serious.

"There were eight chiefs," he said, "representing eight clans. We meant to go directly to Sertorius and resolve our differences as we always did in the past. We never got close."

"Why?"

"Perpenna." Aras spat in disgust. "May he be thrice cursed. He led the assassins. We traveled under a staff of truce, and though we considered bringing a host of warriors, we thought it wiser to keep our numbers low. Therefore, each chief brought but two men."

"Cesada?" Rhonwen asked.

Aras shook his head. "He was the first to fall. When Perpenna and his Roman dogs ambushed us, Cesada charged them. He took a javelin in the chest."

Tears clouded her vision as she worked on Aras' wounds.

"There were too many of them," he said. "Half of us were slain before the battle had properly begun. I looked for Sertorius, but the whoreson didn't show himself." He grimaced as Rhonwen applied pressure to his deepest wound.

"Hold this tight," she said pressing his hand on top of the cloth she used to stanch the bleeding. "I need more bandages."

"A few of us broke free," Aras said. "Had any of the others remained standing, I would never have left." He gasped as Rhonwen replaced the bloody cloth and secured the wound with a fresh dressing. "If you can close my wounds, I'll finish the fight."

"You're already done. The Romans won't be far behind. I'm leaving—come with me."

She helped Aras to his feet and gathered her healer's satchel along with the bag she'd planned to take to the standing stone. Suddenly, men and horses surrounded them, leaving no hope of escape. Perpenna arrived before either of them could move. Aras pulled Rhonwen behind him, drew his sword and faced them.

"Don't be a fool," Perpenna called. "Throw down your weapon. You have no chance."

"I should surrender so you can crucify me?" Aras laughed. "I'd rather die with a blade in my hand."

"As you wish," Perpenna said.

Aras took the first warrior by surprise with a swipe that crushed the man's shoulder and sent him to the ground shrieking. Two more soldiers rushed forward, and Aras gave ground until he backed into the wagon.

The Romans pressed in from behind their shields, shifting them only long enough to stab with their short swords. As he knocked one sword away, another quickly took its place.

Rhonwen searched for anything that might serve as a weapon but found only the old Mauritanian's bow, which she'd saved for Rede. She didn't have time to string it before Perpenna's men swarmed over Aras and hacked him to the ground.

Perpenna climbed into the wagon and backhanded her across the face, knocking her to the floor. He motioned for soldiers to pull her from the wagon. She tried to jerk away, and one of the men slapped her. She tasted salty blood.

"You prove your treachery by consorting with this dog." He kicked Aras, lying in the blood-darkened dirt.

By his vacant stare, she knew he'd already passed through the Cauldron. She raised a hand in a farewell blessing that his spirit would find its way back to avenge his murder. She turned to Perpenna, outrage and grief burning inside. "I'm no traitor, Perpenna, and neither were Aras or the other chiefs you attacked. They traveled under a sign of truce!"

"I saw no such sign," he said. "I quelled an uprising, an attack on Sertorius. I'm a hero."

"There are dead men who would disagree."

"They're welcome to testify," Perpenna said.

✠ ✠ ✠

Perpenna dragged Rhonwen before Sertorius, entering his domain with the sure step of a conqueror. Two guards pushed her to her knees. She waited, hands tied in front of her, as Sertorius sat at his table in conversation with an officer while a dozen toga-clad members of the senate-in-exile hovered nearby. Men at arms and Roman servants lined the walls as if their sole task was to avoid the intense afternoon sunlight flooding through the windows. Again, she saw no Iberians among those surrounding the general.

"Thank the gods you've returned safely," Perpenna said. He saluted his superior crisply, the slap of hand on chest serving to complete his call for everyone's attention. "Your talks with King Mithradates went well?"

"Well enough," Sertorius said, his eyes on Rhonwen. "What's she doing here? The equinox isn't until tomorrow."

"That's true, General," Perpenna replied, "but I couldn't be sure you'd return in time and therefore had to act on your behalf."

Sertorius looked puzzled. "What are you talking about?"

"There's been an uprising by no fewer than eight barbarian tribes you honored as allies."

Rhonwen struggled against her bonds. "You lying pig!"

"Who is this woman?" asked a fat man in a purple-trimmed toga.

Sertorius studied her, his mood and intentions unfathomable. "An acquaintance," he said, "a healer."

Rhonwen seethed. "A driad."

"A traitor," Perpenna said, clapping a hand over her mouth. "Though her scheme failed."

She bit at his fingers, but he gripped her jaw more tightly and covered her nose to cut off her breath.

"What scheme?" Sertorius asked.

"I caught eight conspirators on their way here, disguised as envoys. They planned to attack your command post from within." He observed the lounging soldiers with open contempt. "Though they brought few men, I've no doubt they would've caught your guards napping."

His words dissolved the guards' lethargy. Many scowled as they straightened to alertness, but none dared speak.

"Release her," Sertorius said.

Rhonwen gasped and stretched her jaw. "Perpenna lies!"

"Silence!" Sertorius bellowed. He signaled Perpenna to continue.

"My men and I met the conspirators on the road, where I hoped to speak with them, address their complaints, and end the crisis. They attacked without warning, and it was only by the greatest good fortune that we repulsed them. Too cowardly to stand their ground, the traitors fled. We pursued them, cutting down all but one."

Rhonwen could not believe her ears. Surely Sertorius, with all his years of fighting with Celts in Iberia and against them in Cisalpine Gaul, would see through Perpenna's fabrication.

Sertorius listened intently, his hands balled into fists on the table and his eye narrowed. "Who was it?"

"The Trepani chief," Perpenna said. "But since he was wounded and his native soil lay so far away, I had no doubt where he'd go. After dispatching the last of the renegades, I sent the bulk of my force here and rode directly to Osca." He looked at Rhonwen and shook his head. "I caught the two of them trying to sneak away together. Can you imagine anyone so callous that they'd abandon family for the company of traitors? Is it any wonder barbarians have no souls?"

Rhonwen wanted to shriek against Perpenna's lies. Instead she muttered a fervent prayer the gods would let him die slowly, and in such great pain he'd dishonor himself in public.

Sertorius' face betrayed his feelings. The muscles of his jaw lapped like ocean waves as he held Rhonwen's defiant gaze. "I once held you in regard."

"May I speak?" Rhonwen asked. "Or is truth unwelcome here?"

"Truth is always welcome, but treachery isn't," Sertorius said.

She took a deep calming breath, knowing anger in the face of a schemer like Perpenna could only suit his purposes. "The Aras I knew was an honorable man."

"That ended the day he took up arms and rode against me," Sertorius said. "There can be but one leader in this land, and I am that leader. There can be but one purpose, and I have already defined it. Speak no more of traitors."

"But Aras—"

"Not another word of him!" Sertorius slammed his fist on the table.

Rhonwen held her chin high although she trembled in outrage and the fearful realization Sertorius did not want to hear the truth. She turned toward Perpenna. "Was I riding with the men you ambushed today?" she asked.

He scowled and cleared his throat. "I did not see you among those who attacked us."

"You knew Aras was wounded. Is it so strange he would come to me? I'm one of a few healers in Osca."

Perpenna sneered. "If his arrival was so innocent, why were you attempting to run away?"

"I wasn't running away," Rhonwen said. "I was on my way to retrieve the hind Sertorius commanded me to return to him, or did you not know tomorrow is when night and day are balanced?"

"After this, do you still think we'll believe your nonsense about the hind?" Perpenna laughed.

"Enough," Sertorius said, his voice weary. He turned to the senators. "To achieve our aims, we must be of one purpose, and we must act in concert. There can be no question of the law. Those who rode against me violated my trust. This cannot go unpunished, for to ignore it only encourages more of the same."

Rhonwen bristled. "Those you would brand traitors are dead. They can pay no greater price."

"You're wrong," Sertorius said, his face a granite mask. He turned to Perpenna. "Return to the school at Osca and arrest the sons of the chiefs who rode against me."

"They're children!" Rhonwen cried.

"Be silent!" Sertorius said, his voice rumbling like summer thunder. "Attend me, Perpenna. I command you to put every one of them to the sword."

The strength left Rhonwen's legs.

"Take care," Sertorius said, "that none of the bodies is disfigured. When their families claim them, there must be no questions about who died, or why."

"Monster," Rhonwen whispered.

"And you," Sertorius said, finally responding to her, "you will bring the hind to me tomorrow. If she is healthy and eager to feel the stroke of my hand, you and yours may go free, otherwise you'll suffer the same fate as the traitors."

What little breath Rhonwen retained fled with his words. She fell to the floor in despair.

Perpenna nudged her with the toe of his sandal. "Rather than prolong the pretense of keeping the deer alive, you could prevail upon Sertorius for the justice of Mars."

Rhonwen stared at him in uncertainty.

"Admit the deception now, and offer your own life for your son's."

"I have until tomorrow to return the hind," Rhonwen said. She turned her head sharply to address Sertorius, but he had led his small retinue from the room, leaving her alone with Perpenna and the guards. She staggered toward the door. "I need a horse," she said. "I have far to go before I return."

"We have none to spare." Perpenna shrugged in mock helplessness. "But during your walk, you'll have plenty of time to think about the consequences of your actions."

"No," Rhonwen said, "I'll spend the time finding the curse you'll carry to your grave." She held her bound wrists up, expecting him to release her, but he turned and followed Sertorius out of the room instead. Furious, she strode toward the nearest guard. "Untie me," she demanded.

He hesitated, looking in the direction Perpenna had taken.

Rhonwen held her fists close to the man's face, a warning finger raised a thumb-span from his nose. "Unless you want to carry the same curse, cut me loose!"

The man reluctantly obeyed, sawing at her bonds with a knife. Once free, she left the building, and paused outside to catch her breath. She had little time to reach Osca and take the spellbound hind to the sacred stones for transformation. The horses Perpenna and his men had ridden when they brought her stood tethered to a row of posts in front of the building. The one she'd ridden from Osca was nowhere in sight, but she walked toward the first horse in line, a tall gray Perpenna had ridden.

A soldier who'd joined in the murder of Aras stepped from behind the horses and barred her way. "*Barbari* aren't allowed near these horses," he said, bringing the tip of his spear level with her chest.

She pushed the iron spearhead away with the back of her hand. "Nonsense. I rode one of them not two hours ago."

"It'll recover in time," he said and once more lowered his spear to emphasize his meaning.

She stared at him. "Pray you never need a healer." She pushed past him and down the lane that led to the paved road. The sun promised a few more hours of daylight. If she walked briskly, she might make it to Osca and then on to the nearest standing stones before dawn. She refused to think about tiring.

She let her rage fuel her steps but forced herself to bottle it up inside for every guard she met. Soldiers who allowed Perpenna's band to pass unchallenged now seemed eager to thwart her progress. Each demanded to know her business before allowing her to proceed, and she knew a sharp tongue would only make matters worse. Every stop meant time wasted and miles not covered. When she finally reached the main Roman road, the setting sun lay but one fist off the horizon.

"State your business," said yet another guard as he stepped from the side of the road.

Rhonwen swallowed her impatience, but wondered if any men remained in the ranks. Had the entire army been turned into watchmen to impede her journey? She took a deep breath to explain her purpose one more time. "I'm—"

"I know who you are," the man said.

Rhonwen felt faint with relief when she recognized the Iberian man smiling at her. "Milo," she whispered and sat wearily in the middle of the road. "The gods have not forsaken me after all."

The gentle Bateri farmer knelt beside her. He uncorked his water skin and handed it to her. The water, although warm from the day, soothed her parched throat. Milo offered her a handful of dried figs, which she gratefully accepted. She ate slowly and related the terrible events of the past weeks.

"Perpenna killed Aras?" he asked.

"He didn't wield the blade," she said, "or Aras would have sent him to his ancestors."

Milo grunted. "Even they'd want nothing to do with Perpenna. I didn't like Aras, but I respected him. It troubles me that Sertorius would turn his back on such a man. What keeps him from doing the same to me?"

"Nothing," she said, "so long as Perpenna advises him." She shrugged and reluctantly got to her feet. "But that's no longer my concern. I have only one task left, and that will likely take all night."

Milo looked off into the distance. When he turned back to her, he offered a hopeful smile. "Will you wait here a moment?"

She shook her head sadly. "I can't, Milo, I have so little time."

He took her hands in his, his face close and his eyes intense. "Trust me now, as you once asked me to trust you. I'll be gone a few minutes at most."

Rhonwen capitulated with a great sigh, and Milo disappeared into the growing shadows of early evening. A nightjar trilled overhead, and at a distant campfire men sang a melancholy tune. The minutes dragged by, and she worried that Milo had lost his way. Though grateful for the food he'd shared with her, she grew convinced she would have done better not to have encountered him at all.

"Driad?" he called.

Thank the gods, she thought, he's finally returned. "I'm here," she said.

"Then let me hold this horse steady while you get on."

She scrambled toward his voice, and when she reached him, hugged his neck. "Where did you get a horse?"

"I borrowed it from my centurion. I told him I wanted to buy wine in Osca."

Rhonwen clambered into the saddle then leaned forward as Milo mounted and settled in behind her.

"I'm not much of a rider," he said, hands on her waist.

Rhonwen grinned. "I'll show you everything you need to know." She pushed her heels into the horse's sides and guided it out onto the Roman road. Its iron-shod hooves clattered on the stones. She feared the noise would draw too much attention, but Roman patrols passed them regularly. They hailed Milo but never stopped them. She finally relaxed.

"How can I ever thank you?" she asked.

"For what?"

"Helping me!"

"I'm not helping you. I've no idea where Osca is. I'm bringing you along so I won't get lost."

Energized by hope, Rhonwen laughed. "You've saved lives this night, my friend. I'm in your debt."

They rode to Osca without incident. When they reached the school, her wagon was undisturbed. The ground had been scuffed, the dirt mixed with blood in a symbol of oneness with the earth, and someone had left a wreath of ivy on the spot. She closed her eyes and quietly blessed those who had taken Aras away for proper burial.

She scrambled into the wagon and retrieved the hind's stick.

She embraced Milo. "Thank you," she said before resuming her journey to the standing stones alone.

Milo stopped her. "I've come this far, Driad Rhonwen. What kind of man would I be if I didn't stay with you?" He mounted and held a hand down to her.

Rhonwen smiled. "Won't your centurion expect you back soon?"

"Not until tomorrow," he said.

She retrieved blankets from the wagon and climbed up behind him.

"Your wife is a lucky woman," she said as they traveled under a brilliant starlit sky.

"I hope you'll tell her that when next you see her," he said.

Rhonwen told Milo which trails to follow and then dozed with her cheek pressed against his back. He woke her only rarely to ask directions, and by the time they reached the standing stones it seemed to her only a few moments had passed. It was hours until dawn. While Milo tended the horse, Rhonwen made camp and built a modest fire to ward off the spring chill. More relieved than she thought possible, she placed the hind's stick at the base of the east face of the largest standing stone and then curled up in her blanket.

She woke before sunrise and watched in trepidation at the first hints of Lugh's light in the eastern sky.

"Milo," she called, "come watch a miracle."

He stumbled toward her, rubbing his eyes and stretching the kinks from his spine.

"Sit beside me," she said, pulling her blanket close around her. She wondered whether she could remain calm. Orlan had described the process, but she had never seen it.

They waited nearly an hour for the day to develop. Several deer moved along the edge of the forest, their delicate ears flipping back and forth as they snipped a new leaf bud here or a bit of grass there. Rhonwen touched the stick once just to make sure it was still the right one. Milo tested it with a finger, too, but felt nothing unusual.

As the moment of sunrise approached, she cautioned him to silence. "Behold," she said, "the magic of the gods!"

The sun crested the eastern horizon, and sunlight chased the shadows away. Bright light fell first on the stones and then on the stick. Rhonwen held her breath as it began to pulse and swell. She heard Milo gasp and gripped his arm.

Accompanied by the same popping sounds she had heard weeks earlier when the hind had been transformed, the stick continued to grow.

The change was complete, and the diminutive white deer lay asleep in the morning light. Milo, trembling and on his knees, stared through his fingers at the magnificent animal. "Is it alive?"

The question startled Rhonwen into movement. She knelt forward. The deer's belly, once distended and bloated, now lay soft and quiet. When she pressed her ear to the animal's chest, the heartbeat sounded strong and even. She never knew anything could sound so good. The hind's life assured that of her son. She embraced the animal and wept.

"What's wrong?" Milo asked.

She stroked the deer's neck as it blinked its soft brown eyes. "There's nothing wrong," she said, happily. She ignored the tears of joy dripping down her cheek as she slipped a soft leather collar around the animal's neck. "There's nothing wrong at all."

The doe rolled gently to its side, extended its neck, and licked Rhonwen's tears with its long pink tongue.

23

After the death of Fyrsil, it became my duty to watch and wait for the Ageless Man. I expected him to come to Gillac the day of the Midsummer celebration. Though I had my students watch for strangers, and left word at the enclave, I never met him. I will leave him the same offering Fyrsil bade me give, on the eve of every summer solstice, and hope to see him once before I return to Iberia.

— *Stave One of Orlan, 40th Master of Mount Eban Enclave*

Armorica

Dierdre struggled to keep up with Mallec and Leuw as they led Arie and two other students over the guardian boulders of Mount Eban. She had to follow slowly to avoid being seen, although neither Mallec nor Leuw had even once looked back.

She'd done everything possible to undermine Gar and prayed for Mallec's death at the hands of the warrior-druid. Using Caradowc's little band, she had spread the word that Gar was too weak to fight the raiders himself. If Mallec and Setaine had perished, it would have guaranteed Gar's downfall and her own elevation to Enclave Master. It would have been a simple matter for Caradowc to lead a band of warriors and mercenaries in pursuit of the raiders. Once he'd brought their heads back to the clanhold, his place as chief would have been assured.

She gritted her teeth and clambered over a boulder, scraping her knuckles. She sucked at the blood and spat it out. Unfortunately, Mallec had survived and returned with Setaine to Gillac in triumph. Worse, Gar had also prospered from the victory.

As Mallec and the warriors re-entered the clanhold with war horns blaring and the warrior-druid's head held high, Dierdre could only fume. She vowed to take the enclave for herself and deliver the clan to Caradowc before another year went by.

The gods must have looked upon her oath with favor, for less than a week later Caradowc overheard Mallec appeal to Leuw to stay at the enclave and assist him with an initiation.

"Won't Dierdre help?" Leuw had asked.

"I no longer trust her," Mallec had said.

When Caradowc relayed the conversation, she railed against Mallec for denying her the secret of woadsleep.

Caradowc had laughed at her. "If you know what he's going to do, and where he intends to do it, how difficult could it be to discover his secrets?"

Perhaps there was hope for Caradowc after all.

She thanked the gods Mallec had been injured in his battle with Brucc. Had he been healthy she might not have been able to stay abreast of the others as they wound their way up Mount Eban's hillside. Even so, she cursed the corpulent bard and the wounded druid for maintaining a pace she found taxing. Pausing to catch her breath, she wished she'd brought a water skin. She squinted to see how far ahead they were. She couldn't fall so far behind she would need a torch to traverse the narrow passage to the cavern where the ceremony would take place.

She caught sight of Arie's green-and-red tunic. It irked Dierdre that the girl was to assist in the woadsleep ceremony, even though she hadn't been through it herself. When the flash of color disappeared over the first of the boulders guarding the entrance to the Cavern, Dierdre climbed faster.

By the time she reached the entryway, the others were already deep into the passage, and only scuffling and the faint flicker of the last torch marked their passage. She bolted into the hole like a ferret after a rat.

Hurrying in the dark on her hands and knees to keep up with the dim flame leading the way, she gouged herself twice on jagged rocks. When she finally reached the main chamber she leaned against the cool rock wall and rested, her breath coming in shuddering gasps. She watched the preparations.

Mallec wasted no time. The two young men about to undergo the transformation waited in the same flat space Orlan had used. A small fire, well away from the students, already blazed. Arie and the students faced Mallec and Leuw as the Enclave Master gave them instructions.

Keeping to the deepest shadows, she crept nearer. The only sound in the Cavern was the sleepy rhythm of Mallec's voice as he intoned the proper procedures for the students. The pompous fool was likely making up the rules as he spoke.

Arie and Leuw flanked him as he beseeched the gods. When his voice dropped, she could not make out his words. The two initiates lay on either side of the fire, and Mallec and Leuw traced a pattern on their chests. When Arie handed Mallec a censer with the baneweed in it, Dierdre held her breath. She watched as he lit the dried herb and with a feather waved the smoke into the faces of the young men.

As the popping that heralded the transformation began, her stomach lurched. Allowing oneself to be reduced to such a state was hideous. She hoped to avoid it and still learn the secret of reversing the metamorphosis. Surely Mallec would say something that would give her the clue she needed to transform the stick she believed to be Cullinor's Ancient One.

Mallec lowered his voice again, and as Dierdre wriggled closer to hear him, she stepped on the hem of her cloak. She tripped, crashing to the ground.

Everything went quiet. She squeezed her eyes closed, willed Mallec to continue speaking, and prayed they'd mistake her fall for some natural cave sound.

Approaching footfalls ended her hopes of watching the initiation in secret.

"Dierdre?" Mallec stood over her, a torch in one hand. Leuw stood behind him, scowling.

She forced a sob and swallowed the curse she wanted to make. "Thank the gods, Mallec, I found you!"

He offered her his hand and she grasped it, not needing to pretend fatigue to struggle to her feet.

"What are you doing here?"

She wiped at her sweaty face and maneuvered closer to the fire. The pot of baneweed still smoldered, but she saw nothing else notable. "I came to tell you I've had a change of heart. You were right to require the woadsleep ceremony for members of the enclave. I was selfish to refuse." She smiled humbly at him. Surely he would see how contrite she was. "Forgive my earlier fears. I'm ready now."

The flickering torch light made Mallec's face impossible to read.

"No, Dierdre. You're too late."

"Surely not, Mallec. I see the baneweed still burns."

"The ceremony is over. No one but Leuw and I will continue from this point."

She pointed at Arie. "Gar's daughter is here, and she's not even a druid yet. How can you allow her and not me?"

Mallec paused, and Dierdre recognized the mistrust in his eyes.

"You must allow me to participate!" she cried. "I'm more worthy than that nothing of a girl!" She stepped toward the baneweed.

Mallec grabbed her arm. "You may not!"

Dierdre wrenched herself free. "You dare deny me? I worked hard for what was handed to you on a platter. I've twenty years more experience than you. I have a right to know the secret of the baneweed."

"I will not allow you to defile this sacred place with your demands. There are rituals to follow, observances to be made."

"You're an idiot," she snarled. "I should be Master of Eban, not you. Your silly rules mean nothing."

Mallec drew himself upright. "Fyrsil and Orlan knew what they were doing. This ceremony derives from them."

She lunged for the censer beside the fire. Mallec grabbed at her but only ripped her cloak. She scrambled on the ground, gripped the censer and cradled it. It burned her hands, but she didn't care. With a triumphant smile, she buried her face in the smoke and inhaled deeply.

⌘ ⌘ ⌘

"I like her better this way," Leuw said as he followed Mallec down the mountain trail toward Cad Cerrig's standing stones.

Mallec stopped and turned to stare at the bard behind him. "What do you mean?"

Leuw chuckled and brandished the stick Dierdre had become as if it were a wooden sword. "In this form, Dierdre gives off a rather pleasant tingling sensation."

"The stick tingles?"

"Of course," Leuw said. "Can't you feel it?"

Mallec held the stick in both hands but felt nothing. He shook his head and gave it back.

"It's not unpleasant," Leuw said, "and how often can one say that about Dierdre?" He pondered the stick. "Couldn't we just leave her like this?"

Mallec laughed. "I think not, my friend. It's our duty to restore her."

Leuw's face grew somber. "I wonder. We prohibited Arie from attending the revival ceremony because she wasn't ready. Is Dierdre any more ready?"

"You doubt her sincerity?"

Leuw gazed at him as if he'd lost his mind. "And you don't? She seemed terrified at Orlan's change, and now suddenly she wants it for herself. Why would she sneak in to observe us? She wants something, and being woadslept isn't it."

"She's merely jealous of Arie. Dierdre's been passed over too often. In her place I'd feel betrayed if I thought someone as young as Arie was being considered for a position I wanted."

"Her ambition does her no credit. There hasn't been a master here in over a hundred fifty years who truly wanted the job. Even Fyrsil, who spent his whole life here, wanted something else. He hated record-keeping more than you do!"

He grimaced at the pull of healing skin on his back and arms, unhappy reminders of his encounter with Brucc. "What do you suggest we do with her, then?" he asked. "We can't carry her with us every day, and if we leave her lying around, someone is likely to use her for kindling."

"Why not let her rest with the gods for a while? We'd all be better off not having to worry about her. Perhaps in this state she can talk the gods into being kind to Gillac in the coming year."

Mallec smiled. Leuw was right about one thing. She should spend some time making amends to the gods for her disruption of the baneweed ceremony. "The problem remains. What do we do with her until the next equinox?"

Leuw grinned. "Why not put her in Caradowc's hands? She is his mother."

Mallec shook his head. "We can't let Caradowc know about the ceremony."

"We won't tell him how we did it. We merely give him the stick with the charge that he makes certain it remains safe, that his mother's life and the future good will of the gods depends upon it."

Mallec considered the suggestion. It seemed reasonable. Next equinox they would restore Dierdre, and perhaps by then her time in the Otherworld would have brought her peace. "Yes," he said at last. "We'll give the stick to Caradowc."

✠ ✠ ✠

Caradowc lounged in the shade of a beech tree watching Borwyn throw his knife. The Helveti was good at it, but knife-throwing was a talent Caradowc did not share.

"Real men don't use throwing knives. They fight face to face with nothing between them but skin."

Borwyn pulled his blade from the bundle of straw he had used as a target and tested its edge with his thumb. He sat beside Caradowc, removing a whetstone from his waist pouch. He spat on the stone and worked the blade.

"You Armoricans have strange notions. In a fight there are no dishonorable weapons or tactics."

Borwyn nudged him and jerked his head toward the road. "Here comes your sister. And judging from the scowl on her face, she must be looking for you." He chortled. "Were she looking for me, she'd be wearing a smile and little else."

Caradowc turned away from him to look up the road. He toyed with the idea of rising to meet her and then dismissed it. Let her come to him.

He could not see what Borwyn found so fascinating. In spite of her comely face and well-muscled thighs, she was nearly as great a pain as his mother. If nothing else, her dedication to Gar sickened him.

She stopped, expressionless, in front of them.

"What do you want, Arie?"

"I want to know the truth," she said. Her eyes flashed with anger and she waved at Borwyn and the others. "I heard these men of yours—"

"I'm my own man," Borwyn said. "Come to my house and I'll show you." He laughed, but she ignored him and faced Caradowc.

"Your friends said Father lacked the courage to hunt down the raiders. You know that's not true."

Caradowc shrugged. "He's failing in his duties. You know he would've done nothing about the Redoni raiders unless forced. I can't help it if the gods punish us until he's replaced."

She frowned, and he knew she'd recognized the truth in his words.

"Can't you see it's his grief that saps his strength? The gods don't punish us for things like that."

"Yes, Arie. That's exactly the sort of thing gods do."

"Is that based on all your long years of study?" Mallec asked from behind.

Caradowc spun around in surprise. Mallec and the fat bard, Leuw, approached. "I didn't see you coming."

"That's often the way of things." He smiled at Arie. "Will you be returning to the enclave with us?"

"I can't leave Father just now. I doubt he'd even eat."

"Then go to him," Mallec said with a smile. "We must speak with Caradowc."

The young warrior tried to think of anything he had done that would have angered the druids. He'd been careful to keep up the appearance of a good son to Gar.

"Come," Mallec said, nudging Caradowc toward the altar on the commons.

"I've done nothing wrong," he said.

Leuw chuckled. "The first words of any man with a clear conscience."

Caradowc tensed. "It's true!"

"We haven't come to chastise you," Mallec said.

Caradowc kept silent, regretting that he'd spoken.

"We have troubling news about your mother," Mallec said. "Yesterday, she forced her way into a ceremony to which she had not been invited."

Caradowc relaxed when he realized they weren't angry at him. "Go on."

"The ceremony involves a most profound ritual," Mallec said, "and because she was not properly prepared, we can't be sure how the gods will react to her participation."

Leuw handed Caradowc a cloth-bound bundle, which he unwrapped. Inside he found a length of wood with smooth bark and no branches. It reminded him of the stick he'd found in the Giant's Tomb. "What's this?"

"It's your mother," Mallec said, shifting uncomfortably.

Caradowc laughed. "Do you really expect me to believe this nonsense?"

Mallec sighed deeply. "I wish it were not true."

Caradowc stared at the bundle, suddenly uneasy. If they could turn his mother into a stick...

"When you touch it, do you feel anything?" Leuw asked.

"No," Caradowc replied, remembering the similar question his mother had asked when she told him to carry the stick from the Tomb. Perhaps there was something unusual about that stick, too. No wonder she had guarded it like a treasure. "What should I feel?" he asked, hiding his sudden interest.

Leuw shrugged. "It's not important. What matters is that she be kept safe until she's restored."

"Since you're the only family she has, we thought it best to leave her with you for safekeeping."

"How long will she stay like this?" Caradowc asked.

"At least until the next equinox," Mallec said. "Return the stick to us a few days before then, and we'll finish the preparations. Otherwise, there's no chance she can be restored."

Caradowc nodded, and stared at the stick in his hand. "Can she see or hear us?"

Mallec shook his head. "Fire seems to be the only thing that penetrates." He shuddered. "I suggest you keep the stick bound in that cloth so it won't be mistaken for kindling."

The druids bowed slightly to Caradowc and then turned away as if they had utterly dismissed him from their thoughts. He snorted. He should be used to it after all the times his mother had done the same thing.

He wrapped the stick carefully and walked back toward his companions, then stopped. Who was imprisoned in the stick he pulled out of the Giant's Tomb?

Ignoring the questions from Borwyn, Pugh, and the others as he walked past them, he continued until he reached the stable. He thrust the stick into his belt and saddled the horse Gar let him use.

He rode hard and pushed his horse to reach Eban enclave by mid-afternoon. When close enough for someone to hear his approach, he left the horse tethered out of sight in the trees and walked the rest of the way. Circling behind the enclave buildings, he crept into Dierdre's quarters.

He searched through her belongings. At the bottom of a great wooden trunk he found a stick bundled in plain white linen. He removed the cloth and rested the stick across his palms, but still he felt nothing.

A comparison of the sticks likewise yielded nothing significant. Neither the pale color of the bark nor the smooth texture was different, nor was there any significant difference in the length, girth, or weight. In fact, as he stared at them, one in each hand, he realized he could no longer tell which was which.

"Lugh's balls!" he muttered. What would the druids say if he returned the wrong one? He couldn't return them both. If his mother had wanted the druids to know of the existence of the other stick, she would have told them herself. After all, she'd had it in her possession for years.

He sprawled in one of the elaborately carved Roman chairs Dierdre had obtained in Vannes and tried to resolve the dilemma, but the only thing he felt sure of was a sense of relief that she'd no longer be able to make demands on him. Perhaps he could tell the druids he'd not believed them and had discarded the stick on the first pile of firewood he saw. He grinned recalling Mallec's reaction to the idea of burning.

With that happy thought in mind, he left the building as cautiously as he'd entered it and ran to his horse in the cover of the trees. If he hurried, he could get to the disputed lands before dawn.

He traveled unseen, even when he left the main road and cantered toward the Giant's Tomb. He splashed across the shallow river that marked the boundary, secured the horse in the forest shadows, and crept toward the mound.

The work site appeared as he'd last seen it. No new laborers had been there to dismantle his handiwork. He smiled as he passed the crude statue covered with dried blood. The sheep's head had fallen off, and only scattered bony fragments remained. A short search of the mound brought him to the sheltered hole through which Dierdre had pushed him so many years ago. He brushed aside the overgrown grasses and uprooted a large bush that blocked the hole, and then he peered into the blackness. He would not venture in. Once had been more than enough.

He pulled the two sticks from his belt and addressed them as if they were one.

"I've brought you to your old home, Mother, and I've decided to leave you with the treasure you so eagerly sought. I hope you're happy together."

With both sticks in one hand, he held them over the dark opening. "Sleep well," he said, and let them fall.

24

*With delight I read the staves of the Druid Masters of Eban.
Yet I am saddened to know the Ageless man no longer visits. For
all my time here, not one stranger has come to us. I pray the gods
have finally given him the answers he sought.*

*I too seek answers, and although I honor these staves, for
tradition lends them the weight of history, I shall record what I
learn elsewhere.*

— *Stave One of Mallec, 41st Master of Mount Eban Enclave*

Iberia

Orlan tossed on his pallet, half in and half out of sleep,
the result of a battle between fatigue and a nagging
concern for the hind's recovery. He jerked wide awake
as he realized the morning sky was already bright. Today was
the equinox! Though he lacked the power to alter the outcome,
Orlan prayed anyway, beseeching the gods to revive the deer
and protect Rhonwen as she delivered it safely to Sertorius.

Rede lay peacefully asleep on his pallet beside Orlan's, a
concession wrought from the new master of the school.

Orlan felt badly for the students, whose studies had all but
ended when he and Rhonwen were forced out. No doubt some
of the older ones would teach the younger, but without guidance and encouragement, their efforts would likely fail. How
could Sertorius be such an idiot? He had allowed Perpenna to
discard one of the finest opportunities for creating life-long allies.
Sertorius could not long continue to ignore the foolishness of
the man claiming to act on his behalf.

Shouts from the courtyard roused him, but he could not leave
the room to investigate. Someone called out clan names. Orlan
recognized many of them and pictured the boys he once taught:
sharp-tongued Volio and his brother Pentas of the coastal Laletani,

slow-witted Bragga of the Carpetani, and stout young Hefron whose Bastuli clan lived in the south. Eight clans were called, although he could not make out all the names.

He heard footsteps echo in the corridor and down the stairs leading to the courtyard, then silence for a time. One of the clan names was repeated. After a long quiet, an armed guard unlocked the door to his room and thrust it open.

"We seek the son of the Trepani," the man said with an accent so pronounced Orlan struggled to understand him.

"There are none," Orlan said. "Aras, the Trepani chief, has no heirs."

"How stupid do you think we are?" the guard snarled. "We know all about the Trepani's affections for the healer. Since the traitor Aras is dead, his son will represent the Trepani."

Frightened screams rose from the students in the courtyard. Rede, awakened by all the noise, crawled from his bed and clung to Orlan's calf.

"He is not Aras' son."

"Give me the boy," the guard said, stepping forward.

"No." Orlan faced the armed man defiantly. "You advance at your peril." He made a warding sign at the warrior, who only laughed.

"I've nothing to fear from your curse, barbarian. Move aside."

Another scream from the courtyard ended abruptly and Orlan backed away, keeping himself between Rede and the Roman. The boy pressed close behind him.

"He comes with me," the guard said, brandishing his sword.

"Touch him, and your balls will rot like bad fruit," Orlan said, signing another curse.

A second guard appeared in the doorway, and Orlan made his decision. Perhaps this was the day Rhiannon meant to meet him. He blessed himself, prepared to die before he gave the child to the Romans.

"What's he up to?" asked the second guard from the doorway. "Just go in there and grab the boy. If the old man gets in your way, kill him." With that, the second guard pushed the first from behind, propelling him across the room.

Orlan attempted to dodge out of the way, but Rede didn't move, and Orlan tripped over him. Both crashed to the floor as the mumbling guard stepped over Orlan and grabbed Rede by the hair.

Orlan rammed his foot up between the guard's legs. The man gasped in pain and dropped to the floor with both hands clutched around his testicles.

"The rotting begins now," Orlan said as he struggled to stand and face the remaining warrior. Rede huddled in the corner.

"What kind of man makes war on children?" Orlan asked as the second guard advanced.

"I don't choose my enemies. Do you?"

The question caught Orlan by surprise.

The guard rushed in and brought the pommel of his sword down on the top of Orlan's head, driving him to the floor. Pain exploded in his belly as the Roman kicked him. He struggled to get up but could not make his body move, even when he heard Rede crying out his name as the room went soft, dark, and silent.

✠ ✠ ✠

Milo left Rhonwen and the hind a safe distance from the building where Sertorius waited. Rhonwen thanked him profusely for his help and sent him on his way with an embrace and a kiss she intended him to remember until he returned home. Aras would've been shocked, she thought, smiling. Then she grimaced with regret. Had she accepted his first proposal, they might all now be alive and content in the mountains. She shoved the thoughts aside and put the blame where it belonged, on Sertorius and his sycophant, Perpenna. She spat into the dust.

Though wearing collar and leash, the hind stayed at her side as she walked the last half mile. Known to every man in Sertorius' service, the animal drew stares of awe from everyone they passed. Only when they came close to Sertorius' quarters did she have to restrain its eager pull forward.

The guards at the doors parted silently to let them through. No one dared slow their progress until they reached the room Sertorius had occupied the day before.

It appeared no less crowded this time, even without Perpenna, whose absence made her breathe easier. Senators and Roman officers clustered around the room like patrons at a market, speaking all at once rather than like a deliberative body. Only the servants remained quiet. Sertorius leaned over a table studying maps as the two men on either side of him argued. The general seemed oblivious to them.

Rhonwen stood in the entrance to the room and waited until Sertorius noticed her. Gradually the room fell silent, and the general looked up. He pushed aside a pair of senators who blocked his view. At his first sight of the deer, a smile spread across his face, and he moved away from the table to leave a clear path between them.

Rhonwen released her hold on the hind's collar and it trotted daintily toward Sertorius.

"You've done it!" he said, dropping to one knee to let the doe lick his cheek.

She nodded. "As promised, and now I want my son and my uncle returned to me."

"It will be done," Sertorius said without looking at her. "You're free to go."

Rhonwen stood firm. "I want them returned now."

Sertorius instructed a warrior to ride to the school in Osca. "Bring them directly here," he said. "I will brook no delays."

The man saluted and left, nearly colliding with Rhonwen in his haste to begin his mission.

"Does this not prove the value of my word?" Rhonwen asked.

Sertorius looked up from the hind. "It proves your prowess as a healer."

She swallowed. "We both lost a great friend yesterday, for Aras was an honorable man."

Sertorius silenced her with a wave of his hand. "That issue is done. Sentence has been passed, and nothing is to be gained by going back over old ground."

"That's not true," Rhonwen said. "Mistakes can be corrected. Errors—"

"I've made no mistakes," Sertorius said. "A commander cannot lead if he must constantly rethink everything he does. A good leader makes decisions and moves on, as I have done."

"But there was no conspiracy!" Rhonwen cried. "There's no reason to harm the children of the envoys."

"By now, Perpenna has already carried out my orders," he said.

"But—"

"Don't try my patience," he said. "I've sent a rider to return your family. Wait for them elsewhere. I have nothing more to say to you."

Like hens come for corn, the senators clustered around him and resumed their discussions. Rhonwen stalked out of the room. She found the spot against the exterior wall where she and Orlan had been forced to sit so many weeks earlier, but she ignored it in favor of a place that offered a bit of shade and took up her vigil there.

After a while the guards no longer paid attention to her. It was just as well as she had no desire to converse with them. Her heart filled with the joyful expectation of holding her son once again after so long. The sooner she could get him away from Roman ways, the better, but she smiled thinking how excited he would be to pass by the busy military camp.

As the hours blended together, she turned her thoughts to the future, to Armorica, greener than anything Iberia offered, Orlan had said, and at peace for forty years. She wondered what a battle-weary healer would do in a country without war.

A rider on the horizon captured her attention, and she stood to improve her view. Instead of the three or four horsemen she expected, a line of mounted men appeared. Rhonwen squinted but still couldn't pick out any faces. She waited impatiently as they drew closer and she could make out individual riders, all soldiers. Where were Orlan and Rede?

Perpenna rode at the head of the column, the other riders trailing behind. He ignored her as he drew to a stop in front of Sertorius' headquarters. Rhonwen stepped to the side and finally spotted Orlan near the back of the line. He sat on the horse like a broken old man with a bundle clutched tightly to his chest.

The dark hand of fear squeezed her heart as she ran toward him, ignoring anyone who got in her way. She stopped a dozen paces from the horse and shrieked at the sight of the massive red stains on Orlan's robe.

Orlan looked up slowly. Fresh tears streamed down his blood-spattered and grief-stricken face as he presented her with the limp body of her son.

Rhonwen moaned, all her hopes dissolved. She grabbed Rede and fell to the ground with the dead child clutched to her chest.

Orlan slipped down from his horse and joined her on the ground. "I tried to stop them," he said, pausing for a strained breath. "They said he was Aras' son."

She staggered to her feet, still cradling Rede, and walked back toward the place where she'd last seen Sertorius.

Perpenna had already dismissed his men and entered the building. When a guard moved to keep her out, she met his gaze evenly before looking down at the blood-soaked little body in her arms. It was enough. The man backed away, allowing the druids to pass inside.

Once more the room fell silent at her entrance, and once more Sertorius was the last to look at her. When he did, surprise flitted across his face.

She held out her burden as if offering it to him. At the sight of the child's bloody tunic, he rose from his chair.

"This is my child," she whispered, shuddering through the words. She surveyed those in the room. No one spoke. She moved forward slowly like one condemned to a gallows.

When she reached Sertorius, his hand still resting upon the slim neck of the white hind, Rhonwen lay Rede's body on the table in front of him.

"For what treachery was my son responsible?" she asked, making a knife of every word. "What threat did he offer to the great Sertorius?" She glared at the senators drawing away from the bloody child. "What did he do to deserve this?"

For the first time she could remember, Sertorius appeared uncomfortable. She leaned over Rede's body, her face close enough to his to feel his breath. "You've killed your own son!"

Sertorius stared down at the horror in front of him. "My son?"

"Yes!" Rhonwen hissed.

Sertorius looked up in astonishment and then turned his gaze to Perpenna who stepped forward shaking his head. "Everyone knows Aras was the child's father. If Aras had truly cared for the boy, he would never have turned against us."

Rhonwen's last shred of restraint drained away as she lunged at Perpenna and drove him to the tile floor. Screaming, she gripped his neck in both hands and squeezed, forcing her knuckles white with the effort. She heard only the blood in her ears as she strove to crush the life from the murderer in her hands.

She sensed, rather than saw, other men thrown to the ground as Orlan fought to protect her, but she refused to let go. Perpenna's face purpled as he flailed and kicked, but she would not be denied. The more he struggled, the harder she squeezed. She rejoiced when his eyes widened in the realization of impending death. She saw nothing else until something hard and heavy crashed into the back of her head, and she went numb.

When Perpenna's guards pulled her away she was too limp to resist, slumping sideways as paralysis gave way to pain. Orlan lay a few feet away bleeding from fresh wounds to his head. Rhonwen pressed her hand to the base of her skull and felt blood already wetting her hair.

Perpenna had scuttled away and stood with toga-clad senators supporting him on either side. He pointed a shaky finger at her and said, "Not only is she a traitor, she tried to murder me!"

Rhonwen attempted to rise but was pushed down by the same soldier who'd clubbed her with his javelin.

"I demand justice!" Perpenna cried.

"Silence!" roared Sertorius.

As the room fell quiet, for Rhonwen it also slowly returned to focus. Sertorius stared intently at her.

"Are you certain this was my child?"

She managed a nod.

"Who else knew?" he asked, rising from his seat and looking about the room.

Amid a sea of averted eyes, Perpenna stared straight at him. "She's lying."

"No, she's not," Orlan said through swollen lips.

"Aemelius knew it, too," Rhonwen said. "He left his post to tell you, because I wouldn't. He said I should have faith."

Perpenna laughed. "No Greek dramatist could have said it better."

Rhonwen crawled toward the table on her hands and knees. She pulled herself up and lifted Rede into her arms. Her eyes locked on Sertorius. "He's dead because of you."

"He's dead because of Aras," Perpenna hissed. "Even if Sertorius had fathered the child, the time for accepting him is long past. You condemned him yourself."

Rhonwen spat. "Tell me, Sertorius, how many more children will you let Perpenna kill before you're done?"

Sertorius crossed his arms. "You've said enough."

"I demand justice," Perpenna wheezed. "I want them executed, both of them!"

"Do it," Rhonwen said. "Do you think I care? Do you think you can hurt me worse than you already have?" She licked her thumb and tried to rub some of the blood from Rede's face.

Perpenna grabbed a sword from the hand of a nearby guard and stepped toward her. "I'll do it right here," he said.

"No," Sertorius barked. "She consorted with traitors, but in exchange for the hind's safe return, I promised her life. For this attack, she surrenders her freedom. Put them both in chains and deliver them to the slave dock at Tarraco."

"You're a fool," Rhonwen said. "You don't know your friends from your enemies. You are blind in both eyes, and now you're cursed. May you die at the hands of those closest to you, and may your last thoughts be of those you betrayed!"

It took three men to drag Rhonwen away from Rede, and she cursed each of them as well. By the time she felt the cold iron collar around her neck, and the weight of the chains she shared with Orlan, she had no strength left to curse anyone else.

25

This chronicle is meant to record what we have learned, though of the knowledge itself, it is mere shadow. It begins where life began, with the Goddess. All of everything—birth, death, each pause along life's road—stems from the Goddess of a Thousand Names. She is known to all and seen by few. She is the question that cannot be answered, the thirst that cannot be quenched, and her gift, more precious than myrrh, is given freely.

For all things, the Goddess provides life to fill the void, love to fill the heart, and time to settle accounts.

— The Book of Mallec

Iberia

The Roman soldier shoved Rhonwen onto the dock. She fell against Orlan, who steadied her as best he could with his hands chained to the metal ring around his neck. Another chain linked their collars together.

She did not cry out. Her face, etched with a grief he could only imagine, showed no other emotion. When they pushed her, she walked, and when they struck her, she fell. She made no sound save a deep sigh that wrenched his heart every time he heard it.

He'd prayed to be killed along with Rede so that he might hold the boy's hand as they passed together into the Otherworld. That Rhonwen wished the same, he had no doubt. She'd not spoken other than to inquire once whether he was seriously injured. He'd tried to forestall her ministrations, but she'd insisted on doing the little she could without water or bandages.

It had taken them two weeks to march from Sertorius' camp near Osca to Tarraco on the coast. The blue sea greeted them with the invigorating smell of ocean. Gulls and terns circled lazily above the low swells and cried to each other like lovers.

Once, when Rhonwen looked up, her gaze followed a black-billed tern as it wheeled and dove to flit just above the water's surface.

Soldiers guarded a collection of enslaved men and women from all over Iberia on the crowded dock. Orlan recognized some of the colors of the prisoners, especially those of clans once allied with Sertorius. He recognized several children from the school. If only Rede had been made a slave instead of being executed, they'd be on their way to Armorica rather than waiting to be loaded like cattle into a ship.

"What're those?" asked a Roman slaver.

"Iberian slaves, Scotus," said one of the soldiers. "You should recognize that sort by now."

Scotus, shorter than the soldier by a head, laughed without mirth. "I'm no fool, Timotheus. Those aren't the usual stupid farmers or luckless warriors. Those two are different."

"Because of the marks all over them?"

Scotus nodded as if his patience ebbed. "You are ever vigilant. Do you know what those marks mean?"

"That they're priests, I suppose, but who can keep up with all the gods of the provinces? Were it left up to my master, Perpenna, we'd have killed them, but Sertorius ordered them enslaved."

"They're special, you know. I have a use for druids." He approached within two arm lengths of the prisoners. Rhonwen did not move, but Orlan looked the slaver in the eyes.

"Unafraid, old man?"

Orlan shrugged. "Kill me, and I will be where I should be. Enslave me, and I will live to exact revenge on the man who sent us here. Either way, I win."

"Well said, druid. What's your name?"

Orlan licked his cracked lips. "I'm Orlan."

Scotus nudged Rhonwen with his toe. "And this?"

Orlan moved to shield her. "My niece, Rhonwen, a healer."

"Excellent!" Scotus said. "She's guaranteed a safe place for herself. What about you? What can you do for me?"

"I know history and herbs. Little else interests me."

Scotus smiled with great charm. "I'd wager you know a great many useful things. We'll have a lot of time to find out." He looked around, sniffed the air in an exaggerated fashion, and then stepped away. "Gamala!"

A black man stepped off the deck toward them. Stripped to the waist, he wore only red and blue breeches and an iron slave collar. He bowed to Scotus.

"Take these two and clean them up, then chain them on the deck. They'll make our voyage entertaining."

Gamala nodded and herded them off the dock to a low water trough, where he unlocked the chains that held them together.

Orlan massaged his wrists where the iron cuffs had rubbed his skin raw. The collar remained in place.

Rhonwen looked around with a start. "What's happening? When will they kill us? Rede needs me."

For lack of anything to say, Orlan hugged her until Gamala doused them with a bucket of water.

There was no soap, only the trough water with ashes and grease. At Gamala's silent insistence, they poured more water over each other and rubbed away an accumulation of grime.

As Rhonwen washed, new tears streamed down her face. "My son is dead. Mother, Telo, Aras, Aemelius too. You're in chains instead of on your way to Armorica. All because of me. I'm so sorry, Uncle. I was wrong. Foolish. Selfish." She buried her face in her hands and wept.

"You did what you thought right. We live in a dangerous world."

"I caused Rede's death."

"No, Perpenna did, and Sertorius allowed it."

"I should've killed him long ago, in spite of what I thought was love. Had I avenged Telo, we wouldn't be here now."

"Undoubtedly not. You would've been killed outright, along with Baia, me, and anyone else who knew us well. You would never have known the joy Rede brought to you or experienced the gratitude of the many whose lives you saved." He paused. "Next time you fall in love, choose a better man."

She gave him the shadow of a smile as she scraped the ashes and dirt from her body with her hands, then rinsed with another bucket of trough water. "Next time?"

"Yes, after we escape to Armorica."

At that notion she smiled. "He won't be a Roman. Or a warrior. I'm done with that."

Orlan thought of Mallec, so different from his niece. Yet it had always seemed to him Mallec would have been a good match for her. He shrugged. The gods had never shown him what the future held. Still, he had faith. They would never give life to someone like Rhonwen only to let her be wasted in slavery.

A second slave appeared with a water jug and two rough-woven tunics. Gamala motioned for Orlan and Rhonwen to wear the new clothes. As Gamala drank from the jug, Orlan stepped in front of the other slave and gathered up the rags they'd worn previously. He surrendered Rhonwen's garment but pretended to lose his balance and fall.

Rhonwen shouldered the slave aside to reach him. In the moment he was shielded from view, Orlan retrieved his last druid token from its hidden pocket. Only two remained: the one with Mallec and this one. A sign?

Later, as they sat aboard Scotus' purple-sailed slave ship awaiting departure, Orlan pressed the silver disk into Rhonwen's palm.

"What good is this?" she said. "It has no worth."

"Yes, it does. As we do," he said softly. "You more than I."

She bowed her head. "I wish only to cross into the Otherworld and be with my son."

"Aras will care for him."

She looked up at him with a flicker of hope in her eyes. "Aras would do that, wouldn't he?"

"Of course," he said gently. They're safe where they are, and you have another task. We're alive, Rhonwen, and we must do whatever it takes to stay that way. The gods have something larger planned for us, and until our path is clear, we must bide our time. If you swear anything, swear that you will live."

She stared at him, but he sensed she looked past him into the Otherworld.

"I'll never lose Rede," she said. "He will always nestle close to my heart. I won't allow any more innocents to suffer."

"And Sertorius? Can you let someone else seek revenge?"

"Yes," she sighed. "The blood price has been paid many times over. I leave him and Perpenna to the wrath of the gods." She struggled against the chains to stand and peered into the vacant ocean in front of them. He stood beside her.

"I will live because Rede did not. I will love because he showed me how."

✠ ✠ ✠

Armorica

On the third day of his fast, the dawn arrived warm and clear. Mallec realized with a start he'd been asleep. He yawned, licked dry lips, and allowed himself a sip of water.

He studied the sky in disappointment. Three days of prayer had not brought him the oneness with the gods he'd expected. More than anything he wanted another vision. Why had it been so long since he'd dreamed of the dark-haired woman?

Now, like a supplicant, he waited in the rocks at the mouth of the Great Cavern for a sign. It had not come. He tossed the water pouch to the ground. If the gods would not reveal her, he would seek her himself. He closed his eyes and concentrated on her slender silhouette and the wind-tossed fullness of her hair, yet the vision he tried to conjure dissolved in a spray of colored points of light. The harder he squeezed his eyes shut, the brighter the colors became, and the further he drifted from his goal. Weary and disappointed, he leaned back against the great boulders and tried to sleep.

And then she stood in front of him. Her healer's tattoo swirled upward like the intertwined necks of mated swans. He raised his eyes from her decorated breast, past her sun-browned throat and realized the wind blew her curled hair away from her face. In sunlight instead of shadow, her raven hair glistened. Her full lips frowned at the corners, and her eyes, as brown as dates from Africa, blazed with anger or determination. He couldn't tell which. Then he saw her cheek, its beautiful smooth skin marred by a single shallow scar. His heart thrummed faster than any beat Leuw had ever played, and he feared to look away lest she fade back into mystery.

At last he knew she was neither goddess nor ghost, but a real woman whose life was tied to his as irrevocably as the intertwining spirals of her tattoo. Something inside him whispered: *his woman.*

Tears streamed down his cheeks as his dream self reached for her in a soundless plea that she join him and make his life complete. Slowly she held her hands out to him, and he saw the rust-pitted gray of slave metal around her wrists.

He gasped and opened his eyes. The reality was as hard as the Eban rock he leaned against. The woman he'd known all his life, perhaps even loved, was a slave. He ached, searching his heart and mind for an explanation. As the sun reached zenith and his fast ended, he recognized what it meant.

The gods had finally shown him her face and there could be only one reason why. The time must be right to find her.

Below him the road from Vannes snaked through the valley. Something flashed in the sunlight, and he shielded his eyes for a better look. Someone familiar moved along that route.

He worked his way to the top of an enormous boulder to watch the road and pulled tight the colorful Suetoni cloak Arie had given him. He would know the huge driver of the modest horse cart anywhere. As the cart drew closer he could see it was also occupied by an equally robust woman. To Mallec's great joy, Leuw turned the cart toward the mountain. As it rolled forward, the woman embraced Leuw, and the bard kissed her in return. The back of the cart was loaded with amphorae. It appeared Leuw had secured more than one treasure during his recent journey to Vannes.

Mallec laughed out loud. Surely Leuw's return was also a sign from the gods his decision to find his own mate was correct. He murmured a final brief prayer and eased from his perch to descend from the guardian boulders. He loved the serenity of the great rocks and took his time, stopping often to peer at the thick moss covering the stones like green beards, or to watch a nuthatch search among the willow branches for insects hiding beneath the bark. Once he caught a whiff of brimstone from the hot springs that bubbled from several places near the base of the mountain. No wonder the Ancients had explored it well enough to discover the cave.

An echoing voice hailed him, and he glanced down the trail. "Leuw?"

"Who else?" came the breathless reply. "If I'd known you were coming back down, I'd have waited for you at the bottom."

Mallec grinned at the sight of the heavy bard struggling up the boulder-strewn path. "It's good to see you! How'd you know I was up here?"

Leuw leaned against a tree, one hand on his chest as he drew in deep breaths. "Arie stands below like a war hound on guard. She's already worn a path in the dirt pacing back and forth waiting for you. She said she's prepared to wait until tomorrow."

Mallec nodded. "I told her to let no one pass."

Leuw shook his head. "I told her she'd have to kill me to keep me from climbing up here to see you, although after this exertion, I think I've almost killed myself. What are you doing up here anyway?"

"Fasting and praying. The solstice is almost upon us, and I haven't seen Caradowc since we left him in Gillac."

Leuw frowned. "Are you in that great a hurry to restore Dierdre?"

Mallec shrugged. "We'll have to deal with her sooner or later."

Leuw nodded. "Later is soon enough for me. There are others I'm more concerned about." He paused. "How fares Gar?"

"Poorly," Mallec said. "If not for Arie and young Klervie, there'd be little hope for him."

"Perhaps the woman I've brought will help." Leuw brightened. "We've handfasted for a year. She tells me after that she'll think about renewing our marriage."

Here was yet more proof that anything was possible, Mallec thought.

"She's from Vannes and loves the ocean. Do you think she'll like our little corner of Armorica?"

Mallec straightened with a wide smile and gestured to the rolling hills all around. "How could she not? The ocean-sprayed lands to the west cannot compare to the warm nurturing these Black Mountains provide. They're proof of the Great Mother's love for us. How could anyone want to leave here?"

Leuw chuckled. "Orlan always claimed Armorica was too cold and damp."

Mallec reached into his tunic pocket and pulled out the token Orlan had given him long ago in Mona. If not for the Iberian, he never would have come here and might not even have finished his training. He flipped the disk into the air and caught it. It disappeared from his palm only to reappear when he snapped his fingers.

"I wish you wouldn't do that," Leuw said. "I know it's a trick, but it makes me dizzy to see it vanish like that."

"I wish I could make Orlan reappear. I miss him, as I've missed you, my friend! When I left Belgica so long ago, I thought a home and family were things I'd never have. There's an abundance of folk here who've cared for me more than anyone I ever knew. Though Orlan and Willa are gone, others, like you, come to fill those empty places." He chuckled. "Arie trails after me as if she were my little sister rather than my pupil. I have a family here, Leuw, real family. For once in my life, I belong."

"With all this family you speak of, I'm surprised you haven't found a mate."

"Even that may come to pass, my friend, though I've doubted it for many years."

Leuw brightened. "You've found someone?"

"In a manner of speaking."

"Well, don't keep it a secret! Who is this lass, and when will I meet her?"

"I don't know her name," Mallec said.

Leuw shrugged. "Names are more important to bards than anyone else. How did you meet?"

"We haven't," Mallec said, "at least not outside my dreams." When Leuw gave him a suspicious look, he hurried on. "Until today, the gods had never shown me her face. I only knew that she was slender and had dark hair. Now I know what she looks like." He gripped the bard's shoulder. "I've got to find her, Leuw."

"Did you see anything besides her face, some clue about where she might be?"

Mallec concentrated. "I saw white buildings and the sea."

"That narrows it down," Leuw said. "Next you'll tell me her arms and legs come in pairs and that she sways her behind when she walks!"

Mallec ignored him. "I know several things." He smiled nervously. "She's a driad."

"Ah! That does narrow it down."

"And a slave."

Leuw stared at him. "That's not a combination one hears too often. I hope the gods reveal more than that."

"They will," Mallec said. "I'm sure of it."

Leuw clapped him on the back. "So be it! At least you know what she looks like. Most men have no idea. Now, hurry and finish your business here. There's someone I want you to meet."

"Would this someone be the person who rode with you in your wagon?"

Leuw chuckled. "Her name's Hildur, and she's from the far north."

Mallec frowned. "I thought you went to Vannes."

"That's where we met." He smiled and put his hands on his broad hips. "For the first time in my life, Mallec, I can say with confidence the gods are pleased with me."

"Oh?"

"I have two proofs. First, Hildur's madly in love with me."

"And second?"

Leuw grinned. "She's the widow of a wine merchant."

Mallec roared a deep, soul-cleansing laugh. He stood and wrapped an arm around Leuw's shoulder. "Come, my friend. Let's go back to the enclave."

"What about your fast?"

"I'm done." Seeing the soft eyes and lovely face of the dark-haired driad flit across his consciousness, he had received far more on this vision quest than he'd come for. "The Goddess smiled on me today, reminding me I have friends like you, and Arie, and all the others who've welcomed and loved me here. I'm prepared for whatever is to come."

Leuw gave him a smile of understanding.

With an open palm, and his heart fully soothed, Mallec motioned toward the path home.

EPILOG

... When all the confederates had consented to it, they provided a messenger who brought feigned letters to Sertorius, in which he had notice of a victory obtained, it said, by one of his lieutenants, and of the great slaughter of his enemies: and as Sertorius, being extremely well pleased, was sacrificing and giving thanks to the gods for his prosperous success, Perpenna invited him, and those with him, who were also of the conspiracy, to an entertainment, and being very importunate, prevailed with him to come. At all suppers and entertainments where Sertorius was present, great order and decency was wont to be observed; for he would not endure to hear or see anything that was rude or unhandsome, but made it the habit of all who kept his company to entertain themselves with quiet and inoffensive amusements. But in the middle of this entertainment, those who sought occasion to quarrel fell into dissolute discourse openly, and making as if they were very drunk, committed many insolences on purpose to provoke him. Sertorius, being offended with their ill-behavior, or perceiving the state of their minds by their way of speaking and their unusually disrespectful manner changed the posture of his lying, and leaned backward, as one that neither heard nor regarded them. Perpenna now took a cup full of wine, and, as he was drinking, let it fall out of his hand and made a noise, which was the sign agreed upon amongst them; and Antonius, who was next to Sertorius, immediately wounded him with his sword. And whilst Sertorius, upon receiving the wound, turned himself, and strove to get up, Antonius threw himself upon his breast, and held both his hands, so that he died by a number of blows, without being able even to defend himself.

Upon the first news of his death, most of the Iberians left the conspirators, and sent ambassadors to Pompey and Metellus, and yielded themselves up to them. Perpenna attempted to do something with those that remained, but he made only so much use of Sertorius' arms and preparations for war as to disgrace himself in them, and to let it be evident to all that he understood no more how to command than he knew how to obey; and when he came against Pompey, he was soon overthrown and taken prisoner. Neither did he bear this last affliction with any bravery, but having Sertorius' papers and writings in his hands, he offered to show Pompey letters from persons of consular dignity, and of the highest quality in Rome, written with their own hands, expressly to call Sertorius into Italy, and to let him know what great numbers there were that earnestly desired to alter the present state of affairs, and to introduce another manner of government. Upon this occasion, Pompey behaved not like a youth, or one of a light inconsiderate mind, but as a man of a confirmed, mature, and solid judgment; and so freed Rome from great fears and dangers of change. For he put all Sertorius' writings and letters together and read not one of them, nor suffered any one else to read them, but burnt them all, and caused Perpenna immediately to be put to death, lest by discovering their names further troubles and revolutions might ensue.

— *Excerpt from Sertorius, by Plutarch (75 A.C.E.), Translated by John Dryden*

Our titles are available at major book stores
and local independent resellers who support
Science Fiction and Fantasy readers like you.

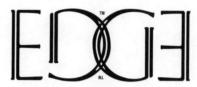

EDGE Science Fiction
and Fantasy Publishing

Tesseract Books

Our titles are available at major book stores and local independent resellers who support Science Fiction and Fantasy readers like you.

Alphanauts by J. Brian Clarke (tp) - ISBN: 978-1-894063-14-2
Apparition Trail, The by Lisa Smedman (tp) - ISBN: 978-1-894063-22-7
As Fate Decrees by Denysé Bridger (tp) - ISBN: 978-1-894063-41-8
Avim's Oath (Part Six of the Okal Rel Saga) by Lynda Williams (pb)
   - ISBN: 978-1-894063-35-7

Black Chalice, The by Marie Jakober (hb) - ISBN: 978-1-894063-00-7
Blue Apes by Phyllis Gotlieb (pb) - ISBN: 978-1-895836-13-4
Blue Apes by Phyllis Gotlieb (hb) - ISBN: 978-1-895836-14-1

Children of Atwar, The by Heather Spears (pb) - ISBN: 978-0-88878-335-6
Cinkarion - The Heart of Fire (Part Two of The Chronicles of the Karionin)
   by J. A. Cullum - (tp) - ISBN: 978-1-894063-21-0
Clan of the Dung-Sniffers by Lee Danielle Hubbard (pb) - ISBN: 978-1-894063-05-0
Claus Effect, The by David Nickle & Karl Schroeder (pb) - ISBN: 978-1-895836-34-9
Claus Effect, The by David Nickle & Karl Schroeder (hb) - ISBN: 978-1-895836-35-6
Courtesan Prince, The (Part One of the Okal Rel Saga) by Lynda Williams (tp)
   - ISBN: 978-1-894063-28-9

Dark Earth Dreams by Candas Dorsey & Roger Deegan (comes with a CD)
   - ISBN: 978-1-895836-05-9
Darkness of the God (Children of the Panther Part Two)
   by Amber Hayward (tp) - ISBN: 978-1-894063-44-9
Distant Signals by Andrew Weiner (tp) - ISBN: 978-0-88878-284-7
Dreams of an Unseen Planet by Teresa Plowright (tp) - ISBN: 978-0-88878-282-3
Dreams of the Sea (Part 1 of Tyranaël) by Élisabeth Vonarburg (tp)
   - ISBN: 978-1-895836-96-7
Dreams of the Sea (Part 1 of Tyranaël) by Élisabeth Vonarburg (hb)
   - ISBN: 978-1-895836-98-1
Druids by Barbara Galler-Smith and Josh Langston (tp)
   - ISBN: 978-1-894063-29-6

Eclipse by K. A. Bedford (tp) - ISBN: 978-1-894063-30-2
Even The Stones by Marie Jakober (tp) - ISBN: 978-1-894063-18-0
Evolve edited by Nancy Kilpatrick (tp) - ISBN: 978-1-894063-33-3

Far Arena (Part Five of the Okal Rel Saga) by Lynda Williams (tp)
   - ISBN: 978-1-894063-45-6
Fires of the Kindred by Robin Skelton (tp) - ISBN: 978-0-88878-271-7
Forbidden Cargo by Rebecca Rowe (tp) - ISBN: 978-1-894063-16-6

Game of Perfection, A (Part 2 of Tyranaël) by Élisabeth Vonarburg (tp)
   - ISBN: 978-1-894063-32-6
Gaslight Grimoire: Fantastic Tales of Sherlock Holmes
   edited by Jeff Campbell & Charles Prepolec (pb)
   - ISBN: 978-1-8964063-17-3

Gaslight Grotesque: Horrific Tales of Sherlock Holmes
    edited by Jeff Campbell & Charles Prepolec (pb)
    - ISBN: 978-1-8964063-31-9
Green Music by Ursula Pflug (tp) - ISBN: 978-1-895836-75-2
Green Music by Ursula Pflug (hb) - ISBN: 978-1-895836-77-6

Healer, The (Children of the Panther Part One) by Amber Hayward (tp)
    - ISBN: 978-1-895836-89-9
Healer, The (Children of the Panther Part One) by Amber Hayward (hb)
    - ISBN: 978-1-895836-91-2
Hell Can Wait by Theodore Judson (tp) - ISBN: 978-1-978-1-894063-23-4
Hounds of Ash and other tales of Fool Wolf, The by Greg Keyes (pb)
    - ISBN: 978-1-894063-09-8
Hydrogen Steel by K. A. Bedford (tp) - ISBN: 978-1-894063-20-3

i-ROBOT Poetry by Jason Christie (tp) - ISBN: 978-1-894063-24-1

Jackal Bird by Michael Barley (pb) - ISBN: 978-1-895836-07-3
Jackal Bird by Michael Barley (hb) - ISBN: 978-1-895836-11-0
JEMMA7729 by Phoebe Wray (tp) - ISBN: 978-1-894063-40-1

Keaen by Till Noever (tp) - ISBN: 978-1-894063-08-1
Keeper's Child by Leslie Davis (tp) - ISBN: 978-1-894063-01-2

Land/Space edited by Candas Jane Dorsey and Judy McCrosky (tp)
    - ISBN: 978-1-895836-90-5
Land/Space edited by Candas Jane Dorsey and Judy McCrosky (hb)
    - ISBN: 978-1-895836-92-9
Lyskarion: The Song of the Wind (Part One of The Chronicles of the Karionin)
    by J.A. Cullum (tp) - ISBN: 978-1-894063-02-9

Machine Sex and other stories by Candas Jane Dorsey (tp)
    - ISBN: 978-0-88878-278-6
Maërlande Chronicles, The by Élisabeth Vonarburg (pb)
    - ISBN: 978-0-88878-294-6
Moonfall by Heather Spears (pb) - ISBN: 978-0-88878-306-6

Of Wind and Sand by Sylvie Bérard (translated by Sheryl Curtis) (pb)
    - ISBN: 978-1-894063-19-7
On Spec: The First Five Years edited by On Spec (pb)
    - ISBN: 978-1-895836-08-0
On Spec: The First Five Years edited by On Spec (hb)
    - ISBN: 978-1-895836-12-7
Orbital Burn by K. A. Bedford (tp) - ISBN: 978-1-894063-10-4
Orbital Burn by K. A. Bedford (hb) - ISBN: 978-1-894063-12-8

Pallahaxi Tide by Michael Coney (pb) - ISBN: 978-0-88878-293-9
Passion Play by Sean Stewart (pb) - ISBN: 978-0-88878-314-1
Petrified World (Determine Your Destiny #1) by Piotr Brynczka (pb)
    - ISBN: 978-1-894063-11-1
Plague Saint by Rita Donovan, The (tp) - ISBN: 978-1-895836-28-8
Plague Saint by Rita Donovan, The (hb) - ISBN: 978-1-895836-29-5

Pretenders (Part Three of the Okal Rel Saga) by Lynda Williams (pb)
- ISBN: 978-1-894063-13-5

Reluctant Voyagers by Élisabeth Vonarburg (pb) - ISBN: 978-1-895836-09-7
Reluctant Voyagers by Élisabeth Vonarburg (hb) - ISBN: 978-1-895836-15-8
Resisting Adonis by Timothy J. Anderson (tp) - ISBN: 978-1-895836-84-4
Resisting Adonis by Timothy J. Anderson (hb) - ISBN: 978-1-895836-83-7
Righteous Anger (Part Two of the Okal Rel Saga) by Lynda Williams (tp)
- ISBN: 897-1-894063-38-8

Silent City, The by Élisabeth Vonarburg (tp) - ISBN: 978-1-894063-07-4
Slow Engines of Time, The by Élisabeth Vonarburg (tp)
- ISBN: 978-1-895836-30-1
Slow Engines of Time, The by Élisabeth Vonarburg (hb)
- ISBN: 978-1-895836-31-8
Stealing Magic by Tanya Huff (tp) - ISBN: 978-1-894063-34-0
Strange Attractors by Tom Henighan (pb) - ISBN: 978-0-88878-312-7

Taming, The by Heather Spears (pb) - ISBN: 978-1-895836-23-3
Taming, The by Heather Spears (hb) - ISBN: 978-1-895836-24-0
Ten Monkeys, Ten Minutes by Peter Watts (tp) - ISBN: 978-1-895836-74-5
Ten Monkeys, Ten Minutes by Peter Watts (hb) - ISBN: 978-1-895836-76-9
Tesseracts 1 edited by Judith Merril (pb) - ISBN: 978-0-88878-279-3
Tesseracts 2 edited by Phyllis Gotlieb & Douglas Barbour (pb)
- ISBN: 978-0-88878-270-0
Tesseracts 3 edited by Candas Jane Dorsey & Gerry Truscott (pb)
- ISBN: 978-0-88878-290-8
Tesseracts 4 edited by Lorna Toolis & Michael Skeet (pb)
- ISBN: 978-0-88878-322-6
Tesseracts 5 edited by Robert Runté & Yves Maynard (pb)
- ISBN: 978-1-895836-25-7
Tesseracts 5 edited by Robert Runté & Yves Maynard (hb)
- ISBN: 978-1-895836-26-4
Tesseracts 6 edited by Robert J. Sawyer & Carolyn Clink (pb)
- ISBN: 978-1-895836-32-5
Tesseracts 6 edited by Robert J. Sawyer & Carolyn Clink (hb)
- ISBN: 978-1-895836-33-2
Tesseracts 7 edited by Paula Johanson & Jean-Louis Trudel (tp)
- ISBN: 978-1-895836-58-5
Tesseracts 7 edited by Paula Johanson & Jean-Louis Trudel (hb)
- ISBN: 978-1-895836-59-2
Tesseracts 8 edited by John Clute & Candas Jane Dorsey (tp)
- ISBN: 978-1-895836-61-5
Tesseracts 8 edited by John Clute & Candas Jane Dorsey (hb)
- ISBN: 978-1-895836-62-2
Tesseracts Nine edited by Nalo Hopkinson and Geoff Ryman (tp)
- ISBN: 978-1-894063-26-5
Tesseracts Ten: A Celebration of New Canadian Specuative Fiction
edited by Robert Charles Wilson and Edo van Belkom (tp)
- ISBN: 978-1-894063-36-4
Tesseracts Eleven: Amazing Canadian Speulative Fiction
edited by Cory Doctorow and Holly Phillips (tp)
- ISBN: 978-1-894063-03-6

Tesseracts Twelve: New Novellas of Canadian Fantastic Fiction
    edited by Claude Lalumière (pb)
    - ISBN: 978-1-894063-15-9
Tesseracts Thirteen: Chilling Tales from the Great White North
    edited by Nancy Kilpatrick and David Morrell (tp)
    - ISBN: 978-1-894063-25-8
Tesseracts Q edited by Élisabeth Vonarburg & Jane Brierley (pb)
    - ISBN: 978-1-895836-21-9
Tesseracts Q edited by Élisabeth Vonarburg & Jane Brierley (hb)
    - ISBN: 978-1-895836-22-6
Throne Price by Lynda Williams and Alison Sinclair (tp)
    - ISBN: 978-1-894063-06-7
Time Machines Repaired Whie-U-Wait by K. A. Bedford (tp)
    - ISBN: 978-1-894063-42-5